THE THREAT OF
A FORBIDDEN PASSION

Pulling her close, Stephen whispered in her ear, "Just let me say what I have to say, and I'll let you go. Stop struggling!"

She looked venomously into his eyes, and he laughed lightly. "That's it, little mountain cat, just listen. You're sleeping with the old man now. You were a virgin and the old man can satisfy you for a little while, but you'll tire of him soon, honey, and when he slows down and can't keep you happy anymore, I'll be here waiting."

"No!" cried Melanie, her eyes sparking amber.

"Yes." Twisting his fingers in her hair, he held her head fast as he traced the outline of her lips with his tongue before covering her mouth again, swallowing deeply of its sweetness.

When he drew away this time, she could feel him trembling. His voice was husky with emotion. "Remember, come to me, Melanie. I'll be waiting for you. We can ride high together, you and I—but don't wait too long, damn you—or I'll come and get you myself!"

AMBER FIRE

ELAINE BARBIERI

LOVE SPELL BOOKS NEW YORK CITY

LOVE SPELL®

December 1998

Published by

Dorchester Publishing Co., Inc.
276 Fifth Avenue
New York, NY 10001

ISBN 0-505-52290-X

The name "Love Spell" and its logo are trademarks of Dorchester Publishing Co., Inc.

Printed in the United States of America.

Prologue

In 1763, the end of the French and Indian War brought both the return of settlers to New York and New Hampshire and the renewal of hostilities between the two colonies. Differing opinions as to the actual course of the Connecticut River, perpetuated by faulty maps and the Crown's indifference, were the main causes of the dissension.

Unchallenged for fifteen years, Governor Benning Wentworth of New Hampshire granted townships west of the Connecticut River to friends, relatives, and those willing to pay large sums of money for the land. Freed from the pressure of war, New York began to feel deprived of the revenue from the "Hampshire Grants" and instituted an organized campaign to evict the families within the grants from their homesteads, negate all land titles, and resell the property. The heated controversy that ensued, during which both colonies petitioned the Crown for their legal rights, resulted in the New Hampshire settlers holding fast to their titles, while the colony of New York, in defiance of a royal mandate to the contrary, began issuing its own patents to the lands.

Challenged by the powerful colony of New York, New Hampshire was obliged to form a "militia" for its own protection. The resulting wild, guerilla band of some 300 rough woodsmen, led by the colorful Ethan Allen, was scathingly referred to as "The Bennington Mob" by the Yorkers, while within the grants it was known as "The Green Mountain Boys."

Years of torn loyalties followed, during which neighbor often turned against neighbor and lives were often unalteringly disrupted in the wake of the violent dispute.

A vague uneasiness disturbed her dreams. Perspiring and still groggy, she awoke to the unfamiliar sensation of a male body curved around her in sleep, the warmth of naked skin pressed tightly against her back, and a large, calloused hand lightly stroking the delicate whiteness of her stomach. She stirred, and the fondling became more deliberate, sensually seeking her secret places, enlarging the circle of caresses until he moved to cup one rounded breast. Suddenly pressed to her back, she was seized by a moment of panic when a warm, moist mouth closed over its crest.

"No! Please . . ." But her frantic whisper trailed away as the fogginess of sleep left her mind and the previous hours spent in the bed returned with glaring clarity. She was no longer a virgin . . . too late for regrets now . . .

In the pale light of the moon streaming through the window, she caught a glimpse of dark hair streaked with gray and began to relax while he continued to kiss and tease her breast with his tongue. A languorous warmth spread through her veins. She groaned lightly as his mouth left one soft peak and hungrily seized the other, but his only answer was a more violent attack as his body began moving atop hers. There was an unmistakable hardness pressed between her legs, the same hardness that a few hours before had caused her pain, and she flinched instinctively with a low protest.

"Don't worry, darling, it won't hurt much this time. Just relax . . . that's it . . ." his deep voice crooned, "just relax and let me in . . ."

Suddenly his lips were covering hers, his tongue separating her teeth as it drove down into her mouth. Simultaneously lunging deep inside her, he paid no heed to her gasp and began a steady, rhythmic penetration of her body. Without conscious participation, but in answer to the need building within her, she began meeting his thrusts, joining his body with increasing impetus and violence, the wild, throbbing heat he caused within her accelerating, gaining complete control of her senses until her body was responding with spontaneous passion, mounting to a peak that could climax in only one way. Her low, sustained groan when she met his final thrust was drowned out by the deep sound of his own passion as they reached the summit together, only to fall again in a long, breathtaking spiral from its ecstatic height.

His body collapsed heavily atop hers, stealing her breath. He raised himself slightly, straining to see her face in the darkness of the room.

"Melanie . . . Melanie . . ." He began kissing her face lightly, "I've dreamed this so often, and cursed myself each time for daring to allow the thought to even enter my mind . . . but you know I love you, don't you, darling?"

The moon breaking again through the clouds caused a shaft of light to reveal the deep lines the years had etched on his face, and she felt a momentary surge of revulsion and stiffened, as her youthful mind reacted instinctively— He's old . . . old . . .

She stared silently for a few moments at his face until reason returned, and slowly raising her hands, she slid them deliberately into the thick gray hair at his temples, murmuring as she pulled his mouth down to cover hers again, "Yes, I know, darling, I know . . ."

Chapter 1

1770

Wispy clouds stretched lacey fingers across the brilliant cerulean sky, an endless kaleidoscope of fragile, moving patterns woven by the infinite artistry of the brisk spring breeze. Peeking with silent warmth through the gently swaying branches of the forest below, the rays of the newly risen sun danced lightly across the cheek of the petulant thirteen-year-old in gray homespun riding astride her horse on the heavily wooded trail; their delicate grace both

11

unappreciated and ignored. Jerking peevishly at the reins of the trail-weary animal as it followed unalteringly the path set by her father riding directly ahead, the girl deliberately refused to give the unfamiliar landscape bursting with the color of first bloom even the slightest glance. She chose instead to keep her high, clear brow puckered in a heavy frown, and her eyes either riveted on her father's broad back or lowered so far to the ground that her long, dark lashes almost rested against her freckled cheeks. Her full, pink lips had abandoned their usual wide, dimpled smile at the inception of the journey the day before in favor of a straight, unrelenting line that was both uncompromising and surly. Small and slight of frame, her fragile appearance belied the wide streak of stubbornness that was becoming increasingly apparent as the journey along the interminable trail progressed.

"I'll hate Salisbury, I know I will," she mumbled over and over to herself, her low, halting litany keeping time with the heavy, plodding step of the horses as they moved steadily forward. A lone tear, breaking free of the deluge brimming within her amber eyes, slid down her smooth, slightly sun-reddened cheek, and a sudden gust of wind whipping a strand of her fiery auburn hair adhered it annoyingly to the damp path. Impatiently brushing it away, she looked up to see her father turned toward her in the saddle, staring at her openly rebellious expression while his horse moved unrelentingly forward.

"There's no sense in pouting, Melanie." His voice as stern as his countenance. Her father's patience with her attitude was obviously beginning to ebb as he continued, "You might just as well accept the fact that Salisbury is going to be our new home. Poultney is just a part of our past now."

Halting his horse, he allowed her to draw up alongside as he directed his angry gaze into her wide eyes. "We are committed to go on to Salisbury. I've accepted a job there and am expected, and if you would allow yourself to reason clearly, you would realize that you'll probably be happier in Salisbury where you can be with children your own age. Besides, it's time you learned to be with people and act like a lady!"

"Mama taught me all I need to know about being a lady!" she burst out, suddenly vexed at her father's attack on her. "I can read, write and do sums, and I can cook and weave and sew . . ."

Her heated defense of her virtues brought a slight smile to his face, and he said in a lighter tone, "Yes, I know, Melanie, you are very accomplished. Your mother was a very able teacher."

The hint of sadness in his voice at the mention of her mother was familiar. He had not yet overcome his grief at her death the previous winter, and pressing her advantage, Melanie interjected quickly, "But Mama's grave, Papà, who'll take care of it now? It'll get overgrown and lost and . . ."

"I told you, Melanie, Poultney is part of our past now. I'll say no more about it!" His anger, returning with frightening abruptness left no doubt as to the finality of his decision. He urged his horse forward again, turning to say over his shoulder, "I'll have no more pouting from you, either. And that's my final word, do you hear me?"

His harshness brought new tears to her eyes, and gulping slightly, she mumbled obediently, "Yes, Papa, I hear you."

But once she was certain he was far enough ahead to be out of earshot, she stared straight at his back and mumbled obstinately under her breath, "But I'll hate it . . . I'll hate Salisbury, I know I will!"

Taking one last look over his shoulder at his unhappy daughter, James Morganfield shook his head slightly and again urged his horse onward. Melanie was such a strong-willed child—sometimes he feared too much so for her own good. It was unfortunate her mother had not been able to instill some of her own gentleness into her spirited daughter. At times it was unfathomable to him that a daughter could be so unlike a mother in so many ways. Oh, she has inherited her mother's charm, to be sure; the little imp can charm the birds out of the trees with a little effort, he thought, a small, brief smile moving across his lips despite himself. And she was going to be a beauty, like her mother in that way also. But if the adolescent Melanie was any indication of the woman she would someday become, it was going to take a strong man to handle her, and shaking his head with a small laugh, James admitted to himself that he did not envy the fellow the job!

But in the meantime, it was no good trying to explain that he was doing this for her own good. His own life was inexorably tied to the grants. He was totally committed to his homestead where he had brought Sara as a bride seventeen years before. A quiet minister's daughter of delicate health, she had

14

been totally unsuited to the rigorous life of homesteading in the wilderness. The landscape was too unyielding and the living too devastatingly hard. He was again assailed with a sharp pang of guilt. Each successive Poultney winter had taken its toll on Sara's health, as had the numerous miscarriages before and after Melanie's difficult birth. She had been uncomplaining, but the constant Yorker threat also preyed on her peace of mind, further debilitating her; and the last winter, the worst James could remember, had finally claimed her as its victim. He had learned a hard lesson. He did not intend to commit Melanie to the harshness of a backwoods life. He dared not explain to her that as far as he was concerned, his departure from their homestead was only temporary, that he would sooner give up his life than the land he and Sara had loved so well, and that had become her final resting place. Or that he intended to stay in Salisbury only until Melanie was old enough to find a husband and live the comfortable town life he had denied her mother. She would have her choice of young men, he was certain. She was growing more and more lovely each day, and when her future was finally secure, he would go back to Poultney—and Sara.

Yes, he thought with a small, silent sigh of resignation, Salisbury is the logical choice for us now. It held all the answers to his most pressing problems. Situated further south, by Lake Wononskopomuc, it had a gentle climate. Its rolling plains and golden meadow had already enticed the population to over eleven hundred, making it the hub of northwest Litchfield County. Located there also was one of the largest foundries in the area, owned and run by a friend, Asa Parker. James shook his head sadly. He was forced to concede his friend had made a wiser choice than he when they had been young men together. When the hills were found to have deposits of low-grade iron ore, Asa had settled there and opened the foundry. He had married one of the local women and was now considered one of the wealthiest men in the county. He and Asa had seen little of each other though the years, but when James had written him of his decision to leave Poultney, the return letter had offered him a job and a place to stay as long as he wanted it.

The fact that Asa had invested heavily in land within the grants and was totally dedicated to victory over the usurpers from the colony of New York also heartened him considerably. His foundry employed a number of men whose wages supplemented the meager living their families managed on farms within the grants, and who also doubled as Green Mountain Boys when the situation demanded. With the fine network of spies they had developed, no Yorker activity went unreported, and his homestead's security while he remained there was almost guaranteed.

No, it would do him no good at all to try to explain all this to Melanie. She was too young . . . she would never understand.

The waning light of late afternoon elongated the shadows of the two mounted travelers against the narrow, cobbled streets of Salisbury as they moved steadily toward Weaver's Row. Determined to hold on to her resistance, Melanie refused to raise her eyes to the sights and sounds of the town that, despite herself, so titillated her youthful curiosity. Having had few neighbors in Poultney, she had never before been in a crowd larger than that of about six families during holiday celebrations; but in the one, brief glimpse she had stolen from beneath downcast eyes as they had entered the town, she realized to her amazement that one short street would probably hold twice that number and more!

After trailing down what seemed to Melanie endless streets, the lateness of the hour and the steady beat of the horses' hooves reverberating against the cobblestones had begun to mesmerize her when the rhythm began to slow, and she raised her gaze. They had entered a new street where there stood only two houses. But what houses they were! The one that they were approaching was made of red brick, and was huge—bigger than any she had ever seen, with four large pillars supporting a great portico over a massive front door. Dismounting before the house, James lifted Melanie to the ground, admonishing her quietly as he did, "You will behave yourself, Melanie, do you understand? You will not disgrace your mother's upbringing in a friend's house."

Waiting only long enough for her nod of acknowledgment, he turned to climb the graceful, graduated steps that led to the front door. Melanie, stumbling closely behind, jumped with a start as her father lifted the shining brass door knocker and rapped loudly. Within a few moments the door opened and succumbing to curiosity just long enough for a peep, Melanie was startled to see a great mass of a woman

17

standing in the doorway, her immense size almost completely enveloped in a spotless white apron.

Hastily slipping back behind her father, she heard him say politely, "I would like to see the master of the house. Tell him, please, that James Morganfield and daughter are here to see him."

"Come in, Mr. Morganfield. Mr. Parker has been expecting you for several days." In contrast to her great proportions, the woman's voice was surprisingly light and pleasant. Sneaking another look as they stepped into the foyer, Melanie saw that the round face, framed in neat, graying hair that sat atop the huge body, bore a warm, friendly expression.

Moving surprisingly fast for a woman of her size, she disappeared momentarily into a doorway across the hall from where they stood, and within moments a tall, ruddy-skinned man emerged, walking toward them with his hand extended in greeting.

"James, you old rake! You certainly took your time in getting here! I was beginning to think you had changed your mind."

"You know better than that, Asa." Her father smiled as he took the hand and shook it warmly, "I'm a man of my word . . . always have been."

Just one glimpse of her father's face showed plainly his pleasure in seeing his old friend, and Melanie's spirits began to rise despite herself. She hadn't seen him smile like that in a long, long time.

More interested in her surroundings than their conversation, Melanie's gaze began to drift around the house in wide-eyed wonder. She had never seen such a beautiful house and stared with open fascination at the chandelier hanging directly over them as the flames of its many candles reflected and sparkled in the bits of cut glass swaying elegantly from its tiered bottom. The little sparks of color reflected on the shining wooden floors and on the glossy surface of the furniture lining the walls, and she was in silent awe of the many hours that she judged must have been spent polishing those surfaces to such a high sheen. Her eyes then moved directly across from them to the gently curving staircase rising gracefully to the second floor, where, unbelievably, there appeared to be many more rooms! She was still staring incredulously when the use of her name jerked her attention back to the two men, and she suddenly realized her father had been speaking to her.

". . . and this is my daughter, Melanie, Asa. The picture of her mother, is she not?" Pride and sadness were evident in her father's tone as he spoke.

Suddenly embarrassed by their attention and stubbornly reluctant to part with her resistance, Melanie raised her eyes just far enough to acknowledge the introduction with a bob of her head, and returned them immediately to the floor.

"Well . . . if you say so, James. I suppose she must be her mother's image, but so far all I've been able to see is the top of her head!"

Crouching down in front of her, the tall man raised her chin with his forefinger until her wide amber eyes looked directly into his. The face only a few inches from hers was craggy, distinctly homely, with large, undistinguished features; but the dark eyes beneath shaggy brows were warm and friendly, and Melanie had to fight her spontaneous response to their warmth. Still smiling, he exclaimed in a deep, surprised voice, "Well, what do you know! She really is a beauty, James! Lucky for her she didn't inherit *your* looks!" Then, laughing again, "Welcome again to my house, pretty Melanie! I'm pleased to meet you at last!"

Begrudgingly, Melanie uttered an acutely formal, "How do you do, sir."

A small smile twitched at the corners of his mouth as Asa continued to look seriously into her unsmiling face. "Well, Melanie, if I didn't know better, I'd think you're not as happy to meet me as I am to meet you. As a matter of fact, if I didn't know better, I'd think you're downright unhappy to be here!"

The warning glance directed her way by her father shriveled the corners of her adamant resistance and she dropped her eyes a notch lower as James said apologetically, "She's just tired, Asa."

Lightly waving his explanation aside, Asa continued directing his comments to Melanie. "I sure hope your father is right and you're just tired, because we've really been looking forward to your father's and your visit here. Emily and I haven't had houseguests in a long time."

Beginning to feel distinctly uncomfortable with her ungracious behavior, Melanie glanced away, only to catch the thunderous look on her father's angry face. Gulping slightly, she stubbornly managed a few more words of feeble resistance.

"It's just that . . . I didn't want to leave Poultney. It's my home. I'm going to hate Salisbury . . ."

An angry grunt from her father startled her into jumping a little closer to Asa, and stifling a laugh, he slid a protective arm around her. "Well, I guess it'll be up to us to make you like Salisbury then, Melanie. Why don't we start by you calling me Uncle Asa?"

Darting her father another short look, Melanie finally conceded to his superiority and shot him a small, weak smile. Then turning back to Asa with inherent female instinct, she raised wide golden eyes to say in a soft compromise, "Well, I don't think I'll *ever* like Salisbury, but I *do* think I'm going to like you . . . Uncle Asa."

For a moment Asa looked startled, and then with a short laugh rose to his feet, a wide grin growing on his face. Turning to James, he clapped him on the back and said laughingly, "Don't you worry about Melanie, James. She'll do all right!" Then taking her hand, he winked at her and said, "I think Melanie and I are going to be great friends."

Glancing quickly to her father's face, Melanie was relieved to see an approving smile had begun to replace the scowl that had been directed at her most of the day.

A small sound on the stairs then caught their attention and they turned to see a small, dark, dreamy-eyed woman descending the staircase. Asa's smile seemed to dim for the shortest second before he stepped toward the staircase, saying as he did, "I thought you were sleeping, Emily. I hope we didn't awaken you."

The woman continued to descend with an oblivious air, hardly seeming to realize that her husband had spoken. As she came closer, Melanie noticed that she was painfully thin, with an unnaturally white color that emphasized the dark shadows under her strange, light eyes. Her gaze moved lightly from her husband to James, and came to rest on Melanie, a small frown wrinkling her unmarked brow.

With a jovial manner that began to look considerably forced, Asa attempted to draw his wife's attention back to himself. "As you can see, Emily, James and Melanie have finally arrived."

"It's good to see you again, Emily."

James' greeting went unheeded as Emily continued to stare at Melanie, her frown deepening.

"Melanie, this is your Aunt Emily. She's . . ."

"I had a daughter once . . ." Emily's words were as vague and distracted as her appearance. She continued speaking in spite of her husband's obvious efforts to get her attention, ". . . but she died. She would have been eight years old now . . . but she died . . . Are you going to be my daughter? . . ."

Noting the girl's apprehension as she stepped back to take her father's hand, Asa said gently, taking his wife's arm, "No, Emily, James and Melanie are only going to stay with us for a little while, until they can find a place of their own. You remember, I told you, James is going to be working at the foundry now. They'll be living in Salisbury."

There was no acknowledgment from Emily as she continued to stare at Melanie, and frightened, Melanie took a step closer to her father.

"Martha!"

Within an instant the large woman appeared in the hallway, and with a quick, appraising glance took the smaller woman's arm and said gently, "Let's up upstairs now, Mrs. Parker. I think you should rest for a while."

"But Martha, we have company . . ."

The woman's wan answer was overruled as Martha gently guided her toward the stairs. "You can come down again tomorrow. You'll be more rested tomorrow."

As the two women ascended the staircase, the silence was broken as James inquired quietly, "She's no better, Asa?"

"No, James . . . worse."

Melanie's inquiring glance moved between the two men. Seeing it, Asa took her hand and said brightly, efficiently shaking off his gloom with the practice of years, "We've delayed supper hoping you'd arrive tonight. You must be hungry. Come . . . let's eat."

The following morning Melanie was awake at the first light of day, her eagerness to see her new home the greatest cause of her sleeplessness. Still, she lay back, running her hand over the soft cotton sheets and enjoying the luxury of the thick, downy mattress under her back. Her own room! A real canopy bed, a dresser with a mirror, a chest of drawers, and matching footstool, all decorated with tiny hand-painted rosebuds along the borders; white lace curtains at the window and hanging from the graceful canopy over her; and a soft, flowered rug to warm her feet when she stepped from her downy haven. She could hardly believe it was really she lying in the midst of all this grandeur! The room had obviously been furnished with a young girl in mind, and Melanie wrinkled her nose unhappily at the reminder of Aunt Emily, mentally resolving to be kinder and more understanding in the future.

As an aroma of fresh bread wafted up from the kitchen, Melanie was unable to decide which was gnawing harder at her, her curiosity or her hunger. She dressed and made her way cautiously to the kitchen, finding it was not difficult, simply a matter of following her nose as her stomach gurgled in anticipation; but when she finally arrived at the threshold, she hesitated uncertainly. Martha, with her characteristic quick movements so unexpected in a woman of her size, was moving agilely from table to hearth in her daily, well organized morning ritual. Suddenly feeling out of place, Melanie moved to turn away as Martha noticed her and turned a cheerful flushed face toward her.

"Good morning, Miss Melanie. Come right on in here. You're a bit early for breakfast, but you can sample one of my sweet rolls if you're of a mind not to wait."

Quickly walking forward, Melanie answered with a bright, "Good morning!" simultaneously accepting the sweet roll held out to her in Martha's wide, plump hand. Within minutes she was seated at the corner of the table, a glass of milk in front of her and the remains of the roll in her mouth as Martha continued her work and chatted amiably. Slowly, as the minutes passed, a strange sense of uneasiness came over her. Unable to find the source inside the friendly kitchen, Melanie turned her head to glance at the windows and door. A frightened gasp escaped her mouth as a shaggy head staring in the window disappeared the moment she turned her face toward it.

24

"Martha, there's someone peeking in the window at us!"

Martha's pleasant face showed annoyance for the first time as she called loudly, "Tom, Tom, are you out there? Come in here immediately!"

Within moments a tall boy, not much older than fourteen in Melanie's judgment, shuffled through the doorway, and Melanie frowned. He was so strange looking. Tall and husky, the boy walked with an awkward, uncoordinated gait. His features were pleasant and in good proportion, but his eyelids hung heavily over dull blue eyes. He had a vacant expression and a laxity of facial muscles that caused his mouth to hang open stupidly while a small drop of spittle ran from its corner down his chin. His well trimmed blond hair was in wild disarray, and although spotlessly clean, his clothes were carelessly donned; his shirt buttoned unevenly in front, and the tail hanging out childishly in the rear. Where at first she had been frightened at the unusual sight he presented, Melanie suddenly found the awkward, ambling creature coming toward her quite comical and laughed out loud.

"What a funny looking boy!"

Seeing her smile, Tom stopped and grinned foolishly, his wide pink lips curling up in a bow, suddenly making him appear more ridiculous than before, and Melanie laughed wildly. Quite the contrary to taking offense, Tom began to laugh in a deep, dull voice that only convulsed her further, and within moments the two of them were laughing uproariously. It was only when Melanie saw Martha's flushed face and pained expression that she stopped abruptly.

"Miss Melanie, this is my son, Tom," Martha said quietly.

Acutely embarrassed and uncertain of what to say, Melanie said politely, "I'm pleased to meet you, Tom." Once again his cupid's bow grin flashed, and Melanie found laughter bubbling up inside her. How funny he is, she thought. Instinctively reaching out her hand, she took his and pulled him toward the table where she sat.

"Martha, may Tom have a roll and sit with me for a while?"

Not waiting for his mother's reply, Tom slipped into the chair beside her, stuffed a roll into his mouth, and smiled blissfully. Turning back to her milk with a smile, Melanie thought, I've never met such a funny boy!

In the weeks that followed, the brick house on Weaver's Row became as familiar as home to her, and Melanie began to assume her place in the household and in Salisbury. Against Asa's protests, Melanie found ways to make herself useful in the kitchen during the day while her father worked at the foundry. Delighting in the daily marketing trips with Martha, she related them in detail to Asa and her father at the supper table each night with an exuberance that delighted the former and often wearied the latter. Aunt Emily remained almost a complete mystery to her as she passed most of the day in her room content in her own little world. Surprisingly, at the end of the first month, Melanie found it hard to believe she had ever expected to be unhappy in her new home.

Her one regret was her first friendly overture to Tom. From the day of their first meeting, Tom took to following her like a lovesick puppy, jumping to her every command, smiling at her in his adoring, idiotic manner, until she felt she did not have a moment's peace. The children in the neighboring houses began to ridicule "Melanie's tail," laughing at the way the "dimwit" had attached himself to her until she flushed with embarrassment every time his foolish face appeared behind her. Finally in desperation, she began to avoid him, scattering out of his way when he approached, and hiding each time he attempted to follow her. She firmly decided she would not allow herself to be ridiculed because of his simpleminded adoration.

Melanie's wardrobe had grown considerably by the end of the first month in Salisbury, due to Asa's overriding of her father's protests. The girl who had never before owned more than two dresses at one time now had an exceedingly fine wardrobe of five dresses, and as she returned home from an afternoon with her new friends, her only thought was which one she would wear for supper that night. In Aunt Emily's absence, it was she who played unofficial mistress at suppertime, a role which Asa enjoyed, but often left her father shaking his head despairingly.

"I have a feeling you're going to miss this fine house when we move from here next month and you can no longer play the grand lady, Melanie. I just hope you don't think yourself too fine to be the daughter of a poor working man again after spending so much time in the biggest house in town."

Cut deeply by her father's remark, Mélanie responded in an injured voice, "Of course I won't Papa. What makes you think I'll be unhappy?"

Raised eyebrows and a knowing expression were her only answer, and it was his expression that nagged her unmercifully.

So engrossed in her thoughts was she that she almost missed the soft, muffled sound coming from the corner of the yard as she walked toward the kitchen door. Stopping, she listened again and heard low moans coming from behind the woodpile. She walked hesitantly toward the sound, uncertain what she might find hidden by the towering pile of wood, and gathering up her courage, quickly peeked around the corner.

Curled up in a sodden, miserable mound was Tom, his head hidden in his arms as low, heartrending sobs came from deep inside his chest.

"Tom, what is it? What's wrong? Are you sick?"

Startled, he turned a tear-streaked face toward her. His eyes were swollen from crying, his clothes muddy and disheveled from lying on the damp ground, and there were deep, bleeding grooves in his cheeks, where he had torn at his face in despair.

Melanie's own eyes filled with tears and she begged softly, "Tell me what happened, Tom."

Turning his face away from her he said roughly, "No! You're not my friend anymore! You don't like me!" Turning back again he said bitterly, "You won't let me come with you . . . you just run away.

You're not my friend at all . . . I'm all alone . . . I don't have a friend anymore. . . ." Putting his head back on his arms, he began sobbing anew.

Tears brimmed in her own eyes as guilt assailed her, and she turned away, unwilling to witness the anguish she had caused any longer. But Tom's deep, gulping sobs tore unmercifully at her conscience.

Suddenly straightening up, she swallowed hard and turned back toward him. Taking a deep breath, she grabbed his arm and shook it angrily.

"What are you talking about, Tom? Wasn't I looking all over for you this afternoon while *you* were hiding behind the woodpile? I called and called, and you didn't answer. I should be the one that's angry! But since you're sorry, I'll forgive you this time if you promise not to do it again, *and* if you'll wash your hands and face right now and help me ready supper with Martha."

Tom raised his head and blinked wonderingly as she continued to rail at him, a small smile picking up the corners of his mouth as he brushed the tears away.

"But just you remember, Tom," she said, frowning deeply and shaking a warning finger in his face, "the next time you hide from me all day, I won't forgive you, do you understand?"

Taking his arm, she struggled to pull him to his feet, looking at him sternly as his smile grew. "Remember, I'll only give you one more chance. Now hurry up and wash your face." And as he ran awkwardly toward the water pail in the corner of the yard, she called at his back, "Martha will be angry if we're late!"

Within a few minutes, his face still puffy but clean,

his clothes hastily tidied, and his blond hair plastered darkly back with water, Tom obediently followed Melanie into the kitchen, exceedingly happy that she had decided to forgive him for whatever it was that he had done. In those few short moments, Melanie had managed effectively to reattach her tail, and it was wagging happily behind her.

Asa Parker walked briskly along the well-traveled road from the foundry to his home. A tall man, his broad back and shoulders well muscled from the strenuous years in the foundry, he had the leanness and carriage of a much younger man, although the hard work and cares of his forty-two years had etched a fine network of lines on his pleasantly homely face. The warm afternoon sun beat down on his uncovered head, catching lightly on the gray hairs generously sprinkled among the dark. Possessed with an enthusiasm for living that the bitter experiences in his own life had dimmed but could not extinguish completely, he took heart once again with the onslaught of another season . . . another new beginning. He was suddenly immensely happy that his hard work had earned him the right to come and go as he pleased, for the day was too beautiful to be spent indoors, and he felt too distracted to do anything that demanded any degree of concentration. Whistling softly, he stopped occasionally to exchange friendly greetings with those he passed. He was a very popular, well-known man in Salisbury. And very much envied, he was sure—the owner of one of the largest industries in Litchfield County, living in the most elegant home in town, and certainly he was one of the richest men most of its residents knew. He would be richer yet, when the grants were settled. And yet he himself was envious . . . of his friend who had nothing he could claim as his own but his child.

It was unbelievable how Melanie had brightened his home, made it come to life again. After many years he had finally accepted the fact that Emily was lost to her own little world, and that they would never have another child, when a kind fate had seen fit to bring Melanie into his home. He was spoiling her terribly, even though James cautioned him against it, but he had so many years to make up and so little time. They would be moving to their own house at the end of the month. He envied James that sassy little chit of a girl who alternately cajoled, pouted, bossed, and wheedled her way around his house . . . and himself. In the short time she had been in Salisbury, Melanie had wrapped Martha, Tom, several assorted immature young swains, and himself around her little finger, and managed it with an inborn, instinctive charm and impudence that left them powerless against all her entreaties. James alone could hold out against her . . . and when she was really trying, not without considerable difficulty. Bounding agilely up the steps of his home, he thought with a degree of pleased amazement, that little girl's potential is formidable, absolutely formidable! Seeing her as he entered the hallway, he scooped her up and whirled her around with a roar of laughter, accompanied by her loud squeals of delight.

The warm April sun shone on the bared head of the

young man laboring furiously over his sextant. Slapping unconsciously at the gnats buzzing around his head, drawn by the beads of perspiration slipping unheeded down the sides of his face, he cast a nervous glance over his shoulder toward the road and in the direction of his horse. The animal was grazing peacefully on the new grass, oblivious to its owner's anxiety, and satisfied the surrounding countryside presented no immediate threat, he returned to his work. This was a job Hugh Monroe had started several times in the past year, only to be caught and ushered firmly from the territory with grave warnings as to his punishment should he return to do the Yorker "dirty work" within the province of the Hampshire Grants. Still, stubborn pride in his authority as an authorized surveyor of the colony of New York, as well as his snobbish resistance to being pushed about by the uneducated, wild woodsmen comprising the Bennington Mob, caused him to return again and again to complete the work he had started.

But he was not without fear, which he realized belatedly and only too vividly, as the sudden pounding of hooves on the road behind him caused a stab of panic to close his throat.

"Lord, it's them again!" was his first thought as he drew his slight figure up, smiling, feigning a boldness he did not feel as the group of riders drew alongside.

The faces surrounding him as they looked down from horseback were neither friendly nor smiling. Their leader, a huge, dark man in buckskins, was livid with anger at the sight of the familiar figure.

"So, you've chosen to ignore our warnings, Mr. Monroe. You stand there smiling, waving your defiance in our faces, flaunting your foolish sextant like a weapon of the righteous! Well, this is what I think of your 'weapon'!" Spurring his horse forward, he deliberately rode it down, causing it to crash and shatter beneath his horse's hooves, while he turned and rode forward again, the veins in his forehead bulging in a mask of fury. "You've been warned and escorted civilly from this territory three times, but our patience with you is now exhausted. You will pay for your devious part in this plot to steal our land!"

The smile had fallen from young Monroe's slightly sunburned face, and his body began a slight trembling as sudden realization of his vulnerability overwhelmed him.

The man is mad! he thought wildly, mad! Making an attempt to still the chattering of his teeth, young Monroe proclaimed in a loud voice, "Mr. Allen, I am an authorized agent of the colony of New York. I have been instructed by Governor Tryon—"

His use of the hated name was the final straw that flung the huge man from his horse in a rapid movement to stand towering a full head and shoulders above the surveyor while he bellowed wildly, "Tryon be damned!" and struck him to the ground.

Dragging him roughly to his feet by the back of his shirt, where he stood wavering uncertainly, Allen turned to his men.

"What do you say, men," he roared, "shall we try him now in our own court? The time for warnings is long past with this man. Action will speak louder than words to this damned fool who is deaf to our threats!"

"Yes, we'll be the judges."

"And I'll be your first witness," shouted another dark-haired, buckskin-clad figure as he dismounted and came to face the fear-ridden surveyor squarely. His dark eyes as they stared down at the slight, swaying young man were also filled with burning anger. "I'm witness to all three of his previous offenses. Each time he attempted to affix a semblance of legality to the Yorker swindle, he was warned not to return, but he has . . . and for the last time . . ."

"That's right, the last time . . . you tell him, Steve!" Angry shouts came from the other men as one at a time, four more stepped forward to testify. Finally appearing to have heard enough, Allen spoke out.

"You've heard the evidence . . . what is your verdict? Is this man guilty or not guilty?"

"Guilty! Guilty!" Emphatic shouts echoed in the vastness of the mountain meadow, and the surveyor's body began quaking visibly. With unbelieving ears he listened as his sentence was pronounced.

"Flogged! I'm to be flogged!" was his shocked reaction to the unanimous decision rendered by the "military court." "You men must be insane. I am an agent of the colony of New York, fully authorized . . . you can't do this . . . it's illegal . . . immoral," he shouted wildly.

Bound to a tree and stripped to the waist, he was still shouting wildly when the lash hit him for the first time. He continued screaming his disbelief, shouting his outrage while the strokes continued. Finally, mumbling of their inhumanity, he lost consciousness for the first time. But he was revived, and the flogging continued while he berated them, speaking incoherently of their presumption, until he fainted a second time. Once again he was revived, and the flogging continued. This time he did not speak at all and remained silent, except for the small whimpers of pain escaping his throat until he was unconscious again.

The young surveyor opened his eyes, dazed and disoriented, his body throbbing with pain, as a sandy-haired man bound his wounds. The burly, buckskin-clad men surrounding him were faintly familiar, but the deep booming voice coming from Allen, standing in their midst, struck terror anew in his trembling frame.

"You'll not disregard our warning again, Mr. Monroe. But in order that it may be firmly impressed upon your mind, I will repeat it once more. Your wounds have been dressed and you will be escorted back to Yorker territory. Do not venture here another time with your puny devices to steal our land in the name of the colony of New York. Your sentence today is mild in comparison to the one you will receive if you return."

Turning to the sandy-haired man he said loudly, "Put him on his horse, Josh." And turning back to the semiconscious fellow, eyes blazing, he railed, "Now you will remember that the gods of the hills are not the gods of the valley!"

The pitiful young man, his body limp and bleeding, was loaded onto his horse and led away, his last glimpse of the raging giant burned forever into his memory.

The men remaining watched the two figures move slowly down the road until they were out of sight, then, turning toward each other, mumbled and grunted their approvals of the proceedings and the manner in which they had been handled. That particular surveyor would not bother them again. They were all in agreement on that, and another attempt by New York to chart the land within the grants had been thwarted.

Satisfied with the success of their mission, the infamous band of Green Mountain Boys slowly dispersed to find their individual ways home. Two men separated from the group, their destinations the same. Both respected lieutenants of Ethan Allen; one was exhilarated, his sense of justice fully satisfied, having had the opportunity to strike a physical blow against his declared enemy; the other slightly revolted by the excessive measures necessary to defeat the Yorker threat. Both engrossed in their own thoughts, they silently followed the road back to Salisbury.

Chapter 2

1773

Standing as tall and erect as she could, Melanie turned from side to side surveying herself critically in the full-length mirror that dominated the corner of her room. She had come to take for granted the extravagance the expensive mirror represented, as well as the dainty, custom furniture that filled her room in the small house she and her father had rented for the past three years, and the extensive rack of dresses that caused the livid jealousy of so many of her friends. The consistent frequency of Uncle Asa's gifts during that time had long removed their novelty, and she had almost come to think of them as her due.

At the age of thirteen, the gilt-edged mirror had provided a curious Melanie her first opportunity to observe her own body in its entirety, and what a vast disappointment it had been! Flat and slender as a stick, she had been aghast at its colorless, sexless appearance. With complete clarity she remembered her mother's lovely womanly appeal, and railed aloud at her reflection, "You are an ugly, skinny, white thing! No man will ever look twice at you!" Turning again to view herself from the rear, which had proved to be no more appealing than the front, she had shaken her head sadly. "You'll end your days as a skinny, old spinster, with a doddering old Tom still trailing at your heels!"

The vision had been so vivid and so frightening that she returned to her mirror weekly in a stringent ritual to assess her naked body for its first signs of womanly development. The first year had proved a series of unending disappointments, while her body seemed determined to remain a child forever; but the following year showed a burst of improvement that caused her to flush with pleasure each time her weekly assessment was completed. In that time her small frame stretched amazingly to a few inches past five feet; and while her height stopped there, she continued growing in other ways. The delicate bone structure of her childhood remained, but her body began to curve appealingly around her breasts. The narrow rib cage seemed to narrow even more at the waist as a slight rounding appeared on her hips and rear portion. And her very legs seemed to lengthen in size! Slowly, the sharp angles and bony awkwardness of puberty began to disappear and the first signs of the woman Melanie would someday become began to emerge.

Previously pleased with the reflection staring back at her in the mirror, this day, at the fully blossomed age of sixteen, she was downright proud of what she saw. The small, heart-shaped face smiling back at her was dominated by huge, amber-colored eyes, heavily fringed with dark brown lashes right up to their provocatively slanting corners. All signs of freckles had disappeared from her short, straight nose, but her pink, finely drawn lips still spread into the wide, enchanting smile of her childhood, the small dimples dancing gracefully in her smooth, ivory cheeks. She had not only retained the auburn hair of her earlier years, but it now radiated a deep, warm glow as it gently framed the graceful contours of her face and fell to a length below her waist. Pleasing her the most, however, were the splendid proportions her body had developed; the slender, graceful column of her throat and the smooth, soft contours of her shoulders, arms, and hands. Her young, high breasts were full, beautifully shaped, erect and pointed, and the still narrow rib cage tapered to an even narrower, minuscule waist. The line of her body traveled smoothly from neatly curved hips and tempting buttocks to long, shapely legs that perfected the symmetry of her form. Extremely pleased with what she saw, she was reaching for her chemise when she heard a low, familiar voice calling from the kitchen.

"Melanie . . . Melanie . . . are you home, Melanie?"

Suppressing a small stab of annoyance, she called out loudly in return, "Yes, Tom, I'm here. I'll be there in a few minutes."

Tom had been coming to pick her up at the same time in late morning almost without exception for the past three years, and still called as if he half-expected her to be gone. But Tom was a child . . . he would always be a child . . . practically her child.

"Imagine that!" she thought, laughing to herself, "Here I am, sixteen years old with a seventeen-year-old child! Well, no one else I know can claim such a feat!"

"Melanie . . . Melanie . . ."

"I said I'm coming, Tom."

Moving to the large wardrobe almost completely covering one wall of her room, she unhesitantly took a soft, blue and white dress from the rack, knowing full well that its gently scooped, modest neckline still provided the opportunity to show the tempting swell of her full breasts and emphasized the narrowness of her waist. Slipping it over her head, she peeked again in the mirror. Yes, the softness of the pastel blue was a perfect foil for her coloring. Leaving her brilliant hair parted in the center and streaming down her back, she merely lifted the front two locks and pulled them to the back of her head, fastening them with a blue satin ribbon. Quickly sliding her dainty feet into soft black slippers, she took one last look, twirling around to be certain everything was perfect. The young men at the foundry had suddenly begun to pay her an inordinate amount of attention when she brought her father's noon meal, and there was one fellow in particular, Stephen Hull, whose wicked, teasing eyes sent little tremors up her spine. The knowledge that he and his friend Josh Whitmore were members of the Green Mountain Boys only added to his romantic appeal. She hadn't been able to make up her mind whether she liked their colonel, Ethan Allen, even though he was a good friend of her father, but it mattered little for she rarely saw him.

"Oh, well, I'll give that Stephen Hull something to look at today!" she said to her reflection with a mischievous laugh. Then calling to Tom, who was once again bellowing her name, "I'm coming, I'm coming . . . don't be so impatient, Tom!" She hastened toward the kitchen where Tom awaited their daily ritual walk to and from the foundry.

Escorting her was a task her father had entrusted to him, to his everlasting and total delight three years ago, and which he intended, with the limited horizons of the dimwitted, to fulfill forever. As her eyes caught sight of the grown Tom, smiling adoringly as she entered the room, her heart gave a little wrench of pity. Tall, muscular, fair-haired and fine-featured, he could have been a beautiful man had not some cruel twist of fate caused a childhood disease to limit his brain and bestow on him that perpetually foolish expression that distorted his handsome features.

Snatching up the basket she had prepared earlier, she feigned an impatient expression. "Papa will be wondering where his lunch is today, Tom. You always make me wait for you!"

41

Tom's startled expression was comical, and bursting into laughter, Melanie grabbed his arm and pulled him with her through the doorway, not able to resist one last tease. "Come on now, Tom, that's enough of your dilly-dallying."

Aware from years of experience that her father would not put up with her tardiness, and realizing her vanity had set them behind schedule, she pulled the door shut, and laughingly rushed Tom across the street. Not really understanding the reason for her laughter, but delighted as her merry, sparkling eyes were raised to his to be included in her joke, Tom's low, dull laughter boomed loudly as they moved quickly across the street.

Benson Road was only one street removed from Weaver's Row, where Uncle Asa resided, but the two streets could not have been more different had they been miles apart. Uncle Asa's house and well-kept grounds occupied most of Weaver's Row, sharing it only with one other house of the same stature; but on Benson Road, the small frame houses ran in straight lines down the street, one against the other, appearing to depend upon each other for support like a flimsy house of cards, where the removal of one would cause a chain of collapse all along the line. Privacy was a difficult commodity in this situation where the closing of a window, the raising of a voice, or the slam of a door so easily caught the attention of the insatiably curious busybodies that inhabited the neighboring houses.

From the corner of her eye, Melanie could see a figure at the window two houses down from hers, and realized that the insidious Mrs. Harriet Sims was at her window watching her departure. Morbidly preoccupied with sin, the old woman saw it everywhere and in everyone, especially in Melanie, whose vivacity and enjoyment of life was to her a sin in itself. Responsible in the past for vicious rumors about Tom's ritual visits after James' departure for work, Mrs. Sims had considered it a personal defeat when James' openminded realization of the harmless, lonely boy's adoration and need for Melanie's friendship had allowed him to continue his visits. The spiteful woman's insistent intrusion into her life in the years since had only inflamed Melanie's stubborn resistance to her unsought advice, taking every opportunity to wave her defiance in the outraged woman's face.

"The old witch is spying on us again, Tom," she whispered. "Well, I'll raise her blood a little bit today, the jealous old crone . . ."

Slowing her step so abruptly that Tom, in his awkwardness, almost tripped, Melanie raised her eyes apologetically to his questioning gaze and winked companionably. Tossing her shining auburn hair flirtatiously, she continued walking slowly, increasing the provocative sway of her slender young body, and swinging her basket gayly. She could feel the vicious woman's heated stare on her back, but was not aware that true, venomous hatred burned in those eyes.

As soon as they had rounded the corner, however, and Melanie was certain she was no longer in Mrs. Sims' sight, she grabbed Tom's hand, jerking him forward, and began to run, simultaneously saying over her shoulder, "Come on, Tom, hurry! You're too slow! Papa will skin me alive if we're late again!"

A short distance from the foundry, they slowed their pace enough to catch their breaths. Smoothing her hair and dress carefully, Melanie and Tom entered the yard, showing no signs of the wild dash that had brought them there on time.

A light gust of wind ruffled James Morganfield's lightly graying hair as he emerged from the foundry for his noon break. The first sign of change from the winter's cold usually brought the fifty-odd workers outside to take their lunch under the few trees left standing behind the foundry, giving them an opportunity to escape for a brief period the oppressive heat generated inside. Wearily wiping away the beads of perspiration covering his forehead and upper lip with the back of one well-calloused hand, he walked slowly to his customary spot beneath the farthest tree, and sat down on the ground, stretching out his long, still slim frame in exhaustion.

The further the better from that blasted heat, he thought, wondering why it was such a drain on his strength the past few weeks. "I'm just not feeling up to snuff these days . . . what I need is to get away from this bloody town and breathe some cool, fresh mountain air again."

Each fall, during the three he had spent in Salisbury, James had returned for a few days to his homestead in Poultney, and each time it had been harder for him to come back. Never a town dweller at heart, with each passing day his life here palled a little more than before. But it won't be long now, he thought with an amused chuckle, as the first two of the group of young men that he usually found gathering around him during lunch began moving in his direction. It was amazing how popular he had suddenly become with the young bucks at the foundry since Melanie had blossomed into woman-hood. Within a few minutes he would be casually surrounded. Biting back a chuckle, he watched as the young men began filtering toward him and shook his head. Like bees toward honey . . . and then with a frown he thought, and the "honey" is late today . . .

As if in answer, two figures suddenly emerged around the side of the building; Melanie, small and graceful, and Tom, lumbering contentedly beside her. Inwardly he was tickled even further when all heads turned simultaneously in her direction as Melanie began walking briskly across the yard toward him; but his frown deepened as he watched eager eyes following the bobbing of her voluptuous young body, almost devouring her with their glances.

"Darn that brazen little miss," he fumed to himself, "I've warned her countless times to walk more sedately. I've half a mind to start bringing a cold lunch."

Misreading his angry glare and fearing she had arrived late despite her haste, Melanie increased her pace, unknowingly causing the group surrounding him to almost pant.

Groaning to himself, James called aloud, "Melanie, please take your time. I'm not very hungry this afternoon."

Momentarily taken aback by his unexpected remark, Melanie looked questioningly at her father,

45

and noting his uneasy expression as he glanced toward the young fellows around him, she suddenly smiled, and slowed her pace. The effect her slowed, unaffected but undulating walk had on the group surrounding him as she approached was even worse than before, and hearing a low, stifled groan coming from within the group, he turned to see all eyes riveted in her direction. Rising to his feet, he thought defeatedly, as the group around him rushed to make small talk with his lovely daughter, I'm going to have to marry her off quickly, before she turns the whole bunch of them into slavering fools!

With a surface calm that belied the rising heat in his loins, Stephen Hull lazily scrutinized Melanie's arrival. Leaning his brawny frame indolently against the tree, he remarked caustically to his friend, his inner turmoil betrayed only by the sarcasm of his words, "Well, the show is about to begin again. Here comes Miss Sweetness and Innocence with her drooling watchdog trailing faithfully behind. Look at those stupid bastards," he said, indicating the group that watched and waited expectantly, "they're eating it up! The damn fools!"

"What do you have against Melanie Morganfield, Steve? You hardly know her."

"I don't have to know her. I know her type—the virgin pure—teases a man to death, but stops him just short of the bed. He has to marry her to get her body. But pity the man that gets that sultry little piece—"

"You don't know what you're talking about, Steve. James Morganfield is a good man, and as far as I

46

know his daughter's reputation is spotless. Just look at the way he's eyeing that bunch!" Josh suddenly started to laugh. "He looks like he'd scalp the first one that made a false move!"

Speaking as much to himself as to his friend, Steve mumbled softly, "They're all the same. The 'good women' freeze their men to death in bed, thawing just enough to produce heirs at modest intervals; and the others, the ones that like the feel of a man's body inside them, are like bitches in heat once they have a taste of it. Then they don't care where they get it, as long as it's available."

"Steve, you're insane, do you know that!" There were times when Josh found his friend completely unfathomable, and he never ceased to be amazed when Steve started off on one of these wild tangents. Shaking his head in bewilderment, he said unbelievingly, "Where do you get these ideas?"

His eyes still glued to Melanie, Steve answered angrily, "I know what I'm talking about, believe me. I can attest to it first hand. My own mother was one of them. Drove my father to his grave with her endless whoring . . ." In his mind Steve could still hear his father's drunken voice . . . "She was a good woman, Steve, a good woman. . . . What happened? What did I do wrong?"

"Take a good look at her, Josh. Oh, she's still a virgin, I don't doubt that, but you can tell just from the look of her that she'll be a hot little bitch in bed."

Josh's eyes narrowed in anger, but he bit back his retort. Steve was a bastard when it came to women, but he was a true friend of three years standing, and he had no desire to argue with him about a girl neither of them really knew. "Just do yourself a favor, Steve. Stay away from her. She's marriage material, and you're not the marrying kind—"

"You're damn right I'm not! No woman will ever get a yoke around my neck. I'll rot in Hell before I make that mistake!"

Watching as Melanie effortlessly whipped the heat in the group around her up another notch, Steve swore under his breath, his eyes raping her viciously. Turning casually, Melanie caught and held his torrid gaze for one long second. Flushing brightly, she looked away from him, and Steve's voice trembled with the passion of his muttered vow as Josh shook his head helplessly.

"Mark my words, Josh, here and now. I might not be the first to have Melanie Morganfield, but I'll have her, damn the little bitch, and when I do, she'll come begging for more . . ."

Quickly swinging her attention back to the men surrounding her, Melanie's heart was beating so fast she was almost weak. What was the matter with that Stephen Hull? She had barely exchanged more than a few words with him, and he was looking at her now almost as if he hated her! As if he—but I hardly know him!

Not that she hadn't been aware of him the moment she had entered the yard. She could feel his presence whenever he was near. All other men paled in comparison. She had never seen a more handsome man; black, waving hair that gleamed in the sunlight; black, dangerous, unforgettable eyes; a strong, masculine face with firm, sensual lips that

48

only occasionally smiled to show straight white teeth. And his stature, tall and broad, narrow waisted and flat hipped, those strong, muscular thighs—he was beautiful! But in the one moment their eyes had met, the thrill that had swept over her was replaced by a cold chill crawling up her spine . . . it was almost as if he hated her. . . .

At the window of the foundry, observing but unobserved, stood Asa Parker. His eyes, too, were riveted on Melanie, his emotions torn in so many directions at once that he was almost ill. Was it only three years since she and James had come to Salisbury? Three years for that precocious little chit to become the center of his life? In the years since he had been forced to put Emily into an institution for her own safety, Melanie alone had provided the impetus for living. Now, as he watched the scene in the foundry yard, he was overwhelmed with jealousy. He was bound to lose her soon, and he didn't have a father's prerogative to remain a part of her life. He wouldn't be able to spoil her any longer, or be subject to her merciless wheedling, which he enjoyed more than he cared to admit. She'd have a husband and father . . . there'd be no place for him. . . .

His heart was suddenly pounding, racing so fast that he had difficulty in breathing. Struggling to regain his composure, he remained at the window until his breathing returned to normal, and then turned toward the door. He had just reached the yard, when Melanie, tugging Tom by the arm, turned to leave.

"So, you can't spare any time for your Uncle Asa these days, is that it, little lady?"

The sound of his voice whipped her around, her pleasure obvious in her broad, spontaneous smile. "Uncle Asa!" Running forward, she hugged him impulsively. "You know Papa has strictly forbidden me to bother you at your office, or," she whispered in his ear, "you wouldn't be able to get rid of me!"

Inexplicably, a lump caught in his throat, and he was unable to reply. But his momentary problem went unnoticed as Melanie turned toward her father and gave him a bold wink. Laughing as he shook his head in exasperation, she turned back to her uncle, and slipping her arm through his, urged him along with her.

"Walk with me a little way, Uncle Asa. I'd better start moving out of here fast before my father assists me with the toe of his boot!"

Suddenly they were both laughing together, and Asa felt the warmth only Melanie could kindle within him.

"When are you and James coming for supper again, Melanie? Martha just this morning remarked that she hardly ever sees you anymore."

"Well, a girl usually has to wait to be invited, you know," Melanie said, fluttering her long, gold-tipped eyelashes wildly.

With a hoot of laughter, Asa bowed slightly. "Consider yourself invited, my dear."

Curtsying gracefully, Melanie replied lightly, "Consider yourself accepted, sir!" Then laughing wildly as she grabbed for Tom's arm, she said over her shoulder as she pulled him away, "We'll be there tonight. Tom will tell Martha."

With a short wave she was off. Asa turned back to

the foundry, his heart pounds lighter. He'd see her tonight . . .

The square, unpainted wooden building in the Bennington hills was alive with activity. The Catamount Tavern, operated by Stephen Fay and his two sons, had seen the birth of the Green Mountain Boys and remained their favorite courtroom and meeting place. A stuffed, fawn-colored catamount, the silent, deadly cougar of the forest, stood outside the entrance to the tavern, facing west. It was the symbolic guardian of the Hampshire Grants against all threats from Yorker claims, and a fierce, bold reminder that the buckskin-clad and homespun-clad men inside would defend with force of arms the rights to their property within those grants.

Remember Baker and Seth Warner, both lieutenants under Ethan Allen, sat at one of the tables, conversing in low tones sprinkled with intermittent laughter. Steve and Josh joined the other members of the band filling the remaining tables and standing around the room awaiting Allen's arrival, their brotherhood expressed solely by the sprig of evergreen all wore in their caps.

Momentary silence fell as the door opened to admit a familiar, dark-haired giant well over six feet two inches tall and broad of shoulder and muscle. An impressive figure in his well-worn buckskins, moccasins, and homespun shirt, he was a man who was quick to smile and quick to anger, a glib talker and a born revolutionary, as well as the most respected and feared woodsman and fighting man in the territory. Within seconds the silence was broken by loud, raucous shouts of greetings.

"You sure took your time getting here, Ethan!"

"What happened, did some sweet, young thing delay you?"

"No, but I'll wager her old mother did!"

Riotous laughter followed that remark, and Ethan's sober face broke into his familiar smile as he replied in a casual, booming voice, "No, as a matter of fact, that isn't what happened. Actually, my horse went lame on the trail when I was halfway here, and I had to carry the damned animal the rest of the way!"

Wild merriment rang in the room as the men convulsed in laughter. Accustomed as they were to Ethan's exaggerated stories as well as his actual, almost inhuman feats of strength and endurance, his wit never failed to raise their spirits, proving to be a wellspring of strength in trying moments.

Allowing only a few moments for the laughter to die down, Ethan turned toward his men, his face once again deadly serious, commanding attention with his earnestness.

"We have another problem to solve tonight, men . . . that damned old turncoat, Dr. Samuel Adams, has been flaunting his Yorker talk in our faces again. He's taken to criticizing our tactics and our justice. He carries two pistols, threatening to shoot any one of us who interferes with him. He's a menace to our cause. What shall we do about it?"

"Fifty lashes will fix him!"

"Hang him from his thumbs!"

"We can tar and feather him!"

Angry voices came from all corners of the tavern, showing the instant hatred that flared against all who would rob them and their families of their life's work by submitting to New York's demands. Ethan surveyed his impassioned men, feeling the heat of his own anger which boiled at the doctor's Yorker leanings. With unusual restraint he again assumed the floor.

"Ah, but this is not our average turncoat, men. He's sheathed in respectability, armored in good looks, and protected by our own people's need for him. Any harsh action we take against him will only convince the people that he is right, and bring their wrath down upon us. We already have a Yorker price on our heads . . . we need the confidence of our own people."

"If he goes unpunished it weakens our cause!"

"Just give him twenty-five lashes, then—"

Ethan's roar of laughter interrupted the shouting. "Twenty-five lashes would lay the reprobate low for a month and turn half the community against us!"

The heads at the tables turned toward each other, begrudgingly nodding their agreement, but anger still burned in their eyes.

"Damn the old geezer! Let him pay just like the rest of the traitors!"

"Yes, . . . fifty lashes!"

Holding up his thickly muscled arm, Ethan called for silence. His was a devious mind and he had not come to the meeting unprepared. "We must first decide one thing . . . is he to be ignored or punished for his treachery?"

"Punished!"

"He can't go free . . ."

Shouts echoed from all quarters, demanding

retribution, and Ethan surveyed the crowd, carefully assessing the heat of their reactions. Finally satisfied they were all in accord, a slow smile spread across his broad features. There were a few moments of silence before Remember called out in a deep voice, "All right, Ethan, out with it. What do you have in mind? I can tell by your face you have our answer for us."

"Well, gentlemen," Ethan's voice was pure cunning, "we'll put him on trial—"

"All right, a trial. But what then?"

"First the verdict . . . and let the punishment fit the crime . . ."

Ethan's cryptic statement was met with puzzled stares, but as his smile grew, his men's spirits lightened. Ethan could be relied upon to have a trick up his sleeve, and all present had experience with his mastery over difficult situations.

"We're with you, Ethan."

"Let the punishment fit the crime . . ."

"Yes, we're all with you . . ."

For all his swaggering, the unworthy doctor's brace of pistols proved useless against the Green Mountain Boys. Within an amazingly short lapse of time he was taken, tried and convicted of traitorous conduct—and served his sentence. To a spot twenty-five feet high in the air outside the tavern, the libelous doctor was hoisted, still tied securely to a chair; and there he hung, in full sight of all Bennington for two humiliating hours, staring down into the snarling fangs of the catamount to contemplate the power within those jaws, and the fury and damage that could and would be reaped by those who dared defy them.

In those two, long hours, Dr. Samuel Adams' loyalty, as well as his silence, were won.

Slowly going through the small rack of ready-made dresses in the rear of Carter's store, Melanie heaved a small sigh of relief. Tom had not been able to stay with her this afternoon, and she finally had some time to herself. He was a dear, but sometimes a girl just wanted to be . . .

A sharp electric tingle coursed down her spine as a hand closed on Melanie's shoulder and turned her around. Suddenly staring up into the enigmatic black eyes that had not left her thoughts since that afternoon in the foundry five days before, her heart began racing wildly and she was at a sudden loss for words.

"Well, if it isn't Melanie Morganfield," Steve's deep voice purred as he moved forward another step, effectively backing her up against the rack of dresses she had been examining. "I just stopped in for some tobacco and spotted you back here all alone . . . Where's your watchdog? Did someone tie him up behind the house for a while?"

Suddenly livid at Steve's demeaning reference to Tom, Melanie spat out angrily, "If you're referring to Tom, he had some chores to do at home. And I'll thank you not to refer to him in that manner again, Mr. Hull!"

Her eyes sparking pure fire, she attempted to remove his hand from her shoulder, but he quickly slipped it up and under her hair to cradle the back of her neck as his eyes moved warmly over her face, coming to rest on her soft, moist lips. His own lips parted, and she could see the pulse throbbing in his throat as he spoke softly. "We could come together with real beauty, you and me, Melanie. You feel it, don't you?" Moving even closer until their bodies lightly touched, he began caressing her neck lightly, his other hand holding her arm fast.

Melanie gasped at the searing heat that rushed through her veins as his body touched hers, and whispered hoarsely, "Let me go! You'll have the whole town talking about me! Your reputation certainly can't worsen, but my father—"

"There's no one in this part of the store, Melanie . . . no one will see anything unless you call their attention to us."

Without her realization, the hand on her arm had slid around her waist, and suddenly pressed her tight against him. His heart was thumping against her breast, echoing her own erratic heartbeat, his lips only inches from hers as a muscle twitched in his cheek and he whispered hoarsely, "I want you, Melanie . . . I can make you very, very happy . . ."

He lowered his mouth slowly over hers and groaning suddenly, he appeared to throw caution to the winds and wrapped both arms around her in a binding embrace, his mouth plunging deeper, separating her lips, his tongue wildly probing her mouth.

Struggling desperately against his demanding kiss, Melanie was assailed with a strange weakness in her knees that gradually increased until she was clinging to him for support, her body transfused with a wild, pulsating heat that seemed to overwhelm her senses. Without her realization, Melanie's arms slid around his neck, clutching desperately as his mouth plundered hers.

When finally he drew his mouth away, they were both trembling visibly, their breaths coming in deep gulps as their bodies heaved against each other. Melanie could feel the swell of his manhood bruising her as he continued to hold her fast against him, and her face flamed.

"Please let me go, Mr. Hull."

He gave a short laugh, not bothering to even loosen his hold. "I think you can call me Steve now, Melanie." And after a few seconds, "No, I won't let you go . . ."

His tongue came out to lick lightly at her lips, and another tremor shook her small body. His quiet laugh bore a victorious ring as he whispered against her ear, caressing it with his mouth as he spoke, "I'll let you go now if you'll promise to meet me behind the boardinghouse in ten minutes." There was easy access to his room from there and his body was screaming to take her.

"No! Let me go, please . . . someone will be back here in a minute—"

"Not until you promise to meet me. You know you want to, Melanie. You want to know what else I can do to make you feel really good. I can make your body sing, Melanie," he was covering her face with short, hot kisses as he spoke, "I can make you glow . . . you want me . . . you know you do."

"No, please," Melanie could feel that same weakness slipping over her and she fought wildly, desperately. "No, let me go I said . . . let me go—"

"I won't let you go."

"Oh yes you will, Steve." A low voice sounded quietly from behind them, suppressed violence obvious in each word he spoke.

Jerking around at the sound of the voice, Steve moved enough to allow Melanie a chance to see a broad, sandy-haired figure standing eye to eye with him.

"This is between Melanie and me, Josh." Steve's voice was low with anger as he faced his friend. "She doesn't want me to let her go, do you Melanie?"

"Oh, yes, please make him let me go," Melanie sobbed, embarrassment and shame finally spilling the tears down her cheeks.

"Let her go, Steve, or you'll be a damned sorry man, I warn you." Josh's eyes glared darkly into Steve's and held his gaze until Steve suddenly blinked, and turned back to Melanie as he released her.

"This isn't the place to take this any further, but you can be sure we'll be meeting again, Melanie," he said, his eyes staring deeply into hers, "and again."

Suddenly realizing she was free, Melanie broke away and rushed toward the front of the store. Stopping only a moment to brush her face clear of tears she lifted her head, and walking as sedately as her trembling legs would carry her, left the store without looking back.

"Who in blazes gave you the right to interfere in my business?" Steve's face flamed with fury as he turned to face Josh.

"She's just an innocent girl, Steve. Leave her alone."

"That's where you're wrong. You should have felt the way she came alive in my arms. I told you she's a hot little bitch, and now I'm certain of it. Somebody's going to get her soon, and it might as well be me!"

"I said to leave her alone!" Josh's fury was quickly mounting to match Steve's as they faced each other squarely.

Slowly a smile came to Steve's face, and he shook his head in apparent amazement. "Well, I'll be damned . . . you want her, too, don't you?" Not waiting for a denial, his face grew suddenly vicious as he whispered venomously, "Well, that's too bad, because I've got that little bitch staked out for myself, and she's hot for me, too, let me tell you. So stay clear of her and out of my business, Josh, if you know what's good for you."

Turning abruptly on his heel, he strode away, leaving Josh staring heatedly at his retreating figure.

Crossing the street in long, angry strides, Steve was shaking inside with frustration. Damn him . . . damn that Josh! Just a few minutes more and I'd have had her just where I wanted her! God, she's a beautiful little wench! he thought, as he saw her face looking up into his in his mind's eye. Those eyes . . . yellow fire . . . and that body . . . He could feel himself hardening, and he cursed Josh again.

He hadn't been able to successfully drive Melanie out of his mind since that day in the foundry the week before. The picture of her had come sneaking into his mind at the most inopportune times—at the tavern while Ethan was talking, during the trial, afterwards, when he should have been enjoying the doctor's embarrassment—and on the trail home, all he could think about was the way she came swinging into the yard, that fiery hair bobbing, her breasts moving beneath the fabric of her dress. Her nipples were probably still pink . . . virgin . . .

Opening the door of his rooming house, he slammed it hard behind him and took the stairs to his room two at a time. Damn him! Damn that Josh! If he thought he was going to get her first, he was dead wrong! When he was finished with Melanie Josh could have her, but he had a feeling he wasn't going to tire of her too easily. There was a lot he could teach her, and he was going to enjoy every minute of her lessons.

But in the meantime, he thought, his glance following the progress of the ripe little maid as she made her way down the hall, his eyes roaming her full curves as she carried the dishes into the dining room, you're in for a real workout, Peg. It's going to take you half the night to wear the heat out of me tonight. Catching her eye as she looked up the stairs toward him, he winked, his good humor beginning to return as she returned his wink boldly.

Another time . . . another place, Melanie . . .

Standing outside the doorway to Carter's Store, Josh's eyes followed the tall, dark man striding angrily down the street, his heavy brown brows drawn together in a frown. He slid a large, calloused hand through his already tousled hair in a revealingly weary gesture. Although he and Josh were a match in size, both standing a shade over six feet and heavily muscled, there the similarity between them ended. Steve's dark good looks had a sensuous, threatening air, his moody, morose nature drawing the women he so scorned like flies. Josh on the other hand was light haired and lighter complexioned. His disposition, taking cue from his appearance, was good-natured and his brown eyes beneath gathered brows, now so dark and thoughtful, sparked with spontaneous humor and wit at the slightest provocation. Although his strong nose bore a slight lump at the bridge from a bone broken in a fight, testimony that his good nature could not be abused, his wide, unsmiling mouth was usually spread in an irrepressible grin.

His eyes followed the figure striding away until it turned to the doorway of their rooming house and disappeared through it with a vicious slam. He wasn't taking any chances that Steve would suddenly change his mind and go after Melanie again. A sudden resurgence of anger flashed over him at the thought. That bastard! Did he really think all women were like the whores he whiled his time away with every night? Not that he himself was one to remain celibate. Hell, no! But he damn well knew the difference between a whore and a virgin, and knew how to treat each!

He began walking slowly toward the rooming house, a picture of Melanie coming into his mind. That long auburn hair, her jaunty, uninhibited walk, and that bright, beautiful face. He wondered how her face would look at very close range . . . how deep was the gold in those amber eyes . . . how those dimples would feel under his fingertips as they played across her smooth cheeks. He'd like to fit his hands around her narrow waist and run them up her straight white back, pressing her against him . . .

Hell, he thought, with a short laugh at the path his own thoughts had taken and the heat he could feel building in his own loins, I'm no better than Steve! He had no right to start thinking about a girl like Melanie now, as tied up as he was with visits back to his homestead where his mother and three younger brothers still farmed the land that Yorkers had already attempted to claim twice since the trouble started. His future wasn't his own and wouldn't be for a very long time. So, why am I getting myself all heated up over a girl who is definite marriage material and, he admitted with a strong twinge of resentment he couldn't suppress, who looks through me like glass whenever Steve is around.

Well, I'll stay clear of that little piece of fluff and, damn it, I'll make sure Steve does, too! Finally having come to a settlement with himself, Josh began walking a little faster. Steve had had some time to cool down a little. He might just as well make his peace with him now . . .

Melanie hurried all the way home, her frantic pace just short of running, and entered to slam the door hard behind her. Running wildly to her room, she threw herself across the bed, burying her face in the softness of the comforter as her body shook uncontrollably. She was perspiring, her dress damp and clinging, her hair warm against her neck. She had had a narrow escape. If Josh Whitmore hadn't interfered at that minute, she really wasn't certain what would have happened. She was going to have to thank him when she saw him again. Thank him . . . a narrow escape . . . but had she really wanted to escape? Her face flamed at her own rioting thoughts. Then why did she still feel Steve's body against hers, still taste his tongue in her mouth, feel the strength of his arms crushing her against him, that hard bulge pressing against her stomach. She had had no experience with men and knew only through the whispers of her friends and the warnings of her father and Martha what to expect and avoid. Turning over, she lay for a few minutes staring at the ceiling, and began to imagine Steve lying beside her . . . his hands touching her, his face lowering over hers. The trembling began again and she felt a warm moistness between her legs. Slowly getting to her feet, she began removing her clothing, coming finally to stand naked before her mirror. Her hands moved lightly over her breasts and along the curve of her waist and hips. If Steve could see her like this, would he be pleased with what he saw? Her eyes traveled down to the small triangle of reddish brown curls nestled between her thighs. How would it feel to have his hardness inside her? Suddenly ashamed, she turned away to cover her face with her hands. What was the matter with her? Was she a wanton? Slowly her hands moved away from her face, and she turned back to the mirror, the question in her mind reflected on her beautiful, frightened face. If he caught her alone again, and he had said he would, would she . . . did she really want to escape?

Morning came too soon to a weary Melanie who had spent a restless night wrestling with her emotions. Adding to the strain she felt was the effort of keeping up a normal facade for her father, to avoid any suspicions. She needed no further complications in a situation that was already too complex to suit her. Walking slowly beside Tom on their way to the foundry, Melanie absentmindedly slipped her arm through his. She was not at all certain how she would react if she ran into Steve again so soon in the foundry yard, but she couldn't and wouldn't be coward enough to run away from the confrontation. But knowing in her heart she really had no alternative, she sighed deeply.

"Melanie . . ."

"What is it, Tom?" Her face was strained and serious as she looked up at him, devoid of its usual sparkle, and Tom was suddenly alarmed.

"Are you sick, Melanie? Does your stomach hurt?"

Taken by surprise with his question, Melanie laughed lightly. "No, why do you ask, Tom?"

"Because you're not happy. It's a pretty day and you always say you like to walk with me." Suddenly putting his free hand on her forehead, he unconsciously mimicked Martha's tone as he said solemnly, "I don't think you have a fever—"

Suddenly it was back, her wide smile and the twinkle in her eye, and Tom was happy again. He was always happy when Melanie smiled, and sad when she didn't.

"I'm all right, Tom, just a little tired, that's all." Realizing how her mood had affected him, she impulsively reached up to kiss his cheek lightly. "And you are a good, dear boy for worrying about me. I'm very lucky to have a good friend like you, Tom."

His bright, answering expression, as they turned the corner of the foundry yard and approached James, spoke for itself.

The usual group of young men stood nearby, waiting, and Melanie gave them the full warmth of her smile. Darting a quick look out of the corner of her eye to the spot Steve usually occupied during the lunch break, she saw his knowing smile as he caught her glance.

He's laughing at me!

Her face flaming, she turned toward her father while she fumed inwardly. What an infuriating man! I'll show that Steve Hull that I'm not like the rest of the tarts he winds so easily around his finger!

"I've brought your favorite lunch today, Papa. I baked you a fresh meat pie and it's still hot. Hurry and . . ." Melanie's words trailed away as her father turned his face in her direction.

"Papa! What's wrong?"

James' face was an odd gray color, and although there was a fresh spring breeze blowing, he was sweating profusely with beads of perspiration running from his temples down the sides of his face.

Answering her in a low, warning voice, he said quickly, "There's nothing wrong with me. Don't make a fuss, Melanie." Turning back away from her he sat on the ground, his attention directed to the lunch basket. Realizing she would not get an answer while the others stood so close by, she said in her sweetest voice, "Would you excuse me today, fellows? I have something to discuss with my father." Not waiting for an answer, she turned away and sat beside him.

"Papa, what's wrong?" Watching nervously as the perspiration continued to stream down his averted face, a note of fear entered her voice. "Please tell me, Papa. Don't you feel well?"

Realizing she was near panic, James turned and attempted a slight smile. "It's just a bad headache and a touch of indigestion. You won't be offended if I don't eat your pie this afternoon, will you?"

His obvious attempt to relieve her tension brought tears to her eyes, and seeing them, James spoke more sternly. "Melanie, you will not embarrass me by making a scene over a small case of indigestion. Sit there and wait until the lunch period is over, if you wish, but behave yourself. I'm beginning to feel better already."

Even as he spoke, his color appeared to be slowly returning to normal, and Melanie began to feel slightly relieved. Slipping her hand into his large, calloused palm, she whispered lightly, "I can see you are feeling better, Papa, but you did give me a fright for a moment." Smiling brightly as he gave her small hand a tight squeeze, she suddenly realized how much she had always taken his steady presence for granted. Impulsively leaning over, she kissed his damp cheek lightly, eliciting a low growl as he glanced around self-consciously for any witnesses to his daughter's show of affection.

"Melanie Morganfield, you will sit there quietly and behave yourself, or you will leave immediately for home, do you hear me?"

Satisfied that his color was once again almost

normal, she sat the remaining time in silence. When finally he arose to join the men returning to work, he looked almost his old self, and she ventured a hopeful, "You're sure you don't want something to eat, Papa?"

His good humor apparently restored, James smiled, pinching her cheek affectionately, "No, honey. Save the pie for me for tonight. I'll eat it then."

Melanie watched until he had disappeared through the doorway of the foundry, finally satisfied that his slight indisposition had corrected itself. Another thought suddenly struck her wandering mind, and Melanie quickly glanced around. No, there he was. Josh Whitmore hadn't gone back in to work yet. Snatching up her basket, she walked hastily toward him.

"Mr. Whitmore . . ."

Turning at the sound of his name, Josh met the full impact of the warm golden eyes turned up to his and was momentarily stunned. His startled expression caused a fleeting smile to cross her lips, and dimples danced across her cheeks before she said in a serious tone, "I want to thank you for what you did yesterday, Mr. Whitmore. You saved me from a very embarrassing situation, and I appreciate it more than I can say."

Regaining his outward composure while his heart pounded like a sixteen-year-old, Josh said lightly, "You needn't thank me—"

"Oh, yes. I have a feeling you did me a greater favor than even I realize now." Blushing lightly at her own words, Melanie continued earnestly, "If there is

67

anything I can do for you in return, please don't ever hesitate to ask, Mr. Whitmore."

"Well, there is one thing . . ."

Her slender brown brows rose in surprise. "There is? Well, what is it? What can I do for you?"

"Now that we are friends, you could do me the favor of calling me Josh instead of Mr. Whitmore." At her surprised expression, his wide grin flashed, and his eyes twinkled mischievously, "And allow me the privilege of calling you Melanie. Is it too much payment to ask, do you think?"

Suddenly laughing gayly, she extended a dainty hand. "I should say not, Josh."

Closing his big hand over her small one, he held it a trifle longer than necessary, despite himself, when Tom's stumbling voice beside him swung his attention to another hand extended in his direction.

"If you are Melanie's friend, then you are my friend, too."

Melanie's quick glance begged Josh's understanding, and releasing hers, he accepted the stubby hand held out to him, saying as he did, "It's my pleasure, Tom. A man can never have too many friends."

The appreciation in Melanie's eyes at his gesture could not be misinterpreted, and sent a flash of pure pleasure surging through him. "Damn!" he said, astonished at his own warm reaction as she turned and walked away, "Damn . . ."

Steve's gaze rested hotly on Melanie and Josh during the entire exchange, his stomach twisting in jealous spasms as her face relaxed into a wide smile. His heart pounding heavily in his chest, he barely registered the urge to stride forward and rip their hands apart. Stirring his anger even further was his realization that she had succeeded in penetrating his indifference, and his deep resentment blew his jealousy into a steaming flash of hatred.

Trembling with suppressed violence, Steve's heated gaze followed Melanie's slim figure until it was out of sight, all the while vowing softly under his breath, "Bitch . . . bitch . . . you'll pay for this . . . you'll come crawling to me . . . you just wait and see . . . and then it'll be my turn to laugh. . . "

Oh, that terrible, terrible man! Melanie thought as she unconsciously followed the routine of preparing the table for her father's evening meal. She had had more time than usual to herself this afternoon, since she was only warming the uneaten pie for supper; but the excess time had been to her disadvantage. Having caught Steve's gaze on her as she had turned from Josh, the one brief glimpse had been sufficient to drive all other thoughts from her mind. Closing her eyes for a few seconds to regain her composure, she only succeeded in gaining a clearer picture of Steve in her mind, a more vivid memory of his mouth pressed against hers, his tongue invading her mouth . . .

"Stop this, stop this now!" she demanded aloud, her eyes springing open in exasperation with herself. "What is the matter with you? He's told you what he wants from you . . . not love," and angering at the sudden knot of excitement the thought produced inside her, she slammed the cup onto the table, shattering it into a dozen small pieces.

"Oh, now see what you've done," she pouted, "you foolish, stupid girl."

"Melanie! Melanie!" Tom's frightened voice coming from the street suddenly penetrated her preoccupation, startling her into movement. She had just reached the door and thrown it open when Tom came bounding up the steps, his hair askew and eyes blazing wildly in fear, his chest heaving as he struggled for breath.

"What is it, Tom? What's happened?"

"It's your Papa, Melanie . . . It's your Papa."

Fear turned her next words into a sob as her heart began pounding wildly. She shook his heaving shoulders. "Tell me, Tom, what is it? What's happened to him?"

Still struggling for his breath, Tom turned and pointed a shaking hand at a wagon coming slowly down the street. Uncle Asa was driving with another man seated beside him, and on the flatbed in back two men were crouched over a reclining figure.

"Papa! Oh, no!" Frozen into immobility from fear, she watched as the wagon drew up in front of the house, her eyes wide with shock. In a quick flurry of movement she was suddenly down the steps and onto the back of the wagon, kneeling beside her father.

Her teeth chattering so hard she could barely speak, she whispered, "Papa, what is it? What's wrong?" His eyes were closed, his chest moving in deep heavy breaths, and he did not seem to hear her. "But he's alive . . . I can see him breathing . . . he's alive!" Suddenly she was laughing wildly while tears streamed down her ashen face. The man beside her father took her firmly by the shoulders and gave her a

70

hard shake.

"Get hold of yourself, Melanie. Your father has had some sort of an attack. He'll need you to remain calm."

Wild, golden eyes looked up into a familiar steady gaze, and she blinked momentarily, "Josh, will he be all right?"

"I don't know, Melanie."

"All right, come on, men, let's lift him down slowly . . ." Uncle Asa's familiar authoritative voice took command.

"Uncle Asa—"

"Get out of the way, Melanie. We have to get him inside. Dr. Pierce is on the way."

Following closely behind as the four men lifted the makeshift stretcher and carried him inside, she kept her eyes on her father's heaving chest. "He's still breathing. Just as long as he's still breathing everything will be all right . . ."

Within a few moments his still form was placed on the bed, and Asa turned toward her, his face drawn with concern.

"What happened, Uncle Asa? What's wrong with him? Why doesn't he wake up?"

"I don't know, Melanie." Reaching out, he enclosed her comfortingly in his arms. "He just collapsed, and no one could bring him back to consciousness. We've sent for Dr. Pierce. He should be here any minute, but you're right, honey. He's breathing evenly. He's going to be all right, you'll see."

"He has to be, Uncle Asa," Melanie said slowly, staring at the still figure on the bed, "he just has to be."

Pulling her closer, Asa turned to the men. "You can go now, boys. Thanks for the help. I'll take it from here."

Two men turned to leave, but Josh spoke quietly. "I'd like to stay a little while to see how he comes along, Asa."

Asa dismissed him with a quick look. "That won't be necessary, Josh. I can handle things from here on. Tom is here if I should need any help in moving him, and anyone else would only be in the way."

Josh hesitated, directing another look at Melanie, who rested passively against Asa's chest, still shivering with shock. "But I'd—"

"Please leave now, Josh."

As he opened his mouth to speak, Martha's wide form brushed past him, and moving to the bedside, immediately assumed control of the sickroom.

"Melanie, get me some warm water in a basin, quickly . . . Mr. Parker, Tom, help me undress him, please. Everyone else, please get out of the room."

Everyone snapped into movement with her orders. Feeling a complete outsider as Melanie brushed past him without a word and ran toward the kitchen, Josh turned slowly and walked out the door.

Melanie fell into bed exhausted. For the first time in her life, she was profoundly grateful they lived in such a small house, with the rooms all on one floor. Otherwise care of her father would be impossible. A month! Had it really been a month since he had moved of his own accord, spoken a word? She had been so hopeful at first, certain he would come around. She knew he could hear her when she spoke. He could open his eyes, and followed her movements around the room. He could swallow the broth she slipped between his lips, and in the past week had been able to swallow the porridge she fed him. But he was getting thinner and thinner, and despite his weight loss, it was still almost impossible for her to turn him as often as Dr. Pierce had suggested to avoid lung congestion. She really wasn't sure how much longer she could go on.

Uncle Asa had willingly left Martha and Tom to help her with his care, but after the first week, she had insisted on their return to their own duties, and assumed full responsibility. She had thought it strange at first that none of the neighbors had come to volunteer their help, but Mrs. Sims had been active with her vicious tongue, and from what Uncle Asa had determined, had convinced the weak-minded matrons that James Morganfield was justly suffering the Lord's judgment for allowing his daughter her wild, heathenish ways. Josh's concerned visits had only seemed to confirm her obscene accusations, and Uncle Asa had forbidden her any further contact with him. To make things worse, the small reserve of money Papa had managed to put aside was fast running out. With her father in need of constant care, Melanie was not in a position to earn more. How much longer would she be able to handle things? Close to tears again, Melanie covered her eyes for one long moment, struggling for control. Well, perhaps it wouldn't be necessary. Maybe Papa would begin getting better tomorrow. Best not to think of it now. Best to take one day at a time . . . sleep now . . .

sleep now . . .

Suddenly she was awake, springing from a deep sleep to a sitting position in bed, where she sat blinking in an attempt to clear her head. What had awakened her? A noise? A shout? Suddenly frantic with fear, she jumped from bed, not waiting to don her slippers and wrapper, and ran into her father's room.

"Papa!" Her shocked scream emerged as a ragged whisper. Lying face down on the floor, where he appeared to have fallen from bed, was her father, a small pool of blood forming under his face. Sobbing hysterically, she ran to his side and turned his face toward her. Blood was streaming from his nose and mouth, and his face was beginning to swell.

"Papa, Papa," she cried, willing him to open his eyes. Slowly, miraculously it seemed, his eyes opened. Clarity and recognition shone from their depths, and relief flooded her senses. He isn't dead . . . he isn't dead. Smothering her sobs, she began cleaning the blood from his face with her gown. "Don't worry, Papa, I'll get you back in bed and then I'll take care of your face."

After a few moments' struggle, she finally succeeded in turning over his stiff, inert form, and then attempted to lift him back into bed. Small beads of perspiration appeared on her upper lip and forehead as she struggled again and again to lift him to no avail. Absentmindedly pushing a strand of hair away from her face, she looked helplessly at her father to see his eyes blinking as tears streamed down the sides of his face.

74

"Oh, Papa, Papa, don't cry," she soothed, beginning to sob again herself. "I'll get you back in bed, you'll see. You'll be all right."

But his body was stiff and unyielding, and blood still streamed from his nostrils as she attempted time and time again to lift him. Finally desperate and sobbing anew with frustration, she wiped her eyes and said softly, "I'll get Uncle Asa, Papa. He'll help me get you back in bed."

It seemed he was pleading with her with his eyes, and she whispered, "Don't worry. I won't leave you alone for long. I'll be right back." Quickly she bent to kiss his cheek, and ran from the room and out the front door.

In her night rail, her feet still bare, she ran across the deserted street and around the corner, and began banging breathlessly on Asa's door. Please let him hear me quickly, she prayed, biting her lip frantically. Within a few moments, she heard a noise from within and the door jerked open to show Uncle Asa, still clothed, his hair unruly as if he had fallen asleep in his clothes.

"Melanie! What happened? What's wrong?" His face paled visibly at the sight of her in her bloodied night rail.

"Uncle Asa, please—hurry. It's Papa. He fell, and I can't pick him up. He's bleeding—"

Within minutes they were back by her father's side, and Melanie was watching anxiously as Asa cautiously lifted him back into the bed. Running to the kitchen, she returned a few seconds later with a basin of water, and began cleansing his face as Asa watched sympathetically. During the process, James' glance

75

moved steadily between Melanie and Asa, attempting to speak to them with his eyes while Melanie spoke soothingly to him. Within the hour, his eyes closed in exhausted slumber, and picking up the basin, Melanie stood for a few long moments staring sadly down at her father's motionless form before she turned toward the kitchen, with Asa following a few feet behind.

Wearily she walked to the bucket, and drawing out some water, washed the blood from her hands. She dried them silently, tears streaming down her face, and turning, walked into the arms Asa held out to her. Then sobbing in earnest, her voice coming in deep gasps, she said again and again, "What am I going to do, Uncle Asa? How am I going to take care of him? What am I going to do?"

Laying his cheek against her fiery tresses, Asa held her comfortingly until her sobbing stilled. When she was once again silent in his arms, he released her and cupping her chin in his hands, tilted her face up to look into his eyes. Her beautiful face, so close to his, robbed him of speech for a few seconds, and not trusting himself to speak, he slowly wiped the tears from her soft cheeks with his calloused palm until he was able to go on.

"You'll come and live with me for a while, Melanie. You can have your old room, and James can have his room down the hall. It'll be the best answer for everyone."

"No, Uncle Asa. I can't impose on you. It will mean more work for everyone in the house, Martha and Tom—and we'll be in your way . . ."

"Nothing could be further from the truth, Melanie. Once you're where we can watch out for you and James, Martha, Tom, and I will know the first peace we've had in the month since James was stricken. As it is, Martha spends the whole day fretting how you're getting along, and Tom spends more time running back and forth between our houses than he does in either one. And how do you think I feel, Melanie? Now that James is ill, there is no one to look after you, to protect you from unwanted advances, wicked gossip . . . I insist that you move in with us tomorrow."

The word insist brought a slight frown to Melanie's brow, and seeing it there, Asa laughed reluctantly, "All right, I'm asking you to come, Melanie, please, for my peace of mind if for nothing else, dear."

Melanie hesitated a moment, staring at his familiar sympathetic face. Uncle Asa . . . she had always taken so much from him without any hesitation. Why was she hesitating now? This was the same dear man she had loved on sight, her father's good friend . . . and he was right, living in his house would make things easier on everyone. Martha was getting too old for the constant running back and forth that she insisted upon against Melanie's protests. And Tom, bless him, considered it his privilege to help her with her father. Yes, it would be easier for all involved and on Uncle Asa's peace of mind.

With a small smile, Melanie nodded her head slightly. "All right, Uncle Asa, we'll come tomorrow if you're sure you want us."

His smile broadening, Asa had to suppress the

surge of pure joy pulsing through him. She's coming tomorrow . . . With a small salute, he said softly, "Tomorrow, then, Melanie," and turning quickly walked out the door. He had gone only a few feet down the street when full realization struck him for the first time. He was happy that his good friend lay helpless in bed because his illness was bringing Melanie close again . . . where no one else could take her from him. . . .

The first week in Uncle Asa's house proved indisputably that he was right. The elimination of simple household chores allowed Melanie more time to devote to her father, and the move had come just in time, for James seemed to take a turn for the worse a day after they had taken up residence in Uncle Asa's house. Spells of erratic breathing seemed to come over him without warning, during which he perspired profusely, his eyes wild with fright. He still could neither move nor speak, and Dr. Pierce continued to be vague about the possibilities of complete recovery. Her father's tall, muscular frame appeared to have shrunk in the time he had lain silently within the bed, his features becoming so gaunt that he was beginning to lose all resemblance to the man he had once been—except for his eyes, those direct, alert eyes that tried so hard to speak to her.

Melanie moved silently in the dark corridor outside her room toward her father's door. Her experience a week before had left her unable to sleep through an entire night without getting up to check his safety. The sight of him lying face down on the floor in a pool of his own blood had been burned into her memory, and continually intruded on her sleep. The day had been hard, and she was exhausted and discouraged. Papa had had several attacks in the afternoon and evening that had drained her mentally and physically, and she had a growing feeling that something must happen soon to improve the state of their lives before she went completely mad. Slowly she walked to his bedside, where a lone lamp burned dimly. Suddenly his eyes sprang open, appearing to bulge from his very head, and he began gasping wildly, his breath coming in deep, heaving gulps as he struggled and choked for air.

"Papa!" Overcome with panic, Melanie began trembling wildly, rooted to the spot with fear. Seeming to appear from nowhere, Asa suddenly brushed past her, and moving to James' bedside, slipped his arm under his back, raising him gently.

"Quickly, Melanie, push the pillows under his back and head . . . yes, the blankets, too. We have to raise his head so he can breathe more easily . . . yes, that's right," he said calmly as she hastened to do as he instructed.

"That's fine." Still watching him carefully, Asa began dipping a cloth into the basin beside the bed to cool James' brow and face. Slowly, while Melanie stood helplessly nearby, James' breathing began returning to normal, his eyes going thankfully back and forth between Melanie and Asa, before they closed in sleep. Checking the pillows once again, Asa turned toward Melanie.

"He's all right now, Melanie. We can go back to sleep. He should be fine until morning."

As he turned to face Melanie, Asa was struck by her terrified expression. She appeared to be frozen in a state of shock, and taking her arm, he pulled her physically from the room.

Once in the hall, he said quietly, "What is it, Melanie, what's wrong?" When she did not answer, he shook her roughly, demanding again, "What's wrong, Melanie?"

Slowly raising her wild amber eyes to his, Melanie said in an unbelieving voice, "I couldn't help him . . . if you hadn't been here, he might have died . . . and I couldn't help him . . . Oh, Uncle Asa, what would I do without you?" Throwing her arms around his neck, she pressed herself tight against him, her body trembling violently. "Hold me, please Uncle Asa, hold me, I'm so afraid." When he appeared to hesitate, she pressed herself even tighter against him. He could feel her firm, unbound breasts against his chest, the warmth of her body moving against him when he withheld his arms. Suddenly his arms seemed to close around her of their own accord, pulling her close. He was beginning to feel lightheaded with desire, the sweet scent of her body intoxicating him, confusing his senses.

His lack of response panicked her even further, and in her near hysteria, she imagined he was turning away from her.

"Uncle Asa, please . . . you're not angry with me—"

"No, I'm not angry, Melanie."

The strain in his voice sounded suspiciously like anger, and Melanie went over the edge of despair, crying wildly as she began covering his face in kisses.

"Please, Uncle Asa, don't send me away. Don't be angry with me, please. What will I do if you send me away . . ."

Her body was shuddering, shaking against his, and his own body began to tremble wildly. He could feel his control slipping, and said almost pleadingly as he wound his hand in her long, soft hair, delighting in the feel of its silkiness against his skin, even as he despised himself for his weakness.

"Melanie, please—"

"Hold me, Uncle Asa, please hold me."

Her soft vulnerable lips were only inches from his own as she pleaded with him, and with a soft groan, he lowered his mouth to cover and conquer hers in a long, deep kiss.

Stiffening momentarily, Melanie slowly relaxed under his kiss, opening her mouth to the warmth of his tongue, pulling his head even closer as he crushed her against him. She felt so safe, so warm . . . he wouldn't send her away now . . .

Slowly, unwillingly he drew his mouth away, whispering softly against her lips, "Melanie, my darling, my love . . ." his heart pounding, his body throbbing with passion.

Feeling suddenly bereft and alone without the warmth of his mouth against hers, Melanie longed for the sweet, beautiful oblivion his kisses induced inside her, the all-encompassing heat that drove away her fear.

"Uncle Asa, please don't leave me, I want to be with you. I don't want to be alone . . . please."

"Melanie, you don't know what you're saying, darling."

"Please, Uncle Asa, please." Suddenly standing on tiptoe, she pulled his head down again to meet her searching mouth, separating her lips to invite the invasion of his tongue, her body rubbing and twisting against his in an urgent, silent plea.

Suddenly his arms pulled her crushingly close, as his hands roamed her back, one coming to rest on her firm buttocks, pressing her tightly against the bulge of his manhood.

Warmly, she rubbed against him, murmuring over and over, "Don't leave me, I want to be with you . . ." until in one swift movement he scooped her into his arms against his heaving chest, whispering softly as he walked rapidly toward the door to his room, "No, darling, my darling Melanie, I won't leave you tonight . . . I'll stay with you," and entering, pushed the door firmly shut behind them. . . .

A vague uneasiness disturbed her dreams. Perspiring and still groggy, she awoke to the unfamiliar feeling of a male body curved around hers in sleep, the warmth of naked skin pressed tightly against her back, and a large calloused hand lightly stroking the delicate whiteness of her stomach. She stirred, and the fondling became more deliberate, sensually seeking her secret places, enlarging the circle of caresses until he moved to cup one rounded breast. Suddenly pressed to her back, she was seized by a moment of panic when a warm, moist mouth closed over its crest.

"No! Please . . ." But her frantic whisper trailed away as the fogginess of sleep left her mind and the previous hours spent in the bed returned with glaring clarity. She was no longer a virgin . . . too late for regrets now.

In the pale light of the moon streaming through the window she caught a glimpse of dark hair streaked with gray and began to relax while he continued to kiss and tease her breast with his tongue. A languorous warmth spread through her veins. She groaned lightly as his mouth left one soft peak and hungrily seized the other, but his only answer was a more violent attack as his body began moving atop hers. There was an unmistakable hardness pressed between her legs, the same hardness that a few hours before had caused her pain, and she flinched instinctively with a low protest.

"Don't worry, darling, it won't hurt much this time. Just relax . . . that's it . . ." his deep voice crooned, "Just relax and let me in . . ."

Suddenly his lips were covering hers, his tongue separating her teeth as it drove down into her mouth. Simultaneously lunging deep inside her, he paid no heed to her gasp and began a steady, rhythmic penetration of her body. Without conscious participation, but in answer to the need building within her, she began meeting his thrusts, joining his body with increasing impetus and violence, the wild, throbbing heat he caused within her accelerating, gaining complete control of her senses until her body was responding with spontaneous passion, mounting to a peak that could climax in only one way. Her low, sustained groan when she met his final thrust was drowned out by the deep sound of his own passion as they reached the summit together, only to fall again in a long, breathtaking spiral from its ecstatic height.

His body collapsed heavily atop hers, stealing her breath. He raised himself slightly, straining to see her face in the darkness of the room.

"Melanie . . . Melanie . . ." He began kissing her face lightly, "I've dreamed this so often, and cursed myself each time for daring to allow the thought to even enter my mind . . . but you know I love you, don't you, darling?"

The moon breaking again through the clouds caused a shaft of light to reveal the deep lines the years had etched on his face, and she felt a momentary surge of revulsion and stiffened, as her youthful mind reacted instinctively—He's old . . . old . . .

She stared silently for a few moments at his face until reason returned, and slowly raising her hands, she slid them deliberately into the thick gray hair at his temples, murmuring as she pulled his mouth down to cover hers again, "Yes, I know, darling, I know . . ."

The first light of dawn slowly inched its way through the window, engulfing Melanie's sleeping form in its soft, silvery glow. Firey tendrils of silky hair spread across the pillow framed her remarkable beauty in brilliant color, emphasizing the creaminess of her unmarked skin and her small, perfect features. Her soft, appealing lips held a slightly bruised appearance, an aftermath of the frenzied night of love; and as she sighed slightly in her sleep, a fleeting dimple danced across her cheek, only to disappear as her long, brown lashes fluttered gracefully. Then she was still again, breathing steadily, her small, dainty hand flung palm upward, resting on the pillow beside her head. So beautiful, so vulnerable. Asa lay beside her, unsleeping, the warmth of her body as it touched his still unable to convince him that this dream was indeed reality. Feeling the need to touch the vision lying beside him, Asa lightly stroked the silken curls only inches from his hand, careful not to awaken her and end his opportunity to drink in her loveliness unobserved. A swell of emotion choked his throat as his eyes roamed her face, the smooth creamy throat his lips had caressed so tenderly, slipping down to follow the outline of her slender young body under the light coverlet that covered them both. He felt a growing need to touch her more intimately, awaken her and bring her to life again under his caresses; but the onslaught of dawn was relentless, limiting the time remaining in which he could return her to her room without anyone becoming aware where she had spent the greater part of the night. But he didn't want her to leave the warm circle of his arms, to be alone once again in the bed that she had brought to life for him.

God, he loved her! He loved her so completely that the enormity of the tumult she created within him both elated and frightened him. She's so young . . . The thought tore viciously at him. For any man of his years to love such a young, lovely woman was in itself a tender burden, but he could not even offer her marriage. After taking her virginity so selfishly, he could not give her his name. Emily . . . poor, dear Emily, the love of his youth who had slowly lost her mind after the death of their child. She was his wife, and would be until she died. The very nature of her sickness made divorce impossible.

You fool, he muttered viciously to himself, as another thought entered his mind. What makes you think she'd marry you even if it were possible? Just because in her hysteria last night she allowed you to make love to her? She wasn't responsible last night, you knew it then, and know it now.

Covering his eyes with his wide hand, he pleaded softly, "Oh, Lord, don't let her hate me, please, I love her so . . ."

Whatever happened, he couldn't allow her to be found in his room, and slowly, taking care not to awaken her, he rose and slipped quietly into his clothes. Hesitating only one minute more to seal a final image in his memory, he lifted her small, naked body in his arms, tucking the coverlet securely around her, and carried her quietly to her room. Her exhaustion was so complete that she stirred only slightly as he placed her on her bed, before slipping immediately back to sleep.

Melanie awoke with a start, a shaft of bright sunlight against her closed lids filling her instantly with guilt. "Papa—it's so late—he'll be waiting for me." Suddenly memory returned to sting her even more strongly. "What have I done? Uncle Asa will despise me for the wanton that I am!"

Looking around, she realized she was in her own room. Perhaps it was only a dream. But her nude, aching body was silent testimony to the reality of her dream. Slowly she rose from the bed and walked to the night stand, still naked, to pour water into the basin, where she scrubbed herself fastidiously from head to foot, wishing with all her heart the same water could wash away her deeds of the night before. Afterwards, dressing herself in clean clothing from the skin out, she walked quietly down the hallway and into her father's room.

Carefully striking all other thoughts from her mind, Melanie spent the entire day in strict attention to her father's needs. Neither Martha's entreaties nor Tom's pleas could move her from his side. She refused to eat a meal that would take her from the room. Her conscience would give her no rest. Shortly after she had come to her father's room, she had heard Uncle Asa's door open, and his footsteps approach her father's door. There they had hesitated briefly before proceeding firmly along the hall and down the steps. Listening intently, she heard him murmur a few words to Martha, and immediately leave the house. It was obvious he did not want to see or even speak to her . . . and she really couldn't blame him. Through her foolish fear she had created an impossible problem for a dear, wonderful man. How he must despise her. A small sob caught in her throat, and she glanced toward the bed to see her father's eyes resting on her. Forcing a bright smile, she walked over to caress his cheek lightly.

"I'm going to be all right, Papa. We're both going to be all right, you'll see."

She stared thoughtlessly toward the muted light of evening streaming through the window when a soft knock on the door shattered the unnatural quiet of the sickroom and startled Melanie to her feet. Martha's broad figure filled the doorway, her friendly face bearing the same concerned expression it had carried the entire day. Melanie's strange behavior worried her. It was so completely unlike her to isolate herself from Tom and herself for an entire day, almost as if she were hiding.

"Mr. Parker would like to see you, Melanie. He wants you to come down to the study." Anticipating her excuse, she continued firmly, "I'll stay to look after Mr. Morganfield until you return. He'll be perfectly all right. Now go downstairs. Mr. Parker is waiting."

Unable to find any recourse, Melanie silently left the room, her mind racing wildly as she descended the staircase, dreading the confrontation that awaited her in the room at the foot of the stairs. As her foot touched the bottom step, the door to the study swung open. Asa stood in the doorway, as if he had been listening for her approach.

"Melanie, come inside, please. We have some things we must discuss." Asa's lined face was unsmiling, his eyes avoiding hers, his hand shaking slightly as he closed the door behind her. His expression as he turned back to her was filled with torment. "Melanie dear, Martha tells me you've been in your father's room all day, and haven't even left to take your meals. Dear, you don't have to hide from me . . . I know after last night . . ." He was stammering slightly, emotion blocking his words, ". . . but you mustn't think . . . you don't have to be afraid of me, Melanie. I'd never force you . . ." Looking directly into her eyes, he said suddenly, with great emotion, "I love you, Melanie. I'd never do anything to make you unhappy . . . not purposely. Last night was beautiful, and I cherish it, will always cherish it. I just hope you don't find its memory so distasteful that you will turn away from me completely. You needn't worry that I'd press you to continue the relationship. I realize you're young and beautiful . . . last night was just . . . it just happened."

Seeming to run out of words for a moment, Asa stood staring into her lovely, incredulous face. Then he slid his hand wearily over his eyes for a few seconds before dropping it lifelessly to his side.

"Just try to forget last night, if you can, Melanie. Nothing need change here, and no one need know."

"But I don't want to forget it." Melanie's voice was a soft whisper. He didn't hate her . . . he loved her . . .

Asa blinked. Surely he hadn't heard correctly.

Longing suddenly for the warmth of his arms around her, the security of his embrace, Melanie stepped forward, placing her palms against Asa's chest. "It was beautiful for me, too, Uncle Asa. I felt happy and warm and . . ." Unable to express her other feelings, she blushed revealingly. When he still made no move to touch her, Melanie slowly slid her arms around his neck, whispering as she did, "I thought you were angry with me. I was hiding from your anger, not your love."

It was true . . . she didn't want to forget last night.

With one quick movement Asa pulled her into his arms, crushing her against him in the wild surge of happiness coursing through him. "Melanie, Melanie darling, I love you so."

When he made no further move but continued merely to hold her, she pushed herself slightly away

89

from him and slid her palms against his cheeks, deliberately touching the deep furrows there as she pulled his mouth down over hers. There was a sweet longing singing through her veins, and she felt a deep need for his intimate touch. It was sweeter still to know the need was mutually felt and desired.

His mouth finally closed over hers, sending waves of heat surging through her as her body began reliving the sensations of the night before. But it was over too soon, and Melanie felt strong regret as Asa moved away. His voice shaking with emotion, he said softly, "Thank you, Melanie, for your understanding."

Before Melanie could comprehend his cryptic remark, Asa released her, maintaining only a hold on her arm, pulling her toward the door as he made a visible effort to regain his composure. "I didn't stop in to see James today, Melanie. I couldn't face him this morning, but now I'd like to see him before he falls asleep for the night. Come with me, please."

Wordlessly they left the room.

Their visit was, of necessity, short. James fell into an exhausted slumber only moments after their arrival. Seeing the weariness in Melanie's face, Martha whispered in a concerned voice, "I'll stay a few moments longer to make sure he's off for the night, dear. Why don't you go to bed now. You look very tired." When she hesitated a moment, Martha shooed her off in a motherly voice. "Go on, off with you now."

The house was in total darkness as Melanie and Asa walked down the hallway. Melanie's heart pounded harder with each step she took, and when they finally stopped at her bedroom door, the sound of her own heartbeat in her ears was almost deafening. She turned to look up at Asa as he lightly touched her cheek with the tips of his fingers. He seemed unable to speak at that moment, but the love shining so openly in his eyes touched off a pulsating tide of desire for him within her. Strong memories of the night before and the new sensations he had aroused within her while he had held her so securely in the circle of his love returned to set her blood afire.

"Uncle Asa . . . do you want to say goodnight to me now or do you want me with you tonight?"

She knew he would never have opened the possibility himself. A flash of pain crossed his face as he said softly, "Melanie, you needn't feel obliged to continue. I realize you're a young, lovely woman, and you deserve a young man worthy of you, not an old, worn-out fellow that can't even offer you marriage."

"Obligation is not what I feel, Uncle Asa." Sincerity and desire kindled a flame in her soft amber eyes and Asa felt consumed by the blaze.

This is wrong, wrong, he argued with himself as his willpower was slowly consumed by his hunger for her, the same hunger that had plagued him the entire day. It's desperation, not love that is driving her into my arms. But even as his mind acknowledged the truth, his body, with a will of its own, could hold out no longer. With a soft groan of surrender, Asa clasped her against him, whispering softly against her hair, "Melanie, please don't ever hate me for this. Just remember I have always loved you, ever since you were a child. . . . but you aren't a child anymore, and, God help me, I'm only a man."

Swinging her up into his arms, he carried her to his room and through the doorway. Laying her gently on the bed, he turned and locked the door, stopping to light the lamp as he returned to the bed. He whispered softly as he kneeled beside the bed and began removing her clothing. "This time I want to see you clearly, Melanie. I want to see you and remember every detail." His hands began working at her clothes efficiently, systematically, until she was naked and trembling beneath them. His voice slightly touched with wonder, he whispered, "You are the loveliest woman I have ever seen, Melanie." His fingers lightly trailed down her neck, coming to rest on the rounded swell of her breast.

His touch caused little electric tingles to travel up her spine and she whispered hoarsely, "Uncle Asa . . ."

Smiling slightly, his mouth slowly lowering toward the erect pink crest, he whispered, "I will ask only one thing of you, Melanie . . . please don't call me *Uncle* any longer."

Her small answering smile was quickly wiped away by a gasp of ecstasy as his mouth claimed her breast and for a long time afterward that night, she was not capable of reasonable thought.

In the month following, James' attacks seemed to occur less frequently, although his general condition remained unchanged. But the pale shadow of desperation that had cast its gloom over Melanie had disappeared in the brilliant light of Asa's obvious happiness. She had been ineffective in helping her father, but the inner joy that Asa inadvertently displayed consoled her lagging spirits. Her own pleasure grew unbounded in the new world Asa had opened up to her, one in which each night her senses were reawakened and her desire rekindled as she was introduced tenderly, gradually to the delights of passions finely cultivated and gently indulged. Yet she remained unaware of the subtle changes occurring in the household around her, of the manner in which Asa's eyes followed her covertly, resting on her unobserved, as if they could not drink their fill of her beauty. She was also unaware of Martha's knowing glances at Asa's inability to keep his hands from her in a straying caress, or Tom's growing sulky behavior, until it manifested itself in outright defiance.

Having taken the first opportunity of the morning to leave her father's room while he slept, Melanie moved quickly down the stairs and toward the kitchen. She was annoyed that Tom had not come upstairs to help her bathe her father, as was his usual custom. Despite his gradual weight loss, Melanie still found it almost impossible to move her father's stiff frame, and she was in absolute need of Tom's assistance to accomplish the task. Anger flared anew when she saw Tom alone in the kitchen, sitting morosely at the table and staring dumbly out the window.

"Tom, you lazy wretch! What are you doing sitting down here twiddling your thumbs when I need you upstairs? You know it's time for Papa's bath and I can't manage it well without you!"

Turning on her quickly with open hostility, Tom

answered belligerently, "Well, you can take care of Mr. Morganfield by yourself, or get Mr. Parker to help you. He's your friend now, not me!"

"Tom! What are you talking about?" Melanie was aghast at the heat of his anger.

"You don't have any time for *me* anymore, just 'Tom do this or Tom do that.' You only talk to Mr. Parker. You only smile at Mr. Parker. You even stay with Mr. Parker at night. You only have time for your papa and Mr. Parker, no time for Tom anymore." Tears welled in the full blue eyes staring rebelliously into hers. "Tom is alone again, Melanie isn't *his* friend anymore . . ." Lowering his head to his arms resting on the table, Tom began sobbing, his big, muscular body heaving as low, gasping sounds escaped his throat.

Feeling the heat of tears beneath her own lids, Melanie raised her hand to brush a straying tear from her cheek. Had Asa and she really been that obvious? Had she really been that thoughtless and unfeeling to Tom? Her questions were answered only too clearly by Tom's deep sobs, and moving forward, Melanie lightly rested her hand on Tom's rumpled hair for a second before slipping it down to his wide shoulder to rub it consolingly.

"Tom," she whispered softly, "I'm so sorry if I've hurt you, but you've always been such a true friend to me that I guess I just took you for granted." Tom gave no answer, but his sobbing slowed almost to a stop, an indication that he was listening. Taking heart, Melanie continued, "But whatever happens, Tom, nothing will ever change between you and me. You will always be special to me . . . my adopted brother, and if you will let me be your sister, we can truly be a family."

Tom slowly raised his head, the light of hope shining on his dull features. "My sister? You will really be my sister, Melanie?"

"Yes, I will."

"Then Mr. Parker won't be able to take you away from me."

Tears again smarting her eyes, Melanie whispered hoarsely, "If I am to be your sister, I will be your sister forever."

The sagging corners of Tom's wide mouth slowly turned up into his comical smile, and he rubbed the tears roughly from his face. "And you will go for walks with me again?" Noting her hesitation, he added soberly, "When Mr. Morganfield is better?"

"Yes, when Papa is a little better."

"All right! All right! You will be my sister!" Then his eyes moved past her toward the door. "Melanie is going to be my sister. I'm going to have a sister!" he said happily.

Turning, Melanie saw Martha in the doorway, and realizing she had been witness to their entire conversation her face flamed brightly. So they both knew about Asa and her . . .

"That's fine, Tom. Now go draw some fresh water so Melanie can finish bathing Mr. Morganfield, like a good boy."

Without hesitation, Tom jumped to his mother's command, and grabbing the bucket, ran out the door.

Melanie turned to face Martha squarely, her face still bearing a trace of scarlet as she asked boldly,

"Do you think ill of me for what I have done, Martha, now that you know I share Asa's bed?"

"What you do with your own life, Melanie, is your own concern, but what you do to affect the lives of those I respect and love are my concern. Mr. Parker is a good, honest man. He took Tom and me in when no household in Salisbury wanted a woman with a fatherless, idiot boy. He has known very little real happiness or love in his life. He loved his wife and was very good to her, but she is lost to him forever. I think you have taken a very unwise and dangerous step, but you have made Mr. Parker happier than I have ever known him to be and given him hope for the future. I can't fault you for that. Tom is my son, and he loves you in his own simple way. You've made him a very happy boy, and I know the burden of his love isn't easy to carry, Melanie." Shaking her head slowly, tears filled her friendly eyes for the first time. "No, dear, I don't think ill of you. You are Tom's sister now . . . you are a part of my family."

Touched beyond words by Martha's generous statement, Melanie stifled a short sob and rushed forward to slip her arms around the woman's ample waist in a short embrace. Whispering a soft, "Thank you," she fled the room quickly to gain some privacy before allowing her gratified tears full reign.

The month passed without change in James' condition. Dr. Pierce continued his visits, but remained noncommittal, and Melanie began to be suspicious that he was just as much in the dark about the possibility of her father recovering as they were. Melanie continued to labor quietly, keeping up a cheerful, one-sided conversation with the wasted figure in the bed, but it was only in that room that time seemed to stand still. Outside, summer was in full bloom, and events continued moving at a steady pace. The warm summer weather was ideal for increases in activity against landholders within the grants. Teams of surveyors were dispatched to different parts of the disputed land by the colony of New York, and the Green Mountain Boys were extremely busy dispersing them. In most cases, simply the words that "the wild man, Allen, and his mob" were on the way were sufficient to scatter the teams, but in some cases direct action was needed, and it came quickly and prudently. Ethan Allen and his men were aware that they could not afford a direct confrontation with the militia from the powerful colony of New York. In the woods and hills the rough woodsmen reigned supreme, and it was necessary that their battleground remain there.

The stepped-up activity of the Green Mountain Boys reduced the work force at the foundry considerably as the summer progressed, necessitating extended hours on Asa's part. Beginning to chafe at his absence, Melanie snatched at the opportunity offered by Tom to accompany him to the foundry to bring Asa his lunch. Melanie had not been out walking for almost two long months, her only excursions in the world outside the sick room being brief trips outside to hang the laundry and a few quick marketing trips for Martha. Feeling a sudden burst of enthusiasm, she rushed to her room to change her dress. Slipping on a light green cotton dress, and stopping only a moment to brush her hair lightly and take a brief peep in the mirror, Melanie hastened downstairs to join Tom. Within minutes they were on their way to the foundry. The warm sun against her skin felt unbelievably good after so many days indoors, and the fresh summer breeze lifting the fiery tendrils of hair from her shoulders, lifted her heart with them. Smiling broadly, she glanced up at Tom, happy to see that he, too, was feeling the joy of the moment. Walking briskly along the street, she attempted to extend a greeting to two matrons she knew, when they surprisingly turned their heads and walked past her. Stunned at the snub, Melanie felt her elation dim momentarily, but firmly putting them out of her mind, she continued on into the foundry yard.

A strange, sudden silence filled the yard at her entrance, and Melanie felt the weight of all eyes upon her. The group of young men who usually rushed forward to greet her, all kept their distance, eyeing her in an oddly hostile manner. "What's wrong?" she thought, unable to understand the situation as she continued toward the foundry door, when suddenly a familiar voice interrupted her worried thoughts.

"Melanie! Wait a moment!"

Melanie turned to see Josh rushing to catch up to her, a wide, friendly grin creasing his face. Tom continued on into the foundry to drop off the basket and sneak his usual tour of the work in progress while the foundry was emptied for lunch. Extending his hands, Josh took both of hers within them, staring down into her face warmly. "It's good to see you again, Melanie. I was beginning to think you had disappeared from the face of the earth. I stopped by to see you and James several times, you know, but was told you weren't receiving visitors."

"Oh, I'm sorry about that, Josh, but Mrs. Sims was busy stirring up the women against me again, and Asa didn't think it wise at the time to have any men visiting. I hope you weren't offended."

"No . . ." The expression on Josh's face was puzzling, but Asa's appearance at the office doorway drew her attention away.

"Melanie . . ."

Absentmindedly considering Asa as he approached, she thought proudly, He is still a fine figure of a man. Broad and tall, his body free from the usual fat and sagging muscles found in a man approaching middle age, Asa had the spring and vigor of youth in his stride, and a youthful glow in his eyes as they rested on Melanie. Slipping an arm around her shoulder, he said offhandedly, "Would you excuse us, Josh," as he pulled her toward the office door.

Shooting Asa an assessing look, Josh mumbled, "Of course," before turning away, and Melanie blushed with embarrassment.

"Asa," she whispered as he led her firmly toward the office door, "that was very rude. Josh wanted to know how Papa was doing."

"Then let him ask me, and I'll tell him."

"Asa!"

Ushering her firmly inside, he closed the door behind them and pulled her possessively into his arms. His mouth as it closed over hers was rough and demanding, bruising her lips with the fierceness of his ardor. When he finally released her, she was breathless and shaken and looked up at him with a surprised, questioning expression. She could feel his heart pounding against her breast, and observing her startled expression, he gave a short, self-derisive snort before shaking his head. "You think I'm crazy, don't you, Melanie?"

"I just don't understand what's wrong. Didn't you want me to come here?"

Suddenly pulling her close, he held her fast against him, whispering softly into her ear as he stroked the back of her head with his wide palm. "I'm jealous, Melanie. I'm so damned jealous it's making me crazy. I looked out the window and saw you talking to Josh, and I wanted to shout, 'Get away from her, she's mine!', but I couldn't do that, so I did the next best thing and came out and pulled you away. Oh, Melanie," he said, moving slightly back to look into her face, "Are you sorry, honey? You could have had just about any one of those young men out there that you wanted. I used to watch them all crowd around you when you brought your father lunch. Are you sorry that you let an old man love you, Melanie?"

The pain in his eyes cut her deeply and, responding with warmth, she lifted her parted lips to his and slid her soft arms around his neck. "No, Asa, I'm not one bit sorry."

This time his kiss was gentle and searching, stirring her response and raising the level of her desire. When he drew away they were both trembling. Looking deep into his eyes, she said softly, "Don't work late tonight, Asa. I want to show you how happy I am with my choice."

Laughing lightly, he put her from him, relief

shining in his eyes. "You little witch." His voice still slightly shaken with desire, he said purposefully, "Now let me see what you brought me for lunch."

Within a few minutes lunch was completed and the office was filled with people. Bidding him a hasty goodbye, Melanie left in search of Tom.

Knowing Tom's sneak tours of the foundry usually lasted until the men returned to work, Melanie started walking around the deserted floor in search of him. Unable to see him anywhere, she was just about to call when she was pulled roughly into a corner and crushed against a hard, strong body as a mouth savagely plundered hers. Struggling wildly, she fought the binding embrace, only to have an iron grip hold her head firmly as a mouth covered hers. Her desperate struggles proved useless and Melanie slowly succumbed to the superior strength of the man holding her captive in his embrace while the heat of his kiss deepened. Slowly unwillingly, he drew his mouth from hers and Melanie was able to pull far enough away to see the scorn reflected on Steve Hull's face.

"Let me go . . . let me go this instant or I'll scream!" she warned hotly through clenched teeth.

"No, you won't scream, Melanie. You don't want your lover to come out here with all those men in his office and see you in someone else's arms, do you? After all, what one man gets so easily, he might think another man could get just as easily."

"Oh, you!" Gulping with fury, Melanie began twisting and scratching in his arms, and when all else failed, tried stamping on his feet . . . all to no avail.

Finally, shaking wildly with anger, she said in a low voice, "I told you, let me go right now. Take your filthy hands off me this instant, you vile man or I will call Asa!"

"Oh, so it's not 'Uncle' anymore. Well, I suppose it would be strange calling him 'Uncle' in bed."

Unable to deny the truth of his words, Melanie struggled all the harder, while he laughed softly at her ineffective attempts to free herself. Then pulling her close, he whispered in her ear, "Just let me say what I have to say, and I'll let you go. Stop struggling!"

She looked venomously into his eyes, and he laughed lightly. "That's it, little mountain cat, just listen. You're sleeping with the old man now. You were a virgin and the old man can satisfy you for a little while, but you'll tire of him soon, honey, and when he slows down and can't keep you happy anymore, I'll be here waiting." Twisting his fingers in her hair, he held her head fast as he traced the outline of her lips with his tongue before covering her mouth again, swallowing deeply of its sweetness. When he drew away this time she could feel him trembling. His voice was husky with emotion. "Remember, come to me, Melanie. I'll be waiting for you. We can ride high together, you and I—and don't wait too long, damn you . . . damn you . . . or I'll come and get you myself!"

Then glancing toward the door, he released her, giving her a small push away from him. "Now get moving out of here before your boyfriend finds out what's been going on."

Her breast heaving heavily, she backed slowly

away, spatting venomously under her breath just before she turned, "You're an animal."

His soft laughter followed her as she walked out the door, her head held high. His eyes followed Melanie while she located Tom and until she was out of sight of the foundry yard. Contrary to the casual, mocking facade he had assumed for Melanie's benefit, Steve's emotions were raging, barely in control, as he watched her slim figure recede from his view.

Damn her to Hell, he cursed to himself while still straining for the last glimpse of her disappearing figure despite his self-disgust. She draws me like a magnet . . . pulls me toward her . . . Suddenly the sensation of her firm, ripe body twisting against him, the silky texture of her hair between his fingers, the soft, moist wonder of her lips under his, and the sweet taste of her mouth returned so vividly that a flash of heat pulsating through his body set his wide, muscular frame to trembling helplessly.

"Maybe they're right. She must be a witch set on driving me wild with wanting her." No other explanation seemed plausible for the way she had filled his thoughts for the last two months, intruding on his more intimate moments with other women, and into every other aspect of his life. His sense of exhilaration had been so great when she had walked into the foundry yard just an hour earlier, that he had been appalled by her power to dominate his emotions.

Asa Parker was a friend as well as his employer, and he had always liked him; but the thought of Melanie sharing his bed twisted and cut at Steve's vitals like a knife. That old man had gotten to her first, damn him, but he wouldn't hold her long. He had felt Melanie respond to him despite her protests. Hot little bitch, he thought heatedly. She'll come . . . His stomach tightened . . . reluctantly he admitted to himself that he was beginning to lose control, and if she continued to haunt his thoughts, he wasn't sure how much longer he could wait. She had better come to him soon, or he wouldn't be responsible for the outcome.

Standing in another section of the yard, Josh's unhappy eyes also followed Melanie's receding figure, a knot in his throat so tight he could barely swallow. There was no longer any doubt in his mind that the rumors were true. Asa's expression when he had dragged her away from him had been the ultimate proof. The old man was wild about her—and jealous. His possessive manner and casual dismissal of him had been deliberate, to set the record straight without the use of words. Melanie belonged to him, and he wasn't about to let her go.

Josh's stomach heaved so strongly at that moment that he was almost sick. "Melanie . . . Melanie . . ." his mind repeated over and over as he felt the rise of a wave of desperation so great that it threatened to inundate his senses and overcome him. Sweet, beautiful Melanie . . . I was beginning to dream such dreams for us . . .

Melanie and Tom began their walk home in silence. The afternoon had been frightening, and she was truly shaken, but despite her revulsion at Steve's obscene proposals, Melanie could still feel the little tremors of delight that shook her as his lips had touched hers.

"He is wicked, vile, only interested in seduction," yet the searing memory of his heated kiss and the feeling of his body straining against hers would give her no respite. Searching her mind for a refuge from her frightening thoughts, she deliberately summoned the picture of Asa's face, and with it came a gradual return of stability.

Oh, Asa, she thought desperately, help me, please.

Tom's sudden, nervous jerking on her arm interrupted her confused thoughts.

"Melanie, look over there." Stopping, he pointed at a group of women waiting on the street corner. Harriet Sims stood in the center of the group, speaking in an inflammatory manner, while the women surrounding her nodded their agreement at frequent intervals, their manner becoming more and more agitated.

"I don't like that lady, Melanie." Indicating Harriet Sims with a nod of his head, he continued in a worried voice, "she always says bad things about you. I heard her talking to some ladies in the store last week. She said you were a witch! She said the Lord had punished Mr. Morganfield and had paralyzed him for the black magic you practiced. I got mad and I told them she was a liar, but she just laughed at me and said you had bewitched me, too. Then she said it was up to the good women in town to stop you. But I told them that they couldn't hurt you because I would protect you during the day, and you were with Mr. Parker all night and he would protect you then!"

"Tom!" Melanie's mouth dropped open in dismay

as her face flushed a bright scarlet. Tom could not have done a better job of spreading Asa's and her secret if he had shouted it from the housetop. No wonder all the men at the foundry had looked at her so accusingly, and Stephen Hull had approached her with his revolting offer. For a long moment she covered her face in shame while Tom whispered in a soft, encouraging voice she had so often used with him, "Don't be afraid, Melanie, she's just jealous because you're so pretty and she's so ugly. I won't let them hurt you. I'll kill all of them if they try to hurt you."

The menace in Tom's voice shocked her abruptly from her self pity and, touching his arm gently, she attempted a small smile. "I'm not afraid, Tom. They can only hurt me if I let them." Then slipping her arm under his again, she said with false bravado, "Come on, Tom, who cares what those old busybodies say, anyway?"

Yes, who cares? she repeated to herself lifting her head proudly. Was she really ashamed of what had happened? Asa loved her and needed her, and she needed him terribly. Aunt Emily was lost forever, as good as dead, and Asa would marry her if he was free. She wasn't the scarlet woman they made her out to be and she would not let them intimidate her. Let them talk and whisper among themselves, she wasn't afraid, and she wasn't ashamed, either!

Unable to avoid them, Melanie and Tom approached the muttering group. Harriet Sims began speaking louder as they neared, fixing her venomous stare on Melanie. "Witch . . . witch . . . she is a witch!"

Concealing the slow, encroaching fear creeping up her spine as the woman continued spewing forth her tirade of hate, Melanie walked past her with no apparent heed to her words. Incensed, Harriet Sims hissed heatedly, "Adultress . . . adultress . . . you will rot in Hell for your sins!"

Face to face with the heat of the woman's hatred, Melanie's smile became stiff and false and her step faltered momentarily. She wanted to shout at her, "No, no, it isn't true!" but determined not to allow the woman any satisfaction, she walked on, managing to toss a contemptful sneer at her twisted face.

"Witch . . . Adultress!" The woman screeched behind her. "The Bible says you shall be stoned!"

Within moments stones began whizzing by their backs and heads. One of them struck her squarely in the shoulder and she stumbled again, feeling a strange weakness slipping over her as the blood drained from her face. Tom attempted to turn back toward them, but Melanie clutched his arm tighter and whispered weakly, "No, ignore them, Tom. We're almost home."

The barrage of stones slowed to a halt as they quickly moved out of range and within minutes Melanie and Tom reached the kitchen door.

Freed from the need of pretense, Melanie's facade crumpled, as did the last of her strength, and she tumbled to the floor and unconsciousness.

A whirling kaleidoscope of faces swirled around her head as Melanie fought her way back from the oblivion that had engulfed her in temporary shelter from the frightening events of the day. Slowly recognizing the faces as they settled, she saw Martha and Tom on one side of her and Dr. Pierce on the other. Looking a little further, she saw furniture with pink rosebuds painted on the borders. She was in her own room. What was she doing here? How did she get here? Her throbbing head and the slow wave of nausea slowly slipping over her caused a low groan to escape her lips.

Dr. Pierce's deep comforting voice penetrated her confused veil of thoughts. "Drink this, Melanie, come on. That's right, it will help you to rest. You've had a frightening experience, and a nasty jolt when you fell. You'll feel better if you sleep a little while."

Strangely unable to respond, she drained the cup, wincing at the bitterness of the taste, and managed a small, meager smile before darkness again overcame her.

Melanie opened her eyes again. She was still in her room, but it was empty this time. No, glancing toward the chair she saw Asa sitting quietly, his hand covering his eyes in a weary, disturbed gesture.

"What's the matter, Asa? What's wrong?" Melanie's voice sounded hoarse and parched in the quiet of the room, and startled Asa to attention.

With a small smile, he came to sit on the side of her bed, slowly smoothing the fiery wisps of hair away from her face. As he spoke, his eyes moved slowly over her young, perfect features. "How do you feel, Melanie? Doctor Pierce gave you something to make you sleep and said you'd feel better when you awoke."

"I'm fine, Asa. What am I doing in bed? I'm not

sick." She was feeling better, now. Was she a child that she should be put to bed because she had a fright?

"No, you're not sick, but the doctor would like you to stay in bed until tomorrow at least. You had a nasty fall when you fainted and he—"

"Fainted! I fainted!" Melanie found that extremely hard to believe. "No, Asa, I must have tripped, that's all. I've never fainted in my life!"

"And you've never expected a child before, either. Melanie, why didn't you say something . . . tell me?"

Stunned, Melanie protested wildly, "But I'm not expecting a child! I can't be!" She hadn't had her monthly flow in the two months past, and was expecting it any day now, but her flow had always been a trifle irregular . . . she hadn't thought . . . "Who said?"

"Dr. Pierce examined you. There's no doubt in his mind. You're almost three months gone."

"Oh!"

His eyes suddenly filling with tears, Asa scooped her small body against him, pressing her close as he murmured against her hair, "Melanie, darling, what have I done to you? I've been so selfish, thinking only of the joy you've brought me, never facing the possibilities . . . unwilling to face what people would say when they found out. Now, soon, there will be no hiding from the consequences. Oh, there'll be no repetition of what happened this afternoon, I'll make sure of that. The husbands of those vicious women are beholden to me for their livelihoods and they'll not resume their attack on you."

"Are you ashamed of me now, Asa? Now that everyone is talking about me and speaking of my shame? Would you rather I went away somewhere?" Her voice choking on the words, she determinedly asked the questions that had been first to enter her mind.

Suddenly slackening his hold, he pulled away, saying in a shocked voice, "Is that what you think?"

Swallowing hard, Melanie said softly, "I don't want to leave you, Asa. I don't want to go away."

"And the child, Melanie, are you unhappy about the child?"

Slowly lifting her tawny eyes to stare fully into his, she whispered in a hushed voice, "I feel privileged to bear your child, Asa."

Unable to speak, Asa stared at her in wonder. Finding his silence unbearable, Melanie threw herself forward, her arms around his neck as she asked frantically, "Are you happy about the child, Asa? Please be truthful and tell me quickly. I must know."

Pulling her arms away from his neck, Asa held her slightly away from him so she might see his sincerity as he spoke. His loving, homely face torn by emotion, he said simply, as a tear slipped down his weathered cheek, "Melanie, my darling, this is the happiest day of my life."

Suddenly they were both sobbing happy, elated tears, clinging together, refusing to allow the outside world to sully the beauty of the miracle that would soon be born of their love. Slowly Asa drew away, pausing to wipe away her tears first and then his own.

"Sleep now, darling. You can get up tomorrow."

"But what about Papa?"

"He's been taken care of and is sleeping. Rest now. I'll see you tomorrow. I'll miss you beside me tonight, darling," he said softly as he pressed her back against the pillow.

Looking full up into his face, Melanie held up her arms and said simply, "Then take me with you, Asa. I'd be lonely without you beside me, too."

Deeply touched by the open declaration of her need, Asa swallowed hard. Bending down, he scooped her into his arms, holding her fast against his chest, his lips against her shining hair. Turning, he carried her through the doorway and down the hall toward his room, whispering softly against her hair as he did, "I love you, Melanie . . . God, how I love you."

Melanie stirred from her sleep the following morning with a sense of peace. The night had been filled with troubled dreams, but she had awakened each time to find Asa's arm holding her protectively against him. Asa was her rock, her lifeline to safety while a tide of public condemnation rose against her. She had no fear while he was there to protect her.

Reaching out once more for the security of his presence, she was startled to find the bed beside her empty. Suddenly fully awake, she started to rise when she saw Asa in the corner, quietly dressing.

"Asa, is it late? Why didn't you wake me?"

Smiling, he approached her, bending to press a light kiss on her parted lips. "I wanted you to sleep a little longer, Melanie. You needn't worry about James. Martha and Tom will take care of him today so you can rest."

"But Asa, I'm not sick. I'm just expecting a child."

"And a very important child, and don't you forget it," he said emphatically, with a broad wink.

"Oh, Asa." Laughing helplessly as he left, Melanie stared for a few moments at the closed door before pulling back the cover and getting to her feet. There wasn't anything wrong with her, and she wasn't going to let Martha shoulder a double burden for the day. The time would come soon enough when she would have to split her time between her father and her child. Her child. Suddenly stopping to glance down at her stomach and running her hand over its flat surface, she whispered aloud to the empty room, "Can it really be true?" Then laughing at her own disbelief, she said with emphasis, "It had better be true. Asa's counting on it."

A few moments later, dressed and ready for the day, she slipped from the bedroom and made her way quietly down the hall toward James' room. She felt elated and pleased with the world—at least with her portion of the world inside this house on Weaver's Row. She was about to open the door when a mumbling sound inside caught her attention. Pausing for a moment, she recognized Asa's voice and hesitated, not desiring to interrupt what appeared to be a very earnest conversation. A few moments more revealed the conversation was completely one-sided. Asa was talking to James.

". . . I make no excuses for myself, James. I should have been stronger, and not allowed myself to take advantage of Melanie's need . . . but, what should have been is gone, and what's done is done . . . and I must admit to you, in my heart I'm glad that the circumstances are irreversible. I just couldn't make it without her anymore. But I want you to know I'll take care of her, James, whatever happens in the future. I'm going to my lawyer today to make sure Melanie and the child will be provided for." His voice a bit lower, shadowed with shame, he continued, "I can't marry her, God forgive me, but I'll make her happy, James, I promise you that . . ."

Asa's voice slowly dwindling off in an anguished spiral wrenched Melanie's heart, and pushing open the door, she came to stand beside him, her hand on his shoulder as she stared pleadingly at the wasted shadow lying helpless in bed.

"Papa, please understand, and don't hate us . . . Papa . . ." Slowly moving to the bedside, Melanie took her father's limp hand in hers. "Papa, I'm happy, I really am, and you're going to have a grandchild."

Still clutching his hand, awaiting a reaction he was incapable of making, Melanie stared into her father's unfathomable features, a deep sob escaping her lips as his eyes, still looking into hers, slowly filled with tears and overflowed their corners onto the pillow beside his head.

The stark, defoliated November woods of Clarendon were alive with unusual activity. One hundred mounted Green Mountain Boys, their nervous, snorting horses pawing at the ground, awaited silently the command for the night ride to begin.

His deep voice echoing in the stillness of the night, his face illuminated by the flickering light of many

113

torches, Allen's broad frame exuded an aura of violence; the living, breathing spector of imminent retribution.

"Clarendon will learn its lesson tonight, Boys! Its double-dealing will not be tolerated. First on our list is that old traitor, Benjamin Spencer. He has well earned that position by his pretentious claims to being the justice of the peace for the colony of New York in Hampshire Territory, and with his audacity in attempting to rename Clarendon by the Yorker name of Durham. The damned traitor would sell us out!" Raising his fist with visible rage, he exploded, "There's not a stout heart among them! Cowards that would let us do their fighting and turn on us the moment it profits them! We'll show Spencer and his weak-kneed followers they've gone too far this time. Durham will disappear forever before the sun rises tomorrow, and Clarendon will stand unchallenged in its place. Justice will be done—Hampshire justice!"

Loud, enthusiastic cheers followed Allen's rousing speech, and within minutes the horses thundered down the road to Clarendon. Moving quickly with the precision of those joined in strong, mutual purpose, they arrived at the residence of Benjamin Spencer in record time and charged wildly up the front steps. Making a shambles of the front door, they continued with single-minded direction up the staircase to the second floor. Locating Spencer's bedroom, they hauled him from his bed.

Roaring like the voice of the Almighty, Allen declared, "You are a damned old offender, Spencer! Put on your clothes before we drag you out of here to stand trial in your night rail!"

"By whose authority do you enter my house?" demanded the arrogant Spencer.

Incensed to the point of rage by the defenseless man's gall, Allen combined word and action in one blow with his gun butt, sending the protesting prisoner into unconsciousness with the words, "By the authority of the people, and the power of my almighty right arm!" Turning back to Josh and Steve, he said emphatically, "The whole town needs this kind of treatment! Now take him away and let's get on with our work and clean up this Yorker's nest!"

No longer capable of protest, the unconscious Spencer was bundled down the stairs and onto a horse and hauled away to await trial. With grim determination the Green Mountain Boys rode the town. Houses were burned, traitorous families chased and threatened with violence, and malingering protestors moved by unrelenting force. Their work for the night done, Allen and his men mounted up, shouting to the quaking crowd of dispossessed settlers, "What has happened tonight you have steadfastly earned with your treachery and guile. Now is the time to mend your ways, for should we be forced to act again, every house will be reduced to ashes and every inhabitant will be a corpse!"

Leaving them with that emphatic, unmistakable message, the force of one hundred rode out of town. Clarendon had paid its dues for the night, but the fee had not been paid in full. Returning the following day the Boys began erecting a podium and grandstand on Benjamin Spencer's land. At the completion of the project two days later, Benjamin Spencer was solemnly returned to his property, a defendant in an open air court. Herding in the townspeople as unwilling spectators, Ethan Allen, Remember Baker, Seth Warner, and Robert Cochran sat as judges as the charges were read.

"Do you admit to representing the New York government in the heart of the Hampshire Grants, and following New York law?"

The pale defendant responded pluckily, "I have, but I ask a question in return. Have I been unfair to any man?"

"No," was Allen's reply, "but fairness does not wipe away traitorous conduct!"

Following a stream of witnesses testifying to his execution of an illegal office, deliberation was short, and the sentence pronounced. There would be no horsewhipping. The begrudging respect the man had earned spared him that, but he and the spectators would witness the burning of his house while they stood powerless to intervene.

With great deliberation the roof of the Spencer house was set aflame. Allen eyed the grim-faced but resolute man, his dark brows drawn together with the weight of a pending reversal. In the snap of a second he made a decision.

Standing to his full height, Allen waved his brawny arms with the authority of an undisputed leader and shouted, "Knock off the roof, men. We'll save this man his house and his land . . . he has suffered enough this day!"

Stunned, Allen's men hesitated only the briefest second before following his command, and within minutes the house was saved. Turning to the relieved but weary Spencer, his eyes intent and piercing, Allen fixed his gaze on him.

"You have felt our mercy, but the well has run dry for you today. You will never taste it again. Your choice is simple; either leave the grants or resign your Yorker commission. It is your decision, and we leave it with you."

Turning back to his men, Allen signaled them to their horses, and within a few minutes they were gone.

But not forgotten. The very same day a letter was dispatched to the colony of New York containing Spencer's resignation of his commission. Clarendon had paid its dues in full and would not put itself in similar debt again.

The weary band of one hundred slowed to a stop to rest their horses. A tall, broad, fair-haired fellow dismounted and strode forward to heartily slap the leader on the back, laughing loudly as he did.

"Ethan, you old fox! There are times when your devious mind amazes me! Do you never stop thinking?"

The dark giant turned, a wide smile breaking over his features. "You know, of course, Josh, that it takes a devious mind to appreciate a devious mind." Suddenly he was laughing uproariously. "There I thought I had everyone fooled . . . it was just too good an opportunity to pass. Ethan Allen has been drawn the black villain too many times of late. It was time to temper my justice with mercy. And after all, what is feared more than my unpredictability? I have today added a few more inches to my stature on both

117

those counts! And to tell the truth," he said, slinging his brawny arm across Josh's shoulder and speaking in a more confidential tone, "that is one cocky old rooster! I have to admire a man with spirit and a strong gut. It's far better to have a man like that as a cool friend than a bitter enemy. We have to live in the present with an eye to the future."

Nodding his head in full agreement, Josh laughed to himself. Ethan Allen a wild reactionary! How very widely this man was underestimated. And it had proved to his advantage again and again. Even this false opinion he had come to use against his enemies. Shaking his head, Josh said aloud, "Ethan, the better I come to know you, the happier I grow that we pursue the same end."

Not to be outdone, Ethan said softly with a wink, "And I feel infinitely safer, Josh, knowing that a man with such keen vision that he can see right through me, fights on my side."

Standing a few feet away, Steve eyed the two men as they laughed companionably, his dark, handsome features drawn into a deep frown. He was irritable and out of sorts. Unlike Josh, he was not at all satisfied at the turn of events. Had he been in command, Benjamin Spencer would have been horsewhipped like the traitor he was, and his house burned. Mercy? Would that old man have shown them mercy if they had been hauled up to be judged by him? But he wasn't in command, and Allen's word was law.

Wearily, he stooped to sit on an old log at the base of the tree, and ran his hand through his thick, black hair. Just a few months previous he had been quite satisfied with the direction his life was taking. He had overcome his bitterness after his father's pointless, alcoholic death by using his brotherhood with the Green Mountain Boys to take out his anger on the enemies of the grants. There he was also fighting for the only thing Thomas Hull had valued in life other than his wife—his land. His mother . . . his beautiful, faithless mother, who had taken his father's will to live with her when she left. Never, never would he let a woman get such a hold on his emotions. His father's love for her had become a weakness, a fatal weakness . . .

Gnawing relentlessly at his peace of mind was his realization that despite his strongest efforts, he was unable to drive Melanie Morganfield from his thoughts. He had caught only a few, brief glimpses of her in the last two months, and those because he had deliberately ridden down Weaver's Row on one pretext or another and had seen her once in the back yard, and another time talking to her shadow, Tom Hartley. She had been laughing up into his stupid face, her hand lightly resting on his arm, and the fierce stab of jealousy that knifed through him had burned for days. Stunned at the effect she still had on him, he had finally come to the conclusion he would have to make the first move. His desire for her had become a fixation that threatened to overcome him. Melanie had eluded him too long.

Relying on the harsh rigors of the season to protect the grants from enemies from without, Ethan Allen dismissed his men. He did not reckon on enemies from within who continued insidiously on their determined course. One such person, the Reverend Mr. Benjamin Hough, Baptist minister of Clarendon, consumed with the fury of the righteous, rode silently out of town shortly after Allen's brigade had left for a secret audience with Governor Tryon. Narrow-minded, inflexible rules had been engrained into his puritanical mind from early youth. By his logic, Allen's use of Scripture was blasphemy, his refusal to accept the authority of New York a crime, and the methods he used in securing the grants for the settlers residing there were illegal and sinful. The ultimate conclusion of his reasoning—Allen must be stopped, and he, Benjamin Hough, would stop him!

It was a sober-faced, upright, grimly determined man who presented himself to Governor Tryon and the Council. His address was persuasive and effective.

"I appeal to you, Governor Tryon, gentlemen, in the name of the Lord and for the sake of humanity, to expend all your efforts to bring the brigand, Ethan Allen, and his crazed followers to justice. I have just come from Clarendon, where your legally appointed justice of the peace was tried in mockery and sentenced to dire punishment for fulfilling his duties. And this was done after the entire town was terrorized by that Bennington mob that calls itself the Green Mountain Boys. That madman has destroyed the peace that prevailed within our town, and spread a mantle of fear over its citizens. If our people are to respect your laws, governor, then they must be protected from those who defy them! If you wish respect for your authority to prevail, you must bring to justice those that flaunt their defiance in our faces.

Justice, gentlemen, justice is what we ask and demand as our right!"

Appearing to weigh the reverend's impassioned appeal, Governor Tryon hesitated a few moments before speaking. In truth, his previous assignment had been in North Carolina, where he had gone through a chastening experience in quarreling with backwoods settlers, and he was not eager to leap again into a military adventure. His reply was a cautious question.

"Your words are very persuasive, Mr. Hough, and we greatly respect your courage in coming to us, but what is it that you would have us do?"

"I should think the answer would be obvious! Send your troops to the grants, and take them once and for all in the name of New York. Maintain law and order, demand it with the power of your office and the strength of your troops! Keep this evil brigade from overrunning your territory and keeping it in constant terror!"

"But you must realize, Mr. Hough, that winter is upon us. Would you have us send our men to spend the winter chasing shadows in the forest and freezing in the attempt?"

"Sir, I do not ask the impossible. I, too, realize it would be ill advised to send troops when the winter snows are about to beset us. But spring, and the thaw, would remove that objection. I merely ask your commitment to action when it is once again feasible to act."

Once again Governor Tryon studied the clergyman's zealous face. He was wary of the circumstances, and Allen's reputation made him a man almost as feared as he was respected. As a backwoodsman, Allen had no equal, and the grants were his home territory. The Governor was only too aware that Allen's backwoods gang could run his soldiers around in circles in the unfamiliar mountains.

Allen's other talents had also begun to bear fruit. An accomplished pamphleteer as well as a fiery orator, Allen had deluged the surrounding colonies with propaganda that had even reached the Crown. Before making a move of such outright aggression, he needed to be surer of his footing. He needed time . . . Slowly he began his carefully worded reply.

"Ah, sir, you stir the conscience of this good council with your words. We have long been aware of our obligations in the grants, but a decision of this magnitude cannot be decided in the heat of the moment. It has also long been our desire to subdue the wildman, Allen, but, alas, our attempts thus far have proved unsuccessful. Fortunately, we have until spring to formulate our plan of action. We beg your indulgence until then. However, at present we have a more pressing problem. We have only just received Benjamin Spencer's resignation of his office of justice of the peace, and are now totally without legal representation within Clarendon. I would like to offer an appeal of my own that I am sure my council members will endorse. Surely a man of your moral fiber would be ideal to fill the post vacated by Mr. Spencer. Would you consider, Mr. Hough, the position of justice of the peace in the interim?"

A slight flush of pleasure transfusing his stern countenance, Mr. Hough replied proudly without hesitation, "It would be an honor, sir."

Within the hour and after considerable discussion, Justice of the Peace Hough left the council chambers with the firm conviction that he had accomplished his purpose and troops would be dispatched in the spring.

But the loyal followers and agents of the Green Mountain Boys were everywhere, and a report that Hough had taken the Yorker post and attempted to foment an uprising of the people against Allen's authority reached Allen's ears before Hough reached his home. The self-righteous Reverend Justice Hough had almost reached his land when he was overrun and taken captive by the Green Mountain Boys and transported thirty miles into Sunderland, in the heart of the grants, to stand trial.

The day of the trial dawned clear and mild and, following the usual procedure, the Green Mountain Boys herded the townspeople in to attend. The charges read, witnesses heard, judgment was pronounced by a livid Allen.

"You, Reverend Mr. Hough, have been found guilty of all charges made against you! You are a traitor to your neighbors and friends. You deserve and will receive a sentence fitting your crime! Two hundred lashes will impress upon you and all others who have Yorker leanings that duplicity will not be tolerated!"

A spontaneous gasp went up from the crowd upon Allen's thunderous pronouncement of the sentence of two hundred lashes.

Drawing himself up to his full height, Allen stood and faced the crowd, his dark brows drawn together over black eyes sparking with anger. Using the full reaches of his powerful voice, he made a sober proclamation to the startled spectators.

"So that there may be no misunderstanding, let it be understood that this man is being punished for attempting to hold an office under the colony of New York within the Hampshire Grants. Let this be a long remembered lesson . . ."

Long after the cracking sound of the lash had ceased, and the bleeding man was hauled off to be treated by the town doctor, the look in Allen's eyes remained to haunt the faint-hearted. Ethan Allen's point was won again.

Frowning slightly, Melanie clutched the folds of her voluminous cape closer around her. She hadn't realized the November wind had turned so bitingly cold, but it made no difference. She still would have come out walking. In the last three months she had seldom budged from her father's sickroom, realizing he was close to the end. But still he hung on. He was no longer recognizable as the man he once was, his skin stretched thin over what was the mere skeleton of his body. And his eyes, even they now had a fevered, wandering quality, as if he no longer comprehended the passage of events around his bed. Oh, God, she didn't want him to die, but she couldn't bear to watch his life slowly fading away! If it were not for Asa . . . his genuine sympathy and understanding, his loving arms, she would not have been able to go on. And the child within her . . . strangely, it had begun to be the only bright spot in her future. Where she should feel shame and contrition, she felt only hope. It mattered little to her what people said or did, Asa would not allow them to affect her in any way. Sliding her hand under her cape, she ran her palm over the rise of her stomach. Midway through her sixth month, she was starting to round well, but was well below the usual proportions of a woman that far into pregnancy. Dr. Pierce, who continued to attend her father, had only laughed when Asa voiced his concern over her proportions.

"Tell me, Asa, do you have a fetish for fat women? Melanie is a strong, healthy young woman who will give you a strong, healthy child. In another month she will be large and awkward enough to satisfy even you, so have patience, my friend."

A small smile crossed Melanie's lips as she recalled Asa's flushed face as he mumbled, "At my age, David, I can't afford anything but caution," and slipping his arm around her shoulder he had hugged her lightly.

"You are a braver man than I, Asa," Dr. Pierce had commented soberly, shaking his head. "I would have sent Melanie away to have her child rather than confront this community head-on with your illegal offspring." Seeing the tears that sprang to Melanie's eyes, he had offered quietly, "I do not mean that as a moral judgment, Melanie, merely as a legal fact."

"Melanie wants to be near her father, and I want Melanie to be near me." The decisive ring to Asa's voice brooked no argument, and Dr. Pierce had turned away, shrugging his rounded shoulders in surrender.

But Papa had suffered two severe spells so far this day, and Melanie had felt a sudden desperate compulsion to get away. With great deliberation she had donned Martha's cape to disguise her spreading figure and left the house. But even now, walking alone in the bright November afternoon, Melanie was not free of the sick room. Determined to provide herself a brief respite from her cares, she lifted her head, simultaneously pulling her cape a little closer. The autumn snap in the air had brought a bright color to her cheeks, and she tossed her blazing mane back from her face as she chastised herself mentally. Stop feeling sorry for yourself, Melanie, or you'll drown in your own misery. You've taken some time for yourself, so enjoy it while you can.

Succumbing to a sudden impulse, she turned onto the main street. The shops should take my mind from things for a short time, she thought. But she had not gone more than halfway down the street when she began to regret her impulsive act. Striding directly toward her in deep conversation with another woman was Harriet Sims. The hag had not spotted her, and although Melanie's condition was not yet obvious in her cape, an overwhelming wave of dread swept over her. She was not up to a confrontation. I cannot face that virago this afternoon! she thought in desperation. Glancing around for a safe retreat, she noticed an alleyway about six feet wide between two buildings. Jumping inside, moving well down into it to flatten herself back against the wall so that she would not catch the women's attention as they passed, she held her breath, her heart pounding in suspense, her eyes intent on the street. Slowly the two women moved past the entrance, still engrossed in their conversation, sending not even the briefest glance her way.

Quietly exhaling a small sigh of relief, Melanie started to inch her way toward the street when a tall figure moved from behind her to clamp a hand over her mouth, slapping her head back against the wall, and pinning her there effectively with his body. A deep, familiar voice in her ear sent tremors of fear up her spine.

"It's been a long time, Melanie. Did you finally decide to pay me a visit? The back staircase to my boardinghouse is only a few feet away, you know."

Laughing as Melanie's eyes widened to large golden pools, he continued, his voice growing cold and menacing, "I'm going to take my hand away from your mouth now, Melanie. If you make any unwise sounds, I'll knock you senseless. Besides, you don't want anyone to find you in a deserted alleyway with me, do you? Your reputation could never stand the blow . . . and your lover . . ."

Enraged by his remarks, Melanie attempted to strike out at him, only to have him catch her hand and twist it down to her side. His low laughter infuriated her even further and she began struggling wildly, twisting and biting in his grasp while he continued to laugh in a low voice, enjoying the writhing of her body against his as he pressed her even tighter against the wall. Suddenly a strange, incredulous expression spread over his face, and he jerked away from her. Seeing her chance to escape, Melanie attempted to run, only to be snatched back roughly and slammed again against the wall. There was a slight ringing in her ears as she struck her head against the stone, and stunned, she merely stood weakly as Steve ripped open the front of her cape and stared down in shocked disbelief at her slightly distended abdomen.

"You stupid fool! Why did you let him do this to you? Or did you drive the old man so crazy he couldn't think straight?" Hot, blind fury swept over him, turning his raging desire momentarily into seething hatred of the small, beautiful woman in front of him. In a frenzy of jealousy, he raised his hand and began striking her repeatedly back and forth across the face while he hissed a malevolent litany. "Whore . . . slut . . . witch . . ."

Unable to block the stinging blows, Melanie's head snapped back and forth sharply, sending her senses reeling and her vision whirling into a spiral of dimming light. The sound of his voice slowly began to fade away, allowing darkness to gain control.

Melanie awakened slowly, her eyelids lifting to see a darkly handsome face staring soberly down into hers. Black, wavy hair tumbled onto his wide forehead, and penetrating black eyes beneath dark, arched brows looked into hers.

Strange, she thought idly in her vague, disoriented state, how thick and long his lashes are . . . Her eyes touched on his sharp, straight nose, down along the line of his jaw and up to his mouth and those warm, seeking lips she could remember so well.

Her glance then moved to wander around the unfamiliar room. Medium sized and bright, there was a small washstand in the corner, small dresser and mirror, a hook behind the door on which hung a change of clothes. Her wandering glance then touched on a much abused desk and chair, over which were thrown Steve's buckskin traveling clothes, and under the one window in the room a nightstand supported a large, smudged lamp. She was lying on a wide bed in the center of the room, with Steve on his side beside her, staring thoughtfully down into her face.

Strangely, it was difficult to speak, and she stumbled uneasily over her words as she managed in a weak voice, "What . . . where am I, Steve? What are you doing here beside me? What has happened?"

Moving his hand to tenderly caress her cheek he answered in a hoarse voice, "I lost my temper and struck you, and you fainted. I brought you here to my room."

He didn't tell her of his panic as she collapsed into his arms, of his hectic flight up the stairs, the wild surge of happiness he felt having her in his arms as he closed the door behind them . . . or the ensuing tenderness that engulfed him as he lay her on the bed. She was all right, just frightened, he was certain, and he lay beside her, unable to tear his eyes from her face. Beautiful, her brilliant auburn tresses spread across the pillow; slim, slightly slanted brows; delicate, almost transparent lids covering those bright tawny eyes; the long, sweeping lashes lying against white flawless cheeks. Her nose was beautiful, too, perfect, slender and straight, and her mouth . . . he had dreamed so long, so very long about that mouth. He touched her chin lightly, smiling at its stubborn tilt, and she began to stir.

Frowning slightly, she said in a soft voice, "Please, Steve, I'd like to go home now."

"You are home."

Looking at him with a puzzled expression, she said questioningly, "Home? What do you mean? What are you talking about?"

"You are home, now. This is where you belong, Melanie, here with me. Not in an old man's bed."

Anger came back into Melanie's eyes, lighting a familiar golden spark and she started to rise, "I'm going ho—"

Pushing her back roughly against the pillow, Steve said with sudden menace, "You're not going anywhere."

Anger flared at his tone. "Take your hands off me this minute! I will be missed very shortly and Asa will come searching for me. I don't want to have to tell him that you kept me here against my will."

"And will you tell him, also, that I made love to you against your will? Because I intend to make love to you, with or without your consent. And I'll tell you now, Melanie," his fingers dug mercilessly into her cheeks as he held her face firmly by the chin, "I'll kill the old man . . . dead . . . if he tries to take you away from me before I'm ready!" His voice was a low growl, his face suddenly contorted into a vicious mask as he hissed, "Do you believe me, Melanie?"

Faced with his heated rage and the innate savagery in his eyes, Melanie experienced true, unreasoning fear. He would—he would kill Asa . . .

"Do you believe me, Melanie?" he demanded again, his fingers biting cruelly into her cheeks.

"Yes, I believe you."

"Good, then we understand each other."

Slowly his mouth descended to cover hers, and a wild happiness seared through Steve's veins.

Roughly he grabbed her, pulling her tight against him. This was what he wanted, what had been missing all these months. Melanie . . . God, my Melanie . . . With bruising force he separated her lips, driving his tongue down deep into her mouth. The sweet, warm taste of her was driving him mad, and he strained and pulled her against him, his fingers biting into her arms and back. He wanted more, he wanted all of her, and began fumbling madly with the buttons on her dress front, but his hands were shaking so badly he could not manage them.

"If you don't want this dress ripped off, Melanie, you had better help me do this. My patience is very short right now."

Her hands moved up to the buttons at her neck, and Steve moved away slightly to allow her room to move. Seeing her opportunity, Melanie was almost off the bed and to her feet when she was jerked back cruelly by the hair to sprawl helplessly backward as Steve glowered over her in a burning rage, twisting and turning his hand in her hair, almost tearing it from her scalp. She cried out in pain and his grip tightened further.

"Start unbuttoning your dress—now!"

Reaching up with shaking hands, Melanie loosened one button after another, until her chemise was completely exposed. Sliding his hand inside the neckline, Steve lifted out one rounded breast. Closing her eyes against her shame, Melanie could not see the look of wonder that transfused Steve's face. Overwhelmed by an emotion he had never before experienced, his mouth slowly closed over the soft, pink crest, eliciting a low gasp from Melanie. Almost beside himself with desire, Steve was shaking wildly. Straining for some semblance of control, he released her slowly.

"Get up, Melanie, and take your clothes off. They're in the way. I want to see all of you."

She made a move to rise and he whispered in a low voice, "Don't try anything, Melanie. I'll kill you before I let you get away from me this time." Even as he spoke the words, Steve realized he meant them, they were no idle threat. He'd kill to keep her if he had to.

"Steve," Melanie's voice implored a return to sane reasoning, "I'm six months gone with child. My body is swollen and ugly to look at. Surely some other woman could—"

"It's you I want, Melanie . . . you."

Melanie rose slowly to her feet and began undressing. Within moments she stood naked before him while his eyes moved shamelessly over her. Her skin was so smooth and white, her breasts so perfect. He looked at her stomach and frowned, but she'd only be that way a little while longer, and then he'd have her to himself again. He rose to stand beside her.

"Lay down on the bed, Melanie."

Quaking violently, Melanie obeyed, and he began to undress. Within moments he stood naked before her, his manhood firm and erect, frightening her with its proportions. Unable to stand anymore, she closed her eyes, and felt the bed beside her give with his weight. Suddenly she was in his arms, and he was kissing her madly, showering her face with kisses, raining them on her neck, shoulders, breasts, taunting, teasing her, his hands everywhere at once, smoothing, teasing, hurting, straining her against him. Slowly without her realization or conscious consent, her reaction began to change. She was no longer pushing him away, but pressing him against her, reveling in the touch of his hands, the taste of his lips, straining, crying, pleading for him to continue. Finally, when she could stand no more, she begged for release, kissing his face and neck as he arched himself over her, pausing for a long moment before driving down full and deep inside her. With a low groan she savored the moment, and then raised her body to meet his, welcoming his savage thrusts, meeting, pushing, glowing, until in one showering burst of ecstasy they reached the peak, caught breathless at the summit for an endless, mindless eternity, to fall gasping and spent . . . content in each other's arms.

For a few brief, mindless moments, Melanie lay basking in the glorious aftermath of their passion until the slow, relentless intrusion of reality interrupted her euphoria. What had she done? What was wrong with her? Her father lay dying in Asa's home. She carried Asa's child inside her . . . what . . .

A warm, firm mouth closing over hers interrupted her thoughts, the intensity of his kiss wiping the words from her mind, his hands caressing her breasts stirring anew the flame they had extinguished so perfectly just moments before.

"Melanie, darling, come away with me. We'll go to the grants, to my homestead. We can stay there and live together for as long as this thing between us lasts."

"This thing?"

"This madness, Melanie, you drive me mad with wanting you. And I know you want me, too . . . you do, darling, you do." Lowering his mouth, he covered her breasts with kisses, filling her body with wild tremors that shook her to the very soul, and she found a new, silent desperation. He was right. She did want him.

"Tell me. Tell me, Melanie," he whispered against her tortured flesh, "tell me you want me."

"Yes, I do want you, Steve," she groaned, tears overflowing the corners of her eyes and dampening the pillow beside her head. "But it wouldn't work. I'm going to have Asa's child."

"Come with me to the grants. You can have the child there and keep it or send it back to Asa. Whatever you want."

"And how long would we be together, Steve?"

"Until this flame burns itself out but, Melanie, Melanie, the times we will have . . ." He paused to press another deep kiss against her mouth, searing and searching, until she was once again almost over the brink of reasonable thought.

"Come with me, Melanie."

"I can't come, Steve. My father . . . he won't last much longer. I have to be with him at the end."

Steve was suddenly silent. He could find no answer for that and stared thoughtfully into her eyes before speaking. "All right, Melanie, we'll wait. No matter how long it takes, but when he dies you'll come away with me."

"Yes, yes."

"And in the meantime we'll meet or you'll come

here. We can be careful, change our meeting places. No one will know."

"Yes, Steve, yes," Melanie answered, pressing wild kisses on his face and neck, savoring the heady man smell of his body. "But I must go now, or it will all be ruined. They're probably wondering where I am now."

"I don't want you to leave yet." Somehow Steve could not face separation from her so soon.

"But Tom will be out looking for me soon, and then . . ."

Considering her words, Steve's eyes traveled her beautiful face. She was right, a little caution today would make their future meetings far less hazardous. With great reluctance Steve rose from the bed. Pulling Melanie unceremoniously to her feet, he pressed her body flush against his, reveling in the beauty as their flesh and mouths met. Then pushing her lightly away, he said in a soft voice, "If you're going, you'd better go now or I'll keep you here all night."

Realizing the truth of his statement, Melanie with shaking hands hurried to dress as Steve slipped on his britches. When she stood ready at the door, he adjusted her cape over her shoulders, his eyes lingering on her beautiful face, moving slowly as he memorized each adored detail. "Tomorrow, you'll come here tomorrow same time. All right?"

"Yes, tomorrow."

"Melanie—"

One last searing kiss and she was down the hall and back steps, running until she could not catch her breath. Shaking and exhausted, she at last walked through the rear kitchen doorway of Asa's home.

"Melanie, what happened to you? We were worried to death! Almost frantic! I was just about to send Tom for Mr. Parker!"

"I'm all right, Martha. I just walked too far, that's all, and I'm exhausted. If you don't mind, I'll rest until Asa comes home. He'll understand."

"Of course, yes, of course, Melanie." Martha's voice was strange, but Melanie made no effort to explain any further, and numbly walked up the stairs to her own room. Closing the door behind her, she walked to the chair and dropped her cape, then slowly lay down on her bed.

Her grief started with a slow whimper, building in intensity to deep, heartrending sobs, shaking, tearing her body, continuing with an intensity and violence that almost drove her past despair. She thought of Steve's face, his touch, and desire rose again inside her. Softly she whispered to the image in her mind's eye. "Steve, darling, that was goodbye . . . goodbye, darling."

Steve watched Melanie disappear around the end of the corridor, and turning, reentered his room and closed the door behind him. He leaned back, feeling the roughness of the wood against his bare back, and closed his eyes.

"Melanie . . . Melanie." His whisper echoed in the silent room. Even the sound of her name on his lips inflamed his desire, and his heart pounded heavily in his chest. She was gone only a few minutes and already he ached to hold her again. He had had countless women in his life, but never had he felt so powerless against his absolute need. Why had he let her go so soon? He should have kept her with him a little longer.

Suddenly he was laughing, and walked forward to lie down on the bed. "You're acting the fool, Hull," he said aloud, still unbelieving of the joy he felt inside him. He turned his face against the pillow. The soft, sweet scent of her still remained, and he breathed deeply, drawing in her fragrance. With a short, rueful laugh, he mumbled to himself, "I will go mad before tomorrow if I continue on this way!" But, Lord, she intoxicated him! He was not really certain when he would come down to earth, or if he really wanted to.

Another thought struck him, and he shook his head in wonder as he turned it over in his mind. He was mad with desire for a woman who was six months gone with another man's child. Melanie would probably sleep in Asa's bed tonight, and for many more nights until they would be free to go away together. Would she allow him to make love to her, sleep in his arms. Pounding his fist against the bed, he said aloud, "No . . . no! I will not think of it!" But even as he spoke, livid jealousy tied his stomach into painful knots. "Tomorrow I will make her promise that she will find an excuse to sleep alone until we can go away together! He'll never have her again, she's mine . . . mine, now."

An uneasy feeling penetrated Melanie's restless dreams and her eyes snapped open to see a familiar, lined face looking down worriedly into hers.

"How are you, darling? Martha told me you

weren't feeling well and came upstairs to lie down." Asa toyed absentmindedly with a lock of her brilliant hair as he searched her face avidly. "You must have been sleeping for hours, supper is ready. Do you feel well enough to eat?"

A wave of guilt sent a flush of color to her face, and tears stung her eyes. "I'm fine, Asa. Please don't fuss over me."

"Are you certain? I mean, it's not like you to do this. You're not ill and hiding it from me, are you?"

His concern was too heavy a burden to bear, and Melanie burst out angrily, "Stop asking me questions, will you, Asa? I told you I'm all right! Just leave me alone."

Asa's shocked, hurt expression brought her sudden tirade to an abrupt halt, leaving her staring into his face for a few wordless moments before she burst into tears, throwing herself against his chest and holding him in a tight, unrelenting embrace.

"Oh, Asa, I'm sorry. Please forgive me. I'm a wicked, ungrateful girl. I don't deserve your love." Turning her bright, golden eyes up to his as tears sparkled on the long sweep of her lashes, she said softly, "Oh, Asa, what have I done? I'm a worthless wanton. I've ruined your peace, brought shame to a household that was respected by the entire town. You must be sorry my father and I ever crossed your threshold."

Melanie's words dwindled off as Asa's hands moved to cup her cheeks with his hands. His voice thick with emotion, Asa whispered softly, "Melanie, darling, you've given me back my life. You are worth any pain you could ever cause me. I love you, darling.

Nothing you could ever say or do could change that. My only unhappiness is that I'm not free to make you my wife." A small smile brightened his unhappy expression as he continued. "But I've been working on a little surprise for you with my lawyer. If all turns out well, you and our child will be secure for the rest of your lives, no matter what happens to me."

"Asa, I don't want—please don't talk like that."

Asa searched her face for a few moments, seeming to read her mind with his eyes, and suddenly overcome with guilt, Melanie turned her head away.

His sudden, fierce, possessive embrace startled her. She could feel the pounding of his heart and the trembling of his hands as he held her tight against him. She was almost breathless with the strength of his embrace, and still he tightened his hold, crushing her against his chest, caressing her long, silky curls with his shaking hand. When he finally spoke his voice was hushed, heavy with emotion.

"Melanie, darling . . . please don't leave me . . . please don't ever leave me."

She was unable to speak when finally she extricated herself from his frantic embrace. She swallowed several times against the huge lump in her throat that stole her words, and paused to touch the familiar creases in his cheek, finally managing in a hoarse whisper, "I'll never leave you, Asa, never."

Raising her mouth, she offered him her trembling lips, and he claimed them possessively, passionately as his own.

Pacing the floor restlessly, Steve wandered to the window of his room to check the street again. Where is she? he wondered helplessly for the hundredth time that afternoon. She's late, damn her! We won't have much time together this afternoon as it is and she had to cheat us more by being late. But she'll come, I know she will.

His steps slowed to a stop as he began to relive the afternoon before in his mind again. He hadn't been able to stop thinking about her, and his desire was so strong it drove every other thought from his mind.

"Hurry, Melanie, hurry, will you?" he said aloud to the empty room, "My darling, darling Melanie."

The room was dark. Hours before, the sun had sunk into the horizon, taking with it the fiery warmth streaming through Steve's bedroom window . . . and the last of his hopes. She wasn't coming. She had never meant to come. She was a superb actress, he had believed her completely, the love in her golden, glowing eyes; the throb of passion that caught in her voice; the soft, warm kisses she had pressed on his face and neck, her ultimate surrender. "Yes, I do want you, Steve . . ."

Those words cut viciously into his gut, and he sat limply on the bed, resting his elbows on his knees as he covered his face with his hands. The pain he felt was deep and excruciating, almost physical in intensity, starting in his chest, squeezing and choking him, moving up to convulse his throat and tighten until a low sound escaped his lips. And then there was another, until he was sobbing, sobbing with the desperation of frustrated desire, jealousy, and the death of the supreme tenderness that had

140

been growing inside him for his beautiful Melanie . . . his Melanie.

"Melanie, you look so preoccupied, darling. What's wrong? What are you thinking about?"

Startled out of her reverie, Melanie turned away from the darkness outside the study window and walked to the chair where Asa sat, a neglected book on his lap. Bending, she lightly kissed the frown lines on his forehead. "I was just thinking what a very long day this has been, especially the afternoon. I'm glad it's over."

Taking the book and putting it on the table beside him, she slipped lightly into his lap, smiling at the flush of pleasure that stole over his face as she kissed him lightly on the lips. She snuggled against him and felt his body's immediate response to her closeness. Feeling an answering need growing inside her, she raised her hand to touch the gray hair at his temples and run her fingertips lightly along the deep lines at the outside corners of his eyes. His skin was tough and creased like old leather as she slid her fingers down his cheek and across his lips in a fleeting caress. Looking deeply into his eyes she took his hand and kissed the calloused palm gently before placing it on her breast, moving it lightly across its fullness.

"Asa," she whispered hoarsely, "I'm tired. I'd like to go to bed now. Shall we check on Papa and turn in?"

With great deliberation Asa lifted her from his lap and stood beside her. Sliding his arm around her waist, he pulled her against his side and said softly, "I'm tired, too, Melanie. That sounds like a good idea."

Arm in arm, her head resting against his shoulder, they crossed the study floor and opened the door to walk down the hallway toward the staircase to the second floor.

The loud clanging of the lunch bell echoed painfully in his head, and in an effort to shut out the reverberating din, Steve dropped his tools on the floor to cover his ears with the palms of his hands. A few of the men around him chuckled at his agonized grimace, and shaking their heads laughingly, walked toward the rear of the foundry to eat their luncheon meal. The late January cold precluded any effort to take their lunch outside in the fresh air, and as soon as the clanging ceased, Steve followed the group toward the rear, his stomach beginning to heave at the mere thought of food. Now I know why they call it 'that demon, rum,' he thought ruefully as he walked, his main objective to find a quiet spot to rest his heavy head.

"Another long night at the tavern, Steve?"

Turning toward the voice, Steve's glance met a pair of worried eyes staring levelly into his. "Since when did you become my nursemaid, Josh? Besides, you're wrong. It was a party of three in my room last night. Peggy, me and a bottle of rum; and you can bet old Peg's head is hanging this morning, too!" He started to laugh, but the effort only caused him more pain, and holding his head tightly, he sank into the nearest corner to rest his head against the wall. But when he closed his eyes, it wasn't Peg's bold features that came to haunt him. Bright amber eyes seemed to burn before him in his mind, while soft, parted lips tempted his kiss. A small dimple flashed in the smooth cheek, and his eyes snapped open in anger. Damn! Would she never stop haunting him? Was there no way he could strike her image from his mind?

". . . Just look at him . . . the old man seems to be getting younger every day. Hell, he never gets tired!" Steve caught a few words of the conversation progressing beside him as Asa strode vigorously across the foundry floor toward his office.

"Well, Bart, if you had what he has at home to keep him young, you wouldn't be sitting here like yesterday's campfire . . . you'd have a red hot blaze going, too!" Loud laughter followed the remark as Steve slowly moved his ominous gaze in their direction.

"And I hear the old man's going to be a papa! That Melanie must be a witch the way she's rejuvenating the old war-horse!"

Josh's head snapped up at the last remark, an incredulous look on his paling face.

"That's right, Josh. Didn't you know the dear, sweet child, Melanie, is expecting Asa's baby?" Steve's insidious tone was low, directed solely for Josh's hearing. "Just an innocent girl, Josh, that's what she is; but that innocent child is good enough to keep that old man's blood running hot. Look at him, the bastard!" Steve's spiteful gaze followed Asa into the office, and then turned back to Josh, enjoying his shock and the dawning of obvious

143

misery on his white face. "Really had you fooled, didn't she? But I told you from the first what she was—a hot blooded bitch, whore."

"Shut up, Steve!" Josh's voice was ominously low.

"But if we're patient, we'll all have our chance. The old man can't keep performing too much longer. She'll be out looking—"

"I said shut up!" In a flash, Josh was to his feet and, grabbing Steve by the shirt front, picked him up to slam him against the wall, holding him there with one hand as the other balled into a fist. "One more word and I'll smash your filthy mouth!" Enraged, Josh looked heatedly at Steve's amused expression, his chest heaving, his body shaking with a myriad of emotions. "Damn you! Shut your filthy mouth before I close it for you!"

Startled, the other men stared wordlessly with no attempt to interfere in the violent exchange.

Staring levelly into Josh's eyes, Steve said in an amused voice, "I don't consider her important enough to fight over, Josh, so just take your hands off my shirt." And then as Josh slowly released him, he continued in a low voice, "So, little Miss Gold Eyes has you tied up in knots, too." His laughter was cold and without humor. "But I have to say you're more the fool than I am. I always knew what she was. You're just finding out!"

Josh's sudden flare of anger was suddenly interrupted by shouting at the foundry door as Tom's excited figure bounded through and toward the office.

"Mr. Parker! Mr. Parker! You have to come home now!"

Within seconds, Asa had the frightened boy by the shoulders. "What is it, Tom? What's happened?"

"It's Mr. Morganfield . . . Melanie's crying . . . Mama told me to get you."

Throwing on his coat, Asa followed Tom out the door, leaving the men staring curiously behind him.

Josh's expression was filled with pain, while Steve stared with overwhelming hatred at the retreating figures, his mind torturing him, This was to be our beginning, Melanie, our time together . . . bitch, lying bitch . . . you'll pay, if it takes me forever, I'll make you pay.

Asa's heart was pounding rapidly as he ran up the outside steps of his house; but it wasn't his wild dash home that was causing the tumult within him. James . . . was he dead? Without a moment's pause he continued on up the staircase to the second floor and to the door to James' room. For a long, painful moment he was unable to turn the knob, but suddenly he was across the threshold. With his first glance, the question was answered. There was no longer any life in James Morganfield's body. Mercifully, he was dead at last.

Melanie, grown large in the late stages of pregnancy, kneeled beside the bed, her cheek resting on James' palm. Her face was stained with tears, but she no longer cried, she did not move at all.

Pausing a few moments to regain his breath, Asa moved quietly to the bed and drew Melanie to her feet. "Darling, we knew he couldn't last much longer. You wouldn't have wanted him to linger on this way."

"Asa, why didn't he get better? Tell me, why?"

"No one knows the answer, Melanie."

Her voice soft, she whispered against his chest, "Do you think it's true? Could it be true what they said, Asa?"

"What are you talking about, Melanie?"

"Do you think it's my fault? Do you think my father didn't get any better because I'm a bad person and he was punished because of me? Tell me the truth, Asa, do you believe it is true?"

Fear and sorrow were reflected in the beautiful face looking up into his and without a second's hesitation, Asa answered in a shaking voice, "There's only love inside you, Melanie, and my child. The Lord has been generous, and taken your father home to him. Be happy for him, Melanie. There's no blame to be shared here."

A small, wobbly smile appeared on Melanie's face for a moment before she buried it against his chest, sobbing anew. "But I shall miss him so, Asa, I shall miss him so." Then raising her tear drenched face, she said simply, "Thank the Lord . . . I still have you."

Pulling her suddenly close against him, Asa repeated softly against her gleaming hair, "Thank the Lord, I have you."

Halfway through the long, wakeful night, Melanie's discomfort began to be more physical than emotional. The deep ache inside her grew in intensity until she was convulsed with pain that could mean only one thing. An excited Tom was dispatched to fetch Dr. Pierce, and in the darkness before dawn the next morning, a loud wail shattered the expectant quiet. Asa and Tom, both tensely pacing the hallway outside the bedroom froze in their steps, their eyes riveted on the door. Within seconds the door opened just enough to allow room for Martha's broad smile, "It's a girl, Mr. Parker, a beautiful little girl, and Melanie's fine."

The door closed in Asa's jubilant face, and he felt an overpowering urge to shout his happiness at the top of his lungs. Instead, turning to Tom, he slapped the boy's back heartily, repeating the words Tom had already heard, wanting to test them on his own lips and savor the joy they brought him.

"It's a girl, Tom! I have a daughter!" Suddenly choked with emotion, he said softly, "A daughter . . . and Melanie. How could a man be so lucky?"

"I'm glad it's a girl, Mr. Parker," Tom whispered through his lopsided grin. "Maybe she'll grow up just like Melanie, and then we can have two of her!"

Suddenly Asa was laughing, his happiness flowing out of him in a deep, rumbling sound as he clapped his hand on Tom's broad shoulder, his eyes filled with joyful tears. "Well, Tom, I think that would be too much for either one of us to ask, don't you think?"

The sound of the door opening behind them precluded Tom's response, and Asa moved quickly forward at Dr. Pierce's quiet invitation.

"Come in and see your new daughter, Asa." Dr. Pierce's voice held a distinct note of pride. "She's almost as beautiful as her mother."

Moving forward into the room, Asa saw no one but Melanie. Pale and exhausted, she radiated a glow, her eyes lit with an incandescence that swelled the love

147

bubbling inside him almost to bursting.

"No, no, Dr. Pierce," Melanie said weakly, lowering her eyes to the child resting in the crook of her arm, "*she* is the most beautiful thing I've ever seen, isn't she, Asa?"

Moving to the side of the bed, Asa bent to touch Melanie's lips with a soft, lingering kiss before looking at his child. His throat tight with emotion, he took Melanie's hand and kissed the palm lightly as his heart pounded with the excitement of seeing his child for the first time. The child's head was perfectly shaped and covered with a light copper fuzz; her wide, golden eyes already lined with dark, sweeping lashes; the skin white and clear of the usual splotchiness accompanying birth. A small, perfect fist separated the pink, delicately drawn lips as she sucked madly and Asa fought desperately the happy tears that threatened to overwhelm him.

When finally he was able to speak, he whispered lightly, "Not only have you made me the happiest man in the world, Melanie, you have also made Tom's fondest dream come true. Now there are two Melanies!" And suddenly bending to scoop them into a wide embrace, he whispered against Melanie's ear, "And they're both mine."

Later that same day James Morganfield's body was laid to its final rest. The small contingent at graveside did not include Melanie, who lay abed, the new Sara Morganfield at her breast. Unable to restrain himself, Josh made his way to Asa's side at the conclusion of the service.

"Where's Melanie, Asa? I had expected her to be here. I wanted to extend my sympathy."

For the briefest moment Asa's jealousy flared. This man could give Melanie two things that he could not—youth and his name, and he knew beyond a doubt that Josh's interest was not solely in extending Melanie his sympathy. But his better judgment came to the rescue, and he turned to look Josh squarely in the face.

"She's at home, Josh. She had my child this morning. She gave me a daughter."

Josh paled visibly, and Asa felt a moment's pity for the young man's obvious distress. Extending his hand, Josh offered softly, "You're an extremely lucky man, Asa. I hope you realize the full extent of your good fortune."

Taking it warmly, Asa smiled. "No one knows better than I just how lucky." Then slipping his arm around the younger man's shoulders, he said companionably, "Come on, Josh, let me buy you a drink. James is finally at peace, and a new life has just begun. I feel the need to celebrate."

Not quite matching his mood, Josh nodded his assent, and as they walked side by side, a solemn truce began.

Spring of the new year brought with it a flurry of new legal activity against the Green Mountain Boys. Incensed by the treatment of the Reverend Mr. Hough, Governor Tryon increased the reward on Allen and some of the others, while the New York Assembly passed a law forbidding assemblies of three or more persons for "unlawful intent" and promised to punish violators with a year in prison. Officials were given permission to injure or kill offenders in the course of apprehension without blame, and anyone who interfered with a New York magistrate in any way was subject to the death penalty. Allen, Warner, and Baker were ordered to surrender within the following seventy days or be shot on sight. All and all, it was an impressive document, which met contemptuous sneers in the mountain land of the grants. The general consensus of opinion agreed with Allen's statement that, "words on paper are just words on paper, unless backed by a strong fist or a loaded gun."

If unsuccessful in striking a spark of fear in the hearts of the Green Mountain Boys, the proclamation was successful in another way. In the discussions evoked by its posting, the scandal of Melanie's first appearance with her child was subdued.

The three months of winter had wrought a great change in little Sara. The small, doll-like infant had bloomed into a plump, rosy child, the sparkling, golden glints in her sparse copper curls matching the glow in her inquisitive eyes. A pleasant, merry child, Sara's wide, toothless smile flashed often, revealing a fleeting dimple in her cheek, the final touch in the duplication of her mother's unusual beauty.

Melanie stood, her arms akimbo, staring down at the heavy rug on the study floor. The sudden spring weather had stirred a frenzy of spring cleaning in the Parker household, and purposely putting Sara in for her nap a little early, she had immediately embarked on her first project for the day. She was going to surprise Asa and have his study gleaming before the day was out, but so far, she hadn't been doing so well. The heavy rug was proving more of a challenge than she had anticipated and resisted all her efforts to move it with a seeming will of its own! How was it she had not realized how many pieces of bulky furniture were in the way? But Josh was coming to supper this evening, and when he and Asa went into the study to conduct their business, it was going to dazzle them!

Smiling to herself, she began struggling anew with the heavy side chair on the edge of the rug, her mind wandering aimlessly as she labored. Her life was finally beginning to straighten out. Salisbury was no longer scandalized over Sara's birth. The first furor was over. She was now accepted by most of the men and treated at least civilly, if not warmly, by most of the women. The exception was Harriet Sims and her group of vicious gossips; but she had learned to ignore the heated jibes directed at her by the sick-minded woman who had seemed to make the persecution of Melanie Morganfield her life's work. She frowned a little, thinking of the future little Sara would have to face at that woman's hands, but firmly shook off that unhappy thought. Perhaps by the time Sara was older she and Asa would be able to marry; but that thought, also, seemed unworthy, for the only way that could come about would be if Aunt Emily . . .

Well, at least during the long winter months she had succeeded almost completely in driving Stephen Hull from her mind. She no longer relived that afternoon in her dreams to awake trembling with an emotion she dared not name, and she was certain that with the passage of a little more time she would drive the memory away forever.

151

After Sara's birth, Asa had begun spending more and more time at home, leaving Josh Whitmore to assume many of his duties at the foundry. It was inevitable that Josh would be invited to the house, and during the last months, his weekly presence at dinner had become an accepted ritual.

Grunting in a low, unladylike manner, Melanie tugged again at the stubborn rug pinned by an ancient chest on its corner, only to hear a small tearing sound.

"That does it!" she said aloud, completely exasperated. "Tom! Tom!" she shouted, sending her voice helplessly into the kitchen, "Could you come in here and help me? I'm in need of your strong arm for a few minutes."

Within seconds Tom came running into the room with his familiar, awkward gait, his face filled with stern reproach. "Melanie, you should be more quiet. You'll wake Sara!"

Melanie's annoyance was smothered by a sudden flooding of warmth. Shaking her head, she thought to herself, Sara will never want for love in this household. Between Asa's doting, Martha and Tom's spoiling, and Josh's complete capitulation to her gurgling charms, she is bound to grow up an incorrigible hoyden!

"Very well, Tom, I'll promise to lower my voice if you'll help me move this chest and the rest of the furniture off the rug."

Without a word, Tom bent and moved the chest in an effortless manner and turned to give Melanie the full glow of his lopsided smile. Unable to resist a smile in return, Melanie said lightly, "All right, no gloating, Tom. Let's move the rest of the furniture, and then you can help me roll up the rug and carry it outside. We'll put those muscles of yours to the test today!"

Suddenly the loud rapping of the brass knocker echoing in the wide hallway startled them both. "I'll get it, Tom. It certainly is an unusual time for visitors." Her curiosity piqued, she walked to the front door. Suddenly she was conscious of her appearance. She was a mess! Anticipating a morning of hard work, she had donned her old gray homespun, now a trifle tight across the chest, baggy in the waist, and short in length, and had tied an old cloth around her head to shield her hair from flying dust. In her struggles, a stubborn strand of fiery hair had worked loose to hang annoyingly in her face. In an effort to brush it away, Melanie had smeared a long smudge of dirt up the bridge of her nose and across her forehead. Shaking her head in self-disgust, she mumbled under her breath as she reached for the knob, "Well, I can't go upstairs and change just to answer the door." Swinging it wide, she stood in the doorway as a deep voice said with a definite twinge of amusement, "I would like to see Mr. Asa Parker. Would you be so kind as to tell him that Simon Young, a representative of Governor Tryon of the colony of New York, is here to see him?"

Melanie's mouth dropped open with shock. A representative of Governor Tryon here in Salisbury! He must be insane. Struck speechless, Melanie's eyes slowly swept the elegant figure from head to toe. The fellow's bared head showed brown, well-groomed hair tied neatly to the back of his neck in a queue, the slight touch of silver at the temples imparting a rather stately bearing. His brows were dark, in startling contrast to his extremely light, clear blue eyes that were almost transparent in appearance, giving his glance an extremely penetrating quality. His nose was rather sharp, his features stern, the lips full but unsmiling, with the deep cleft looking strangely out of place in his strong, firm chin. Tall and slender, his clothes were perfectly tailored, the dark blue of his coat falling in a faultless line to his knee, just short of his soft, fawn colored britches. His hose appeared to be a fine white silk and his black gleaming shoes closed with an ornate gold buckle matching perfectly the smaller versions that secured his britches at the knee. The fawn satin waistcoat was delicately embroidered in the pattern of running vines interspersed with clusters of flowers running along the front and skirt, the buttons securing the vest providing rich agate centers for the embroidered blooms. Carefully left unbuttoned a short way down from the neck, the waistcoat displayed an artfully arranged cravat edged in a fine, white lace, the same type of lace peeping discreetly from his slender cuffs. He carried under his arm a dark blue cocked hat, the edge of the brim trimmed with a fine metal lace. Although a bit travel stained, the gentleman standing before her was by far one of the most well-dressed men she had ever seen!

As her eyes slowly drifted back up to the gentleman's face, she flushed at the expression of amused tolerance reflected there.

"Well, child, if you have finished looking me over, I would appreciate your announcing me to your master, now!"

Flushing even darker, Melanie echoed angrily, "Child! Master!"

Before she could respond further, the man, reaching out, took her firmly by the shoulders, turned her around in the direction of the staircase, and with a hearty swat on the behind, propelled her purposefully forward.

"Yes, I said to get your master! I have traveled a long way, have had miserably inadequate bathing and sleeping facilities, and am running short of temper!"

As she turned obstinately back toward him again, he issued a sharp command, "I said get moving—now!"

Incensed by the stranger's overbearing behavior, Melanie stood resolutely on the spot, glaring with the searing heat of amber fire in her eyes as she said haughtily, "How dare you speak to me like that . . . and touch my person. I don't care if you're Governor Tryon himself, you . . . you . . . pompous, dandified bag of wind!" The stranger's brows arched in surprise as she advanced again upon him. "And until you can behave in a civil manner, you can—"

A sudden, loud wail from upstairs interrupted Melanie's words and brought an ungainly flash out of the study and up the stairs as Tom raced to see the cause of Sara's sudden discomfort. Completely forgetting the man standing in the doorway, she started for the stairs and had just reached the first step when Tom appeared at the second floor railing and started down, carrying a tear-streaked but smiling Sara proudly in his arms.

"Sara doesn't want to sleep anymore, Melanie. You put her to sleep too early, and she's finished with her nap now."

"Tom, you put Sara right back to bed. She's only a little baby and needs her sleep to grow."

"Maybe she's hungry, Melanie," Tom was obviously clutching at straws in his attempt to keep from returning her to the nursery where he was certain she would just begin crying again. "Why don't you feed her?"

Inadvertently clutching at her bosom, Melanie flushed brightly. "Tom! I, of all people, should know when it's time to feed Sara! Now put her back to sleep!"

"But Melanie—"

A sudden, impatient bellow from the doorway halted their exchange just as Tom reached the foot of the staircase.

"Is there no order at all in his household? From what I have seen so far of the people north of New York, it is no surprise to me that your affairs are in such a state of confusion! As far as the child is concerned, I strongly suggest that you call the child's mother, and let her decide whether she should eat or sleep, or have her linen changed! Or," he continued with deepening sarcasm, "has the woman fled this chaotic household for a few hours to regain her sanity and left you two . . . children in charge?"

Melanie turned slowly, the heat of blazing anger bringing sparks to her eyes and sudden color to her cheeks. She advanced toward Simon Young with a measured step and whipped the cloth from around her head, releasing a shower of auburn curls to fall gleaming against her proud, homespun-clad shoulders. Coming to stand directly in front of the arrogant figure filling the doorway, she said slowly in her most imperious manner, "I *am* the mother of this child!"

An expression of shocked surprise, and another undefinable emotion flicked over Simon Young's face, and there was a moment's stunned silence. Suddenly, he burst into loud, uncontainable laughter, his body heaving with the effort, his eyes filling with tears as he convulsed with hilarity at her unexpected announcement. Melanie stood speechless for a few moments, enraged by the man's insolent, insulting manner, before she shouted, raising her arm to point toward the street, "Get out! Get out of this house this instant, you arrogant, insufferable boor!"

But the man continued laughing, tears running down his face as he leaned against the door frame for support in an effort to bring his laughter under control.

Never in all her life had anyone incensed Melanie to such heights of fury, and suddenly rushing forward in a flash of temper, she shoved the weak, teary-eyed man out the door, almost knocking him down the steps in the act, and turning sharply, slammed the door in his face!

"And that is the end of you, Mr. Simon Young, representing Governor Tryon of the colony of New York! Humph! Damn him!"

Turning on her heel, she faced Tom squarely, looking him straight in the eye as she said firmly, "Now, put Sara back to sleep this minute, Tom, and

157

come and help me move that rug. We have a lot of work to do before Asa comes home tonight."

Recognizing the resolute expression on Melanie's face, and realizing the discussion had ended, Tom turned and started up the steps. "All right, Melanie, but she's going to cry . . ."

By mid-afternoon, Melanie had completed her work in the study. The walls had been dusted, the dark mahogany furniture polished to a gleaming hue; the windows washed, the window hangings laundered and returned with a fresh crisp look; and the rug, beaten and aired, was back on the floor, completely conquered by her dedication of purpose. All had been accomplished between Sara's feedings and changings, and as Melanie stood back and surveyed the room, she was not quite certain which was stronger, her feeling of pride or her feeling of exhaustion!

Closing the study doors behind her, Melanie started down the hallway toward the kitchen. Suddenly the picture of Mr. Simon Young's startled face as she had shoved him out the door came back to her mind, and she began to snicker. By the time she reached the kitchen, she was laughing uncontrollably. Well, I must have gotten my message across, she thought as she wiped her eyes weakly, because he didn't waste any time getting into that fancy carriage of his and driving away. I wonder if he drove right back to New York, where it's safer. Suddenly she was laughing again as Martha and Tom looked on with wary expressions.

When she was again able to catch her breath, she said weakly, "Don't worry, Martha. I'm not losing my mind. Something just struck me funny, that's all."

"Well, if you say so, Melanie." Martha's voice sounded doubtful. and Melanie was almost coaxed into laughter again.

Exerting a great effort to control herself, Melanie turned to Tom. "Tom, do you think you can drag that old tub out back into the kitchen? I'm afraid I overdid today. I'll really benefit from a warm bath."

"All right, Melanie," Martha replied. "Tom can do that while I change my clothes. I have an errand to run and will need Tom's assistance. Sara should sleep for another two hours, so you should have plenty of time."

Within the half hour, Melanie was stepping into the tub that had been drawn up before the fireplace and filled with deliciously warm water. Feeling a sudden desire for a little luxury, Melanie had slipped a cake of the lavendar soap Asa had given her for Christmas into the bath water, and sliding down into the fragrant warmth, she closed her eyes in silent ecstasy. She lay completely motionless for minutes at a time as the pulsating heat took the stiffness from her limbs. Heavenly . . . absolutely heavenly, and Asa loved it when she smelled of lavender. Her eyes suddenly snapped open as she blushed at her own nameless thoughts! Wanton, absolutely wanton, that's what you are! A slow smile came to her face as she raised her leg and pointed her toe to watch the soft, sweet bubbles racing in a jagged path down its shapely length. And how Asa loved that incorrigible, wanton side of her nature. Giggling to herself, a fleeting dimple flashing across her cheek, Melanie took the washcloth and worked up a thick lather before scrubbing her smiling face. Night would be here soon enough.

Humming softly to herself, Melanie then proceeded to rub the fragrant bubbles into the long, slender column of her neck and across her shoulders. The water came barely to the middle of her breasts and she scrubbed briskly, noting absentmindedly that although she was breastfeeding her child, her breasts were still firm and pointed. A strand of her fiery hair slipped down from the knot she had carelessly tied at the top of her head, and she paused a moment to resecure the straying lock, not realizing the beautiful picture she made framed against the light of the fire, her hair reflecting its brightness while small curls escaped the hastily arranged hairdo to curl appealingly around her face. Her thick, brown lashes, still damp with moisture, curled gracefully, and her skin radiated a soft, rosey glow. Finally realizing the hour was growing late and her privacy would soon be at an end, she unhappily stood up in the tub, stopping for a moment to look down at herself to reassess her proportions. Surprisingly, it was true what Asa said. Having Sara had only improved her figure and, satisfied with what she saw, she turned to take up the cloth to dry herself and met a pair of translucent blue eyes. Shocked, she stood motionless for a few seconds as Simon Young's eyes slowly roamed her body with an appreciative warmth. His voice startled her into movement again as she snatched at the cloth and attempted to wrap herself securely against his gaze.

His tone was surprisingly hushed in the silence of

the room. "Yes, I can see you were right, and I was wrong—you are not a child."

Completely flustered by his presence, Melanie hastily attempted to hide her naked body from his assessing gaze by wrapping herself more tightly in the large linen cloth, but the soft material clung revealingly to her damp body, in its transparency revealing more than it concealed. Suddenly realizing she was still standing in the tub, she attempted to hold the material up from the surface of the water while still clutching it tightly around her, and at the same time step out of the tub and on to surer ground. But she could not manage the difficult maneuver, and completely frustrated, she stood still, knee deep in bath water.

In a few quick strides Simon Young was beside her, and placing his hands on the sides of her waist, he lifted her easily to the floor where he stood very close looking down at her with an oddly disturbing expression on his lean, sharp features.

Too proud to show the trembling that had started inside her, Melanie obstinately stood her ground. "How dare you disturb my privacy? Is this what the gentlemen in New York do to amuse themselves, stand peeping in windows while ladies bathe? And you have the gall to criticize—"

"Do you know where I've been most of the day since you so effectively evicted me from your household?" Simon Young's soft, low voice interrupted her tirade. Not waiting for her answer, he continued. "I've spent the day poking around this miserable town, trying to find some answers to my questions. I've found that your people are quite willing to gossip with strangers, especially about the notorious Melanie Morganfield, who has bewitched the most admirable Asa Parker, and having given him a sorceress' child, continues to hold him in her evil web." Unconsciously, as he spoke, he reached up to touch the burnished auburn curls framing her face so enchantingly, and slid his finger lightly across the high rise of her cheekbone the second before Melanie shook his hand away.

"I must admit," he continued softly, speaking almost to himself as his eyes roamed her face, "I could not imagine the little gray wren in her baggy, worn dress as the seductress they described, despite the spirit she showed when she fought me so effectively, but now, now, Miss Melanie Morganfield, you are no longer disguised, and the little gray wren has shown herself to be a beautiful peacock. Now I can well understand the old man being smitten, sacrificing his good name for you—even taking on the whole town in his determination to keep you."

"I'm not really interested in what you think, Mr. Simon Young, for you must surely be an idiot to so boldly announce yourself as a representative of Governor Tryon while here in Salisbury! Aren't you aware how Governor Tryon is regarded in this territory? Don't you realize that you risk being taken by the Green Mountain Boys to face their justice? I assure you they would not allow you to get off easily. It was two hundred lashes for Governor Tryon's last representative—"

"My dear Miss Morganfield, you certainly do not

think I openly declared my mission here! I dislike disappointing you, but I am not that much a fool. Still, I do believe some of the men became suspicious when I visited the foundry and Mr. Parker rushed me off so quickly. He was interested in hearing more of Governor Tryon's communication, but he felt my carriage and attire were indicative of my position, and asked me to go to his house and await him. Not wanting to cause any more speculation, I told my driver to await me on the road outside town, and I came around the back of the house as he drove away. So you see, my dear, I am an invited guest to this house."

"But you were not invited to peep in the window!"

A small smile curved his haughty mouth. "But my dear, how could I resist?"

"Melanie! Melanie!" Tom's anxious voice preceded him as he rushed through the kitchen doorway. Martha was following breathlessly behind, and stopped in her tracks at the surprising picture that met her eyes; Melanie standing wrapped in a revealing damp cloth, very close to a tall, well-dressed stranger. Tom continued on, completely ignoring the tall man.

"Melanie! A group of Green Mountain Boys is gathering. Mama and I saw them by the stable. They were talking about a suspicious stranger asking a lot of questions. They're going after him!"

Simon Young's head jerked up, the small muscle twitching in his cheek and the sudden narrowing of his eyes the only sign of emotion.

"And you thought you were so clever." Melanie's

voice was a contemptful sneer as she turned the full force of her withering glance on the arrogant stranger.

The sudden thundering sound of many men on horseback riding up the street caught their attention, and Tom ran to the window. "They're coming here, Melanie!"

Spurred into action by the crisis descending upon them, Melanie spoke quickly. "They're coming for this man, Tom. Mr. Parker wouldn't like it if they caught him. If they stop here, just tell them you haven't seen him since this morning, and don't worry about anything else. I'll hide him."

Turning quickly to Simon Young, she motioned for him to follow her, and lifting the bottom of her wrap, she scampered ahead of him up the stairs. When he did not move as fast as she would have him, she whispered hurriedly over her shoulder, "Hurry up, you fool! Two hundred lashes is not a pleasant prospect!"

Running up the steps, she quickly opened the door to her room and pulled him inside behind her. "If they come up the stairs, get under the bed and I'll take it from there—"

"What! You don't really expect me to—"

"If you expect to save your hide, and I mean just that, you will do what I say!" Still clutching the damp cloth around her shivering body, she moved to the door and looked toward her dressing gown on the hook. Glancing helplessly down at herself, she turned to command harshly, "Turn your back so I may put on my gown!" When he made no move to do as she said, she whispered again through gritted teeth, "Turn your back, I say!"

"Sorry, my dear. I would not turn my back now to save myself three hundred lashes."

Mumbling under her breath, Melanie lifted her head a notch higher and deliberately dropped the cloth to the floor. Slowly she reached for her wrap, flushing as Simon Young openly scrutinized her naked body.

A sudden, loud pounding on the front door snapped the building tension, and Melanie jerked on her wrap, saying in a soft voice as she hastily pulled the pins from her hair and sent it tumbling around her slender shoulders, "Now will you get under the bed?"

With a small smile, Simon Young turned and bent to slip noiselessly under the bed. Within moments loud voices sounded in the hallway, and Melanie could hear Martha's indignant voice, "No, there is no one here!"

The sound of scuffling footsteps sounded on the staircase and in the upstairs hallway. There were the sounds of doors opening and closing and, as the footsteps proceeded to her door, she jerked it open and inquired angrily, "What's going on here? What do you think you're doing? I demand that you . . ."

Her words trailed to a stop as she came face to face with Stephen Hull, the burning intensity in his black eyes staggering her angry words to a complete halt.

"We're looking for a man suspected of being an agent of Governor Tryon. He was seen here earlier this morning, and his carriage stopped here briefly again this afternoon. He was asking questions all over town, mainly about you." His eyes roved her alluringly disheveled appearance, the tightening in his groin deepening his anger. "Where would be the more logical place to look for him than in your bedroom?"

Stunned by the deliberate insult, Melanie's hand came up to deliver a stinging blow to his cheek. Grabbing her hand, Steve twisted it sharply, eliciting a small cry from Melanie moments before a deep voice from behind him said menacingly, "Let her go, Steve—now!"

"Not this time, Josh, this time she's not going to get away with it."

"We're not here to satisfy your twisted whims, Steve, we're here to get that stranger and find out what's going on! Now let her go!"

Reluctantly, Steve released Melanie's hand, growling under his breath as he did, "Another time, Melanie. We have much to settle between us."

"I said let's go!" Josh jerked abruptly on Steve's arm, and shooting Josh a warning look, Steve turned and followed him down the stairs. Standing motionless in the doorway to her room, Melanie watched as the last of the men filed out the front entrance, and only after she had heard them ride away, did she turn back to her room, and close the door behind her. It was then that she realized she was trembling wildly, and she leaned back against the door for support, closing her eyes against the weakness that threatened to overcome her.

Suddenly she was enclosed in a warm embrace, her cheek resting against a lace-trimmed cravat as Simon Young said in a surprisingly gentle voice, "Melanie, my dear, you are everything they said you were . . .

and more. My only argument with this town is that they have underestimated you."

Too weak to respond, Melanie rested in his embrace until the pressure of the moment was past.

That evening as Asa participated in a house to house search for Simon Young, Tom returned with his instructions to secretly lead the man to the grove outside town, where his carriage awaited so he could flee the area before sunrise the next day. Following those instructions, Martha had just finished packing some food when Sara's sudden wailing moved her out of the room and Tom slipped stealthily into the shadows in the back yard, waiting for Simon Young to follow after a slight interval. In preparation for his unseen departure from their back door, Melanie blew out the lamp on the table, leaving the fire in the hearth the only illumination in the room.

Fatigued from her long, exhausting day, Melanie whispered softly, unmindful of the tender vulnerability the light circles under her eyes added to her brilliant beauty as the light from the fire was captured and glowed in the mahogany highlights of the hair spilling down her shoulders, and in the heavy lidded amber eyes, "I think it's safe for you to leave now, Mr. Young, and if I were you I wouldn't come back!"

"Not before I do this!" he mumbled the second before he swept her against him in a tight embrace, his lips crashing down to cover hers in a deep, lingering kiss. She struggled briefly as he increased the pressure of his embrace, and protested under his lips, only providing him the opportunity to slip his tongue between her teeth to plunder her mouth. Too tired to resist any longer and realizing he would soon be forced to leave, she suddenly relaxed in his embrace. The intensity of his kiss deepened, seeming endless in its searching, until he finally drew away with obvious reluctance.

"Well, are you satisfied now, Mr. Young?" Melanie's voice was cold.

With a short laugh, Simon Young answered shakily, "Well, not exactly satisfied, my dear, but I could not leave without stealing a kiss from the golden-eyed witch of Salisbury." Then a little softer he whispered, "They're right about you, Melanie, you do cast a spell." Within a moment he too had slipped into the shadows, and she turned to make her way wearily to her room.

Melanie fell asleep within seconds, only to be awakened what seemed minutes later as Asa slipped into bed beside her. Moving to curl against his side, she whispered groggily, "Did he get away, Asa?"

"Yes, he did, darling, but that fine gentleman doesn't realize how close he came to being a living example of righteous wrath."

"What did he want with you, anyway, Asa?" As her mind cleared, the questions she had longed to ask all day surfaced again. "I wouldn't ask that arrogant fop and give him the satisfaction of knowing my curiosity was driving me mad!"

A small smile flicked across Asa's weary face. How like Melanie! Stubborn and proud to the very last, she would allow no one to believe they had bested her, no matter what the cost to herself. Leaning toward her, he kissed her mouth lightly before pulling her closer to rest her head against his chest. "I really don't know why he came to me, Melanie. I can only surmise that my investments in the grants are more well known than I realized. At any rate, in the few minutes we spoke at the foundry, Mr. Young indicated that Governor Tryon was interested in a settlement of some sort. It seems he is also involved in a border dispute with the colony of Massachusetts, and is seeking to ease the pressure."

"That sounds quite encouraging, doesn't it, Asa?"

Hesitating a moment before answering, Asa said slowly, "I think not, Melanie, although I can't be certain, since we didn't have time to finish our conversation. I have the feeling the price of the settlement would have been too high to accept. Mr. Young intimated that certain people could profit from cooperation with the governor, while others would pay the full or perhaps an exorbitant share of the penalty. But," giving Melanie a short hug, kissing the top of her head lightly, "it appears we will never be sure, because I think we can be fairly certain that gentleman will give the governor a true picture of our people's unity against him and his policies. I will be very surprised if he returns again with a proposition of that kind."

Snuggling closer, Melanie flung her slender arm across Asa's hairy chest, kissing it lightly as she mumbled, "Well, I'm glad you believe that fellow came on a useless mission. I would hate to think I threw out the man who could have brought the dispute to an easy conclusion."

Hearing a slight rumbling in his chest, Melanie look up to see a surprised smile that was quickly turning to subdued laughter. "You threw out Mr. Simon Young?"

"Representing Governor Tryon of the colony of New York! Yes, I did! And he's fortunate he caught hold of the railing when he did or he would have landed on his pompous backside at the foot of our steps! Can you imagine, Asa? He called me a *child*— and told me to get moving!" Then lowering her eyes from his, Melanie snuggled back against his chest, saying softly against its warmth, "But he did admit he was wrong before he left. He said I was not a child. You know I'm not a child, don't you, Asa?" Her tongue tracing a warm pattern against his chest, she continued softly, "And I made myself all fresh and pretty for you today, too. I bathed in your lavender bubbles and thought only of you." Her hand was tracing a tantilizing path down to his navel as she listened to the rapid acceleration of his heartbeat. Turning slowly toward her, he whispered lightly against her lips, "Well, Melanie, darling, we can't let all those bubbles go to waste, can we?"

Rubbing her body slowly against his, she mumbled back against his lips, the sweet scent of her raising the level of his desire to a heated pitch, "No, Asa, I suppose we can't. My mother always said, 'Waste not, want not.'"

"Somehow, Melanie," Asa's voice held a momentary twinge of laughter, "I don't believe your mother had this type of situation in mind."

"If there is one thing I have learned, Asa," Melanie's voice held a note of amused finality in it as she dismissed his retort and slid her slender hand into his hair, urging his mouth against hers, "Mama was

170

always right."

Despite their temporary disagreement, within a short while, they found they had reached total accord.

Simon Young's coach traveled rapidly in the direction of New York. The full moon allowed the advantage of using the night to increase his distance from Salisbury; but despite the hour, Simon still found himself unable to sleep.

"It must be this damned, uncomfortable coach!" he mumbled under his breath, vexed at his inability to clear his mind of the events of the day. "When I get back to New York I will immediately replace it with a new one!" Suddenly a spark of amusement lit his weary eyes, and he was chuckling softly, remembering Melanie Morganfield's expression of complete outrage when he called her a child. "Well, Simon, old boy, you sure called that one wrong, didn't you?" he thought, marveling for the hundredth time that he could have been so blind. In the hours since his escape, he had finally conceded to himself that Melanie Morganfield was the most beautiful woman he had ever seen and, for a second, a vision of Charlotte flashed before his eyes. His wife was also an extremely lovely woman, but her beauty was merely physical, and in all too short a time had proved vapid and empty. Her belief that the purpose of marriage was merely to produce progeny had led her to the obvious conclusion, when she found she was incapable of bearing children, that there was no further need for intimacies between them. But his many mistresses had eagerly filled the role she so easily

171

abdicated, and although most possessed not even a portion of her beauty, they had held his interest far longer than the lovely empty shell that was his wife. Thus, being no stranger to beauty, Simon was amazed that the sight of Melanie in her naked splendor had awakened such a strong reaction within him. Chuckling again, he remembered Melanie's contempt as she sneered, "And you thought you were so clever."

"And damned if I didn't think I had been clever," he laughed at himself. "Insolent little witch, the golden-eyed witch of Salisbury." It was going to be a long time before he forgot her, and suddenly he was uncertain if the failure of his mission was the true cause of his irritability. If he were truthful, he would have to admit that in comparison to Melanie, all his present mistresses appeared as dull as Charlotte, and that was a pretty sad state of affairs. Oh, well, he would merely institute a search for a few replacements as soon as he broke the news of his aborted mission to William. There had to be a woman somewhere in New York with at least a portion of that little spitfire's spirit, for Miss Morganfield was certainly out of his reach. No woman, not one, was worth two hundred lashes. "In any case," he thought, allowing himself a healthy portion of sour grapes, "I'd probably tire of her in a few weeks."

"Damn!" he cursed aloud as the carriage suddenly jolted, tilting precariously and almost knocking him off his seat as it sank momentarily into an unseen hole in the road, "Will we never reach civilization?"

The warmth of the bright morning sun against his

172

eyelids nudged Josh into wakefulness. He opened his eyes gingerly, instinctively gripping his head against the ensuing pain as his pupils contracted in the brilliant light, and uttered a low, involuntary groan. The few hours sleep he had managed in his small, airless room that humid August night had provided him little relief. His broad back clung to the sheets with perspiration, as the rising sun elevated the temperature in his room even further, increasing his discomfort to the point where he reluctantly decided to risk getting up. Slowly, still holding tight his huge, pounding head, he lifted himself to his feet with great caution and staggered to the washstand. His mouth and tongue felt dry and cottony, and his stomach churned dangerously with each step. The pain and discomfort only increased as he attempted to pour some water from the pitcher into the washbowl, the sound attaining the volume of a crashing waterfall to his sensitive ears. Realizing it was a time for drastic measures, Josh lowered his head, not without considerable pain, and poured the remainder of the contents of the pitcher directly over it. Reaching for the cloth beside the washstand, he carefully attempted to dry his face and hair.

"Even my scalp hurts!" he murmured under his breath with disgust. "Where in hell did Abigail get that rum?" In truth, if he were to be completely honest with himself, he would have to admit that it wasn't the quality, but the quantity of the rum that had done him in. But dire circumstances had demanded dire measures. His mental and physical distress after spending another evening in Asa's house, covertly coveting his beautiful mistress, had sent him on another of his visits to Abigail, the frequency of which was increasing as rapidly as his love for Melanie. The only problem was, it was taking more and more rum to make the eager young whore a palatable substitute to his frustrated passions.

"You're a fool, do you know that, Josh Whitfield?" Josh murmured indistinctly to his bleary-eyed reflection in the small mirror. "Everyone thinks that Tom is the simple-minded one, but where Melanie is concerned, you don't possess half of his common sense!" Was it only a year ago he had watched Melanie saunter into the foundry yard with her father's lunch and decided so confidently he would dismiss the attraction she held for him in favor of more pressing areas of his life? Hah! That was a laugh! Now, twelve months later, with the same family, political, and money problems pressing him, and with Melanie completely beyond his reach, he had come to the tardy conclusion that he loved her to distraction!

"Fool . . . fool," he mumbled, his mental chastising beginning to cause him actual physical pain. After countless evenings spent in Asa's home, he knew without doubt that Melanie considered herself married to Asa, despite the absence of actual vow-taking. Hardest of all to accept was the realization that Melanie actually loved Asa . . . that homely, gray-haired old man! Beautiful, sparkling Melanie had given herself to Asa without reservation and never gave himself more than a casual, passing thought. He knew instinctively she didn't have the slightest inkling of his violent reactions to the small, dimpled smiles she tossed at him over Sara's head, or the way the golden glow of her eyes melted him inside, the way his heart lurched when she brushed close by his side, or his deep, consuming desire to be in Asa's place, with Sara their child, and him the recipient of the alternating warm, amused, tolerant, and outright loving looks she bestowed on that lucky old man.

Deliberately forcing himself to pull his broad, well-muscled frame to its full height, wincing slightly at the pain, he ran his fingers through his damp, sun-streaked hair, and walked to the bed to pull on his britches. His usual pleasant expression was replaced by a deep frown. The friendly relationship between Steve and him had taken a definite downturn in the last few months as his visits to the Parker household had increased. Steve was only too aware of his feelings for Melanie, having much the same problem himself, whether he would admit to them or not, and his jealousy took the outlet of constant, jeering remarks which he was finding exceedingly hard to bear. Relations between them were now strained to the breaking point.

"Hell!" he thought miserably, pulling on his boots and reaching for his shirt, "Where is all this going to end?" Finally shrugging his broad shoulders into his shirt, he walked to the washstand to cautiously brush his hair into place before heading for the door. Another thought lightly crossed his mind as he closed the door behind him and started down the hall, smiling slightly at its absurdity.

"Maybe they're right, maybe we're all under her spell. Maybe Melanie really is a witch!"

Afraid to trust breakfast on his queasy stomach, Josh strode past the dining room where some of the boarders still lingered and made directly for the front door. Once on the street, he walked leisurely in the direction of the foundry. He needed air to clear his head, and work to occupy his mind, and was tremendously relieved when the foundry finally came into view. Watching as another figure approached from the other direction, he acknowledged Asa's wave with a slight nod of his still aching head, an edge of jealousy slowly eating away at him as he mumbled under his breath, "The old boy has a real spring in his step this morning. Hell! Why not? If I were in his shoes, I'd go to bed early, too."

But strangely enough, his own spiteful observation toward Asa only had the effect of tightening even further the knife of pain twisting in his vitals. Suddenly disgusted with his own unworthy thoughts, he pushed open the foundry door and walked in, his brows drawn together in a dark frown.

"What's the matter, Josh, have a bad night last night?" a voice called laughingly from the corner.

Before he could respond, another voice said in a mock whisper, "Keep your voice down, Jeff, I think Josh is taken again with one of those headaches he's been suffering lately."

"Oh, leave him alone, boys, can't you see the poor fellow has something on his mind? He must have a problem. He's having trouble handling—" Steve's voice, syrupy with false concern, had exactly the effect he had sought as Josh's face flushed with anger, and he growled with a menacing look, "Shut up, all of you!"

Good-natured laughter followed his surly remark as most of the men moved to begin their work, leaving only Steve, who stood and walked toward him, the look in his eyes in direct contrast to his casual, sauntering approach.

"I'm telling you, Josh, you're causing yourself a lot of unnecessary pain." Steve's soft voice had a familiar, taunting ring, and Josh fought the urge to put his hands around Steve's throat and squeeze that knowing look off his face. "You don't stand a chance. You can believe me when I tell you that when the time is right, I'll be the one Melanie comes to. Don't ask me how I know, just take me at my word. You don't stand a chance."

Josh had taken a menacing step forward, his hands balled into fists, when Asa's voice sounded from the doorway of his office. "You fellows had better start moving. That new equipment I ordered should be here soon, and we're not ready by half to put it into position." When his voice did not have the desired effect, and they still stood there, eyes locked in direct challenge, Asa repeated in a firm voice, "It's time to go to work."

A few moments of uneasy silence passed before Josh, suddenly realizing the absurdity of battle over a woman who would ultimately belong to neither of them, shrugged his shoulders, turned his back on Steve's baiting, and walked away. But it was hours later before he had once again established control over his raging emotions.

It was well into afternoon when the wagon finally arrived with the new equipment. The driver slowly backed it in through the foundry doors, reining as close as he could maneuver to the block and tackle. Asa, with unusual anxiety seemed to be everywhere at once, directing the fastening of the lines and shouting instructions. Completely exasperated with the havoc Asa was creating with his endless, barking commands, Josh turned away, seeking a quiet, comfortable corner to rest his aching body, when a sudden, ominous crack snapped him to attention a split second before a sharp outcry turned him around and running. Asa lay pinned helplessly, his face bearing a startled, empty expression, the broken rope dangling overhead as the huge crate laying on his chest slowly crushed the breath from his body. Scrambling wildly, men came from all corners of the room to heave and push ineffectually at the crate.

"Wait a minute!" Josh's voice stopped the disorganized floundering attempts to free Asa, assuming control of the situation. "Everyone take a good grip and when I count to three, we'll all lift. Jeff, Tim, you pull Asa out as quickly as you can."

Acknowledging the affirmative nods, Josh took hold of one corner of the crate, counting evenly. "All right . . . one . . . two . . . *three!*" The crate lifted with agonizing slowness, and the moment it was free, Asa's inert body was swiftly snatched from beneath.

"All right, let it *loose!*" Josh shouted, and the crate crashed to the ground, the earth vibrating beneath their feet.

"Jeremy, quick, get Dr. Pierce," Josh shouted, rushing to Asa's unconscious body, noting the almost invisible throbbing of the pulse in his throat. At the same moment he noticed the ominous bluish-gray cast of the unconscious man's face. A small trickle of blood slowly eased its way out of the corner of Asa's parted lips and down his cheek, and Josh felt the chill of premonition run up his spine. Waiting helplessly in silence for Dr. Pierce's arrival, Josh's eyes quickly flicked over the area, coming to rest on a motionless figure in the corner. There, standing quietly, completely divorced from the frantic scene, was Stephen Hull, his expression unreadable as his enigmatic black eyes remained glued on Asa's still, blue face.

Melanie gazed lovingly at Sara as the sleepy infant struggled to keep her eyes open. Finally losing the battle, the delicate, long-lashed lids fluttered closed over her curious amber eyes, and her small mouth relinquished the nipple at last, allowing a small dribble of milk to slip across her rosy cheek. Easing the child gently onto her lap, Melanie lightly cleaned the milk from her cheek and proceeded to button her bodice, her gaze still fastened on Sara's angelic sleeping countenance.

"My sweet little darling," she whispered softly to the child's unhearing ears, as she lightly touched her fiery ringlets. With a smile she recalled the night before and the light in Asa's eyes as Sara had squirmed with delight at the appearance of her father's face. He had taken the smiling baby from her arms and turned to exhibit her proudly to Josh.

"How do you like my little girl, Josh? A real beauty, isn't she?"

"Asa!" Melanie had been shocked by his boastful manner, and Asa had turned laughingly toward her.

"A man has a right to say what he thinks in his

179

own house. She is a beauty, isn't she, Josh?"

"She certainly is, Asa, but you have to give Melanie the credit for that. If she had inherited *your* looks . . ."

"All right, young man," Asa said with mock severity, "There is such a thing as being too outspoken."

Smiling again to herself, Melanie picked up the sleeping child and walked slowly to the cradle, whispering softly as she did, "You are my little love, and your father's pride and joy."

She had just lain the sleeping child down when a loud pounding on the front door snapped up her head, and her heart began a slowly accelerating pounding. Standing motionless, strangely unable to move, she heard Martha's heavy footsteps moving toward the door with Tom's uneven step close behind.

The low rumbling sound of male voices met her ears as she heard the door open. Martha's sudden gasp jerked her into movement, and running from the room, she dashed down the steps, her eyes on the group of men at the door. Josh stepped forward as Melanie ran toward them, but she brushed past him to look out the front door.

"Oh, Lord, no!" she cried as she spied the wagon drawn up in front with Dr. Pierce working over a prone figure in the back. "Not Asa . . . no, not Asa!" Running down the steps, she scrambled aboard the back of the wagon, gasping with fright at Asa's gray, perspired face.

"Asa, darling . . . Asa," she whispered, bending to touch him.

"Be careful, Melanie, his chest is crushed."

Dr. Pierce's soft warning brought Melanie's frightened gaze to his face, where it remained, seeking some reassurance, only to see him shake his head negatively.

A soft, instinctive sob escaped her lips, and swallowing tightly, she turned back to Asa. "Darling, darling," she whispered softly, caressing his cheek lightly, "Asa, darling, can you hear me?"

Slowly with obvious effort, Asa opened his eyes. They remained fixed on her face as he struggled to speak.

"It's all right darling, don't try to speak."

"Let him talk now, Melanie." Dr. Pierce's soft admonition had an ominous ring, and Melanie swallowed hard again, forcing a smile to her face.

"What is it, darling? What did you want to say, Asa?"

With a supreme effort, Asa lifted his hand, groping for hers, and Melanie snatched at it, lifting the calloused palm to her lips.

Obviously struggling to form words as his eyelids drooped weakly, he gasped with shallow, painful breaths. Asa shot a pleading glance into her eyes, and she leaned forward anxiously.

"Melanie . . . Melanie . . . sorry . . . too soon . . . not ready . . . love you, Melanie . . . tell Sara . . ."

Suddenly there were no more words, and the heavy lids dropped closed. Glancing down at the rough hand clasped so tightly within hers, she released it slowly, to have it fall lifelessly beside him.

"No," she said softly, staring at the lifeless hand. "No, this cannot be." Slowly her gaze moved to Asa's face where she stared for a moment at his motionless countenance. Suddenly jumping to her feet, she screamed, "No! No! *He is not dead!*" Scrambling wildly from the wagon, she dashed past the men still standing on the steps, pushing aside those standing in the doorway, shouting as she raced up the staircase toward her room, *"He is not dead! He is not dead!"*

Chapter 3

Walking out the rear kitchen door, Melanie glanced around apprehensively before putting down the basket of laundry, and it was this apprehension that attested to the fact that she had finally accepted Asa's death. Asa was no longer there to protect her. With a deep sigh reflecting her private thoughts, she commenced hanging Sara's linens to dry, completely oblivious to the beauty of the late September day.

For the first time in her life, Melanie was without someone to fall back on. She was entirely alone, with the exception of Martha and Tom, who couldn't be expected to be responsible for her future, and Josh, who was managing the foundry until the estate was settled. Settled . . . that was if it would ever be decided by the courts. The settlement Asa had left her and Sara in his will was being contested by Emily's brother out of sheer perversity, and never did she believe she would come to the point where she would be anxious for Asa's money. But money meant security, and security was what she drastically needed for Sara and herself. She was being allowed to maintain her residence in Asa's house and live on the proceeds from the foundry until the will was settled, but if the decision went against her, she would be both penniless and homeless. That frightening possibility set her hands to shaking again, and angry with herself for her weakness, she dropped them to her sides and took a deep breath before continuing her chore with renewed determination.

Putting additional stress on her muddled state of affairs was Harriet Sims. Aware of Melanie's sudden vulnerability, the hateful woman had taken the opportunity to seek support within the town in her vilification of Melanie's character. She had gained strength and followers in her suit to have Melanie "punished for her sins against the community," and had raised public opinion against her to an alarming level, to the point that wherever she walked, Melanie was accosted by hate-filled glances and degrading remarks.

"And she has the audacity to call me a witch!" Melanie mumbled under breath, attacking the linens with renewed vigor.

And as if that wasn't enough, there was Stephen Hull. He had not spoken more than a few words to her since Asa's death over a month before, but had made his presence felt each and every day since. It was as if he played a waiting game.

But if he's waiting for me to go to him, he has a long wait in store, she thought, her heart racing at the very thought. In truth, she had never been able to completely bury the memory of that afternoon, but there was Sara to consider now, and any plans Steve had for her were not long range, and definitely didn't include Sara or marriage.

But would anyone ever consider marriage to her now? Melanie Morganfield, the witch of Salisbury, mother of an illegitimate child, scandalous Melanie. Angry with the sudden tears that filled her eyes, Melanie rubbed them away with a quick, furtive movement. She was a scandal simply because she had loved Asa, had given him a child. Asa had told her countless times that she had made him happier than he had ever been in his life. His last year had been his happiest. For that she had no regrets, and if that was her sin against the community, well, the community could go to blazes!

Raising her head a notch higher, she picked up her empty basket and returned to the kitchen. She would find a way to beat those hypocrites yet . . .

Smiling, Josh shook Mr. Pettigrew's hand and turned and walked away, closing the bank's door quietly behind him. He had deposited the weekly proceeds from the foundry with the banker handling Asa's estate and was on his way to bring Melanie her weekly portion. In truth, Josh found it difficult to suppress the smile hovering at the corners of his mouth, he felt so damned good! Momentarily overcome by guilt his brows drew together in a frown, but he suddenly thought, "Hell, there has to be a bright side to every situation." The fact that circumstances had worked to draw Melanie and him into constant contact and Melanie into reliance on him couldn't possibly suit his purpose any better. He was so absolutely wild about her that even the mention of her name set his pulse to racing. He knew she was worried about the future, but it was too soon to let her know of his feelings, too soon to expect her to put aside her grief.

"I'll give her another month." Then he was laughing to himself. How generous of me . . . but I'll be damned if I'll wait any longer and give someone else the opportunity to snatch her away. By that someone he meant Steve, whom he knew in his brazen conceit expected Melanie to run into his arms.

I'll see him dead first! Josh thought in sudden rage, and lengthening his stride, he increased his pace toward Melanie and away from his own blazing jealousy.

Grateful for the opportunity to get his mind off the endless circle it had been traveling in recent weeks, Steve directed the whole of his attention to the tale being recounted so vividly in the crowded tavern. Already in a foul mood, he rested his lean, broad frame against the bar, his dark brows drawing into an even tighter frown, his black eyes sparking dangerously. Finishing off the last of his rum, he slammed his mug down on the counter and signaled a refill before turning to the burly, dark young man who had paused momentarily in his narrative.

"You're telling us Robert McCormick is a damned traitor, Heman?"

"So he is, Steve," Heman declared vigorously, pounding his fist heavily on the bar. Two years Ethan's junior, Heman had long been considered the steadiest of the Allen brothers, but his devotion to Ethan and his cause was inviolate.

"Damned if McCormick didn't find out Ethan and Ira were on their way home from Hartford. The low dog knew they would stop for a family reunion with Zimri and me here in Salisbury overnight, and he must have made his plans accordingly. The price on Ethan's head must have been too much of a temptation for him."

"What made you so suspicious of him, Heman? He's worked for you for a long time."

"Well, I didn't think much of it when he showed up at the house just short of an hour after Ethan and Ira arrived, looking for a place to stay for the night. You know he's done that before; but as luck would have it, Ethan and Ira had gone out on an errand. Robert was just too curious about Ethan—when would they return, how long would they stay, what room was Ethan using that night. Finally, I became convinced something was amiss when Robert refused a second mug of rum."

"McCormick turned down your rum? Hah! You would have had to be a fool not to realize something was wrong then!" shouted a voice in the crowd, and Heman waited for the chorus of snickers to die down before continuing.

"When I heard Ethan's and Ira's footsteps in the hallway, I excused myself and warned Ethan of my suspicions." Suddenly Heman's angry face twitched lightly in an effort to suppress a smile that surprisingly broke into a wide grin. Obviously recalling something that greatly amused him, he began laughing in a low voice, causing an impatient prompting from the crowd.

"Well, what happened then, Heman?"

"Yes, stop that damned laughing."

"Well," Heman continued, "you know Ethan. He burst into the room and attacked McCormick with my suspicions, demanding to know all about it! Boys, you should have seen McCormick's face! The miserable snake blanched pure white! His eyes were bulging with fear! 'Yes, I did hear something about a plot against the Allen brothers, but I don't know anything about it.'" Heman imitated McCormick's nervous twittering response, drawing chuckles from the appreciative group.

"Then Ethan fixed his beady eye on him, and suddenly McCormick jumped to his feet, recalling vital business in Amenia that couldn't wait until the morrow. He dashed out of the house into the night and we haven't seen him since! But," Heman continued, squinting his eyes with the return of heated anger, "he was seen within the half hour meeting with a group of riders, all strangers, just outside town. The men were heavily armed and appeared ready for travel!" Pausing a moment, Heman surveyed the faces in the crowd, his own face darkening, and suddenly shouted emphatically, "I'll be damned if that no good, villainous bastard didn't plan on spiriting Ethan away into Yorker territory to collect the reward!"

"Damned right, the bastard!"

"Filthy traitor!"

Explosive comments were still bursting from the crowd, when Steve's angry voice posed a simple question. "And where is McCormick now, Heman?"

"Damned if he didn't disappear from sight, Steve, the slippery bastard!" was the growling response.

His face set in anger, Steve finished off the last of his rum, and with a disgusted glance turned on his heel to stride toward the door. Slamming it behind him in frustration, Steve took a deep breath and exerted a great effort to control his rage. "Damn! Damn!" he thought, as he strode angrily down the street toward the boardinghouse, "is there no place I can go and relax?" His life seemed to suddenly be filled with endless frustrations that taxed his patience and left him touchy and irritable. There was no doubt about it, he was spoiling for a fight—or something.

Turning into the doorway of his boardinghouse, he took the steps to his room two at a time. Entering, he slammed the door hard behind him and without bothering to light the lamp, flopped on the bed to stare into the darkness.

"Damn . . . damn," he said aloud, staring unseeingly at the ceiling. But he didn't need a lamp to see the vision that was always within his mind's eye, taunting him, teasing him. If he were to be honest he would have to admit that the true reason for his frustration was not the exasperating incident with

Ethan Allen, but the small, fiery-haired, golden-eyed creature that would give him no rest. Reaching out with the aid of long practice, he found the bottle and cup beside his bed and poured himself a hearty portion of rum. It crossed his mind momentarily that he could seek out Peg, she was always available to his summons; but he didn't want Peg, there was only one woman he really wanted.

Melanie stood staring at the sleeping face of her child for a few silent moments before turning toward the door and stepping out to close it quietly behind her. It had been a long, tiring day, and the strain of uncertainty was beginning to be more than she could bear. How she missed Asa, his optimism, his warm humor. She longed to feel his arms around her again, holding her close, to hear his deep voice whispering soft endearments against her hair in the darkness of the night, to feel his lips caress her face, her lips. She longed to touch him, to feel his body against hers. The past month had just been a progression of long, frightening, empty days without him.

Feeling a spark of guilt, she whispered softly under her breath, "Forgive me, Sara, I love you baby, but I need . . . I need. I need Asa."

A small tear slipped despairingly down her cheek and, hastily wiping it away, Melanie continued down the steps and toward the kitchen. The house was especially silent tonight. Martha and Tom had decided that morning to make a trip to Cornwall to see Martha's ailing sister, hoping to be able to return within a few days. Josh had been upset when he realized she would be alone in the house, but she had reassured him she would be all right. If only she felt as secure now in the darkness of the night as she had felt this morning.

You're acting like a child, Melanie! Berating herself silently, Melanie turned into the kitchen. Just lock the doors as Josh said, and go to bed, and morning will be here before you know it!

Sighing deeply, she walked toward the rear door and slipped the lock into place. "Well, that's that," she mumbled as she turned to walk toward the fireplace.

"Not quite, Melanie," a deep voice responded from the shadows a second before the tall figure stepped into the light.

Speechless with fright, Melanie stood still, her gold eyes wide, her body trembling visibly, as Steve walked toward her.

"Don't look so frightened, Melanie," he said softly, reaching out to caress her white cheek.

Suddenly regaining her voice, Melanie shrugged away his hand. "What are you doing here, Steve? How dare you sneak into this house and frighten me this way? You had better leave immediately or I'll call Martha and Tom!"

Steve's low laughter sent tremors of fear up her spine as he casually picked up a curling auburn lock and wound it slowly around his hand, drawing her closer as the shortening length jerked against her scalp.

"You don't have to pretend, Melanie. I know Martha and Tom are gone for a few days. I watched them ride out this morning."

Melanie's throat was suddenly dry, and she

stuttered weakly as Steve's unrelenting grip on her hair drew her steadily closer. "You had better leave right now, Steve. Josh will be by in a few minutes to check on me and he'd better not find—" '

"Don't waste your breath with obvious lies, Melanie." Steve's face stiffened slightly at the mention of Josh's name, and the grip on her hair tightened, "I saw Josh leave half an hour ago, and heard him say he'd see you tomorrow. The fool."

"Please leave, Steve."

"I'll leave when I'm ready, Melanie." Holding her fast with his firm grip on her hair, Steve cupped her cheek with his other hand and drew her mouth to his. Slowly his mouth caressed hers, an intense wave of pleasure sweeping over him as the heady sweetness of her taste sent his blood to racing. As if mesmerized by the softness of his voice, the gentleness of his lips, Melanie remained motionless under his kiss, her own lips gradually parting to allow his tongue entry into the tender wetness of her mouth. Slowly the merciless grip on her hair slackened until in one fluid movement he slipped his arms around her back, pulling her tightly against him. Startled out of her stupor by his sudden motion, Melanie twisted her face away to stutter incoherently against his chest, "Please, Steve, please go away and leave me alone. You don't really care for me. You just want me, to use me . . ."

"You don't really want me to leave," he whispered, tracing the outline of her ear with his lips, exalting in her body's responsive shuddering. "You want me, too, want me to make love to you."

"No, no, I don't."

"You do. You want me to touch you," he whispered softly sliding his hand slowly up her side to cup her breast, bending to nuzzle her neck as he moved his hand in a gentle, caressing motion that sent little shivers of ecstasy up her spine.

Her body quaking violently, she pleaded softly, "Steve, I can't do this, I have a child now to consider. My name is black enough. Please." Feeling the last of her resistance slipping away as his other hand slipped down to cup her buttocks, pressing her firmly against his surging manhood, she uttered a low groan and closed her eyes against the searing rise of passion rushing through her.

"You want me, don't you, Melanie?"

"Steve, please."

His lips were teasing hers, circling her mouth with light, fluttering kisses, driving her mad with the desire to feel them pressed firmly against hers, to taste him again.

Slowly, of their own volition, her arms began moving around his neck as the heat of her emotion increased, until she held the back of his head with her hands and with a steady, positive movement, guided his mouth to cover hers in a deep, searching kiss.

Finally raising his head, his face flushed with passion, Steve stared for a short moment at Melanie's soft, dazed expression before scooping her into his arms, and with long, rapid strides carried her out of the kitchen and up the staircase to the second floor.

With one last feeble effort at resistance, Melanie mumbled against his neck as he opened the bedroom door and stepped inside, "Steve, I can't, I—".

Slowly putting her on her feet, Steve looked deeply

into her eyes, seeing his own passion reflected there, and raised his hands to her neckline to begin unbuttoning her dress. "This is what you want, Melanie, you know it and I know it."

Within seconds her buttons were loosened and, pushing aside her chemise, he lowered his head to her breast, eliciting a deep gasp from Melanie as his mouth tenderly caressed the erect peaks, his arms straining her against him. Moments later he lifted his head to look once more into her face, his heart pounding with the desire raging inside him. "Melanie, tell me, is this what you want? Tell me."

Gradually her passion-drugged eyelids lifted, releasing the full heat of the amber glow beneath on his waiting face.

"Melanie, tell me, is this what you want? Do you want me?"

Struggling to form words, she swallowed tightly, finally responding in a low hoarse voice, "Yes, yes, Steve."

Driven by an urgent need to hear the words he had so longed to hear her say, he demanded again, urgently, "I want to hear you say it, Melanie. Tell me you want me."

"Yes! Yes, I want you," she finally whispered, tears rolling uncontrollably down her face, "Lord help me, I do want you."

Wild with elation, Steve scooped her up into his arms and, carrying her to the bed, laid her down gently and began undressing her in sure quick movements, even as his hands trembled with an overwhelming anxiety to touch the smooth whiteness of her skin once again. Pausing only to light the lamp, he slipped off her dress. Moving quickly, he stripped her of the remainder of her clothes, stopping still when she lay naked beneath his gaze.

"Melanie," he said softly, pausing for that one, long moment to take in her incredible beauty, "at last . . ." He was unable to speak another word past the tightness in his throat, and within moments he was lying beside her, his nakedness pressed tightly against hers, savoring the jolt of sheer, exquisite rapture as their skins touched. Suddenly he was past coherent thought, mad with an emotion that burned out of control, triggered by the simple meeting of their flesh. There was no part of her he didn't want to touch, caress, kiss, and make his own, and he traveled the full length of her body, leaving no spot uncovered in his suit to satisfy the need that had burned so long unfulfilled inside him.

Finally, teased and tortured exquisitely by the finesse of his boundless passion, Melanie groaned and cried out, begging for release from the agony of searing, surging passion brought to the crest time and time again without ultimate fulfillment.

"Is this your revenge, Steve?" she gasped with sudden apprehension, the aching need he had stirred within her stealing her breath and pounding wildly in her breast. Unable to face his reply, she turned her face from his, closing her eyes as tears slid beneath the darkly fringed lids.

Startled by her question, he was completely still for a moment. His body still lying intimately atop hers, Steve cupped her face in his hands and turned it back to his. Still she refused to open her eyes and he perused the beauty lying only inches beneath him as if for the first time. She was even more lovely than he had remembered, than the vision that had haunted him so relentlessly. Moving his hand to touch the brilliant auburn swirls stretched across the pillow, he marveled at its glory, his eyes traveling from the ends of the curling locks to the wispy tendrils at her hairline, framing her face so perfectly. The same smooth, clear forehead, slender, straight brows; delicate, almost transparent lids hiding the glow beneath; that slender, short nose, the nostrils flaring occasionally as passion still reigned her senses; the fine line of her lips, parting in that instant to reveal perfect white teeth in the warm, inviting, voluptuous mouth that transported him to a realm where reason no longer prevailed. Moving his hands, he caressed the delicate contours of her face, suddenly shifting from atop her so that he might allow his eyes the feast his other senses had enjoyed only moments before. Her shoulders, delicately sloped; slender arms tapering to small, graceful hands; her throat, white, soft, inviting; the perfection of her breasts, full, rounded, the nipples still erect, proud, tempting him; the sudden tapering of her ribcage to that incredibly small waist. Without his own realization, Steve's hands followed the path of his eyes, and Melanie gave another involuntary shudder as they slipped beneath her waist. The stomach flat, the skin unmarked by pregnancy, the curve of her hips emphasizing her femininity. As his eyes then moved to the triangle of tight, shining curls, his heartbeat quickened. This at last was his, his alone, and lovingly he bent to press a warm kiss to seal his possession. Steve did not notice Melanie's eyes snap open at his intimate kiss, but continued his gaze down the full length of her shapely legs, to the tips of her small feet and slender toes. Finally, unable to comprehend the combination of pride, tenderness, and humility overwhelming him as he at last knew total possession of such sheer perfection of beauty, and deep, passionate spirit, he finally lifted his eyes to the heated, amber glow trained on his face.

Suddenly recalling her question, he replied softly, his voice husky with emotion. His hand, resting lightly on the warm triangle of curls, began stroking her gently, moving to slip inside the warm crease, knowingly encountering its intimate wetness. Her soft, low groans accompanied his words as he quickly raised her to the peak of passion again. "My revenge, Melanie? Who is the victor here, when passion is mutual, shared."

Suddenly she climaxed, gasping and moaning in the throes of an ecstasy that assumed complete control of her senses. Unable to tear his eyes from her face, Steve watched, fascinated and exhilarated by both his power to incite her to such heights and by the sight of passion suffusing her matchless beauty. When finally she lifted her heavy lids, her body spent, he whispered against her parted lips, "Was it revenge, my darling, or was it love?"

Without waiting for her response, he covered her mouth in a deep, searching kiss, his tongue probing, unbelievably stirring anew within her the desire that had only moments before appeared completely spent. In a quick movement he was atop her again, his manhood probing and finally entering in one deep thrust the warmest reaches of her body.

Smothering her involuntary gasp with his mouth, he stifled the low moans of pleasure emanating from deep within her as he plunged deeply again and again, raising her, raising him to an elevation of climactic sensation that could culminate in only one way. Together they reached the summit, only to fall in a long, breathless plunge from the passion raging uncontrollably within them. Gasping and consumed, they lay side by side, their breathing gradually slowing, their exhaustion so complete that sleep eventually overcame them.

It was still night when Steve awakened. The lamp still burning brightly beside the bed illuminated Melanie's beauty, revealing an aura of innocence and vulnerability not ordinarily noticeable in her usually guarded expression, and Steve frowned at his instinctive desire to pull her even closer still, to hold her protectively close in his arms. He was not going to fall into that old trap, she wasn't innocent; the mistress of an old man, the mother of an illegitimate child. Had Asa not died, she probably would have tired of him within a few months in any case. This was no time to let his defenses down, when he was in the most danger. And begrudgingly as he looked down at her magnificent body curled against his, her face relaxed and guileless in sleep, her mouth soft and appealing, he experienced even more strongly a desire to draw her close, to claim her openly as his own; and he was forced to admit his convictions were in dire danger of crumbling into dust.

And that would be the most stupid thing you could do, you fool! his inner self berated. She shares your desires now, but her type could never be satisfied with one man for long, not even you. Make her take you on your own terms, so when the time comes for a parting, you can walk away a man. Play your cards right and enjoy her for as long as your desire lasts and walk away with no strings.

As if sensing his perusal, Melanie began to stir, opening her eyes to look up into his warm glance. Seeming momentarily startled, her expression quickly relaxed into a small smile, her soft sigh resembling a light, contented purr, and Steve's arousal was immediate. Turning his body toward her in a deliberate, sensual movement, his intention clear, he lowered his mouth to hers, his last thought still ringing in his brain. Yes, enjoy her now . . .

The loud banging on the kitchen door below awoke Melanie to the bright, new day, and she turned to Steve's frowning face.

"Who can that be?" Melanie mumbled softly, suddenly aware of her nakedness and feeling the flush of embarrassment as she pulled back the covering and moved quickly to slip her night rail over her head.

Turning back to the bed, she encountered Steve's black scowl as he said acidly, "Come now, Melanie. You know who it is. It's Josh, your protector. He's come to see if you're all right."

Flushing even more deeply, Melanie was about to retort when Sara's loud wail interrupted her thoughts, and pushing her feet into her slippers, she moved quickly from the room to the nursery.

"Shhhh, Sara, I'm here, baby," she cooed softly to the trembling infant as she scooped her into her arms, wrapped her loosely in a blanket, and moved quickly down the steps to the rear kitchen door.

The pounding continued as she entered the kitchen and she called loudly, "Just a moment, please." Quickly slipping the lock, she opened the door to see Josh's worried face. The sight of Melanie in her ample night rail, her glimmering auburn locks streaming over her shoulders, clutching her wide-eyed, squirming miniature in her arms, changed his expression to a tender smile.

"I just wanted to make sure you were all right before I left for the foundry, Melanie. I know you were a little frightened last night, even if you wouldn't admit it. Did you have a restful night?" His eyes intent on her lovely face, his heart pounding like a schoolboy, Josh felt an overwhelming rush of loving warmth slipping over him when a voice from the kitchen behind her answered coyly, "Melanie had a very good night last night, Josh. It's kind of you to ask."

Steve, stepping beside Melanie, curved his arm around her shoulders, drawing her close against his side. "But you needn't trouble yourself about her. You can see she wasn't quite as alone as you thought last night."

"Steve!" Melanie's voice was an embarrassed gasp, and turning back to Josh, she saw the incredible dismay reflected on his face.

Quickly assessing Steve's appearance as he stood bare chested, wearing merely his britches, his hair still tousled from sleep, Josh said quietly, "Of course. Excuse me for interrupting, Melanie. I'll be going now."

"Josh, please," she whispered, reaching out to take his arm as he turned away, shame flooding her face a bright scarlet. But as he turned back to her restraining grasp, Steve roughly pulled her hand from his arm.

"Goodbye, Josh." Steve's voice was heavy with warning. "Thank you, but I don't think that you'll be needed back at this house again."

Jerking her out of the doorway, Steve firmly closed the door in Josh's face, and Melanie turned toward him, gasping in anger. "Why did you do that? How dare you do that? You had no right to be so rude to Josh. He's been my only friend since Asa's death. He's—"

"He's not needed here anymore," Steve said directing a stinging glance down into her flashing eyes. "Not while I'm here at any rate. Make your choice here and now, because I won't have him hanging around."

"How dare you give me an ultimatum! Who do you think you are?"

Turning back toward her, Steve directed a heated glance her way, deliberately moving his eyes sensually over her face, sliding his glance down her throat to roam warmly over the erect nipples pressing tightly against her night rail. Casually moving his eyes back to her flaming face he said softly, "You know who I am." Then walking away in an abrupt dismissal, he shot a disgusted glance over his shoulder toward the squirming baby, "Now feed the child so we can get her out of the way!"

Fuming inwardly, but unable to do else but follow his command in light of Sara's increasing moans,

Melanie sat down in a brusque movement and, unbuttoning her night rail, put the hungry child to her breast. The infant suckled noisily as Steve moved efficiently around the kitchen, stirring the fire, heating water for tea, and slicing the bread to toast over the crackling flames. Turning back toward Melanie with an annoyed expression, he said tersely, "Hasn't she finished yet?" Then noting the sated child's drooping lids, "She's almost asleep. Put her back in the nursery for now. I have to leave for the foundry soon. I don't have much time."

Afraid further argument would only disturb Sara, Melanie shot him an angry glance before taking the sleeping child from her breast and getting up to march angrily out of the room and up the stairs.

The beast! Inwardly fuming at Steve's commands and his complete dismissal of her child, she gently lay Sara back in the cradle and tip-toed out of the room to close the door lightly behind her. But she reached no further before strong, brawny arms slipped around her, pulling her close, and warm, seeking lips plundered hers. Hungry hands traveled her body intimately, defeating the heat of her anger, and raising the level of another emotion within her. Suddenly scooping her up into his arms, Steve pushed open the bedroom door with his back and moved inside.

"Steve, stop. Wait, I want—"

Depositing her firmly on the bed, he moved his hands inside her open night rail, caressingly, his voice low as he watched the soft, dazed expression move once more across her face. "You know you don't want me to wait, do you, Melanie. Do you?" he urged, feeling his own responsive hardening as her eyelids began to close in submission to her passion. "You don't want me to stop, Melanie, do you?" he demanded, his own breathing heavy.

There was a short silence before Melanie gasped finally, "No, no . . . I don't want you to stop, please don't stop, Steve."

Taking advantage of the early morning quiet of spring for a few leisurely minutes before rising, Melanie's eyes warmly traveled the expanse of Steve's smoothly muscled, naked back as he dressed. Sliding across his broad shoulders, her glance moved slowly down to his narrow waist, strong, firm buttocks, and powerful thighs. Raising her eyes, she noted with a particular tenderness the curl of his short-cropped black hair at the base of his neck, remembering with growing warmth its thick smoothness between her fingers when they made love. Turning unexpectedly, exposing the breadth of his lightly furred chest and wide, muscular neck, he caught her glance and said softly, a glow in the depths of his dark, unfathomable eyes as he gave her body one more appreciative sweep, "What is it, Melanie? Is there something you wanted?"

Annoyed with the revealing flush that colored her face at the veiled innuendo in his tone, Melanie murmured indistinctly, "No, I was just thinking . . ."

His low, knowing laugh as he turned back to dressing caused a momentary stab of anger, and purposefully turning her back to him, Melanie pulled the coverlet over her shoulder and buried her head in the pillow. She wouldn't give him the satisfaction of letting him think she enjoyed watching him dress—even if she did!

But he's such a beautiful man, she admitted to herself with a deep sigh. I'll never tire of looking at him.

The past six months were proof enough of that statement. After countless long and beautiful winter nights spent in mutual enjoyment of each other, as winter gradually faded into spring, the spark between them still burst into a blaze each time their glances met, their bodies touched.

But, a small voice at the back of her mind nagged relentlessly, he's grown too sure of you, too confident of his power to eliminate your resistance, dissolve your anger.

Sudden tears sprang into her eyes. How true that was. Those unexplained nights when he was not beside her haunted her. She still could not understand why he would suddenly absent himself for days at a time, without warning or explanation, only to return expecting to be accepted without protest when he casually returned to her bed. She could understand that no more than she could understand her own acceptance of his casual attitude toward her.

Why do you allow him to treat you this way? It was a question she could read in both Martha and Josh's eyes and one which she had posed to herself countless times. Still, she avoided the answer.

He was intense, moody, changeable. She was not even sure he loved her. Oh, he was careful to impress others with his complete domination over her, in fact had only allowed her Josh's friendship reluctantly and sparingly. Her most casual reference to Asa seemed to stimulate a chain of moody, irrational behavior, and she reluctantly admitted even Sara seemed to be tolerated more than enjoyed. His treatment of her ranged from soul-shaking, loving tenderness, to hateful distrust which manifested itself in malicious barbs directed against her character that cut her deeply. And while at times a simple word or glance from another man could cause his jealousy to rage unreasonably out of control, at other times he went to great lengths to make her understand he cared not a damn what she did!

Still, she ignored all the negative aspects of their relationship as well as the hostility their illicit association aroused in the town, while realizing fully that only fear of Steve's retribution kept her safe from the hatred Harriet Sims spewed forth in her ever increasing, heated tirades. Each day's marketing excursion showed her more clearly the pronounced effect those tirades were having on the townsfolk's attitude toward her. Her conduct had somehow become a matter of the town's conscience, and hidden deep inside her was the fear that the town would someday attempt to cleanse its soiled conscience.

Judging from the sounds behind her back, Steve had finished dressing. Melanie closed her eyes, feigning sleep. Angry with him and angrier still with herself for her own weakness, she steeled herself against him.

"Come, now, Melanie, I know you're not asleep." Whispering coaxingly into her ear, he paused to nibble lightly at the lobe, sending shivers down her spine. "Be a good girl, now, and kiss me goodbye."

When she continued to ignore him, he whispered annoyingly into her ear, "You know you'll be sorry later if you don't."

Steadfastly keeping her eyes closed and her back to him, she could not suppress the small, irritated frown his words evoked, and seeing it he laughed softly, rolling her on her back. "And you're covered up to your neck. It isn't cold in here." Her eyes snapped open as he pulled the coverlet from her grasp and drew it down to her waist. She had not slipped back into her night rail the night before, relying on the heat from Steve's body to keep her warm through the night, and her full, rounded breasts were bared to his view. There was a moment's pause before his gaze moved back up to her face, his expression suddenly sober. Holding her amber gaze for some time, he whispered hoarsely, "Oh, Melanie, I lo—"

Suddenly biting off his words, Steve's mouth descended to cover hers in a long, devouring kiss. Finally drawing away, his breath ragged and uneven, he lifted her slightly to clutch her tightly against him. Reluctantly, he finally released her to lay her back against the pillow, his hands moving to cover the white mounds of her breasts as he spoke. "You make it damned hard for a man to leave you, do you know that, Melanie?" And then in answer to his own question and with an edge of hostility in his voice, "Of course you know it. You know, there are times when I really believe you are a witch and that you've cast a spell over me. How else could you—" Frowning darkly, he again bit off his words, glancing away to avoid the question in her eyes.

Gradually his gaze drifted back to spend a few wordless moments staring unreadably into her face. Slowly raising his hand, he traced the outline of her lips with his fingertip in a tender gesture before moving abruptly from the edge of the bed to leave the room without another word.

Walking down the staircase as fast as his feet would carry him, Steve strode to the front door, slamming it hard behind him. Damn her . . . damn her, he had almost said it again. It had been on the tip of his tongue. I love you, Melanie. I love you, my darling Melanie. He longed to say those words, to hold her close and tell her over and over again how even the mere thought of her set him to trembling, and the touch of her hands sent his blood pounding through his veins. God help him, he was crazy, wild about her! He closed his eyes for a brief second as the tormenting ache inside him swelled, and a small voice in his mind laughed bitterly. You weren't going to be like your father. No, not you. You'd never let any woman get that power over you. But she laughs at your resolutions, seduces you with a glance, melts you with a touch, motivates all your conscious thoughts, and dominates your dreams. You are obsessed by her and you delight in your own obsession. Only one thing stops her from completely owning your soul. Go ahead, fool, tell her that you love her, can't live without her. Tell her you want her to be your wife. Wife—the fatal mistake. She's too beautiful, too filled with a lust for life. She's like your mother, the excitement would pale for her and you would start to die slowly like your father. Knowing everything beforehand, you've made all the same mistakes he made. Don't make the last one!

His hasty retreat had led him to the foundry with unaccustomed speed, and pausing for a moment, Steve entered to look in the direction of the office. Catching Josh's pensive, assessing gaze and reading his thoughts, his own answering gaze was pure, heated venom as a silent vow rang again and again across his mind.

"You'll never get her away from me, Josh, never."

The abrupt explosion of shattering china against the stone kitchen floor rent the afternoon silence and Melanie stood still, staring helplessly down at the broken bowl, tears of frustration welling in her eyes. What a terrible day this was proving to be!

But then, lately, she thought wearily, there has seemed to be a progression of terrible days.

In the past month it appeared that events had conspired to keep her at nerve's edge, and now, she had the uneasy feeling that the slightest push would shove her over the brink. This morning's succession of minor fiascoes, culminating in the breaking of Martha's favorite bowl, had only succeeded in inching her closer to the edge.

If you want to be truly honest with yourself, her mind nudged her relentlessly as she stooped to pick up the jagged remains of the bowl, you will admit your real problem is Steve. Well, it was true. Steve's bouts of moodiness since the turn of the year had increased alarmingly in the past month, and his vacillating behavior toward her, which at first seemed merely an irritating aspect of his personality, had reached an extreme that could neither be ignored nor tolerated any longer. Too often he was silent and uncommunicative, and on too many occasions of late she would turn unexpectedly to find his eyes fastened on her with heated bitterness. She was puzzled, unable to find an honest cause for his sulking animosity, and was hurt beyond words when her attempts to determine the cause were met with vile repulsion. But, then, when it would seem their relationship was at its lowest ebb, Steve would surprisingly turn to her with a loving passion that despite its admittedly desperate quality, nonetheless had the effect of subduing her fears for a short interval.

But Steve's erratic behavior was becoming too wearing on her and the entire household. Martha was more and more obvious in her disapproval. Tom, in his childish openness, discontinued even his former brief conversations with Steve, and even Sara contributed to the tension by screaming intolerably whenever he approached. In the past month her own puzzlement had slowly turned to anger, and now, nearing the end of April, they had progressed to the point where the tension between them was a living, vital force.

Inwardly, Melanie was beginning to feel more and more trapped by the deterioration of her affairs. She realized now, as the tide of public opinion swelled to a new high against her, she had been unwise in the openness of her association with Steve. Alienated by Steve's moodiness, Melanie had begun to rely more and more on Josh's guidance in his position as temporary manager of the foundry, a point that only proved a further irritant in their relationship. Exhibiting his usual sensitivity to her feelings, Josh had realized the complication and hardship his presence was working on Melanie, and, the week before, had taken the opportunity to return to his homestead prior to spring plowing, intending to remain there for an indefinite period. With the responsibility for Sara weighing heavily on her shoulders, Melanie was beginning to believe there was nowhere to turn. More and more each day she realized the value of Asa's complete devotion, and also realized that even in their most heated moments of passion, Steve had never declared his love for her, an uneasy suspicion had formed in her mind that he never would.

So here you stand, you silly fool, her mind berated, a victim of a situation of your own making. There's no one to blame but yourself, and no way to change what has been done, so at this point you must decide if you will allow yourself to drown, or if you will learn to swim.

A heavy footstep on the path outside the door turned her from her somber thoughts, and with the abruptness of all his recent actions, Steve strode through the doorway, the dark expression clouding his handsome face causing a rapid acceleration of her heartbeat.

"What's wrong, Steve? Why are you here so early in the day? Did something happen at the foundry?"

"There has been a battle at Lexington and Concord in the Massachusetts Bay Colony. American blood has been shed for the first time in combat with the British."

The problems of a colony such a distance away seemed of little consequence to Melanie, who was still caught up in the problems of her own survival, and she replied irritably, "What has that to do with us in Salisbury?"

"Your attitude is so typical of a small mind, Melanie."

Steve's stinging words, delivered with a deprecating sneer, sent a flush of anger rushing to her face, and in a voice heavy with sarcasm, she retorted angrily, "And what does your 'great' mind make of the event, Steve? Or do you hesitate to answer in fear of my limited capacity for understanding?"

"Quite simply," he said with aggravating condescension, "it probably means war."

"War!"

Barely acknowledging her response, he continued in an objective voice, "Ethan has sent a call for all the Green Mountain Boys to meet in Bennington as soon as possible. Heman Allen is coming up from Connecticut; Heber Allen is on his way from Poultney; Ira Allen is coming from Onion River with Remember Baker. The whole Allen clan is assembling to lead the Boys. John Brown of Pittsfield, Massachusetts approached Ethan about taking Fort Ticonderoga from the British."

"But why?"

"Fort Ticonderoga is strategically important. It controls traffic on Lake Champlain. It also has the only cannon in this area. Aside from that, do you think Ethan would allow those damn Yorkers to get ahead of us and take possession? Steal the glory and make themselves instant heroes? That wouldn't bode well for the cause of the grants, and whether this present crisis comes to war or not, the fort will be better off in our hands than in theirs."

At this point Melanie was only partially listening to Steve's explanation, the one word drumming over and over inside her head—war. War. War. In the flash of a second she was revisted by the vision of her father lying dead, and then Asa, and the deep fear abiding inside her came to life. All the men who had ever been close to her had been taken from her in death. If Steve were to go this time, she suddenly knew with a startling certainty he would not return. In that second, all her reservations about Steve were swept away in her intense desire to keep him away from the impending battle.

Finally she managed to stammer past her anxiety, "I didn't mean, why take Fort Ticonderoga . . . I meant why do you have to go?"

His exasperation seemed to grow by leaps and bounds. "Can you really be that dense, Melanie? I've always ridden with the Green Mountain Boys!"

"But there are so many of them. They won't miss you if you don't go."

"Of course I'm going!"

"Steve, please don't go. I need you here much more than they need you."

"Melanie." Steve's tone held an impatient ring.

Taking a step closer to him, Melanie lay her palms against Steve's chest, noting subconsciously the pounding of his heart beneath her hands as she directed a smoldering glance into his eyes. "I need you, Steve. I need you here. You don't really want to leave me, do you?"

With the touch of her small, delicate hands against his chest, Steve felt an almost instantaneous draining of his heavily contrived resistance. The prospect of battle far to the north began to feel less and less important as her golden eyes seemed to sear into his. Entranced by the amber glow, his glance slowly drifted to her soft, inviting mouth. She was right, she did need him. Her position in Salisbury was extremely precarious. It was a situation he had encouraged when he flaunted their relationship in the faces of the hostile element in town, knowingly stirring the resentment against her, relying on her fear of reprisal to bind her to him.

Her slender, white arms slowly slid around his neck as that warm, sweet mouth came closer, and she pleaded softly, "Please don't leave me, Steve."

She continued to speak, but her words drifted from his hearing as his body began to swell with desire. God help me, he thought in desperation, I want her even now when I should be . . .

A particular name on her tongue suddenly tugged at his consciousness.

"And now that Josh is gone, too, I don't—"

A flash of jealousy at the mention of Josh's name jerked him viciously from his mesmerized state, and pushing her violently away from him, he knocked her back against the table where she clung momentarily for support. Stepping forward, he glared down into her eyes, growling ominously with an emotion akin to hatred, "If Josh were here now you wouldn't be pleading so tenderly for me to stay. You wouldn't care one little bit if I left then, would you, Melanie? You might even enjoy the opportunity to test Josh's devotion. How would you pay him for his protection? The same way you pay me?"

Gasping with indignation at his degrading insult,

Melanie raised her hand and swung with all her might, snapping his head to the side with the force of her blow. With unexpected suddenness, Steve's hand whipped out, striking her full across the cheek, staggering her almost off her feet. Her eyes smarting heavily, Melanie gazed with wordless fury through the watery mist.

"I would tell you never to raise your hand to me again, Melanie, without expecting a return of the same, but that would be redundant in any case. I don't expect you'll have an opportunity, even when I do return to Salisbury. Your wiles have been ineffective on me this time, Melanie. You've failed, the spell is broken. It wasn't strong enough to turn me into a coward, sacrificing my self-respect to retain your favors."

"What spell? I've cast no spell. I was afraid for you, wanted to keep you safe from battle. My concern was for you, not myself."

"You're wasting your breath, Melanie." Steeling himself against her hurt, disbelieving expression, he continued viciously, "Better yet, save your explanations for Josh when he returns. He may be more susceptible to your wiles. Perhaps you'll have more success with him."

Unable to believe the venomous stranger standing before her was the same man who had loved her long and well over the past seven months, Melanie whispered incredulously, "You can't mean all this."

"But I can, Melanie, and I do!" Turning abruptly on his heel, Steve walked out the door, leaving her staring in wide-eyed shock at the empty doorway through which he had disappeared.

Reaching his room almost breathless from his rapid walk, Steve slammed open the door and kicked it closed behind him. She was a witch all right, she had to be. His sense of purpose had been firm when he had reached her, unshakable, but within minutes he had turned to putty in her hands. Groaning slightly as the vision of her beautiful face turned up to his shook him deeply, even in memory, he sat at the edge of the bed, covering his face with his hands in a futile gesture. Salisbury's Green Mountain Boys were leaving for Bennington in the morning, and he would be with them. Determinedly rising from the bed, he walked to the dresser and retrieved his meager possessions from the drawers, turning to throw them onto the blanket. With great deliberation he rolled the blanket tightly and secured it with a leather thong. In the morning he would pick up some food for the journey and a horse from the stable, and he would be ready to go.

Abruptly sitting again, he had to laugh at his own sense of panic. He sincerely doubted he was capable of maintaining his resolve! He sincerely doubted he could leave her! Nauseating waves of jealousy were already sweeping over him at the mere thought of Josh's exhilaration when he found out Melanie was free. Why had he done it? Why had he broken with her? He was uncertain as to his own motives. But it seemed he was not capable of sound reasoning where Melanie was concerned. He had cleared the way for Josh—Melanie and Josh. The thought caused him such a jolt of anguish that he suffered a sudden heaving sensation in the pit of his stomach. Melanie was his, his! God, he loved her, but his love was consuming him, making him insensible to life-long objectives, his duty. He had to take a stand. If he gave in this time, he'd be lost. He would no longer respect himself. His father, he had sacrificed his self-respect. The weakness must run in the family, but he'd be damned before he would subjugate himself to his passion for Melanie.

Resolutely he pushed the blanket roll to the floor and flopped back on the bed, his hands crossed behind his head as he stared at the ceiling, his dark brows drawn into a deep frown. He must not give in, he could not if he was to survive. Glancing to the table beside his bed, he saw an unopened bottle of rum and, reaching for it with a sense of desperation, he said determinedly, "Well, old friend, it looks like you and I are going to spend the night together."

Hours later, Steve held the bottle high, squinting in the darkening room, disbelieving his own eyes.

"Impossible!" he mumbled, staring at the empty bottle. His voice echoing in the silence held only the slightest touch of slur, and staring at the vessel with abject disappointment covering his handsome face, he said sadly, "Old friend, you've let me down. I'm not drunk enough yet. I can still think," and laughing foolishly, he discarded the bottle beside the bed to cover his eyes with his hand. Still he was unsuccessful in blocking the golden-eyed vision constantly before his mind's eye.

"Will morning never come?" His unanswered question still ringing in his ears, he staggered to his feet and walked to the washstand. He had long since discarded his shirt, and he splashed water liberally over his face and head, finally reaching for the towel

216

as a light knock sounded on the door.

"Come on in," he muttered, suddenly realizing he was a bit more intoxicated than he had thought as he fought to focus on the opening door. A female figure stood hesitantly in the doorway, the light from the hallway behind her shadowing her face, making her features indiscernible. Squinting against his blurring vision, Steve swayed slightly. She said nothing as he fought to focus his eyes, his heart pounding in his chest as he felt a faint stirring of hope.

"Melanie?"

There was a slight pause before the figure in the doorway spoke, crushing his hopes with the first utterance of her sharp, nasal twang.

"Sorry to disappoint you, love, but it ain't Melanie. It's just poor old Peg, coming to see if there's anything she can do for her favorite chum. Shall I still come in?"

Swallowing tightly against the overwhelming wave of disappointment recognition had evoked, he said indistinctly, "Sure, Peg, sure." Still swaying, he grasped the edge of the dresser to steady himself. "Make yourself comfortable. You're no stranger here."

"Oh, but I have been of late, Steve, my boy." Sauntering toward him with a sway of her ample hips, stopping just short of body contact, she whispered again, "I heard you'll be leaving with the Boys in the morning, and it took me by surprise when you shut yourself away up here all afternoon. What happened, did you have a falling out with your new ladybird, dearie?" Her broad, pleasant face was turned up to his as she slowly ran her hand along the surface of his chest and up to the back of his neck where she tangled her short, stubby fingers in his hair.

"If you're in need of some consolation, chum, old Peg'll provide it for old times' sake. She wouldn't want you to go to battle without a proper sendoff." Slowly rubbing the tips of her breasts against his bare chest, her breathing quickening with her growing warmth, she reached down with her other hand to stroke his lagging member. Finally beginning to feel a reaction to her advances, her hand kneaded more vigorously as she cooed, "That's it, we have the old boy interested now, don't we? Come on, darlin'," she coaxed sweetly, "make up your mind now. Will you have a romp with Peg for old times' sake? It's yours for the asking, chum."

Peg's experienced hands had accomplished their objective, and glancing down at the heaving cleavage so well displayed in her deep neckline, Steve roughly pulled her dress off her shoulders to close his hand over one slightly sagging breast.

"Yes, Peg, for old times' sake." He was breathing heavily as Peg's experienced hands emptied his troubled mind for the first time that day. "We'll make the night of it, and you'll send me off a new man. Come on." Roughly jerking her hand away, he staggered toward the bed, pulling her behind him. "You're right, Peg. Your kind of consolation is what I need now."

"I say good riddance to him, Melanie. It was a mistake your ever getting involved with him in the first place." Martha's fair brows were knitted together in a frown, her broad face creased with concern as she removed Melanie's untouched plate from the table. "Mark my words, now. That man's not quite sane where you're concerned. I've had some experience with people going off the deep end, and if ever a man was headed in that direction, he was. Just be glad you're off easy, and be thankful it didn't end up worse for you." Profoundly hopeful they had all seen the last of Stephen Hull, Martha was using her sharpest tone to shake Melanie out of her obvious depression, with no apparent reaction.

"That's right, Melanie." Tom's deep voice took up his mother's cause. "Mama's right. I don't like Steve either. He didn't treat you right. He was nasty and mean, and I felt like hitting him most of the time, but Mama wouldn't let me. I'm glad he's gone."

Directing a brief smile in Tom's direction, Melanie turned back to Martha. "You're both right, I know. Everything you said is probably true, but it doesn't change the way I feel, does it?"

"It should!" Martha's voice was indignant.

"But it doesn't, Martha, and I may never see him again." Her words choking in her throat, Melanie turned toward the window to stare at the waning light of day as tears filled her eyes. "In the morning he'll be gone." Her tone softening, pleading their understanding, Melanie continued, "I have to give it one more try. It was all so quick. I almost don't know what really happened. I'm sure Steve is regretting everything he said now, just as well as I, but is too proud to give in. I can't afford pride now. He'll be gone in the morning."

Snatching up her shawl, Melanie turned back

toward them. "I'm going to try to talk to him. I have to. Will you listen for Sara, Martha?"

Her mouth tightening in anger, Martha's answer was brief. "If you must go."

"I must. Thank you." Throwing on her shawl, Melanie hurried out the door into the darkening twilight.

Anxiety putting wings to her heels, within minutes Melanie stood breathlessly before the back staircase to the boardinghouse. Pausing only to take a deep, sobering breath, she mounted the stairs, and entering the hallway, noted with relief that it was deserted. Old memories returned unbidden as she walked toward Steve's room. The last time she had been here she had not entered of her own free will, Sara had not yet been born, and Asa was alive.

Stopping before the familiar door, Melanie knocked lightly. There was a faint stirring within, but no answer, and she knocked again.

A faint shaft of light slid beneath the door as a slightly slurred voice answered irritably, "Just a minute, I'm coming."

A few seconds later the door jerked open. Steve stood in the doorway, weaving slightly as he stared with a startled expression into her anxious face. His chest and lower legs bare, he had obviously donned his britches with haste. His hair was untidy, and his deep, black eyes were heavy-lidded and dull. A strong odor of rum permeated the room and Melanie hesitated momentarily before speaking. She hadn't expected to find him in this obviously drunken state, and considered the wisdom of beginning a conversation while he was in such a condition.

220

"I'm sorry if I woke you, Steve," Melanie stammered slightly, "but I had to talk."

There was a brief hesitation before Steve's response. "I wasn't sleeping, Melanie."

A low snicker from behind him drew Melanie's eyes to the bed. Gasping audibly as her eyes locked with Peg Carver's amused glance, she watched in horrified fascination as Peg boldly propped herself on her elbow, allowing the covering to fall away from her naked breasts, cooing sweetly with a slight, negative shake of her head, "No, he wasn't sleeping, dearie."

Backing away, her face flooding a deep scarlet, Melanie gasped haltingly, "I didn't know . . . I didn't realize . . ." Her words sputtered into silence and, darting a last look at Steve's unreadable face, she turned on her heel and fled down the hallway. Behind her she heard Steve call her name, but she continued down the back staircase and was in the alleyway before the first deep, shattering sob wracked her body. Continuing to run as fast as her restricted breathing would allow, she sobbed incoherently under her breath, "Oh, God . . . oh, God, I was so sure. In my heart I was so sure he loved me."

Chapter 4

Frowning down from his towering height, Ethan Allen effectively dwarfed the well-groomed man standing confidently in front of him. Openly assessing, his glance flicked over the handsome man's immaculate light blue uniform, purportedly signifying his rank as colonel in the Connecticut Militia, and spared only the briefest dismissing glance for the fellow's valet standing insignificantly in his shadow. Without comment, his eyes returned to the official paper in his hand, to read it again, more slowly, in an attempt to digest more palatably its contents. It was an impressive document, written in a fine hand on long paper by the Massachusetts Committee of Safety, authorizing the gentleman presenting it, Benedict Arnold, to assume command of the force due to strike Fort Ticonderoga the following day.

Ethan himself possessed no such paper, only a document from the Connecticut legislature authorizing the attack, but his efforts in preparation for the assault had been intense. One hundred and thirty Green Mountain Boys had answered his summons to Bennington, and he had amassed provisions, firearms, and ammunition for the entire force. From Bennington he had dispatched Noah Phelps, a bright, young newcomer to the area, to assess the situation at Fort Ticonderoga. Unknown at the fort, Noah had entered on a pretext and determined its condition and defenses before returning with the surprising information that news of the trouble in Boston had not reached Ticonderoga! Enlightened by this bit of intelligence, Ethan had proceeded with his men to their Castleton headquarters at Zadock Remington's Tavern for a prearranged meeting with a group of Connecticut-Massachusetts volunteers and there had begun to formulate the final plan of attack. On the determination that the attack would be launched from Hand's Cove, across the lake from the fort, Ethan had dispatched thirty men to Skenesboro to seize the boats necessary to carry them across the lake. All was progressing on schedule, and from the first the unanimous, undisputed leader had been he, Ethan Allen. Suddenly faced with the impressive document in his hand, authorizing his replacement as commander, Ethan's reaction was surprisingly calm. His face expressionless, he stated in an even voice, "Follow me, Colonel Arnold. I will inform my men that there has been a change in command."

Arnold followed the huge, dynamic figure in the tattered green jacket and fawn britches signifying his leadership in the Green Mountain Boys, among the men squatting and sitting around their campfires. Feeling smug and slightly gratified at the easy turn of command after having heard wild stories of Allen's volatile temper, he took his place beside Allen as the deep, booming voice drew all eyes toward them.

"I'm calling your attention, men, to introduce this man standing here beside me. This is Colonel Benedict Arnold. I have here in my hand," he said, raising the paper high over his head for all to see, "a commission from the Massachusetts Committee of Safety authorizing him as the new commander of the attack against Fort Ticonderoga tomorrow morning. This paper also assures you all that the attack plan will remain the same and your pay will remain the same, two dollars a day; only your leader will change."

The boys in buckskin leisurely scrutinized the immaculately clad gentleman before them, apparently considering the announcement calmly. Their reaction was deceivingly casual as they began gradually moving to their feet, and taking their arms, began stacking them carefully, the symbol of a camp at rest. Preparation for the battle had come to a complete halt.

"I don't know about you, but I'm not following any cockatoo colonel into a shooting war," mumbled one grumbling dissenter as he laid his rifle down.

"He may be the bluebird of the Connecticut and Massachusetts militia, but I'm not following anybody I don't know into a battle," muttered another.

"For all we know, he doesn't know his mustache from his musket!" exclaimed another.

"As far as I'm concerned, if this pipsqueak from Boston is leading, I'm not following," was the final comment of another rangy backwoodsman, who stacked his rifle with the rest and walked away.

The grumbling gradually gained in volume as Colonel Arnold at first watched with obvious unconcern and then in growing dismay as the stacking of arms continued. From amidst the sea of mumbling a single voice called out purposefully, and all eyes jerked to the tall, dark-haired fellow whose black eyes sparked angrily.

"Well, Ethan, and 'Colonel Arnold'," Steve Hull shouted, pronouncing the latter's name acidly, "you have read us your official document, and we have listened like the good soldiers that we are. But now, like the good *men* that we are, we will give you our official response to that flowery paper—Massachusetts Committee of Safety be damned! Ethan Allen has been our commander for four years, and we will go into battle under his command, or we will not go at all!"

Shouts echoing the same sentiment reverberated through the camp as Ethan stood, his great hands on his hips, barely managing to conceal his triumphant grin, while Colonel Arnold eyed the men in shocked disapproval. Directing his penetrating stare directly into the uncomfortable colonel's eyes, Ethan announced solemnly, "The men's response is obvious, Colonel Arnold. They will not accept you as their leader, and I'll be damned before I'll jeopardize the success of this mission by attempting to persuade them against their better judgment."

Raising his voice so that it might be heard by all the Boys assembled, he then announced vehemently, "I will not surrender my command against the wishes of my men. When the attack begins tomorrow, *I* will be at the head of the force leading them into battle!"

Hearty cheers followed Ethan's declaration, formally closing the matter to the contentment of the general assembly. "However," Ethan added, directing his remarks in a magnanimous voice to the perplexed gentleman in blue, "if you would like, Colonel Arnold, you may walk beside me during the attack and watch the progress of the battle . . . provided you do not interfere."

In a brief glance over the expectant faces awaiting his response, Arnold accurately assessed his situation as hopeless and responded politely while controlling his inner anger, "I accept your generous offer, Colonel Allen."

With a satisfied nod in his direction, Ethan then turned and swaggered away to conclude last minute plans, leaving the spotless officer to his own devices.

A few hours later, under cover of darkness, Ethan and his men moved down the lake to Hand's Cove, a mile north of the fort. There the lake narrowed to a point where the men could swim across, were it not for the major problem of keeping their powder dry. The men dispatched to secure a transporting fleet had come back empty-handed, except for one batteau and one small rowboat. It was an inadequate fleet to transport two hundred thirty men and officers before daylight, but, nevertheless, the frantic ferrying commenced. When dawn finally began breaking through the night sky, Ethan realized that they would get no more than eighty-three men across in safety, without alerting the guard to their approach.

Leaving Seth Warner behind to bring up the remainder of the men after the attack had begun, Ethan crossed the lake to assemble his troops. Even under the tension of expectant battle, Ethan's oratory was reliably inspiring.

"In striking this blow against British tyranny over our freedom, we strike a blow for all mankind. Ours is a noble cause, Boys, but a dangerous one. Our number is few, far less than we had anticipated would initiate this action, and because of this, knowing full well that our lessened number increases our danger, I will ask only for volunteers. Those who will participate will signify by raising their arms."

Without exception, all arms were raised, bringing a wide smile to Ethan's dark features.

"Stout hearts and stout men!" The words of Ethan's approval carried distinctly to the furthest man, and turning toward the fort, he continued in a voice frought with determination, "And the devil take any man who stands in our way!"

Efficiently leading his men in a column three abreast, the natty Colonel Arnold at his side, Ethan approached the south wall of the fort. There the wall had been damaged and left unrepaired, and storming it easily, they were soon at the wicket gate of the inner fortress. A lone sentry guarded, and seeing the armed force approaching, the frightened soldier aimed his gun at the huge man heading the column and fired. A hearty hoot of laughter issued from Ethan's lips at the clicking sound of a misfire, and taking off after the retreating soldier, he raised his sword and brought it down forcefully, only to have it deflected against the soldier's gun to allow a small head wound.

Using the sentry's confusion to his advantage as the Green Mountain Boys gave three loud huzzahs to arouse the fort before swarming into the sleeping barracks, Ethan demanded, "Now take me to your commander, boy, or prepare to meet your maker!"

Unable to utter a reply from his frozen throat, the staggering sentry led Allen, with Arnold at his heels, up the steps to the officers' quarters. Arriving at the top and finding no one within view, Ethan shouted loudly in disgust, "By God, someone had better come out here now and surrender this garrison before I kill every man in the fort!"

Ethan's bellow succeeded in bringing a groggy officer still struggling to close his uniform britches stumbling from one of the doors, mumbling irritably, "What in Hell is this ungodly racket? And who in Hell are you?" he demanded of Ethan.

"I, you fumbling clod, will prove to be the grim reaper for the entire fort if you do not surrender it immediately. You fool, this is an attack!"

"And by whose authority do you proceed with this illegal act against the King?" the young officer demanded haughtily.

"In the name of the Great Jehovah and the Continental Congress!" was the bellowed response.

Suddenly another door opened and another irate officer emerged. "I am Captain Delaplace, commanding officer of this fortress. Now, what in bloody Hell is all this commotion?"

This time Ethan's declaration of purpose was delivered with the added volume of rage against the officer's glaring stupidity. "I demand the surrender of this fort in the name of the Great Jehovah and the Continental Congress!"

Sudden realization widened Captain Delaplace's eyes. The significance of the strangers' presence within the fort seemed finally to penetrate his sleep-fogged brain, and he sent a quick, assessing glance to the fort yard. There the Green Mountain Boys were actively and efficiently routing his men and proceeding to secure them under guard. Realizing the force far outnumbered his fifty men stationed in residence, and that for all intents and purposes they had already been defeated, he turned back to look up into Allen's livid features.

Hesitating only a moment and pulling himself together with typical British aplomb, the captain said calmly and clearly, "Sir, it would be obvious to anyone but a fool that our position here is futile. You have us at an insurmountable disadvantage. It is with great regret that I deliver Fort Ticonderoga into your hands."

"Don't be afraid, Melanie, I won't let them hurt you." Tom's voice was paternally protective as he shot a warning glance at the group of women gathering suspiciously a short distance away, effectively blocking their path home from marketing. For a few seconds, as she turned her worried frown in his direction, Melanie allowed herself to be comforted by the imposing picture Tom presented. Pulling himself up to his full height, emphasizing the breadth of his shoulders and chest, his thick blond hair gleaming in the morning sunlight, Tom was a formidable sight to oppose, but the moment he turned to face her, her heart plunged downward in despair. His lopsided smile and vague eyes confirmed sadly that he was just the old Tom after all, who could be depended upon for his strength and loyalty, but could be outwitted as easily as a child; and there was small comfort in that. Unwilling to allow the fear that had begun to grow inside her in the weeks since Steve's departure for Bennington to become obvious to those so clearly seeking to intimidate her, Melanie slipped her hand casually through the crook in Tom's arm, a small, uneasy smile covering her face as Tom grinned, happy in her dependence.

They continued moving forward, pretending to ignore the group rapidly enlarging in their path. Melanie's smile stiffened and she wished desperately she could subdue the wild pounding of her heart and the uneasy, prickly sensation crawling up the back of her neck.

Unwillingly, Melanie had to admit Steve's departure had seemed to release Harriet Sims to actively pursue her greatest passion in life; the vilification of Melanie Morganfield. Preying on the puritanical fears of the overzealous moralists in the community, she had inflamed their dread of divine punishment for allowing Melanie to walk among them without castigation. Having been stoned on two different occasions when she returned from marketing, Melanie knew her fears were not unfounded, and as she and Tom drew nearer the threatening group, she fought hard to control the quaking that had begun deep inside her.

Gathered as ominously as a flock of evil black crows poised to prey on some wounded creature by the roadside, the women in their somber dresses watched unblinkingly as they approached. With a jolt of panic, Melanie realized that the creature they waited to prey upon was her!

"Get out of our way, all of you, and let us through!" Tom's deep voice was angry, his body quivering in prelude to the rage she could sense building inside him. "You are wicked women," he shouted aggressively as they stood their ground. "Melanie and I are going home."

"Send your fool away, Melanie Morganfield." The thin, nasal tones of Harriet Sims came from the center of the group, and Melanie's eyes flew to the face of the wizened old woman. Her small black eyes gleaming with feverish glee, the woman's narrow lips turned up in an unmistakably victorious smile. "We have no grievance against him. You have bewitched him just as well as the other men you have used."

"I have bewitched no one. You are insane!" Melanie exclaimed violently, her face flushing with the heat of anger.

"Get out of our way, I said!" Tom shouted again,

attempting to push a few resisting women aside.

"I said send your fool home, Melanie Morganfield, or he will be on your conscience, not ours. The time of judgment has come. You must pay for your sins and evil ways."

Realizing there was no sense in arguing with the demented old crone, Melanie whispered quietly, "Run, Tom, run!" But no sooner had the words escaped her lips than Melanie felt strong, biting hands grasp her arms to hold her prisoner.

With a bellow of rage, Tom lifted his arm to strike the women restraining her when, with a low groan, he suddenly crumpled into a heap at her feet, blood trickling from a wound in the back of his head.

"Tom! Tom!" Melanie had not seen the blow or from whence it came and began screaming hysterically, "You've killed him! You've killed Tom! Let me go—" Struggling and screaming wildly, she sent a frenzied glance around the street for help, only to find it strangely deserted. They were all in on it, the whole town, and it was obvious that those who did not agree would do nothing to stop the fanatics that threatened her. "Bigots, cowards, lunatics!" she screamed at the venomous faces surrounding her. "You won't get away with this because as long as I'm alive I'll—"

"You'll do nothing!" Harriet Sims hissed with maniacal fervor. "You will be incapable of working your spells on the unsuspecting men you desire! Your beauty has been the lure you have used to draw them to you while you bent them to your will and corrupted their minds. In destroying your beauty, we will destroy your powers."

A sudden, jerking spasm of fear convulsed Melanie, causing the bile to rise to her throat, and she swallowed tightly. Destroy her beauty! Suddenly regaining her voice, she shouted, "You are the evil one, Harriet Sims. You are the evil witch in this group, not I! It is not your zeal for justice that moves you today, but jealousy, you ugly old crone!"

"You are an adultress!" Harriet Sims' eyes gleamed with the fire of hatred. "Adultress . . . fornicator . . . sinner . . . sinner . . ." she chanted over and over, while the restraining hands bit deeper into Melanie's arms, and she struggled harder for release.

Slowly the chant was picked up by the women who had now encircled her, and Melanie began trembling wildly in fear.

"Release me! Release me, I said. I'm innocent of any witchcraft. I've done nothing to hurt anyone! Please!" She finally pleaded, her eyes going from face to face within the crowd, searching for one spark of doubt reflected there, but the chanting continued.

"Adultress . . . adultress . . . adultress . . ."

A flash of sunlight reflecting on metal caught her eye, and Melanie snapped her face back to Harriet Sims who was advancing slowly toward her, a knife gleaming in her clawlike hand.

"We will shear your power when we shear your flaming mane of Satan, and you will wear forever as the reminder of your sins the adultress *A* that we will cut into your cheek today! You will be helpless to work your spells without your beauty, and we will be free of your evil!"

"No! No! You can't allow her to do this!" Melanie was screaming hysterically, tossing her face from side to side to avoid Harriet Sims as she advanced and raised the knife ever nearer.

"Hold her still! Hold her still!" the nasal tones whipped out in sharp command, and immediately unknown hands gripped viciously at her hair and chin, holding her head still. Her eyes bulging ever wider as the knife neared her face, Melanie whimpered softly, "Please don't let her do this, please—"

"Madam!" A deep male voice called in a commanding tone. "If that knife you are holding touches that young lady's face, the ball from this pistol will penetrate your evil heart!"

The raised knife remained poised to cut, and the deep voice commanded again in a warning tone, "Drop the knife! Drop it now! I will give you three seconds before I pull the trigger!"

There were a few moments of hesitation, and suddenly the knife dropped from Melanie's view. Still the binding hands held her firmly, digging into the flesh on her arms and shoulders, bruising her chin and pulling mercilessly on her hair while keeping her from seeing the face of her rescuer.

"Now release her! Release her now!" the voice demanded, finally rising to a shout in obvious impatience.

Gradually the restraining hands dropped away, leaving her swaying weakly as she turned slowly toward her liberator.

First to meet her gaze were assessing, icy blue eyes, immediately familiar in a face that for a moment defied recognition. The cold fury reflected there had transformed the placid, arrogant features of Simon

Young into a mask of outrage. She stared expressionlessly, her golden eyes fastened hypnotically on his face as he commanded sharply, "Now, get out of here, all of you! And should you ever attempt anything of this sort again in the future, remember that each and every one of you will pay, and pay heavily for the sin, yes *sin*, you commit against this young woman! Now GO!"

Within seconds the preying crows had disappeared, and without a word, Melanie dropped to her knees beside Tom's inert body.

"Oh, Lord," she cried aloud, "please do not let him be dead!"

"He's not dead, but it must have been a heavy blow to put this young fellow so soundly unconscious." Kneeling beside her, Simon Young efficiently examined Tom, lifting the unconscious man's eyelid and lightly pressing his fingers against the pulse in his throat. "It doesn't appear that he is badly injured. His heartbeat is strong."

"Could you help me take him home, Mr. Young?"

Without a word, Simon Young rose to his feet and walking a few steps to the corner, raised his hand in summons. Within moments a familiar coach appeared, and with the aid of the driver, Tom was laid upon the seat, still unconscious. Turning to Melanie, who stood beside the coach, Simon Young deftly scooped her up, installed her on the seat across from the unmoving Tom, and sat beside her. The coach immediately sprang into motion.

"Do you think Tom will be all right?" Melanie worriedly fixed her eyes on Tom's face as she lightly

235

stroked his cheek. When Simon Young did not respond, her eyes flew to his face to catch his annoyed expression.

"I have already told you that I don't believe he is badly injured."

Irritated by his tone, Melanie quickly turned her face back to Tom. Now that was the Simon Young she so well remembered.

Within moments they were on Weaver's Row, but before she could scramble from the carriage, Simon Young had opened the door and was lifting her from the coach. Running to the front door, Melanie rang the bell and returned to assist in removing Tom from the coach, only to have Simon Young remark aggravatingly, "Kindly step out of the way, Melanie. You are only making matters more difficult!"

Before she could respond, a gasp from behind turned Melanie toward Martha's white face as the massive woman quickly moved down the steps to the side of her still unconscious son.

"What happened?" Lightly she touched her son's pale cheek.

"We were set upon by a group of women. Tom was struck from behind. Mr. Young saved us both." Striving for an encouraging note in her voice, she continued, "Mr. Young says he's not badly hurt, Martha. He says Tom's going to be all right. He has to be, he was only trying to protect me."

Slowly they carried Tom up the steps and into his bedroom near the kitchen.

"I would appreciate it if you would send your man for Dr. Pierce, Mr. Young." The noticeable quiver in Martha's voice belied her calm facade.

"Certainly, Martha."

A low, forlorn wail from upstairs automatically turned Melanie away from the tense scene as she hurried to answer Sara's summons. Stopping only to change the child's linen, Melanie returned to find Simon Young busily moving around the kitchen. Turning as she entered, he remarked casually, "I've just gotten Martha a basin of water to sponge Tom's face and thought a cup of tea would do nicely right now. Shall I make one for you, also, Melanie?"

Stunned at his casual attitude and quick recovery from the shocking events of the last hour, Melanie nodded her head dumbly. She was still quaking inside from her close brush with disfiguration and terror, and as she sat Sara quietly in her chair, the delayed reaction to her horrifying experience brought tears streaming down her face. Suddenly she was enfolded consolingly in Simon Young's embrace, her face pressed against the fine lawn of his lace edged cravat, the scent of his cologne in her nostrils.

"Why, why do they hate me so? I have done nothing to hurt any one of them. I've bewitched no one." There was a low sound in Simon Young's chest at her statement that went unheeded as she continued sobbing, "If anything happens to Tom now, I will never forgive myself." Simon Young's responsive stiffening went unnoticed as a sound at the doorway turned their glances toward Dr. Pierce, who entered, demanding without ceremony, "Where is Tom?"

"He's in his bedroom, Dr. Pierce."

Dr. Pierce moved toward the door with undisguised haste, and Melanie turned back toward Simon Young, whose arms had dropped to his sides at the doctor's entrance. Brushing away her tears in a resolute gesture, she said politely, "Please be seated, Mr. Young. And you, too, sir," she said referring to his coachman who stood hesitantly near the doorway.

"Yes, Peter, for God's sake, be seated," Simon Young exclaimed irritably.

Attempting to atone for Mr. Young's impatient words, Melanie addressed the balding, slightly paunchy middle-aged driver, "I owe you a debt of gratitude, also, for helping me to bring Tom home, and—"

Interrupting her ungraciously, Simon Young stated in a flat voice, "You owe Peter nothing. He is in my employ and was following my orders, nothing more."

"Nonetheless, thank you, Peter." Shooting Simon Young a deliberate, deadly look, she ignored a small grunt that sounded suspiciously like a chuckle and turned away.

Both men were installed unceremoniously at the table with tea and biscuits, and she was feeding an unconcerned Sara her gruel, when Dr. Pierce finally emerged.

"He is conscious and in remarkably good condition, considering the size of the lump on his head and the blood he has lost," Dr. Pierce remarked in his usual off-hand manner. "And," he said emphatically, "if you aren't in his room within two minutes, Melanie, he will be bursting out here headache and all to make sure you are all right!"

Making a dash for the bedroom, Melanie stopped short to toss over her shoulder at the men sitting by the table, "Watch Sara for a moment, will you please?" and catching Simon Young's raised brow, she added meaningfully, "Please, Peter."

The friendly driver's brief nod sent her scurrying into the next room. Lying on the bed, watching the door intently, Tom smiled briefly as she entered, his smile turning to a grimace of pain as he spoke. "I was afraid they were lying to me when they said you were safe. I'm sorry, Melanie, I didn't protect you at all, did I?"

Swallowing hard at the emotion choking her throat, Melanie ran to the bed to throw her arms around his neck and kiss his cheek lightly. "Tom, you were wonderful, showing them that you weren't afraid. Someone just crept up behind you and hit you when you weren't looking. It was an unfair thing to do, and you mustn't blame yourself. Mr. Young happened to be passing by and sent them away." At Tom's downcast expression, Melanie added vigorously, "But he had a gun and that's the only reason he was successful while you were not!"

Slowly Tom glanced toward the door, saying begrudgingly under his breath, "Thank you for helping Melanie, Mr. Young."

Melanie's head snapped around to notice for the first time that Simon Young had followed her into the room and had heard her brief dismissal of his rescue. She flushed brightly in that moment, realizing she had never thanked Simon Young for having helped her.

Turning back to Tom, Melanie again kissed his cheek. "I'd better go now, Tom, I think it would be best if you rested for a while. I'll be back later."

Nodding sleepily, Tom closed his eyes, and all others left. Only Martha remained to keep a watchful eye on her son's condition.

"I'd like to add my thanks to Tom's before I leave, Mr. Young." Dr. Pierce politely extended his hand. "This young lady has been maligned too often in this town by people who have allowed their jealousy to become obsessions. Of course," he said, lifting a gray, bushy eyebrow to cast Melanie a speculative glance, "she has not always been too wise in her actions, but nothing she had done was with malicious intent, contrary to the vicious slander repeated against her. And," he added in a softer tone, his eyes misting lightly, "she brought a very dear friend of mine more happiness than he had ever known."

"Certainly no thanks are necessary, Dr. Pierce." Simon Young's tone was gracious as he accepted the doctor's hand.

The doctor's burly figure disappeared around the corner of the yard, and Melanie turned back toward Simon Young, extremely conscious of her unforgivable behavior. Glancing toward Sara, who was contentedly pulling on Peter's long, white mustache, she said, self-consciously avoiding his eyes, "Mr. Young, would you step into the dining room with me for a moment? I would like to speak with you privately."

His amused, "Most certainly, Melanie," caused another brief flare of irritation on her part, and she berated herself mentally, Why do you allow him to annoy you so? You owe this man a debt of gratitude and should certainly be able to control your reactions to him for another few hours until he is gone.

Once the dining room door was closed behind them, Melanie found herself at a loss for words. Under the intense scrutiny of those translucent blue eyes, she was suddenly aware of her disheveled appearance, and raised her hand self-consciously to her hair. In the struggle, it had fallen free from the tidy bun she had adopted in an attempt at a more sedate appearance, and was hanging down her back in a shimmering disarray of riotous curls. Certainly her somber marketing dress made her look more like the little gray wren he had remarked on the first time he had seen her, and her eyes were probably puffed and her nose red from suppressed tears, also. All in all, feeling quite the ugly duckling under his keen appraisal, she experienced a hot flare of defiance.

Who is he to stand there in his spotless dress, she thought, eyeing his faultless maroon jacket and still immaculate tan waistcoat and britches, and assess me so openly? I owe him a word of thanks and nothing more, and I need not bow to his condescension! Unknowingly, anger returned the brilliant glow to her amber eyes and the color to her cheeks, and contrary to his calm facade, Simon's heart began pounding disturbingly.

Perhaps those women are right, he thought idly, staring down into the heated amber orbs. She surely must have the power to bewitch, because bewitched I am, and enjoying every moment of it!

Casually he inquired aloud, in a tone that only provoked her further, "Is there something you wish to say to me, Melanie?"

"Yes, there is." Melanie's own tone imitated his

imperious manner, unknowingly amusing him further. "I know you must be anxious to be on your way. My problems have detained you far too long already, I'm sure. But I would like to thank you for coming to my rescue. Were it not for you," she began to falter, the horror of her experience returning momentarily to tighten the words in her throat, "I'm, I'm sure I would now be thoroughly disfigured." Suddenly seeming to realize the extent of the debt she owed this irritating man, she raised her hand unconsciously to her cheek and said sincerely, "I owe you more than I can ever repay."

The cold blue eyes searched her face for a moment, and adjudging her sincere, he said dismissingly, "Enough said. It was my pleasure, Melanie, I assure you. But I am interested now in what you intend to do."

"Do?"

"Yes, surely you don't intend to stay here, until those wretches can work up their courage to attack you again? Tom is a good boy, but you know he can be of no real help to you. Do you expect that Stephen Hull will return to you?"

Stunned, Melanie gasped, "What do you know of Stephen Hull?"

"Melanie," Simon Young whispered softly, "I know everything there is to know about Stephen Hull and you—"

"But how . . . why?" Melanie stammered.

"I must confess, Melanie," Simon exhaled his breath dramatically, "I have not found you an easy person to forget. I have spent many long, pleasant hours reliving my experience at your window, and later in your room." All note of falseness fell away from his voice, and the hint of passion that deepened his tone set Melanie's face aflame as he stated simply, "You are by far quite the most beautiful woman I have ever seen, Melanie. I made it my business to keep track of you, and when Asa Parker died, I had intended visiting you after an initial period of mourning, but you did not mourn very long, my dear."

"That's where you're wrong, Mr. Young," Melanie interrupted angrily. "I did, and still do mourn Asa. I loved him very much."

Looking deeply into her eyes, he whispered surprisedly, "I believe you really did, but in any case," he continued, "before two months had passed you had taken up with Stephen Hull."

Melanie lowered her head. She was not proud of her association with Steve, especially now that she realized he had never truly loved her.

"But he left you, didn't he, dear?" Not waiting for a response, Simon continued. "Asa Parker's will has still not been settled, and probably will not be settled for months, or perhaps years to come. The town has turned against you because of your transgressions. You are truly in mortal danger. Now I ask you again, Melanie," he said pointedly, "Do you expect Stephen Hull will return to you?"

Taking a deep breath, Melanie responded honestly, "No, I don't. And if he did, I wouldn't take him back. I truly believed he loved me, but he did not. It's finished."

"Then I will repeat my other question. What do you intend to do?"

"Do? What can I do? I have no money, no place to go. I can't run away, not with Sara to care for. I must stay here and take my chances." A sudden picture of her dark future caused a chill to slip down her spine, and her slender frame gave a convulsive shudder.

"Yes, you do right to shudder at your bleak future, Melanie," Simon said, accurately reading her thoughts, "But you do have one alternative."

"I do? And what is that?"

"I have a proposition to make you."

"A proposition?" Melanie's brow raised questioningly.

"Yes, Melanie," he laughed, amused by her openly suspicious expression. "A thoroughly reprehensible but straightforward proposition. I would like you to be my mistress."

"Your mistress!"

"That's what I said. But first I must know one thing. Do you have a tendresse for that simple boy, Tom?"

"A tendresse?"

"Yes, a tendresse. Please desist from repeating my words, Melanie," he said impatiently, "I would like to hear your answer, not a reiteration of my own question!"

Suppressing her own irritation, Melanie answered in a clipped voice, "Tom is like a brother to me. I love him dearly, but as someone would love a dear child—"

"Which is what he is, yes, I know, Melanie." His tone softened. "And I apologize for speaking to you so harshly. Sometimes," he faltered, obviously uncomfortable in an apology, "my anxiety expresses

244

itself in sharpness."

"Anxiety? Why should you be anxious on my account?"

Again he stared into her face. It seemed inconceivable but she was sincere. "You really don't know, do you? I was anxious because I have been unable to get you out of my mind since the moment I first saw you, even disguised as a plain little wren, but once I had seen you in your true magnificence, Melanie, I was lost. I have thought of and desired you these many, long months, and no other woman has been successful in driving you from my thoughts. I do not profess love for you, Melanie. Truly, I don't believe such an emotion actually exists between a man and woman. I am married, and have been for eight years. My wife no longer shares my bed, an arrangement we both find quite satisfactory. I have had many mistresses, and will probably have many more, but I will take care of you and your child. During our association you will live in a house of your own, which I will visit from time to time. I will be generous financially, and when our liaison is over, you will be in a position where your child and you will be financially secure. When I am not with you, your life is yours to do with as you see fit, with one restriction. I must make the qualification that you see no other men during our association . . . but do not ask the same of me in return." With a cryptic smile, he added jokingly, "I must, after all, have the upper hand somewhere in this arrangement!"

Astounded at his openness, Melanie stood with her mouth agape, her eyes wide, and for the first time since the early moments of their first meeting, Simon

Young began to laugh. The change that came over his features was quite pleasant, and Melanie remarked with a small smile, "I'm glad I give you pleasure, Mr. Young."

Slowly the smile faded, and he said quite seriously, "I know we could give each other much pleasure, Melanie. I am very certain of that." Gently taking her hand, he said quietly, "I must ask you to give me your answer today, Melanie. I have a very important appointment which I have already put off too long. Others have gone ahead of me, and await my arrival. What do you say, Melanie, will you come with me?"

"How can you expect me to decide such an important issue so quickly?" Melanie's response showed her irritation.

"Quite easily, I think. Just consider the alternatives. You say you love Tom like a brother, yet he barely escaped death today in your defense. You are no doubt fond of Martha. Should something happen to Tom, she would be alone. And what of Sara? Do you want her to be exposed to that old hag's viciousness? If you stay here, will anything change? Do you not owe it to all those you love to absent yourself from this place? And finally, do you stand any chance of leaving in safety and comfort for your child and yourself without taking advantage of my offer?"

There were long moments of silence while Melanie considered all Simon Young had said. It was all true, and she had long since decided she must leave Salisbury. If she refused this opportunity, would she have another before something drastic happened?

But to be on such close physical terms with someone she barely knew.

Keeping his eyes glued on Melanie's expressive face, Simon felt a certain softening inside him. She was so young. Gently he touched her cheek with the tips of his fingers, whispering lightly as he did, "Surely you know, Melanie, that I would never hurt you."

His sensitivity to her feelings was the deciding factor. Taking a deep breath, she directed a steady golden gaze into his eyes and said firmly, "Yes, Mr. Young, I'll go, Sara and I will go with you."

Hesitating only a moment, he corrected gently, "Yes, *Simon*."

Chapter 5

"I still cannot understand why you would not allow me to pack any of my things to bring along with me," Melanie whispered over the steady rumble of the coach. The poor roads over which they had been traveling for the last few hours had bumped and jolted them continually, and she dared not raise her voice for fear of waking Sara, who had spent those hours in an annoyingly fretful mood. Finally, in the late hours of the afternoon, the restless child had fallen asleep, allowing her mother the comfort of laying her down on the seat beside her and resting the weary arms that had held her all afternoon.

"There certainly was no need for such haste that I could not be allowed to pack Sara's clothes as well as my own!" Melanie continued speaking despite the fact that Simon Young in no way acknowledged her whispered comments. Instead, he continued gazing out the window, inspiring in Melanie a desire to take his well-clad shoulders in her hands and shake them vigorously. Deciding on another tactic instead, she said coyly, "Well, I suppose you will be the one to suffer far more than I in the long run. It is, after all, at least two days travel to New York, is it not? After wearing these same clothes for that length of time, Sara and I may begin to offend your delicate sensibilities."

Hiding a small, victorious smile, Melanie then moved her attention to the passing landscape, realizing full well that Simon Young had finally turned his head in her direction. Speaking in a detached manner, he answered her coolly.

"As to your first comment, Melanie, yes, it was necessary that we leave with the most possible haste. After your prolonged goodbyes, it was already approaching two hours past noon. It was of the utmost importance that we spend the remainder of the daylight hours on the road, or be forced to spend the night in exceptionally inferior accommodations. The inn I wished to reach required at least five hours traveling time. At our present rate of travel, we should be there by nightfall."

Pausing briefly for effect in the manner Melanie found so exceptionally irritating, he smiled, satisfied she had finally deigned to tear her glance from the window and was giving him her complete attention. "In response to your second comment, Melanie, you need not worry about clothing for the journey. You will find everything you and Sara will need in a trunk fastened in the rear of the coach."

Too surprised to hide her amazement, Melanie asked unbelievingly, "Were you so very sure I would accept your proposition? Had you no doubts—"

"Melanie, dear," he said patiently, "I told you I was fully aware of the conditions under which you were living. My high opinion of your good sense gave me all the assurance I needed." Simon Young looked casually into the wide golden eyes of the woman facing him, knowing full well that the truth was the exact reverse of his statement. In the short time it had taken Melanie to make her decision, he had suffered a torment of uncertainty, and her consent had given him more pleasure than he had experienced in many years. Their precipitous departure had, in fact, been a result of his fear that she would change her mind, more than the excuse he had delivered so coolly.

"Thirdly, Melanie," he offered nonchalantly, "I don't recall having mentioned we were on our way to New York."

"But . . . I assumed . . . I thought . . ." Melanie stammered in surprise, finally regaining her composure to state slowly, "I remember your statement distinctly, the one you made when you first appeared at our door." Mimicking his officious tone, she continued, "'I am Simon Young, a representative of Governor Tryon of the colony of New York.'"

"And so I was, my dear, but you are a bit behind the times, you know. Governor Tryon was recalled to England in February of this year."

"Well, why didn't you tell me we weren't going to New York?"

"My dear," was the condescending reply, "you never asked."

A flash of temper sent the color flying into Melanie's face. Make sport of her, would he? Satisfying herself to pound emphatically on his knee with her small fist, when she would have preferred to pound the smug expression from his face, Melanie ejaculated angrily, "I demand to be told immediately where you intend taking my daughter and myself!"

When her only answer was a slight raising of his aristocratic eyebrow, she jerked herself to the edge of her seat and pushed her face into his to stare directly into his eyes. "If you do not tell me immediately, Mr. Youn—*Simon*, I will take my daughter, jump from this coach, and walk all the way back to Salisbury!"

Sitting almost nose to nose with the annoying Simon Young, angry amber eyes staring directly into frosty blue ones, she waited defiantly for his reply, only to be stunned when a small smile cracked his enigmatic expression. Shaking his head wonderingly, he said with a laugh, "Yes, Melanie, I believe you would, wouldn't you?"

When she did not answer, he continued easily, "I don't think such drastic measures will be necessary, Melanie. I did tell you I had a very important appointment I must keep. That appointment is in Philadelphia, and will necessitate my remaining there for some time. I maintain a residence in

251

Philadelphia, as my business often brings me there, and I have secured a very nice house that is convenient to both my residence and the area where I will conduct my business. Now, does that explanation suffice, my dear?"

Slightly embarrassed at her own behavior, Melanie inquired politely, "What is your business, Simon?"

"I own and operate a shipping company."

"And this business keeps you in Philadelphia so much of the time?"

"The pressing business I speak of this time, Melanie, is a meeting of the Second Continental Congress. It was scheduled to convene this week, and I had promised to lend my support and advice, but, other personal matters suddenly seemed to take precedence . . ." He touched her cheek gently in a disarming gesture, his eyes flicking for a moment to her soft lips a second before his voice became completely impersonal again. "Now, tell me, Melanie, are there any more questions you would like to ask?"

"I have heard of the Continental Congress, the first one last year. Stev—Steve was a member of the Committee of Correspondence with some of Ethan Allen's other men. It doesn't seem to me that the Congress accomplished very much."

"But it did, my dear. Its conclusions were strictly upheld. Its formation of the Continental Association forbade importing English goods, or export of our goods to England. Since the trouble at Lexington and Concord, there is talk of authorizing privateers, tossing all trade restrictions to the winds, resuming traffic with foreign countries. I am acquainted with all four of New York's representatives, Messrs. Floyd, Lewis, Livingston and Morris, and they have asked for my consultation in the matters where I have expertise while the Congress is in session. Of course, I agreed."

Smiling suddenly, Simon leaned back in his seat. "You will enjoy Philadelphia, Melanie. It is one of the few centers of culture in our colonies, like no city I'm sure you have ever seen. It is unfortunate that the Continental Association of the last Congress also opted to discourage plays and other entertainments. David Douglass had no choice but to take his theatrical troupe to Jamaica, or I could have taken you to the theater. Oh, it was not as grand as Europe's theater, to be sure, but it was stimulating entertainment." Chuckling lightly, Simon continued, "But Philadelphia still manages some entertainment, you will see."

Suddenly moving forward in his seat, Simon took Melanie's two small hands in his and whispered softly, "You have much to look forward to, I promise you, Melanie."

Before she could respond, their attention was drawn by the jerking halt of the coach and Peter's voice as he called inside, "One of the horses seems to have picked up a stone, Mr. Young. Would you like to take a few minutes exercise while I remove it?"

"Yes, we would, Peter."

Without a word, Simon stepped down from the coach and swung Melanie to the ground. From there they separated for a few moments privacy, and when Melanie returned, she faced again the former cool, self-possessed Simon Young. All trace of that brief, elusive warmth had disappeared as rapidly as it had appeared.

Daylight was waning rapidly and Sara's tired, hungry moans were beginning to settle into a series of long, annoying whines, when the coach finally turned off the main road. Within moments, they were drawing up before a large, well-kept inn.

"Well, a bit behind schedule, but here we are." An obvious note of relief rang in Simon Young's voice, and despite her own exhaustion, Melanie was secretly amused. Simon Young may have had many mistresses, but she was certain few of them had put him through the rigors of traveling with an exuberant, and now very cranky, one-year-old child. Her eyes flew covertly to Simon Young's fawn britches and the large stain that spread over the center of both thighs, and she struggled to maintain a sober expression as he graciously assisted her and Sara from the coach. She was also certain he regretted relieving her briefly of Sara's weight during the journey, when Sara took the opportunity to relieve herself while she sat so innocently on his spotless, well-fitted britches. The large, dark spot was so incongruous with the almost immaculate appearance he had otherwise managed to maintain during the long, dusty trip, that Melanie, almost convulsed with laughter as they approached the door to the inn, barely managed to conceal her widening grin in Sara's fiery curls.

Stopping abruptly in mid-stride, Simon faced her and demanded coolly, "Do you find something amusing, Melanie?"

Gulping loudly, she managed to squeeze out the

obvious lie, "No, Simon, no."

Pausing only a moment longer to send her another frigid glance, Simon preceded her into the inn to speak briefly with the keeper. A few moments later he returned and, motioning to a young girl following expectantly at his elbow, he said politely, "This young lady will show you to your room and will assist you in feeding and preparing the child for sleep. After you have freshened up and changed your clothes, I will meet you in the public room for supper. Shall we say within twenty minutes?" Not waiting for her reply, he continued, "Peter will bring your traveling case."

His orders given, he turned on his heel, leaving Melanie to stomp up the stairs at the heels of the energetic young girl. "Twenty minutes! What am I, a miracle worker?" she mumbled under her breath. "I am supposed to bathe and change Sara, prepare her for bed, and then bathe and clothe myself and meet him downstairs in twenty minutes! Well, I hope he's a patient man . . . and not too hungry tonight, because it's my feeling that he's about to have a long wait!"

Upon their arrival in the room, the young maid, shyly introducing herself as Mary, took complete and efficient control of Sara with unexpected ease, bathing the tired child patiently, and as the food arrived, began feeding her with unusual forbearance. Freed to complete her own toilette, Melanie had bathed and brushed her hair to a fiery luster with time to spare. Sara had already been clothed in a fine lawn night rail taken from the traveling case delivered by Peter, and ready to don her change of clothing, Melanie apprehensively opened the handsome leather case. A low appreciative gasp escaped her lips as her eyes touched on the lovely, forest green gown lying atop. Digging down a little further, she came upon a fine lawn chemise, trimmed in delicate lace, miscellaneous other undergarments and—suddenly her heart stopped cold. At the bottom lay a fragile lace night rail, a light, airy transparent veil that caused her heart to begin a nervous pounding. So preoccupied had she been with Sara's fretting for most of the day, that she had not had time to speculate on the hours after dark. Did Simon expect to share her bed tonight? But he had arranged for separate rooms. Would he visit her later during the night? Whatever had possessed her to agree to such an arrangement?

Her stomach's low, rolling growl of hunger interrupted her raging thoughts, and purposefully covering the lacy wisp, Melanie removed the new chemise and gown. It was too late now for regrets. She had made her choice, and would have to see it through.

Within minutes, Melanie was standing before the mirror, appraising her appearance. She certainly could not fault Simon Young for his taste. The dark green of the gown was a perfect foil for her auburn tresses and creamy skin. The neckline, cut in a deep square, was trimmed with several rows of white lace, which lay provocatively against the high, rounded swells of her breasts. Cut as if it had been made to her exact measurements, the bodice dipped to a low, snug point at the waist, where it gathered to flare out gracefully to her ankles. The sleeves, tightly hugging her slender shoulders and arms to the elbow, burst into graduated tiers of white lace that hung elegantly almost to her wrists. On her feet she wore soft green slippers, the exact shade of her dress, decorated around the instep with amber and green stones. In deference to her own individuality, Melanie had disdained the tightly bound hair style adopted by most matrons, and used the large green combs also provided in the case to sweep her hair back from her face in a center part, securing it just behind her ears and allowing the riotous shining curls to hang in a shimmering fall almost to her waist. Her sudden nervousness in realizing she must go down and face Simon Young alone for the first time, sent a bright flush to her face, adding to her beauty a natural luminescence that was reflected in her darkly fringed golden eyes.

Walking quietly to the chair where Mary rocked a gently nodding Sara in her arms, she lightly kissed the fiery curls before walking silently out the door, closing it carefully behind her.

Taking a deep breath, her heart thudding nervously in her breast, Melanie descended the steps in anxious haste, her glowing eyes scanning the noisy groups below for Simon's tall, spare frame. So intent was she in her purpose that she failed to notice the heads turning in her direction following the bobbing of her young, firm body and the gleaming bounce of shining curls against a narrow waist. She was a few feet from the bottom of the staircase when, failing to sight Simon amongst the milling group, her lively step slowed to a halt, and she hesitated, uncertain where to go from there. In a moment a craggy-faced, dark-haired stranger attired in well-worn buckskins, and armed with a definite twinkle in his eye, stepped forward smoothly.

"Little lady, you are a sight to soothe my weary eyes. If you have any trouble finding the fellow you're looking for, I volunteer my services right now. I haven't seen anyone that looks as good as you in—"

"Melanie!" A coldly familiar voice turned her head to meet a frigid stare emanating from the face of Simon Young as he advanced toward her. "You are late. I have secured a table for us. Quickly now," he admonished, extending his hand toward her, "the food will be arriving any minute."

Putting her hand in his, Melanie moved quickly to his side, blushing with a small, dimpled smile as the brawny backwoodsman winked boldly when she passed. Shooting the man a black stare, Simon urged her into the public room a bit less than gently, mumbling irritably under his breath while they walked.

"Why are you so angry, Simon?" Melanie demanded with an irritation of her own. "I was the one left to stand foolishly on the steps until you came forward to claim me at last. I should be the one who is angry!"

Upon reaching the table, Melanie plopped herself down angrily on the chair Simon stiffly held for her, the soft swells of her breasts putting an alarming momentary strain on her revealing decolletage, and turning a few more appreciative eyes in her direction. Seating himself across from her, Simon rested his elbow on the table and covered his eyes with his hand for a moment in an obvious attempt to control his annoyance as a muscle in his cheek twitched revealingly. A few moments later he removed his hand and snapped quietly, "I could tell the exact moment you began to descend that staircase, Melanie. Nothing could hush a room filled with noisy men more effectively than your . . . *uninhibited* step! Melanie, has no one ever advised you to walk more sedately?"

Angered at what she felt was an unwarranted criticism, Melanie hissed in return, "You are neither my father nor my husband, Simon Young! You will please not give me orders in that patronizing tone. If you find me so distasteful, I cannot understand why you extended your . . . invitation."

Pausing for a moment to look into Melanie's lovely, animated face, Simon adversely felt a surge of the same unexplainable attraction that had drawn him to this spirited little vixen the first moment of their meeting and a softening of his own impatience.

"Melanie, dear," his voice surprisingly gentle, he reached his hand across the table to cover the small fist clenched so tensely a few inches away, "it is not that I find you so distasteful. Quite the contrary, my dear. I find you far too delicious to conduct yourself so unconsciously in a manner that stirs a man's baser instincts. If there were a few more steps on that staircase, I fear I would have been forced to battle every red-blooded man in the inn for the pleasure of being at your side tonight."

Her eyes widening at Simon's generous explanation, Melanie quickly scanned the neighboring tables, to find herself the object of many heated male glances, and flushed brightly. Swallowing tightly, she managed a meager smile into those penetrating blue eyes before mumbling an indistinct, "Oh," and turned gratefully for the arrival of the food.

The meal was begun in virtual silence, Melanie's natural vivacity suffering a severe setback with the realization that so many eyes within the room seemed content to rest unalteringly on her person. Unaccustomed to such incessant attention, she became increasingly self-conscious of the neckline of her gown that seemed to dip a little lower with each and every forkful. After several surreptitious and unsuccesfull attempts to adjust it upward, Simon offered softly, "Melanie, dear, I in no way meant to make you uncomfortable with my comment about your appearance. You look extremely lovely, and even if you succeeded in hitching your decolletage up an inch or so higher, every man in the room would still keep his eyes upon you. The only way you would succeed in drawing their eyes from you would be to cover yourself completely from head to toe in a huge sack."

Simon's words drew Melanie's eyes to his and a small dimple danced its way across her cheek as she attempted to conceal the pleasure his words had given her.

Holding her gaze tightly with his own, he continued softly, "Such drastic measures, besides being impractical, would not please me in the least. I am thoroughly enjoying the view afforded me each time you reach for another morsel of food, or piece of bread. I have not enjoyed a meal so well in months . . . Melanie, you are very good for my digestion!"

Laughing softly at her shocked expression, he gave

her a short wink, shocking her even more, so completely out of keeping was it with his aristocratic bearing. After a few minutes of stunned silence, she lowered her head, devoting her attention completely to the food on her plate.

From that point on, Simon also contributed to the silence between them, slightly shocked at his own behavior. How many years had it been since he had given a wench a cocky wink or spoken so gently to a woman from the heart, without the pretentions and guardedness that had become so much a part of his nature? There was something about this golden temptress—an aura of innocence, although he knew she could not be so innocent, that nevertheless stirred within him a tenderness he could not recall having experienced before with any woman, even his wife. Shaking his head slightly, he reached for his tankard. He was going to have to be cautious with this little miss. He doubted very much if this game would be played according to his usual rules. There was nothing usual about Melanie, nothing at all.

The conclusion of the meal was reached in almost total silence while Melanie's anxieties toward the night before her grew. Taking her arm in a casual gesture as they climbed the stairs, Simon could feel the slight trembling of her body, and sensing her apprehension, fought an overwhelming wave of tenderness toward this beautiful girl-woman whose future was so completely within his hands. Stopping as they neared the door to her room, he grasped her shoulders firmly and turned her to stare upward at his serious, pensive expression.

"Sleep well, Melanie. I have instructed the inn-

261

keeper to have the maid awaken you in the morning and assist in preparing the child for the day's journey. I will knock on the door when it is time to go down for breakfast." With a small smile, he added lightly, "We will practice walking down the steps in a sedate manner—together."

Lowering his head, he pressed a light kiss on her parted lips before turning abruptly and walking down the hall to his room.

Each of the following days of their journey was conducted in much the same manner as the first, the only exceptions being that Simon began sharing the burden of Sara on the second day of travel, realizing the strain the active, curious child was on her increasingly weary mother. Preparing his lap cautiously with a covering, and ignoring Melanie's small, knowing grin, he took Sara's sturdy little body onto it, warily at first, as unsure of her reaction as he was of his own. He was unaccustomed to dealing with children, having had none of his own and no attraction whatsoever to those of his friends, and eyed the small, pert face turned so curiously up to his. Up to this point, he had not consciously looked at the child, and really seeing her for the first time, he realized with some amazement that hers was a perfect miniature replica of her mother's face. Unexpectedly, Sara boosted herself to a standing position on his lap, gripping his jacket firmly with one chubby hand against the bump and sway of the coach while the other openly explored his face.

"Sara!" Melanie's voice held a sharp reproach, snapping the curly head around to her mother's face.

"Don't reprimand the child, Melanie." Despite his natural reserve, Simon was as curious about the child as she was about him and watched solemnly as she turned slowly back to resume her close perusal of his face. Beginning a steady babble of baby talk, Sara trailed her hand down his cheek to his mouth, suddenly poking a stubby finger into the deep cleft in his chin and giggling profusely. Unable to suppress his own smile at her inane chatter and spontaneous mirth, he felt an unfamiliar flush of pleasure as the irrepressible child took both his cheeks in her hands and kissed him unexpectedly on the side of his slender, aristocratic nose. Dimpling precociously into his face, she continued her babbling, completely baffling and captivating him at the same time.

Watching his bemused expression, Melanie felt the first thawing of her feelings for the enigmatic Simon Young and ventured softly, "Sara was hopelessly spoiled by Tom and Josh. She is accustomed to male attention. I think she attempted to reward you for your smile."

Consciously noting that Melanie had not included the name Steve in Sara's list of admirers, he directed his sober comment to Sara. "Aha! Buying smiles with kisses at such an early age. Sara, that is not a wise practice to assume." Then, firmly seating her on his lap, he directed his attention once again to the passing landscape, as if she had ceased to exist.

Regretting her brief mellowing toward the unpredictable man staring in such a detached manner out the coach window, Melanie mumbled none too softly under her breath, "Insufferable man!" and then directed a brilliant, encouraging smile into the face of her bewildered child.

By the third day of travel, Melanie seriously began to question the wisdom of her hasty decision. She was heartily sick of the bump and jolt of the coach as it continued on the seemingly endless roads and had begun to miss both Martha's wide, pleasant face and Tom's lopsided grin. Tom had not taken her leaving lightly, but, surprisingly, Martha had not tried to persuade her to stay. And Josh . . . he would be surprised to find her gone when he returned and perhaps a little relieved. She had been nothing but trouble to him from the first, but he had been a true friend. As for Steve . . . a bittersweet pain knifed through her, it was best she was not there when he returned.

Simon had become increasingly preoccupied as the journey progressed, frowning darkly a good portion of the time. After his initial kindnesses the first night of travel his treatment of her, although still kind and considerate, had become extremely formal. He even treated Sara with a kind of light formality, although Melanie had to concede Sara was accepting his treatment in a far better spirit than she.

The closer they came to Philadelphia, the larger loomed Melanie's ignorance of the city, and she began to speculate how she would fit into the society there, if, in fact, she was expected to greet society in her position as Simon's mistress. Shooting him a furtive glance, only to find him still deeply engrossed in his thoughts, she hesitantly broke the silence between them.

"When do you think we'll reach Philadelphia, Simon?"

"Probably before noon tomorrow."

There was a spontaneous tightening in her stomach. As uncomfortable as the journey had proved to be, it still required nothing of her except to endure. When she reached Philadelphia, she was certain it would be another matter.

"I know very little of Philadelphia, Simon, except that it is a very large city. What is it like?"

Slowly turning to direct his full attention to her, he looked vaguely annoyed, as if resenting being disturbed, but he answered in a civil manner.

"Yes, it is a very large city, the largest in the colonies, and I have already told you that it is, or I should say was, the cultural center of the colonies as well. Congress' decision to dispense with frivolity has managed to put a damper on that aspect of life. Still, the very fact that the Continental Congress meets there brings so many men of trained taste and intellect to the city that the Congress is a cultural event in itself. Men like the physician, Benjamin Rush; Arthur Middleton of South Carolina, who is a Latin and Greek scholar, and incidentally, reads Horace during recess; James Wilson of Pennsylvania, formerly a Latin tutor of the College of Philadelphia; Thomas Jefferson, who is a serious amateur of books, music and poetry; and John Adams, who is probably the most learned man there in both ancient and modern literature. Even the old English poets are familiar to him. And of course, Benjamin Franklin."

Melanie was beginning to feel more and more the country bumpkin as he spoke, realizing the acute void in her education. Still, her mind was stimulated and her curiosity grew. "You have said you expect to spend some time in Philadelphia, Simon. Will you stay for the duration of the meeting of Congress?"

"If I feel I can be of assistance. It has already been in progress for over a week. I am anxious to test the climate of the meeting. There has been much talk of breaking with the Mother Country, but most delegates have been reluctant so far to take the step. I, myself, am not certain if it would be wise at this point, although I do feel that the Regent is completely ignorant of our needs here, and probably, in all honesty, could not care less. To him, I fear, we are merely wayward children, whom he must chastise for our disobedience. And, Melanie, if he does not change his manner of thinking, I also fear his children will desert him to strike out on their own."

Stopping momentarily, an expression of extreme sadness covering his lean countenance, Simon allowed his gaze to move slowly over Melanie's bright, interested face. Recognizing her open, inquisitive mind and her eagerness to fill the gaps in her education, he hesitated as she waited for him to continue before saying, "Well, I think we have discussed current events sufficiently for the time being, Melanie. When we reach Philadelphia, if you wish to broaden your knowledge any further, I will see that you are furnished with newspapers and copies of the *Pennsylvania Magazine*, which Tom Paine assists in editing. It is extremely well done, and quite informative." Hesitating a moment, he asked bluntly, "You do read, don't you?"

"Of course I read!" Melanie exclaimed indignantly. Did he think only the people in New York and points south were educated? "And I shall be happy to accept those newspapers and the *Pennsylvania Magazine!*" Raising her chin a notch higher, she finished silently, And I'll be damned before I give you an opportunity to talk down to me again, no matter how my curiosity teases!

Chapter 6

"If you please, Madame, you will turn this way again." Responding automatically to Madame Boniel's instructions, Melanie faced the mirror, her eyes wandering absentmindedly over the unfinished garment being fitted to her slenderly curving figure. She had been twisting and turning to Madame Boniel's instructions for two days and was beginning to tire of being jabbed, pricked and pinched in the name of fashion. Never having been fitted for a complete custom wardrobe before, she had not realized it would be such a chore. But now, in her third day of residence in the rather elegant house on Philadelphia's Walnut Street, she was beginning to realize there would be many things she had not anticipated when she accepted Simon Young's rather vague proposition.

First and foremost, she had not expected to be deposited like a sack of potatoes inside the front door of an unfamiliar house with a hasty introduction to the servants only seconds before Simon Young took an unceremonious leave to "attend to pressing affairs."

"Those affairs must be pressing indeed," Melanie thought again, a frown of annoyance knitting her slender brows, for she had not seen him since, and were it not for his emissaries, she would have been certain he had forgotten her existence entirely. But he left her with no doubt that he fully intended to fulfill his portion of their bargain. The bright, cheerful morning room was bright with sun, and she and Sara had barely finished their breakfasts the day after their arrival when Madame Boniel and her industrious entourage invaded. Taking up temporary quarters in her bedroom, the small, quick-moving French-woman had monopolized Melanie's entire morning choosing sketches, fabrics and trims for her ward-robe. She had brought along with her a number of delicately embroidered garments for Sara, explaining with profuse apologies that her ignorance of Sara's exact size had precluded any further work in her behalf. Also contained in the towering pile of boxes covering her bed and spilling over onto the floor and any other available vacant corner was a breathtaking array of flimsy night rails, banyans, and slippers, all of which the Madame informed her candidly had been ordered by Simon Young prior to her arrival. Stunned into speechlessness, Melanie had merely managed a feeble nod in the woman's direction as she marveled again at "Monsieur" Young's monumental presumption!

Upon Madame's departure at midday, Peter arrived with a large package containing weeks of back issues of the Philadelphia newspaper and the *Pennsylvania Magazine,* along with other periodicals on fashion. With a seething curiosity to find out more about the affairs that occupied Simon's time so completely, she had plunged into the intimidating stack, rousing herself guiltily hours later to spend some time with a fretting Sara.

This morning Madame Boniel arrived for the first fitting, her efficient staff miraculously having cut and pinned her entire wardrobe! In response to Melanie's surprised reaction, the fluttering Frenchwoman had explained with a serious frown, "But Monsieur Young has specifically stated all the gowns are to be finished within the week. He will not countenance a delay. It is most fortunate, Madame," she added with a small smile, "that the monsieur has approved your choice of styles and fabrics with very few exceptions. He was quite upset that you had not chosen a riding habit, but he has selected one from among my sketches. As usual, his taste was flawless. I am sure you will be pleased." Suddenly noticing Melanie's annoyance, she inquired politely, "Is something wrong, Madame?"

"Do you mean you were instructed to have Mr. Young approve my selections before you began work?"

"But of course, Madame!" The woman's narrow brows registered surprise at what she obviously felt was a foolish question. "It is the standard procedure whenever the Monsieur employs my services. He is a man of very particular tastes . . . and an impeccable sense of style."

"And I suppose it was beyond his comprehension that I might be capable of choosing adequately without his help?" Melanie added haughtily, anger flushing her face at the pair's presumption.

Appearing momentarily flustered, Madame Boniel finally answered, avoiding Melanie's heated glare. "It is not for me to say, Madame. I merely follow the Monsieur's orders."

Now, turning once again at the Madame's request, the Frenchwoman's words were echoing hauntingly in her mind. Tossing a look at her already elegant reflection, Melanie warned her splendid image mentally. Don't become too accustomed to all this luxury, Melanie. If Simon Young thinks to employ the same high-handed attitude he has obviously used with all his other mistresses, your stay may be a rather short one.

The fourth day of Melanie's residence at Walnut Street brought her the first three completed gowns and accessories from the extensive collection, as well as her first message from Simon Young. Her hand trembling despite a deliberate attempt to appear unconcerned before the servants, Melanie slowly

271

opened the envelope.

My dear Melanie,

It is my sincere hope that you feel sufficiently rested from our rather exhausting journey to Philadelphia to be able to accompany me tonight to the commencement exercises at the College of Philadelphia. It is usually a rather entertaining as well as educational affair, which I think you will find interesting.

I understand from Madame Boniel that a portion of your wardrobe has been completed, and in the event you are unsure as to the manner of dress for the occasion, the blue organdy should do quite nicely.

Until tonight at seven, I remain sincerely,
Simon

Suppressing a slight resurgence of irritation at his instructions as to her dress, Melanie carefully refolded the note and turning abruptly, started back up the steps to her room. So he was coming tonight at last. Suddenly inundated by a flood of apprehension, Melanie fought to control the nervous tremors beginning to shake her slight frame. It would not do to allow the servants to become aware of her uncertainty. In the short time she had assumed the role of mistress of the rather stately red brick residence, she had come to realize that the servants watched her carefully, taking their cue from her attitude.

Mrs. Walters, the silent, middle-aged housekeeper, whose loyalties were obviously to Simon, apparently withheld judgment of Melanie pending an assessment of the state of affairs between Simon and herself, but Melanie had the feeling the woman considered her just another temporary occupant of the bedroom at the top of the stairs. Helga, the white-haired, red-faced cook, barely acknowledged her presence beyond a formal nod, and Rose and Molly, the two young maids, did their work efficiently with very little comment. Of them all, Melanie sensed the most warmth in Molly, and it was to her she had entrusted the care of Sara while she herself was otherwise occupied. But of the entire household, there was not a one with whom she was sufficiently at ease to share her apprehension.

In her three nights alone in the huge canopy bed in the impressive master bedroom, she had spent long hours reviewing, with conflicting emotions, the last three years of her life. Experiencing afresh all the painful emotions her daring inexperience had led her through, she began to feel that the shock and pain she had suffered at Steve's betrayal was a result of her unwillingness to accept their relationship as it was. Steve had been honest from the start. He did not love her, but she had waited, stubbornly naive, for the declaration of love that had never come.

But understanding still did not alleviate the pain coursing through her each time Steve's dark, brooding countenance was recalled to mind, and she had determined that she would not allow her emotions to run unchecked again. She would keep in mind from the beginning that her arrangement with Simon was of necessity and of a business nature, with each having their own obligation to fulfill. Since Simon appeared to be adhering to their contract with extreme generosity, if not without a firm sense of control, she in all honesty could do no less. Her only doubt as she reached the top of the staircase and turned toward her room, the trembling within her increasing alarmingly, was in her own ability to perform her portion of the pact . . . and in her ignorance of just exactly what her duties would entail. Shaking her most deeply at the present moment was her certainty that tonight all those questions would be answered.

At mid-afternoon while Melanie sought to divert her mind from the evening to come, a tall, imposing woman was ushered into the parlor.

"Mrs. Morganfield? I am Mrs. Bidsley. Mr. Young has retained me to dress your hair for this evening." Eyeing her abundant, gleaming tresses speculatively, the woman stated in a scathing manner, "Shall we begin immediately? I fear it will prove to be a lengthy task."

Irritated by the woman's authoritative manner, Melanie's tone was deliberately imperious. "How do you do, Mrs. Bidsley? And may I ask you a question?"

"Of course."

"Do you attend all Mr. Young's . . . lady friends?"

"Only those who do not have their own hairdressers, Madam."

"I see. Follow me, Mrs. Bidsley." Standing, Melanie proceeded toward the staircase, only to be brought up short by the woman's soft remark.

"Oh, I know the way, to be sure."

Installed a few moments later in front of the large vanity mirror in her bedroom, Melanie watched as the woman began efficiently unpacking the large case she carried, stacking the table high with a variety of jars and wire forms.

"What do you propose to do with those, Mrs. Bidsley?"

Melanie's question appeared to have taken the haughty woman off guard, and she replied hesitantly, "This is merely the pomatum we will need to stretch your hair over the wire shape while holding it fast; the powder and—"

"You needn't unpack any further, Mrs. Bidsley. They won't be needed."

"What?"

Interrupting with a firm glance into the woman's startled face, Melanie continued, "I will instruct you in the manner *I* wish my hair dressed, and none of those will be necessary."

"Mrs. Morganfield—"

"Shall we proceed, Mrs. Bidsley?"

Fidgeting nervously before her large bedroom mirror, Melanie appraised her appearance while shooting repeated glances over her shoulder at the mantel clock.

"Seven o'clock. Simon should be here any moment," she mumbled under her breath, a worried frown creasing her brow. If she was only as certain as she had pretended about the style in which she had instructed Mrs. Bidsley to dress her hair. Having taken an immediate dislike to the false, towering hairdoes favored by so many of the women in

Philadelphia, as well as the popular custom of powdering the hair, Melanie had hastily decided she would not be able to abide having greasy pomades stiffen and stretch her hair into monumental proportion. Instead, she had directed her hair to be rolled away from her face on the top and sides, forming a soft pompador that caught and reflected the glow of the room's soft lights. The remainder of the hair was wound in an expert manner into a turban effect behind the gleaming rise of hair, with two curls released to fall casually against her long, slender neck. Without her realization, the soft, upswept hairdo enhanced Melanie's fine facial structure, drawing attention to the huge, darkly lashed amber eyes glowing so brightly and the perfection of her delicate profile.

The startling amber of her eyes was matched perfectly in the silk of the gown that swirled gracefully about her ankles as she turned to view herself from another angle. The fine, black lace edging of the neckline dipped low in front to expose the creamy swells of her breasts and accent the smoothness of her skin, while providing a brilliant contrast for the light amber silk. The bodice hugged her body snugly to the waist with the sleeves clinging tightly to her slender arms as far as the elbow, where black lace showered out in a profusion of tiers, to hang gracefully to the wrist.

Her feet were encased in black satin high-heeled slippers, bearing a single embroidered amber rose on the instep, and in her shimmering auburn locks a small, black ostrich feather bobbed and weaved gracefully with her movements.

A soft knock at the door broke into Melanie's thoughts, and Molly's small elfin face peeked inside the door.

"Mrs. Morganfield, Mr. Young is here!"

Snatching up her beaded bag and black lace wrap, Melanie took a deep breath, ignoring the nervous tightening in her stomach, and without a word, proceeded slowly out the bedroom door and down the staircase. Not finding Simon in the hallway, Melanie proceeded into the parlor, and upon entering was surprised to find his back to her as he helped himself to a generous glass of port. But of course, she thought, laughing at her own stupidity, this is his own house after all.

The sound of her step in the doorway turned Simon in her direction, his usually guarded expression openly registering his appreciation. Slowly his eyes traveled the full length of her body, starting at the top of her brilliant auburn crown, sweeping downward to linger for a few sensuous seconds to caress the soft, white swells edged in black lace, and continuing slowly with considerable warmth to the tips of her black satin shoes. Carefully lowering his glass to the table, he turned and walked toward her to take her gently by the shoulders.

His voice husky, he whispered softly, "You are a vision, my dear . . . exquisite." Slowly he lowered his mouth to cover hers for a brief moment, laughing lightly at the flush that transfused her face at his unexpected compliment and kiss. The glacial blue eyes looking deeply into hers radiated a surprising warmth, and Melanie's heart quickened, surprising her with its response to his masculine appeal.

"Will you have a glass of wine with me before we leave, Melanie?"

"I'd like that, Simon."

Melanie's eyes followed his retreating figure with considerable interest. Madame Boniel had certainly summed him up perfectly. Even with her limited exposure to the styles of the day, it was obvious to Melanie that his sense of style was truly flawless. The black brocade coat fitted his broad, but slender build perfectly, falling to the knee just short of the startlingly white britches secured with jeweled buckles. His hose was of a fine white silk, and the sides of his black, brilliantly polished shoes were unbelievably fastened with jeweled buckles matching those at his knee. As he turned toward her, she noted a masterfully tied cravat, edged with delicate lace and a simple white waistcoat buttoned with jewels that caught the light as he walked. His dark brown hair tied to the back of his neck in a queue in his usual manner was unpowdered, and his general appearance exuded a powerful aura of masculinity that was unmistakable.

Stopping suddenly in mid-stride, two glasses of wine balanced carefully in his slender hands, Simon said softly, a trace of the old arrogance flashing in his unusual, light eyes, "If you have finished assessing my appearance, Melanie, I will continue forward."

With a small laugh at her undisguised spark of annoyance, he advanced to give her a glass and stand breathtakingly close. "Melanie, dear, you really must learn to guard your expressions more carefully. It was frightfully easy to read your thoughts just then."

"As easy as it was to read yours a few moments ago, Simon?"

Chuckling lightly at her bold response, Simon replied softly, "Perhaps. But that is not the way the game is played, my dear."

Raising the golden glow of her eyes to his in a slow sweep of long, dark lashes, Melanie replied softly, "Then perhaps we will play our game by different rules, Simon."

Hesitating a long moment before responding, Simon's face was suddenly serious, his gaze holding hers with increasing warmth. "Perhaps, Melanie . . . perhaps we will."

The streets outside the College of Philadelphia tingled with excitement as their carriage drew up, and the milling throng pressed to enter and be seated. Apprehension at her first appearance in a sophisticated society froze Melanie into sudden immobility as she viewed the unfamiliar scene with obvious wariness. Extending his hand in her direction, Simon said in a low voice, "Come now, Melanie. Shall we show this enlightened society that we have our own contribution to make with the most beautiful woman that has yet graced this rather astute gathering?"

Melanie's brilliant answering smile precluded comment as she stepped gracefully down the steps of the carriage. Walking in her most practiced, sedate manner, Melanie entered the hall on Simon's arm, a small thrill of pride surging through her when a quick assessment of the room brought her to the sudden realization that she was escorted by one of the most attractive men present. She was suddenly acutely aware that Simon's perfect grooming and almost regal bearing set him apart even in this accomplished, well-dressed crowd, and was immediately conscious that women of all ages were drawn to those startlingly light blue eyes in his thin, lightly tanned face, and the quick flash of warmth in the brief smiles he deigned to cast in their direction. Her almost constant irritation with his manner had previously made her oblivious to his attraction, and with a brief glance into his face, she suddenly began to view him in a completely new light, musing silently, Simon, why haven't I noticed it before? You are a true and accomplished rake!

Amused by her own belated realization, Melanie smiled lightly. Raising his brow in the manner so characteristic of him, Simon leaned down to whisper in her ear as they walked, "Will you allow me to share your private joke, Melanie?"

"Oh, I think not, Simon." True laughter sparked in her golden eyes. "I don't think you'd see the same humor in the situation as I."

Undeniably impressed as each step toward their seats seemed to draw another friendly greeting from within the crowd, Melanie acknowledged each with a small smile of her own, assessing the attention they drew as a mark of Simon's importance. Completely unaware that her unusual beauty brought many a distant friend forward to renew Simon's acquaintance, she was puzzled by Simon's unduly amused, derisive comments whispered quickly into her ear prior to the approach of many.

"Well, here comes old Charlie Blake . . . haven't exchanged a word with him in months."

"Well, I knew Bill Martingale wouldn't let an opportunity like this pass him by."

"If it isn't Fitzhugh Morris . . . I thought he had died!"

Taking her first opportunity, she whispered lightly, "What is it that you find so amusing, Simon?"

Her question was annoyingly dismissed with a brief glance and her own words of a few minutes before. "Oh, I doubt that you'd find the same amusement in the situation, Melanie."

In reality, with each brief conversation, Simon became more amused by the blatant curiosity so openly displayed about his beautiful companion while he easily answered their questions with the prefabrication Melanie and he had agreed upon for polite society.

"Yes, Mrs. Morganfield and her child will be spending some time at my Walnut Street address as my guests. Since the death of her husband a year ago, she has been at a great loss, and her family has sent her to Philadelphia in an attempt to take her mind from her grief," Simon whispered into yet another anxious ear, while observing with some annoyance Melanie's attempt to dislodge her hand from the grip of one of her more ardent admirers. Reaching out, he extended his hand in Melanie's direction, forcing the recalcitrant swain to relinquish his hold and, taking her small hand in his, he raised it lightly to his lips, unexpectedly eliciting from Melanie a bright flush. His smile widening, he leaned forward to whisper quietly, "Come, my dear. Shall we be seated? Should the crowd surrounding us widen any further, I fear we will be trampled in the crush. Let's leave them now to further speculation about the mysterious Mrs.

Morganfield." With a small wink, he led her to their seats and seated her grandly, enjoying immensely the envious stares aimed in his direction by Melanie's court of admirers.

A sudden blast of music interrupted Melanie's thoughts and drew her attention to the entrance of the graduates and the beginning of the exercises. Never having attended an affair of such intellectual magnitude before, Melanie's excitement continued to build with each new presentation, almost stealing her breath despite her unsuccessful attempts to match Simon's apparent indifference to the program.

Finding the ceremonies boringly similar to the previous year, Simon derived his enjoyment from watching the play of emotions across Melanie's beautiful face. At the conclusion of the students' Dialogue and Two Odes Set to Music, William Ellery and George Wythe took up a stylish correspondence, exchanging political opinions, verses, and personal opinions on Homer and Milton, further awing Melanie with their understanding of the diverse subjects. As her eyes widened, Simon's smile grew. He found her freshness exhilarating to his jaded tastes, adding yet another to the long list of unfamiliar emotions she had stirred in him since the first moment of their meeting, and found it truly puzzling that a young woman just out of girlhood could have such a disturbing effect on a man of his sophisticated tastes.

Turning unexpectedly in his direction, Melanie caught his speculative smile, and unable to contain herself, she whispered softly, "It is all so marvelous, isn't it, Simon? William Wythe is the noted jurist from Virginia, is he not? And William Ellery is a Harvard graduate as well as the colony of Rhode Island's representative to the Congress, isn't that so?"

Unwilling to spoil her obvious enjoyment, Simon stifled a biting reference to the reading material he had provided that hovered threateningly on his lips. She had obviously gone to great pains to assimilate as much of the material as possible, and he was deeply touched with her desire to impress him as well as her obviously quick mind.

"Yes, my dear. And there are many other men here tonight whose names you might recognize." Following the direction of his eyes, Melanie listened intently as he continued. "The Congress has attended en masse, you know. That portly, older gentleman with the unbound hair and kind face over there," he indicated with a nod of his head, "He is Benjamin Franklin."

"Oh, yes!" Melanie gasped, obviously impressed, "Of *Poor Richard's Almanac!*"

Once again suppressing a smile, he continued, "And over there . . . John Adams."

"Yes, a truly learned man." Melanie commented unconsciously, craning her neck to get a better view of the astute gentleman, and stirring in Simon an almost overpowering urge to laugh at her earnestness.

"And that man, Simon," Melanie inquired softly, "the tall, handsome red-haired young gentleman, who is he?"

An uncommon prick of jealousy took the smile from Simon's face and he responded stiffly, "He is

Thomas Jefferson."

"Thomas Jefferson! But he is so young to be a full-fledged architect as well as the man of cultivated tastes the *Pennsylvania Magazine* makes him out to be." Then flushing darkly as she unconsciously revealed the source of all her new-found knowledge, she succeeded in her discomfort in restoring Simon's good humor.

"Well, my dear, you are proof that the young can be well informed when properly motivated to become so." His whispered comment was rewarded with another unexpected blush, and bending forward he whispered sincerely into her ear, "Melanie, dear, you are priceless."

Barely able to suppress an almost uncontrollable urge to kiss the warm lobe so close to his lips, Simon then devoted his strict attention to the proceedings for the remainder of the exercises.

"It was a brilliant affair, wasn't it, Simon?" Melanie was still a trifle breathless from the stimulating experience of her first introduction to Philadelphia society and their quick flight from the crush surrounding them at the conclusion of the ceremonies, and smiled brightly in his direction as their carriage moved slowly through the crowded streets. She had not realized that Philadelphia would be so exciting or that Simon had so many friends, all so anxious for just a few words with him before they left.

"Quite honestly, Melanie," he replied caustically, "I found the students' dialogue and musical odes quite joyless, and the discussion only mildly stimulating, but," he continued, lowering his head to whisper confidentially into her ear, a small smile finally breaking through his dry countenance, "I found the company completely stimulating and surprisingly enjoyed myself immensely!"

Hesitating a moment, Melanie's face became suddenly serious. "Do you think everyone believed the story about my being a widow and my family asking you to look after me?"

"Melanie, dear, I'm afraid everyone is quite familiar with my Walnut Street address . . . and all its implications. That fantasy fooled no one, I am sure, but it was necessary to enable you to be accepted as a guest at whatever occasion I choose to escort you. In my position there are, after all, very few people that would dare call me a liar to my face. But I assure you, there is much speculation going on right now, and a very many tongues wagging. You will be the talk of Philadelphia society tomorrow, behind people's hands, of course."

"So, I will be a scandal again," Melanie murmured, her elation dimming in the light of Simon's dousing of cold, hard truths.

"Probably so, Melanie." Lifting her drooping chin with his finger so that she looked into his light, penetrating eyes, he continued softly, "But a beautiful and surprisingly charming scandal, to be sure, and I can promise you truthfully that I am presently the most envied man in Philadelphia right now."

Slowly lowering his mouth, Simon covered Melanie's full, parted lips with his for a warm, moving kiss that startled Melanie back to reality. In all the excitement she had almost forgotten what still lay ahead of her, and for the remainder of the ride avoided his eyes while an uncomfortable silence developed between them.

All too soon for Melanie, Walnut Street came into view, and within minutes Simon was helping her from the carriage and up the front steps. Her expectations were confirmed by Simon's terse instructions to Peter, and pausing just inside the front door, Simon glanced casually in her direction, "Would you care for some wine before we retire, Melanie?"

"I think not, Simon." Her golden eyes held his glance. "It has been a long day."

Turning to Mrs. Walters, Simon said dismissingly, "Peter will pick me up in the morning. I should not like to sleep past nine."

The click of the door latch behind her sounded loudly in the silent room, and Melanie turned to face Simon's assessing glance. His face unsmiling, he was a formidable detached stranger again, and Melanie bit down hard on her lower lips, her doubts looming to towering proportions. Allowing her eyes to move slowly over his unreadable countenance, she searched for a trace of the warmth he had displayed so openly during the long evening; but the cool, penetrating eyes and full, unsmiling mouth gave no indication of his thoughts.

Unknown to Melanie and contrary to his cool facade, Simon was exerting the full limits of his control to steel himself against the amber gaze that seared him with an almost physical force. He had become increasingly conscious of her nearness the entire evening and increasingly annoyed by the fact that her merest touch would set his pulse racing. His anticipation of this moment had been keener than he dared admit to himself, and the present slow sweep of her eyes down his face, touching momentarily on his lips was accelerating his heartbeat until he was almost breathless. He was rapidly advancing to the point past physical control and waged a desperate battle to conceal any signs of the emotions coursing through him.

"Simon," Melanie broke the uneasy silence hesitantly, "I want to say something to you before we . . ." Then continuing with a rush, she said emotionally, "I know you have had many mistresses, but contrary to your probable opinion of me, I have only known two men intimately—"

"I'm not interested in your past, Melanie." Simon began impatiently.

"Please let me finish, Simon." Insistently she continued. "The first was a deep and mutual love, even though it wasn't sanctified by marriage, and the other was—a mistake. But each time *my* love was sincere. This bargain of ours . . . you have been extremely kind and generous to me, Simon, and I truly want to fulfill my portion of our agreement, but I'm not certain how I—" Flushing painfully, Melanie forced herself to continue. "What I'm trying to say is, I hope you will not be disappointed, Simon, I'll do my best to please you, but—"

"Melanie, dear," Simon's face was oddly strained, his voice carrying a strangely hoarse quality she had not noticed before, "I want you only to be yourself, nothing more than that." Slowly taking her into his arms, he began covering her face with soft, warm kisses, mumbling as he did, "I have wanted you from that first day, Melanie, just you . . . I don't want an able courtesan. Thoughts of you have given me no peace, and now that I have you, my little witch, I want you to be just you . . . Melanie."

His hands moved slowly in her hair as he pressed kiss after kiss against her soft, moist mouth, gently removing the pins restraining her auburn curls and dropping them to the floor in his rush to strain her even closer against him. His heart was pounding wildly, his eagerness for her driving him into a passion that suddenly could no longer suffer the intrusion of clothing between them.

Releasing her, he ordered quietly, "Turn around, Melanie, let me help you remove your gown."

Avoiding his gaze, Melanie turned to do his bidding, her trembling increasing as her dress dropped to the floor. Turning her to face him again, Simon efficiently loosened her remaining undergarments despite his trembling hands and finally removing her chemise, left her standing naked before him, her clothing an amber heap around her feet. The hands that touched her shoulders and slowly drew her against him trembled revealingly, and she could feel the heavy thudding of his heart against her chest the moment before he bent to scoop her into his arms and carry her to the bed. With uncharacteristic haste, he stripped away his clothes, revealing a strong, athletic body, and the full extent of his passion. Within moments his flesh was against hers, the startling actuality of its touch stiffening her with fright. Sensitive to her apprehension despite his own overpowering feelings, Simon continued holding her intimately close, but drew his face just far enough away so he might direct an earnest glance into her frightened eyes.

"Don't be afraid of me, Melanie, and don't try to force a response. My own passion for you can carry us through as many nights as will be necessary for you to respond naturally. Just relax, Melanie," he said softly, pressing short, light kisses against her parted lips, "Just relax and let me love you. That's all I ask for now, just to be yourself and let me love you."

Gradually the soft, moist kisses left her mouth to trail to the small pink lobe of her ear that had tantalized him so wildly that evening, and proceeded down the column of her throat. The sweet, warm, womanly scent of her was driving him insane with desire, but exercising stringent self-control, he began a deliberate loving campaign to arouse her frozen emotions. Slowly his mouth trailed the curve of her shoulders, continuing his loving caresses to the firm white mounds of her breasts. They were so perfect, so beautiful . . . Touching them with wonder, he felt the shock of that touch travel the full length of his body, settling in his groin to raise his level of excitement even further. Lowering his mouth once again, he kissed the gleaming mounds lightly, avoiding the inviting pink tips intentionally in an effort to increase Melanie's anticipation. Gradually, persistently, he caressed the warm mounds with his hands and tongue until the stiffness in Melanie's body began to ease and she began breathing heavily, sensuously. Only then did he lower his mouth to cover the enlarged crest, the sound of her low, passionate groan shooting a rapturous thrill throughout him. Almost completely past the bounds of rational thought, he began a wild assault on her breasts, throwing all caution to the winds when her arms gradually closed around him to hold his mouth firmly against her. Trembling violently, he ached for her, wanted desperately to claim every inch of her body for his own, and ran the palms of his hands roughly across her skin, leaving no portion of her untouched; caressing, stimulating, loving her with an intensity that raised him to a euphoric plane he had never realized existed. He felt the warm, moist, inner reaches of her body against his hand, and slipping his fingers further inside the sensuous crease, drew back a moment to watch as tremors of passion shook Melanie's body. She was so beautiful . . . he would never tire of watching, and as he did, the heavily lashed lids raised slowly, unleashing the full power of the burning amber fire beneath into his eyes, and he gasped at the heat of her searing gaze. Slowly she raised her hands, slipping them around the back of his head, and pulled his mouth down to cover hers, opening her mouth wide to his invading tongue, transporting him to a realm of glory that almost pushed him past control. Slowly, reluctantly, drawing his mouth away from hers, he whispered hoarsely, "You want me now, don't you, Melanie? You want to feel me inside you. You want me to join your body with mine."

Keeping his eyes glued to her impassioned face, he slid his hand down her body to enter once again the vulnerable crease, experiencing a surging joy as her eyelids fluttered in passion and a soft groan escaped her lips. Continuing his intimate caress, he whispered against her throbbing lips, "This is the way it was meant to be, little witch."

"Simon . . ." His name was a whispered sigh.

Crushing her lips with his, Simon separated her legs in a quick motion to plunge deep inside her, groaning as her warm moistness closed around his throbbing member. Completely past the bounds of all restraint, he drove deeply inside her again and again, exulting as her body welcomed and accommodated each savage thrust, savoring the impetus of the force that was driving them toward wild, ecstatic culmination. With one last, savage plunge and a deep, passionate cry, Simon carried Melanie over the summit to sink slowly, breathlessly, into the warm abyss of total fulfillment.

So totally had he spent himself that Simon lay for some time, still joined to the beautiful warmth of Melanie's body. Finally able to arouse himself from his passion-induced lethargy, he felt strangely reluctant to separate his body from the beauty that lay beneath him. Slowly lifting his head, he cupped the small pointed chin in his hands, forcing Melanie's face up to his, willing her to open her eyes. Within a few moments the sleepy, love-drugged eyes opened to unleash their amber glow.

"It was good for you, too, wasn't it, Melanie? Truly good."

It was a small eternity before the warm lips beneath his parted to release the faint whisper, "Yes, Simon . . . it was."

The golden glow of morning against his closed lids awakened Simon to the new day, and he turned to view the small woman cuddled near his side in sleep. The delicious scent of her filled his nostrils like a heady perfume and, pulling her closer still, he breathed deeply of her fragrance. Careful not to awaken her, he rubbed his cheek against the soft, auburn tresses, feeling an exhilarating joy in the absolute possession of her.

A soft knock on the door shattered the serenity of the moment, bringing him back sharply to reality.

"Mr. Young, it's past nine o'clock. I rapped on the bedroom door next door for several minutes before realizing you weren't in there."

Awakened by Mrs. Walters' voice, Melanie murmured sleepily, "Why would she knock next door, Simon? She must realize . . ."

Avoiding her eyes, he said coolly, "I sometimes return to a solitary bed when I become restless. Fortunately, I slept very well last night."

The short smile he directed into Melanie's eyes brought a small one of her own as Simon rose to dress. He had skillfully avoided telling her that he usually had an aversion to sharing his bed once his passion had been spent. Uncertain in his own mind about his reluctance to part from her the night before, he hastily decided it was a weakness he could neither afford to display or indulge, and determined to subdue it.

Dressing quickly, he turned as he saw Melanie begin to rise and said offhandedly, "You needn't get up, Melanie. Mrs. Walters has my usual breakfast ready."

Stopping short at the coolness in his voice, Melanie said hesitantly, "All right, Simon. What time may I expect you tonight?"

Completely dressed, Simon turned with a slight raising of his brow, "I have not said I will return tonight. I will send you a message in advance of my coming, whenever that may be. Meanwhile, I'll turn Peter over to your service temporarily, with instructions to acquaint you with the city. You'll find a draft on the desk in the library in the event you may want to purchase some things."

Bending, he pressed a light kiss on her forehead, stifling with sheer strength of will, the urge to kiss away her puzzled frown, and quickly removed himself from the room and the woman drawing him to her so effortlessly.

"Will I never learn?" Melanie mumbled past gritted teeth as the door closed quietly behind him. "The man is an egotist—completely unpredictable." Well, he had really done her a favor. He had set the standards for their relationship in no uncertain terms, and it would be far easier to maintain a balance with no pretense of love between them. She obviously would be treated with utmost generosity if she did not make the mistake of infringing on his privacy or commit the unpardonable sin of presumption!

Suddenly she felt greatly relieved! With all his faults, Simon was a pleasant, generous companion, capable of amazing gentleness. She knew now she could enjoy their association as long as she kept her mind free of the past, and when the time came for them to part, she would find herself in a stable financial condition and able to make Sara's and her way on her own. In the meantime, she would enjoy herself! Philadelphia was really a beautiful city!

Pausing for a moment before she stepped into the open carriage, Melanie glanced up at the brilliant blue sky, drinking in with pure appreciation the beauty of the tranquil June day. Not realizing the breathtaking picture she herself presented, attired in a pale blue, full-flowing organdy gown, her auburn curls softly swept to the top of her head and secured with graceful combs, she unconsciously fingered the perfectly matched pearls clasped around her slender neck and lying provocatively across the gleaming swells of her breasts. Although the pearls were only one of Simon's many gifts in the past month, they were by far her favorite because they had been his first personal gift, and had preceded a long evening and night of exceedingly warm memories that still brought a flush to her face.

"It is a truly glorious day, isn't it, Peter?" She smiled widely into his familiar, pleasant face as he assisted her into the carriage.

"But not as glorious as you yourself are, Mrs. Morganfield." Peter's reply was delivered with a mischievous twinkle and a twitch of his magnificent white mustache. "Mr. Young won't be able to take his eyes off you for sure. I'm certainly glad I thought to take the top down so no one will have to strain their eyes for a glimpse of you when you arrive at the State House to meet him."

"Peter, you are an old flatterer!" Melanie exclaimed with a laugh, her eyes following the portly figure with affection as he climbed into the driver's seat and clucked the horses forward. In the month she had been in Philadelphia, she had formed a real attachment for the old servant and heartily hoped Simon would keep him in her service indefinitely. She sorely missed Martha and Tom and needed at least one person on her staff with whom she could feel relaxed.

Mrs. Walters' attitude had not changed from the first day of residence. Although Melanie could find no fault with her work, the woman was given to subtle innuendos about Melanie's term of residence; her narrow, lined face assuming an annoyingly superior expression when she hinted at her knowledge of the pattern all Simon's former relationships had followed. Although Melanie would give her no satisfaction, the woman was a source of constant irritation.

Rose continued to be an efficient, unobtrusive servant, while Molly, although a sweet girl, at times proved decidedly unsatisfactory in handling Sara. The beautiful, precocious child took advantage of Molly's gentleness to inflict the rigors of her already strong personality on the girl, thwarting her at will. In fact, it was beginning to appear the only person Sara obeyed without question was Simon! Contrarily, his sternness with her misbehavior only seemed to endear him to her, and she welcomed him enthusiastically with each visit.

Carefully arranging the folds of her gown, Melanie smiled absentmindedly. Simon had not presumed to instruct her in her manner of dress since their first outing, and she was generally pleased with the progress of their relationship. Although at first, his visits were almost formally scheduled, delighting

Mrs. Walters by appearing to relegate Melanie to the specific, unquestionable position all his other mistresses had held and not allowing her intrusion into any other facet of his life, he soon began spending increasingly more time at the Walnut Street residence, allowing Melanie her own portion of satisfaction in Mrs. Walters' obvious amazement at the deviation from his usual conduct. He had taken to stopping by unexpectedly, to discuss a daring political action being contemplated by Congress, or just to relax and pass the time in idle conversation; while it was his habit to stare annoyingly at her person, his clear, blue eyes wandering slowly with unconcealed enjoyment over her body, delighting in the heated discomfort his glance usually produced. Their lovemaking itself—Melanie flushed hotly remembering the night before—had matured in the passage of the first weeks into a mutual, almost violently passionate exchange that Melanie had begun to anticipate with undisguisable eagerness. She was constantly amazed that a man of Simon's often frigid, aloof moods was capable of such warmth and gentleness, possessing the capacity for a genuinely beautiful expression of physical love.

Suddenly she was laughing to herself, elusive dimples dancing across her velvet cheek as she remembered with true amusement the evening a few nights before when Simon and she had attended another of the city's political fetes. Strangely, after a few exposures to society, Melanie had become a natural curiosity to the many who found it difficult to believe her quick wit and well-informed mind could quite match her outstanding beauty. That evening, having excused himself to momentarily renew an old acquaintance, Simon had found himself unable to return to her side without the discomfort of forcing his way through the admiring circle that had quickly surrounded her. His irritation betrayed only by the muscle twitching in his jaw, he said in exceedingly dulcet tones, "Do you think these gentlemen could spare me a few moments of your time so that I might take you in to dinner, Melanie?"

Secretly, Melanie felt that despite his occasional possessive displays, Simon maintained a certain sense of pride in the fact that so many of his friends seemed to consider her almost as intellectually stimulating as she was charming. She had become a well-known figure at the State House, having had many occasions at Simon's instruction to meet him there, and she was once again on her way to meet Simon so that he might take her to see the well-known artist, Charles Peale. After visiting the gentleman painter's room the week before, Simon had stopped by to announce he had arranged to have her portrait painted. Taken completely by surprise, Melanie had candidly commented that he might not think the portrait such a good idea at some time in the future when another woman might be installed in the house on Walnut Street. Directing her a deadly look, he had replied caustically, "Well, then, we'll have to make sure you take the portrait with you when you go, won't we?" Contrary to taking insult at his comment, Melanie had been extremely amused and, strangely, only succeeded in irritating him further.

As they moved slowly through the streets of the

city, Melanie mused silently on Simon's increasing thoughtfulness. She remembered earlier in the week when she had remarked on an article in the news stating that John Behrent of Philadelphia had announced the manufacture of the first American-made piano, and that she had secretly always wished she could play the beautiful instrument. A piano had been delivered a few days later, with arrangements completed to have her begin her lessons that same week. Thoroughly thrilled at the prospect, she still shook her head in amazement. Simon Young—a true enigma—because despite all this, he was still a mystery to her, and although she was the only woman he illicitly supported, she knew she was not his only mistress.

A few moments before the appointed time the carriage pulled up in front of the State House, but Simon was not in evidence.

"Peter, it appears Mr. Young's business has not yet been completed. It's far too warm today to wait in the sun. I'll go inside to find him and you can go around the corner and wait in the shade. When Mr. Young is ready, we'll come to the carriage."

"I don't mind the sun, Mrs. Morganfield."

"You'll please do as I say, Peter."

With an obedient nod, Peter descended to help her from the carriage. Noticing his rather dogged expression, Melanie pinched his cheek, saying softly, "We don't want the sun to scorch that tender skin, do we Peter?"

The corners of his mouth finally lifting, he mumbled inaudibly and Melanie started lightly up the steps. Knowing Simon, the wait might be of a long duration, and Peter was getting too old for a lengthy wait in the glaring sun.

The cool, high-ceilinged corridors were a welcome relief after the humid heat of the June day. Walking slowly toward the meeting room, her gown a floating blue mist outlining her delicately curved figure, two brilliant auburn curls swinging lightly against her neck, her eyes glowing in anticipation of her meeting with the renown Mr. Peale, Melanie looked like a gay fairy sprite who had wandered erringly into the somber halls. As she rounded the corner, she noticed two men waited outside the meeting room doors, and her step slowed. One of them looked vaguely familiar, and she continued forward hesitantly, her heart beating a rapid tattoo in her breast. The massive fellow . . . she knew only one man that size.

At her own moment of positive identification, the big man turned in her direction. Slowly raising his huge fists to his hips, he exclaimed with a bellow of surprise, "In the name of the Almighty! It's James Morganfield's little girl, Melanie, isn't it?" His eyes searched her face as she drew closer, and not waiting for her reply, he continued, "Of course it is! I'd know those eyes anywhere!"

Unable to do else, Melanie continued forward, her knees shaking as she was confronted with a specter from her past. Recognizing the man beside him as Seth Warner, she nodded briefly in greeting.

"I'm surprised to see you, Mr. Allen. Aren't you taking a chance coming here with a price on your head?"

"Don't tell me you haven't heard, Melanie! My men and I are heroes now, fresh from victory at Fort

Ti! They can't arrest a hero!" Allen's short hoot of laughter echoed in the hallway as he soundly appreciated his own wit. Then with a sudden change of mood so common to his personality, all trace of laughter disappeared from his face. "But we're not finished yet with our work. There's more to be done, but this time we need the authorization of Congress— a time-consuming business," he mumbled under his breath.

Then stopping in mid-thought, he shook his head, his dark brows knitting together in a frown. "Your departure was a true mystery in Salisbury, Melanie. Either Martha and Tom Hartley didn't know where you had gone, or just weren't telling. One of my men went just about crazy looking for you." Tossing a glance over his shoulder, he mumbled indistinctly, "Say, where is he?"

"I'm right here, Ethan."

The deep, familiar voice that answered from the corner a moment before Steve stepped forward into Melanie's view, shocked her into sudden immobility.

Beginning to tremble visibly as Steve advanced toward her, Melanie clasped her shaking hands tightly in front of her with a supreme effort at control. She had not imagined she could still be so devastated by his mere presence, and closed her eyes in a momentary surge of weakness; but the ringing hatred in Steve's voice snapped her from her moment of shock.

His dark eyes roaming her body in an insultingly familiar manner, he managed to make his complimentary words a deliberate slur, "Well, you seem to have done quite well for yourself, Melanie. It looks like I wasted my time worrying."

Incensed by his attitude, Melanie flared out heatedly, "And what makes you think you had a right to worry, Steve? In the event you don't remember, you forfeited that right. As a matter of fact," she continued viciously, "the last time I saw you your forfeit was laying naked in your bed!"

"Shut up, Melanie!"

"You have no right to give me orders! I won't shut up!" Melanie's voice was rising in volume with her mounting hysteria.

As Steve took a menacing step forward, he growled warningly, "Shut up now, or I'll shut you up! Don't you—"

Steve's malevolent hiss was suddenly interrupted by a low, frigid tone that turned all eyes in the direction of the meeting room door. Immaculately groomed and attired, his tall, slender frame held almost militarily erect, Simon's appearance was in vivid contrast to Steve's broad, homespun-clad figure, the only similarity between them being the violent anger flashing in their eyes, bringing the two men to the same level of volatility as Simon spoke.

"I would suggest you alter your tone when speaking to Mrs. Morganfield."

"*Mrs.* Morganfield! Hah! That is the biggest joke of all! Melanie's no maiden, I can testify to that, but she's never been married! A man would gladly bed her, but no man would be fool enough to exchange vows with a woman like her!"

Moving forward with a furious snarl, Simon had gotten no further than two steps before Melanie was at his side, her eyes turned up to his face. "Simon, please take me home. I want to go home right now!"

"Take her home? Simon? Of course!" His glance at first puzzled, Steve turned toward Melanie in sudden realization, his face frightening in its malevolent display. "Of course! He's Simon Young and you're his new mistress—the one every man in the tavern was discussing this lunch hour—the beautiful, mysterious wench that is the wealthy Mr. Young's latest kept woman. I suppose I should congratulate you, Melanie," lowering his voice to a sarcastic sneer, he dipped his head in mock obeisance before directing the full force of his jealous anger into her flushed countenance, "once again you have managed to become the most well known whore in town!"

"You low, filthy . . ." Simon stepped forward again, only to have Melanie edge effectively between them as she pleaded desperately, "Please, I want to go home. Please, Simon."

"By all means, take her home, Simon." The malicious ridicule filling Steve's voice provided added sting to his searing words, "You've obviously paid a good price for her. Oh, but believe me, Simon," his voice dropped to a confidential whisper, "I can testify from experience, there'll be times when she'll be worth every penny you've spent. Do you know what she really likes? She—"

In a blur of movement Simon pushed Melanie aside and swinging his fist with the full power of his fury, crashed it unerringly into Steve's distorted face to send him sprawling backwards into his friends' arms. His chest heaving heavily, his face frighteningly enraged, Simon growled, "You filth! Melanie is well rid of you. She is far better off."

"Oh, is she better off with you?" Steve shouted, struggling to be free of his friends' restraining hands. "You are a married man, aren't you, Mr. Young? Are you saying you do her honor by flaunting her in this society as your latest whore?"

"I treat her with the respect due the beautiful, intelligent woman that she is." Simon was struggling against the wild desire to put his hands around the man's throat and choke him into silence, and was rapidly losing the battle with his control.

Frightened to despair by Simon's unexpected violence, Melanie interrupted again, "Please—please take me home now, Simon."

"Yes, do take her home, Simon." A small trickle of blood was oozing from the cut on Steve's swollen lip, lending a wildly fanatical appearance to his hate-filled countenance, "and remember to show her your respect when you lay her in your adulterous bed tonight!"

"That's enough!" Allen's deep, emphatic tone jerked all eyes in his direction. "You've said enough, Steve . . . far too much." Turning to Melanie while still maintaining a strong hold on Steve's arm, he said softly, "I apologize for this, Melanie. What you do is your own affair, but James Morganfield's daughter is deserving of better treatment at the hands of her father's friends than she has received today."

With a dark glance into Simon's eyes, he directed his next words to him. "I suggest you do as the lady asks, Mr. Young. These halls are not the place to air the details of her personal life."

Choosing not to acknowledge Allen's solemn advice, Simon turned his eyes in Steve's direction with slow determination, his tone coolly ominous.

"Stay away from Melanie, Mr. Hull. And if you value your life, *never* attempt to see or contact her again, because I give you my oath in the presence of these witnesses, should that happen, I will kill you myself!"

Melanie's gasp was the only sound breaking the silence that followed Simon's declaration until he turned again in her direction and, sliding a supportive arm around her waist, urged in a soft tone, "Come Melanie, it is time we went home."

Finding the sun an invalid excuse to neglect his duty, Peter was waiting outside the building with the carriage. Cursing silently when he saw the top had been rolled down, Simon assisted Melanie to her seat with a curt command.

"Take us home, Peter."

With seemingly steadfast determination, Melanie avoided Simon's glance, keeping her eyes trained on the road with a vacant, doll-like expression. Realizing she strained to suppress the emotions that he was certain were tearing her apart, Simon felt a fierce stab of hatred for the man who had purposely caused her such pain.

The bastard! Simon's mind raged, The low scum! That ignorant backwoodsman could never be worthy of his magnificent Melanie. What had ever possessed her to have anything to do with him? Had she been that frightened and alone? He should have gone to her sooner. She had too much to offer to lend herself for even a short time to an individual of such poor judgment and character that he could not realize Melanie for the rare jewel she truly was.

It seemed the passage of an eternity before Walnut Street came into view. Melanie's bearing had appeared to grow more taut as the minutes passed, and it was only as he assisted her up the steps to the door of the residence that he realized the cost of her stringent control. Completely rigid under his guiding hand, Melanie's body began to tremble wildly as the door was opened by a startled Mrs. Walters, and she only managed a few steps into the foyer before the descending blackness engulfed her and she collapsed into wordless oblivion.

"Quickly, call Dr. Simmons!" Simon's sharp command snapped the immobile Mrs. Walters to life as he caught Melanie's slumping form and, scooping her into his arms, carried her easily up the steps and into her room. Laying her gently on the bed, his heart beating wildly, he touched her ashen cheek, but she still did not awaken. Molly's small face peeped around the doorframe, and he commanded sharply, "Get me some cool water and a cloth, quickly!" Turning his attention back to Melanie, he began to loosen her clothing, mumbling over and over under his breath, "Melanie . . . oh, God . . . darling, Melanie . . ."

Melanie's light, almost transparent lids fluttered with the first application of water against her forehead and struggled open as Simon ran the cool cloth gently down her cheek.

"Simon . . ." Her voice was weak, her glance disoriented, and he hushed her softly.

Almost unable to speak above the lump that had formed in his throat, he whispered as he looked into her tear-filled eyes, "Don't worry, darling, and don't

305

be afraid. I'll take care of you, I promise you that."

Sliding his arms under and around her, he lifted her to pull her close, his face pressed against her auburn curls as he declared fervently, "He'll never hurt you again, darling . . . never."

Groggy and disoriented, Melanie awoke. The first light of morning cast its glowing rays through the corners of the drawn blinds, and her eyes roamed the room slowly, a sudden movement jerking her eyes to the man lying beside her. Simon's clear, pensive gaze studied her unsmilingly, bringing her to immediate recall of the afternoon before, and she flushed hotly.

Lifting himself to his elbow, the light covering falling away from his bare, smoothly muscled chest, he gently stroked her flushed cheek with his long, slender fingers. His face deadly serious, he inquired softly, "How are you this morning, darling?"

With a positive lift of her chin, Melanie replied carefully, "I'm quite well, Simon. The sedative Dr. Simmons provided seems to have done its work well. I feel just as good as new." The slight tremble of her bottom lip belied her words and the confident veneer she had assumed for Simon's benefit.

With a peculiar twist of pain, Simon realized from her reluctance to face his eyes that Stephen Hull had been successful in establishing in Melanie a shade of shame in their relationship, but despite Hull's grossly demeaning words, he, himself, felt nothing that was tawdry or common in the way he regarded Melanie, or the feelings she stirred within him.

Her gaze still averted from his, Melanie whispered with a pretense at lightness, "I think I'd like to get up now, Simon, and—"

Groaning softly, Simon wrapped his arms around her, pulling her close as he whispered against her ear, "Not now, Melanie. Don't get up, yet. We must first heal each other's wounds, darling."

Slowly he turned his face against her cheek, stifling her short sob with his mouth as it closed over hers. There was a moment of stiffness as his flesh pressed intimately against hers, causing a true rise of panic to sweep his senses the second before Melanie relaxed beneath him, allowing her lips to separate and accept his searching tongue. Experiencing true elation as her arms slowly moved around his neck, Simon felt absurdly grateful for her initial reacceptance. His mouth moved lovingly over her face and neck as his hands released the ties of her shift. Having previously thought he and Melanie had touched upon every level and shade of emotion in the brilliance of their mutual expressions of passion, Simon was awed once again with the new, indefinable element introduced into their lovemaking. Touching Melanie's flawless, white skin, caressing the incomparable beauty and perfection of her body, tasting her, breathing her fragrance, he appreciated the joy of loving her, the privilege of being allowed to possess her; and having felt in her one moment of hesitation the possibility of her loss, he experienced true humility in gaining her anew.

Realizing the truly fine balance of Melanie's injured emotions, he was extremely aware of his delicate position in her confused state of mind that Steve's vengeful words had induced, and he took her gently, coaxingly, healingly on his excursion into ecstasy. His gentle, persuasive lips assailed her senses with endless caresses along the long line of her throat and around the creamy mounds of her breasts, seizing on the enlarged pink crests that invited his caress with a tender urgency that left her gasping. Loving, kissing, caressing the firm mounds, he could not seem to get enough of her, each taste, each touch driving him to an insatiable desire for more. Slowly his mouth descended her narrow rib cage to her even narrower waist, its brief expanse providing no relief for his raging passions. His hands caressed her gently rounded hips, the delicate white skin of her stomach as his mouth moved ever lower, seeking, searching, finding at last the brilliant auburn curls nestling between her white, slender thighs. They were soft, smooth beneath his cheek, and he nudged them gently, spreading a shower of kisses on their coppery glint. Melanie was murmuring indistinctly, but Simon was past distraction of any sort, so engrossed was he in his loving quest. His kisses descended lower, lower, seeking and finally finding the other lips awaiting his lover's kiss. Subtly, without her realization, Melanie's legs separated, allowing his entry, a supreme jolt of ecstasy piercing her body as his lips discovered her for the first time. Slowly, with extreme control, Simon began his gentle assault, his lips and tongue, kissing, touching, tasting, lifting her on the wings of ecstasy to a passion so intense that she feared she could not survive in its breathtaking sphere.

"Simon . . . please . . ." she gasped, taking his ruffled brown mane roughly in her hands, forcing a momentary cessation of his tender assault. "Please,

Simon . . . I can no longer breathe . . . I am past endurance."

"No darling, no," he whispered, his mouth still pressed lightly against the sensitive, throbbing lips of her vulnerable crease, "let me take you a little further . . . just a few steps more, my darling, so that we may experience the full limits of ecstasy together, darling."

Melanie's gripping fingers gradually released their binding hold, and freed once again, Simon renewed his loving task, his searing, caressing tongue seeking out, touching and penetrating the last of her defenses. A gasping, tumultuous thunder of ecstasy shook Melanie's body, transporting her in one swift second up and over the precipice of rapture, her beautiful, delicate body shuddering, rewarding with the nectar of passion the lips that loved her so well. Anxiously, greedily accepting her body's tribute, Simon felt a surging sense of joy so complete that he was momentarily awed by its brilliant perfection. When her body was once again still, her breathing almost normal, he slowly slid himself up to cover her perspiring frame with his own. Quickly and smoothly he slid himself inside her, eliciting another gasp as her eyes flew open to look into his impassioned face. The amber glow of her eyes merged wordlessly with his icy blue gaze as he moved inside her, slowly at first, savoring and then titillating once again, increasing and accelerating his movements, raising her swiftly and sweetly to a plane of exhilaration that peaked to hold them suspended in a joyful, mutual explosion of rapture for a split second of timeless eternity before dropping them spent and breathless, still wrapped in each other's arms.

For long, exhausted minutes they lay in wordless communion, their bodies still entwined. Slowly Simon lifted his head to look down into her silent, beautiful face. Cupping her chin gently in his hand, he willed the dark fringed lids to lift and smiled momentarily as they slowly fluttered and raised to release a mellow glow. His lean, pensive face was then sober, his penetrating eyes level and clear as he spoke spontaneously with great feeling.

"Melanie, darling, there has never been a woman like you before in my life, nor have I ever felt for another the feelings I feel for you. You are special to me, Melanie, more than I had dreamed possible. Between us there is true beauty that no words can demean, no matter how jealously delivered. The communion of our bodies and souls was meant to be . . . that was what I sensed from the very beginning—meant to be. Melanie, darling, we have but fulfilled our destiny."

Chapter 7

The empty hallway sounded with the steady, measured tread of the huge, broad man in homespun, as he paced impatiently, his black frown and angry manner only too obvious to his friends' weary glances.

"Ethan, why don't you try to relax? You know damn well they're going to keep us waiting as long as possible out of sheer perversity if nothing else. The truth of the matter is, they're probably still arguing if they should arrest us or not!" A momentary smile flashed over Seth Warner's broad face at his own ironic thought.

No one could dispute the irony of the situation. Having received a signed recommendation from Congress for the New York Assembly to employ the Green Mountain Boys in the New York forces, the three men had boldly presented themselves before the New York Assembly several weeks before, and waited just as boldly for authorization, while the incensed body of men argued violently whether they should be shot, arrested, or authorized! But eyeing Ethan's tense, volatile expression as he stopped his pacing long enough to shoot him a dark scowl, Seth mumbled with a brief grunt of amazement at Ethan's indefatigable drive, "We wait boldly . . . but not patiently."

"Time is passing too quickly, Seth." Ethan's voice was heavy with the impatience so obvious in his bearing. "These fools will delay their decision and play their foolish games, and in the end damage our chances of success in an assault on Canada. Fools!" Ethan's brow darkened even further with the thought, and he resumed his pacing as the two other men exchanged glances with a shake of their heads.

Shrugging his broad shoulders, Steve slumped back on the bench. In all honesty, he cared very little about the outcome of their petition. All the heart had gone out of him. Physically, he followed the visit through to the finish, but his mind strayed not far from the small, pointed face and brilliant gold eyes filled with hate and tears. He had gone over the confrontation in the State House hallway countless times in the past weeks. What had gone wrong? Why had he behaved so viciously when in truth his first instinct was to take Melanie in his arms and never let go. God, she had looked beautiful—more beautiful than he had ever seen her, except after they had made love, when her eyes were soft and warm, her lips vulnerable and waiting. She had awaited his first move, and he had attacked her viciously with words. With a slight shake of his head, he marveled again at his own stupidity, but he acknowledged again with a bitter frustration that he seemed incapable of rational thought where Melanie was concerned. He was a fool! He had effectively destroyed all hopes of a reconciliation with his wild jealousy, and now the knowledge was destroying him.

A sound at the assemblyroom door snapped three heads in its direction as it opened to reveal a somber, unfriendly face.

"Would you gentlemen step inside? The delegates have a few more questions to ask."

Without response, Ethan strode past the man, directly into the meeting room. Waiting only long enough for his friends to join him, Ethan turned to the assemblymen, a broad smile transforming his angry features, and Steve and Seth exchanged surprised glances. Ethan had obviously decided to win the legislators over, and both knew from experience he was an extremely hard man to resist when he extended the full charm of his personality in any direction.

Addressing the assembly in a forthright manner, Ethan announced in his deep voice, "I understand you gentlemen have some questions as to our service. Ask ahead, gentlemen. We are here to answer any and all of your questions."

A sudden, explosive voice was heard from the corner, as a slender, red-haired gentleman jumped to his feet. "Why do you even listen to this ruffian? He is a criminal with a price on his head! He has broken every law we have ever passed, and now has the gall to come asking our authorization? Give me one good reason why we should trust a single word he says!"

Turning his glance in the young man's direction, Ethan answered calmly, "Rather than give you cause to doubt us, the past activities of the Green Mountain Boys should give you cause to respect our word. In the past we were enemies, and with true dedication of purpose we thwarted your assembly efficiently and effectively at every turn. Your wealth and superior forces were ineffective against us because as a fighting force in our own territory we are unmatched and undefeatable!"

Scoffing remarks were mumbled throughout the group, and Ethan moved his gaze over their faces with a confident air. "Come, gentlemen, the mere fact of our presence here today is testimony to the truth of my words. Had not the Continental Congress considered our capture of Fort Ticonderoga a great victory, and had not General Schuyler, who was formerly one of your group and is now in charge of the northern army of the United Colonies of America, realized our value, you would not be faced with the recommendation you find so hard to swallow. But if it will set your minds at rest, gentlemen, I will go a little further to answer this fellow's question," he said, gesturing vaguely to the red-haired fellow who had testily resumed his seat.

"You should trust us now because the emergence of a greater threat has made us allies. We are no longer enemies fighting for property, we are allies fighting for our own personal liberty. There is no greater cause than liberty, and the very fact that ours is in jeopardy makes us brothers of one family, united in the fight against oppression! Come gentlemen," he coaxed proudly, his dark glance moving over the entire group until they squirmed under its intensity, "come, do not let blind prejudice from the past eliminate hope for the future. We are in mutual need of each other right now. It is imperative that we take bold, offensive action against the British in Canada before their position becomes too strong. The necessity is for prompt efficient action that will take them by surprise!"

"You are a wild man!"

"Your proposition is insane!"

Shouts decrying Ethan's proposal came from all quarters of the assembly, necessitating a harsh call for order, but Ethan faced the men squarely, his gaze steady, his purpose sure. "We cannot afford to show weakness now, gentlemen. It is a time for swift, decisive action, and complete unity. You say I am a wild man, insane. Is it wild to demonstrate by the strength of harsh action that we will not be ruled without due representation? Is it insane to believe we must fight to secure our liberty? Search your hearts, gentlemen, how precious is your liberty to you?"

There was a brief, pensive silence as the solemn question touched the conscience of the assembly. Intense self-scrutiny was obvious in the minds of many as his eyes traveled the faces of the delegates, and Ethan experienced a deep surge of relief. He had done it! He had hit upon the key that would eventually release the assembly from their preconceived, unfounded objections to him and allow their common sense to prevail. He knew in that second of insight that all that remained was for him to battle the last of their prejudices before they succumbed to better judgment and his petition was granted.

Hours later the heated debate had drawn to a conclusion, and the delegation of three left the austere meeting room. Once out of earshot of the weary delegates, Seth clapped Ethan heartily on his broad shoulder.

"Ethan, you were never in better form! If anyone had told me two months ago that we would face the New York Assembly and come out free men, I would have doubted their sanity. But you, Ethan, have pulled off the impossible! Hah!" He continued in a whisper, "To come out of those chambers with an authorization for a force of five hundred men that will be paid from the date of attack on Fort Ti, tentative approval for an attack on Canada, and . . . and . . ." he laughed again incredulously, "with a personal advance against your salary! Ethan, you are a wonder!"

Using all his control to stifle the laughter welling in his throat, Seth slapped Ethan's broad back again, shooting Steve a teary-eyed, mirthful glance. Suddenly almost convulsed by the humor of the situation, both men turned to face a completely sober Ethan.

Stopping for a moment, Ethan replied with absolute candor, "Boys, I never had a moment's doubt about the outcome of our petition. The only thing I was a little unsure about," he said slowly, a spark of mirth dancing momentarily in his dark eyes, "was the size of my advance."

"Melanie, you will please follow me into the library. I have some business to discuss with you." Throwing the words over his shoulder in casual command, Simon strode through the front door and past a startled Melanie. Rooted to the spot with the incredibility of his manner, Melanie stared at the open doorway to the library through which he had disappeared.

Within a few moments, he called again irritably, "Do hurry, Melanie. I would like to finish this before dinner."

Shaking her head lightly, Melanie mumbled under her breath, "Simon, you never cease to amaze me." A maze of contradictions was Simon Young! Her encounter with Stephen Hull a few weeks before had preceded several days of the most tender, exquisite lovemaking she had ever experienced, during which Simon took up residence temporarily at the Walnut Street address. Suddenly on the fifth day, Simon arose and announced that he would be returning to his own residence. The passage of the next weeks had followed the same erratic pattern, until Melanie could only conclude pressure from his other mistresses was causing him to spread his attentions a little more evenly. She had long since accepted that she would have to become accustomed to sharing Simon's attentions, and was in fact relieved that his demands on her did not constitute a permanent arrangement. That brief meeting in the hallway of the State House had shown her only too clearly that her emotions were still entangled with the volatile backwoodsman who viewed her so scornfully.

"Simon, I thought it was understood," Melanie said imperiously as she started toward the library door, "that you were to send me word of your intention to visit. I haven't seen or heard from you in two days."

Raising his brow, Simon interrupted caustically, "Why, Melanie . . . have I infringed on your plans for the evening?" His tone clearly dared her to deny his right to presence.

"I had no other plans, Simon, except for an early dinner and bed."

"Well, then, Melanie, my plans tonight are not at all in conflict with yours."

Blushing unexpectedly, Melanie stammered, "But Mrs. Walters is not prepared for another place at dinner. You should have called."

"I'm sure she will manage something. Come in and sit down, now. We have much to discuss." His manner suddenly serious, he pulled out a chair, and when she was seated, turned to close the door behind her. His businesslike manner sent a chill up Melanie's spine, and she was filled with a sudden apprehension. Walking quickly to sit down behind the desk, Simon rifled through the papers, and finally finding the one he sought, lifted his cold azure gaze.

"I have been making inquiries as to the disposition of Asa Parker's estate since your departure." To Melanie's startled expression, he replied easily, "I see no reason why your absence should deprive you and Sara of your inheritance. After all, Sara is Asa's child and deserves her father's legacy."

"Simon—"

"Please don't interrupt, Melanie." Then watching her face closely for her reaction, Simon said bluntly, "The foundry has been sold, Melanie."

"Sold!" Melanie paled visibly. The foundry was part of Asa, his own creation. "Who bought it?" she demanded breathlessly, almost unable to bear the thought of another man at Asa's desk.

"It was bought by a cooperative of men, the employees of the foundry. A man called Josh Whitmore has continued managing—"

"Oh, Josh . . . thank the Lord." A wild surge of relief rushed through her at the mention of Josh's name.

"That's right, you know Josh Whitmore, don't you?" Simon's glance was quietly assessing.

"Josh is the only man I can truly see behind Asa's desk. Asa would have approved of having him there." Her eyes filling unexpectedly at the thought of Asa's well-loved, lined countenance, Melanie stopped speaking abruptly, unable to go on as an old sadness swept over her, and she drifted off for a moment into the past.

". . . Melanie, are you listening?"

The irritated note in Simon's voice as he paused in mid-sentence brought her back from her somber thoughts.

"Of course I'm listening," she responded heatedly, her face flushing at the obvious untruth.

His raised brow showing only too clearly what he

thought of her response, he continued, "Asa's will is still under protest, and the proceeds from the foundry are being held in escrow. I have instructed my lawyer to keep careful watch to make certain nothing illegal is attempted in your absence."

"I sincerely appreciate your help, Simon. I had almost given up hope of ever finding out the disposition of Asa's estate."

"Oh, is that so?" Simon's glance was suddenly hard and penetrating. "And how did you expect to prepare for your future? You did not expect to remain my mistress forever, did you?"

Flushing brightly at Simon's deliberate cruelty, Melanie stated adamantly, "I certainly did not, and I have been taking steps in preparation for my and Sara's future."

"You do not refer by that statement to the pitiful amount of money you have managed to put into the bank each week?"

"How did you find out about my account?" Melanie was enraged at his scornful regard for the sum she had watched grow with loving pride. She already had several hundred dollars saved and considered that a very sizable nest egg.

"My dear Melanie, you must realize that nothing you do is a secret from me. Especially when you use my banker."

"The sneak."

"No, Mr. Rogers was merely protecting his own future."

"What do you care, anyway, about the provisions I'm making for Sara's and my future. Once our liaison, as you call it, comes to an end, my affairs will be my own to do with as I wish." Then paling slightly, she added in a hesitant voice, ". . . or is that what you're trying to tell me, Simon, that our arrangement is at an end?" Melanie knew a sudden fear as her mind screamed, No, not yet! I'm not ready yet.

"No, Melanie, that is not what I was trying to say." Simon's face held a peculiarly blank expression, unfathomable, as he continued speaking. "I was trying to impress upon you that you've been a very foolish girl." At her shocked expression, he said soberly, "Yes, even your acceptance of this agreement with me, it was very foolish on your part."

"But I had no choice! You know that!" Melanie said defensively, "You saw the situation that existed in Salisbury . . ."

"And that was as a direct outcome of your foolish behavior with Stephen Hull."

"I know now that my behavior was foolish, but I did not know it then, Simon, and since it is too late to change the past, I don't wish to discuss it further!" Rising quickly, Melanie turned to leave, but within seconds Simon was around the desk, holding her arm securely.

"I have not said that you may leave yet, Melanie."

"And I do not need your permission to leave the room!" Melanie flashed angrily, jerking her arm free and turning once again toward the door.

Taking her roughly by both arms, Simon turned her back to face him, his countenance white with suppressed anger. His cold eyes staring relentlessly into hers, he said softly, "But you will wait until I have finished speaking with you, just the same.

Someone must straighten out the mess you have made of your life."

"If that is so, Simon, that person will not be you!"

"That person *will* be me!" Simon demanded, jerking her forcefully back to the chair and pushing her down firmly onto the seat. "Now sit there and listen to what I have to say!"

Shaking with fury, Melanie sat rigidly on the chair, her golden eyes smoldering as she stared forward into space, deliberately ignoring him as he spoke.

"Since you have conducted your life in such a foolish and haphazard manner thus far, Melanie, I have come to the decision that someone must take a hand in your future. Aside from assigning my lawyer to study the handling of Asa's estate, I have transferred the deed to this house into your name."

Melanie gasped, her eyes darting quickly to his face to see if he joked, and seeing him in dead earnest, allowed her eyes to remain there while he continued.

"I have made the deed out with the provision that I am not to be denied entrance at any time, and the sale of the premises must have my prior approval." Shooting her a small, undereyed glance, he commented quickly, "I did not feel those precautions to be unreasonable, considering the terms of our present arrangement. I have also put a number of shares of stock into your and Sara's names, with you as guardian of her funds until she is twenty-one years of age. These stocks are particularly stable, and provide healthy dividends, so proper management should give you some future potential." Without waiting for her comment, he continued brusquely,

"Now I will need your signature on a few of these papers before the legal arrangements may be secured."

"Simon—"

Ignoring her attempt to speak, Simon put the pen in her hand, and pointing to an endless sheaf of papers, repeated again and again, "Sign here . . . and here . . . and here . . ."

Following orders like a mechanical doll, Melanie affixed her signature to each appointed spot, only to have Simon say with complete disgust as he gathered the papers together and stacked them into a neat pile. "Well, you have done it again, Melanie. You have signed an endless stack of legal papers without reading one of them. You don't really know what you've signed, do you, Melanie?"

"Simon! What are you saying?" Melanie's eyes were wide with puzzlement.

Staring into her beautiful baffled face, Simon suddenly sighed, covering his eyes wearily with one hand. "I'm saying nothing, Melanie, except that you have once again leaped into a course of action without investigating the circumstances completely."

"But, I trust you, Simon."

"And that is what I'm trying to tell you, Melanie." Simon's voice held a peculiarly sad quality, "You trust . . . you trust too much, Melanie. Everyone is not as honest as you." Looking up, he realized she was completely confounded by his odd behavior, and rising, he took her by the arm and led her to the door. Cupping her face in his hands, he kissed her lips lightly and said, "Go and tell Mrs. Walters to prepare for another for dinner. I want to finish up in here. I'll be ready in half an hour."

"Simon, please, I want to talk to you."

"Later, darling, please. Let me finish up in here first."

Nodding her head, Melanie turned away and started down the hall as Simon's eyes followed her retreating figure. When she disappeared around the corner, he closed the door quietly and returned to sit at his desk. Resting his elbows on the smooth surface, he buried his face in his hands for a few long moments.

What in hell had possessed him to treat Melanie like that? Even though she had refused to admit it, he had frightened her half to death, and he knew it. Had it been her comment about Josh Whitmore that had sparked his jealousy? It had been a hell of a month, damn it! Ever since that day in the State House when he had seen Melanie's eyes while they rested on Stephen Hull, he had suffered the tortures of the damned. Melanie would never look at him that way. To her he was just a temporary, necessary alliance. Nothing he could do could stir her jealousy. Her anger, yes, but that was all. But the reverse was true of him. Never having cared enough for a woman to experience the painful emotion, he suddenly knew the green-eyed monster as his constant companion. He did not question her fidelity—Melanie did not play that kind of game, and strangely, neither did he any longer. Which had brought him to the scene he had just forced upon her.

After forcing himself to face some painful facts, he had acknowledged that Melanie would someday declare her desire to end their relationship. He had developed an uncommon tenderness for her, and worry for her future began to cloud his every waking thought. She was too vulnerable, too trusting . . . a mature, loving woman in so many ways, and an inexperienced child in others. His desire to remove the financial need from her future had motivated the work he had done in her behalf, and his own jealousy had motivated the rest.

Shaking his head in a totally bemused manner, he thought wearily, You did not know when you were well off, Simon, old fool. You had to possess the little golden witch . . . and now she possesses you.

Hours later they lay abed in the bedroom at the top of the stairs. Melanie's head rested comfortably against Simon's smooth chest, the steady, even beat of his heart under her cheek lulling her into a sense of warm tranquility. They had just finished making love, and the delicious aura lingered on. Sliding her hand lightly up the side of Simon's neck and across his cheek, Melanie ran her finger experimentally across the deep cleft in his chin.

To his inquisitive gaze she murmured lazily, "I have always secretly wondered how it would feel to do that." Her eyes brightening slightly, she added, "And what's more, I have wanted many times to do this." Raising herself slightly, she planted a firm kiss on the tempting cleft, inadvertently rubbing her full, naked breasts up against Simon's chest as she moved against him.

"Melanie, dear," Simon said, taking a deep, ragged breath as she resumed her former position against his side, sliding her breasts back down his chest in the process, "do stay still. I have a very full day ahead of me tomorrow, and if you persist in this squirming, I suspect I will not spend the remainder of the night sleeping."

"Oh, Simon," Melanie laughed lightly, "you know you don't come here when you want to get a good night's sleep!" Then blushing at her own bold statement, she avoided Simon's appraising stare. "I suppose becoming a woman of substance has made me suddenly brazen."

"You have always been a woman of substance, Melanie, dear."

"But in that case," Melanie continued, choosing to ignore Simon's flattery, "I will take advantage of my sudden boldness to ask some of the questions that have been pestering my mind."

"Think carefully before you ask, Melanie," Simon cautioned.

Completely ignoring his words, Melanie continued. "First, how old are you, Simon?" Her fingers lightly played with the gray at his temples as he managed to convey his disapproval of her presumption with a slight raising of his brow.

"I did not think age was of any particular consequence to you, Melanie," he began shortly, "since in the past you have demonstrated a—"

"Simon!" Melanie interrupted, a small frown creasing her brow, "you are trying to make me angry, but I will not be put off. I am wise to this particular tactic of yours. Come now, tell me. How old are you?"

Finally smiling openly, Simon touched her soft cheek lightly with the tip of his finger. "I am thirty-six years old, Melanie . . . old enough to know better, but not wise enough to follow my own better judgment." Directing his suddenly sober gaze into her eyes, he continued softly, "And you are eighteen years old, Melanie. Eighteen years separate us . . ."

The peculiar sadness in Simon's glance had a sobering effect on Melanie, and snuggling tightly against his side, she whispered against his chest, "You are wrong, Simon. Nothing at all separates us right now."

The long moments of silence following were finally broken as Melanie whispered again, "I have another question, Simon."

"Melanie . . ." Simon's voice bore a warning note.

"Your lawyer visited Salisbury. Did he, perchance, mention anything of Martha and Tom Hartley? Are they still residing in the house on Weaver's Row?"

"As a matter of fact, Melanie, I did ask Mr. Pringle to inquire as to their welfare. They continue to live in Asa Parker's house, and will stay there until the estate is settled and the house sold." His face softening a bit, Simon added softly, "Tom has recovered fully from the blow on his head the day of your departure, and aside from what Mr. Pringle described as a 'moody streak,' he appears to be quite well."

"He is moody because he misses Sara and me," Melanie mumbled without the slightest pretense at modesty. "I was his only true friend, and Sara was the light of his existence." Blinking back sudden tears, Melanie said in a slightly choked voice, "Well, I miss them too, but there is no turning back the clock."

Simon directed his glance into her tear-filled eyes. "That's right, Melanie, and right now that fact makes me a very happy man."

A small smile picked up the corners of Melanie's full lips, and hoping to raise her spirits a bit further, he teased, "You certainly cannot be accused of having an overly inquisitive mind if those were the only questions pestering you all this time."

"I have another . . ." Melanie was strangely hesitant to approach the next.

"Do you?"

Taking a deep breath, Melanie blurted in a bold rush, "What is your wife like, Simon?"

Simon's features tightened in obvious anger as he answered curtly, "I refuse to discuss my wife."

"Simon."

"I refuse to discuss my wife while I am in my bed with another woman."

Suddenly angry herself, Melanie stated imperiously, "You forget, Simon, this is not *your* house any longer. You are not in *your* bed, you are in *my* bed!"

"Melanie, dear," Simon's voice was insidiously sweet, "I told you I had deeded the *house* over to you. I made no mention of the furniture!"

"That is ridiculous!" Melanie gasped, "What am I to do with a house that has no furniture?"

"I have no idea, my dear," Simon responded lightly with an acid smile, "but I think I can safely presume you will not spend your time asking foolish questions!"

"Simon!"

Unable to think of any further retort in her fury, Melanie stayed staring into his eyes in angry frustration until the absurdity of the situation dawned upon her, and a small smile cracked her frozen facade. Within moments she was laughing helplessly, causing an edge of speculation to enter Simon's glance as he eyed her warily.

"Simon," she gasped finally, still breathless from her uninterrupted mirth, "dear Simon. I don't really care what your wife is like. I can only think one thing. She must be at least seven different kinds of a fool to have allowed you to escape her!"

With a sudden warmth in his clear blue eyes, Simon said softly, his mouth descending toward her with clear intent, "Oh, yes, Melanie, I do agree. At the very least seven."

"How do I look, Simon? Do I look quite presentable?" Her fingers fluttering nervously against her hair. Melanie turned away from the bedroom mirror for Simon's approval, her eyes bright with true anxiety.

Never a man for blatant flattery, Simon's eyes swept her critically. The burning auburn of her hair was brilliantly coiffed into a shining mass of curls atop her head with two gleaming spirals allowed to fall gracefully against her slender neck. His glance trailed the creamy skin of her shoulders, displayed to perfection in the off-the-shoulder gown. Cupping the smooth line gently was a wide ruffle of ecru lace, which hung gracefully to provide a delicately provocative cover for her upper arm. The copper silk of her bodice hugged her slender curves temptingly, dipping to a tight point at the waist to flare out grandly in shimmering irridescence to the hemline, where a hint of ecru lace peeked out just above the brown satin, high-heeled slippers she wore on her dainty feet. As she turned back and forth for his appraisal, a single gold, jeweled butterfly sparkled from a swirl of hair behind her small ear, as if poised in anticipated flight.

His light, penetrating eyes completely serious, Simon replied simply, "You are exquisite, Melanie. Your lovely little butterfly could find no fairer bloom in Philadelphia on which to alight."

"Simon! Thank you!" Melanie flushed at the unexpected extravagance of his compliment.

"But wait!" Putting his forefinger to his bottom lip in a pensive pose, he continued, "there is something that can be improved!"

"I should have known," Melanie mumbled under her breath as Simon turned his back and walked to the dresser drawer.

When he turned back to her he was carrying a small satin case, and stopping in front of her he said softly, "I think this will add the finishing touch to your ensemble."

As he opened the case, a large golden topaz on a heavy antique chain caught the light, and Melanie gasped aloud. Beside it, two smaller topaz earbobs winked appealingly.

"Simon, what is this?"

"It should be quite obvious, Melanie. It is a necklace and earrings."

"Oh, Simon," Melanie's voice was impatient. "You know what I mean. Why have you done this?"

Removing the necklace from the box, he reached around her neck and fastened it easily, answering as he did, "Because I wanted to, Melanie, and because these stones are the exact color of your eyes and called out your name the moment I saw them.''

Turning to glance in the mirror, Melanie's eyes widened, and she reached without another moment's hesitation into the box and, removing the earbobs, fastened them on her ears. Then turning back toward him, she whispered, truly flustered, ''Simon, I have never owned anything so beautiful. Thank you does not seem adequate somehow.'' Suddenly flinging her arms around his neck, she pressed herself against him in a tight embrace. ''You are too good to me, Simon, you really are.''

''Am I really?'' he teased her gently, moving her far enough away so he might look into her face. ''I shall have to remember to remind you about those words at the appropriate time in the future, but now,'' he added, pushing her more firmly away, ''we must go downstairs. Our guests will be arriving soon.''

''Oh!'' Melanie mumbled. She had almost forgotten that she was to entertain Simon's friends at her first dinner party at the Walnut Street address. It did not seem quite proper to her, somehow, and she had protested quite bitterly when Simon had made the suggestion, but he had been adamant.

''Congress will be adjourning for the month of August, Melanie, and I would like to have a few of my friends to dinner.''

''But here, Simon? Surely your own residence is a better choice. Even though most of your friends seem to accept me, every one of them is quite aware of my . . . position. They will not bring their wives to this house, and you know it.''

''I have not invited their wives.''

"And I shall be the only woman present! Simon!"

"You will be my hostess, Melanie. My friends were all delighted with the invitation. As a matter of fact, Horace Wheeler's son hinted so broadly that he should like to attend along with his father that I was forced to invite him also." Frowning slightly, he mumbled, "And I don't really like the young pup."

Young pup is right, Melanie thought with a slight frown. Byron Wheeler had been following at her heels to the point of actual discomfort since she met him several weeks before. Unwilling to bring the matter to Simon's attention, Melanie had attempted to handle it on her own, but had not been too successful in discouraging the arrogant fellow's advances. The broad shouldered, sandy-haired young man had even taken to showing up for her sittings at Mr. Peale's studio, his hungry, dark eyes playing over her body with irritating familiarity for the duration of her sitting, until she was almost ready to wring his neck in frustration. But nothing could dent his staggering self-confidence, and he continued to press his unwanted advances.

Now the night of the dinner party had arrived, and Melanie still had grave reservations about the evening to come.

Noting her frown, Simon said lightly, "Come now, Melanie, stop your worrying. You've planned the evening perfectly, Helga has the kitchen in excellent control, and I have even allowed you to borrow one of my staff to help serve so that Molly will be free to stay with Sara. You are worrying needlessly. Relax and enjoy the evening, Melanie."

His smile coaxed one in return from Melanie, and

relief flooded Simon's senses. He was extremely proud of Melanie, proud of her in every way, and somehow it was very important that his friends realize his esteem for her. Their relationship had far exceeded in depth those of his former alliances, for him at least, and he had a burning desire for his friends to accept that difference.

Offering her his arm, he said lightly, "Shall we go down, Melanie?"

With an obviously feigned expression of shock, Melanie exclaimed suddenly, "Certainly not, Simon. I have not yet given your appearance my approval!"

Walking around him slowly, she put her finger to her lip in the same pensive expression Simon had used earlier. Her eyes touched on the smooth brown of his hair, and smiling at the familiar hint of gray at the temples, she moved her glance over his lean, lightly tanned face, clashing with and holding those clear, translucent eyes for only a few short seconds before continuing her perusal. He wore a fine lawn shirt and cravat, but had chosen to wear a banyan of a deep green Chinese silk in place of his heavy coat, in deference to the warmth of the evening, and in startling contrast, a lightweight waistcoat and breeches in midnight blue. Smiling to herself as she walked around him for the second time while he regarded her with amusement, she thought silently, Simon, you are a devastatingly attractive man. Coming to stand in front of him, she announced finally, "You look quite handsome, but there is something that appears to be missing—Oh! I know what it is . . ." Standing up on tiptoe, she pressed her mouth firmly against his and kissed him thoroughly, scampering out of his reach just as his arms moved up to clasp her against him.

With a small smile, she took his arm and said quietly, "Now you look just right. Shall we go down, Simon?"

The spark of laughter in his eyes was her only answer as they turned toward the door, arm and arm.

The evening was going very well. The buffet had been a tremendous success. In strict accord with Melanie's instructions, delicately browned cold fried chicken, heaped high upon a huge platter, dominated one end of the table, around which various relishes and pickled and sliced fresh vegetables were arranged. The center of the table bore a platter of Helga's finest dark bread, the crust crisp and shining, placed in alternating slices with her special corn bread in an attractive fan pattern. A large wheel of yellow cheese and a crock of freshly churned sweet butter was nearby to tempt the palate even further. At the other end of the table a large ham, expertly spiced and fresh from the oven, stole the scene, complemented by bowls of candied sweet potatoes and fresh peas. All as delicious as it was appetizing, the guests ate heartily despite the heat of the evening, and when it seemed they could eat no more, an elegant tea cart arrived bearing assorted fresh fruits, a towering brandied pudding, and a tantalizing chocolate torte, the sight of which drew loud groans from the men who knew that despite their better judgment, they would make room for more.

Each of the eight men present, visibly impressed with the arrangements and the warmth of Melanie's

hospitality, followed her slender figure affectionately with their eyes as she moved gracefully between
her guests. Extremely pleased as the evening progressed, Simon whispered in her ear, "I am the envy of
all my friends tonight, darling. Neither they nor I can
seem to keep our eyes off you."

Laughing lightly, Melanie whispered in return,
"Since there are no other women present, Simon, you
must admit part of my success could be attributed to a
lack of competition."

"My dear Melanie," Simon responded earnestly,
his gaze locking with hers for long, sober seconds,
"there is never an occasion when you have any true
competition."

Startled by his obviously sincere compliment,
Melanie's gaze held his wordlessly for a few moments, until a frantic movement at the doorway
suddenly drew both their glances to a worried Molly,
holding a tearful Sara just out of sight of the guests.
Before Melanie could take a step toward them, Simon
said with a broadening smile, "Come in, Molly. Are
you having a problem with your little mistress?"

Their entrance drew all eyes in the direction of the
beautiful, fiery-haired child in the long white night
rail, whose golden eyes still welled with stubborn
tears while wide streaks of those she had already shed
trailed down her rosey cheeks. Her lower lip still
trembling with an impending wail, she spotted
Simon's tall figure and immediately stretched out her
arms in irresistible appeal.

"I cannot make her go to bed, Sir. She has been
crying for the past hour, and I didn't know what else
to do with her." Molly's apologetic tone held a touch

of embarrassment.

Barely able to conceal his smile, Simon lifted the child easily from Molly's arms, speaking softly into the small, pointed face turned up to his, "Have you been misbehaving again, Sara?"

The small head wagged furiously from side to side in adamant denial before Sara lay her damp cheek against his to whisper in his ear, "Want Simee . . ."

Working to suppress his smile amid the chuckles of the group that had gravitated around the appealing child, he responded firmly, "It is time to sleep now, Sara. You may kiss your mother goodnight, and then you must go with Molly. I will be here in the morning when you wake up."

Studying his face soberly, Sara began to wag her head negatively, and when her response drew a darkening frown from Simon, she abruptly changed direction and began nodding vigorously, a small smile dimpling her full cheeks. The gale of laughter her actions brought from the group of men surrounding them snapped the child's head in their direction and Simon said lightly, "Gentlemen, I'd like you to meet Miss Sara Morganfield."

The wide, gold eyes so similar to her mother's slowly scanned each face amid glowing responses.

"Beautiful child."

"Saucy little charmer."

"Picture of her mother."

Standing aside from the group, completely stunned by the whole scene, Melanie stood in open-mouthed surprise. When had this transformation come about? Was this the same Simon who had regarded Sara so warily on the trip to Philadelphia just a few months before? She had been aware of Sara's unexplainable attachment to Simon, but the true warmth in Simon's eyes could not be misinterpreted, nor could his undeniable expression of pride as he displayed Sara to his friends.

"Your daughter is quite lovely, Melanie."

Nodding a polite thank-you to Theodore Billings, Melanie heard a soft voice in her ear as a surreptitious, caressing hand crept around her waist. "Almost as lovely as her mother."

Quick to take advantage of the distraction her daughter was creating, Byron Wheeler boldly pressed a light kiss on the corner of Melanie's mouth as she turned.

Anger obvious in the heat of her glance, Melanie firmly jerked his arm from her waist and moved forward into the group, extending her arms toward Sara.

"Come now, you little vixen," Melanie said sternly to her child, propped so comfortably against Simon's chest, "I will put you to bed, and this time you will stay there."

Contrarily, Sara turned from her mother's extended hands to wrap her plump little arms around Simon's neck, as a chorus of deep sounds of approval echoed within the group. This time the smile did momentarily break through Simon's stern facade before he wrestled it down to say firmly, "Goodnight, Sara. I will see you in the morning."

Pulling herself slightly away, Sara stared into Simon's face for a brief second, and suddenly placing a short kiss against his unsmiling lips, she then turned to her mother with outstretched arms.

337

Shaking her head with a small smile, Melanie mumbled under her breath as she took her completely docile daughter into her arms, "Sara, my little darling, you are quite the little coquette." Then turning, she walked unhesitantly from the room, a slightly shame-faced Molly following quietly behind.

Within minutes she was back at Simon's side, having tucked her capricious child firmly into bed and unhesitantly closed the door behind her. An obvious warmth shone from Simon's eyes as he glanced down into her face, and slipping his arm around her waist, he pulled her lightly against his side as he resumed his conversation. It was a tender, possessive gesture that did not go unnoticed by the men surrounding him, and Melanie flushed slightly at their speculative glances. Quite obviously she was not the only person startled by Simon's behavior this night.

Before the hour had passed, Melanie again slipped away from the group and ascended the stairs to check on Sara's status. Finding her child sleeping angelically, with a dutiful Molly seated watchfully in the corner of the room, she quietly closed the door behind her. Reaching the foot of the staircase, she had just turned toward the living room where the men had retired to smoke, when she was snatched roughly into the corner by a pair of waiting arms. Warm lips brushed against hers as she was pressed against a broad chest. Struggling against his overpowering strength, she heard Byron's voice whisper huskily, "Be still, Melanie. Don't make a fuss. I've wanted to hold you in my arms since I first saw you."

"How dare you molest me in my own home, Byron?" Melanie hissed, incensed by his gall. "Release me this minute, or I'll call for help."

"Are you afraid to let me kiss you, Melanie . . . afraid you'll like it too much?"

"Like it too much? Hah!" Melanie exclaimed in soft vehemence. "What makes you think I would prefer the pawings of an immature boy just out of puberty to the lovemaking of a grown and accomplished gentleman?"

Her deliberate barb stung deep, and Byron's dark eyes flashed with anger as he murmured heatedly, "I am quite a few years older than you, but I suppose you force me to prove that I am mature in my passion as well."

Suddenly Byron's arms were ripped away from her as he was jerked around to face Simon's enraged countenance. "You will prove nothing and do nothing, aside from leaving this house!"

Running his fingers through his sandy hair, Byron turned to stubbornly face Melanie. "Do you wish me to leave, Melanie?" His dark eyes bore an unbelievable spark of hope as he faced Melanie's flustered face.

Simon moved toward him with an angry growl, but Melanie stepped quickly between them, blocking his access to the unhappy young man as she whispered quietly, "Please leave immediately, Byron."

Acknowledging her request sadly with a slight nod of his head, Byron turned, lifting his gaze momentarily to the doorway behind them and moved toward it. As it closed behind him, both Melanie and Simon turned to confront Horace Wheeler's embarrassed face.

Completely speechless for a few awkward seconds, the man's flushed face betrayed his discomfort. "Please accept my apologies for my son's unforgivable actions, Simon, but if I may offer a few words in his defense, may I say that a full evening's exposure to Melanie's beauty and charm is extremely intoxicating, and was perhaps too heady for a man of my son's youth to carry off well. I must admit I am somewhat smitten by Melanie's charms myself, and had I still the impetuousness of youth, I might find myself in much the same predicament as my son right now. However," he continued apologetically, "there is no true excuse for his boorishness, and I hope you will not hold his foolish actions against either one of us."

Simon hesitated, looking for a brief moment down into Melanie's anxious face. With a small smile, he slipped his left arm around her waist, drawing her with him toward his embarrassed friend, his right hand extended in truce.

"No hard feelings, Horace." His voice was honestly gracious. "If I am to be completely honest, I must admit I was guilty of much the same boorish behavior the first time I met Melanie. I only hope your son is more successful than I in getting her out of his mind, because I have no intention of giving her up, and," he continued with noticeable emphasis, "I will not be as tolerant a second time."

A few days later Simon arrived unexpectedly in mid-afternoon, announcing to Melanie with a

340

combined air of relief and suppressed anticipation as he strode into the parlor, "Well, Melanie, Congress has adjourned for the month of August." Turning to Mrs. Walters who still stood by the doorway, he issued a quick request, "We would like something cooling to drink, Mrs. Walters," and then turning back to Melanie, took her hand, pulling her down to sit beside him on the sofa as he continued speaking.

"Many of Congress' decisions affect my business directly. Congress has voted to put the colonies in a state of defense; privateers are to be financed to harass British merchant ships, all trade restrictions are to be dispensed with, and traffic resumed with foreign countries. There is even talk of overtures being made to France for her help. In any case, I must return to New York without delay. We shall have to leave tomorrow morning at the very latest. Since Congress is set to reconvene in September, it is vital that my business be concluded and I return for the first session. When she returns you may instruct Mrs. Walters to begin packing for you and Sara and instruct Molly she is to travel with us to assist in Sara's care."

"Simon!" Melanie was aghast, "surely you don't expect Sara and me to accompany you to New York?"

Stiffening defensively, Simon answered sharply, "Is that not what I have just said?"

"But that will be quite impossible."

"Impossible?"

"Simon, surely you remember the hardship our journey from Salisbury to Philadelphia worked on Sara, not to mention the strain her cranky behavior was on both of us. Now, with the heat and humidity

341

of August, it will be impossible."

"This will be a considerably shorter journey, Melanie. Merely a day and a half at most. If we start out promptly tomorrow morning, we should arrive at my residence in New York in late morning of the following day. We will also have Molly along to assist with Sara, freeing the both of us for a good part of the day."

"I'm sorry, Simon," Melanie was adamant, but avoided his eyes as she stated firmly, "It is quite impossible. We will wait in Philadelphia for your return."

Simon hesitated, his observant blue eyes noting the manner in which she averted her gaze, and taking her hand in his, he said slowly, "Melanie, if you are worried that you run the risk of encountering Stephen Hull, you may set your mind at rest. Allen, Warner and Hull received full authorization from the New York Assembly approximately two weeks ago and left almost immediately for Fort Ticonderoga."

Melanie hesitated briefly before responding. She was not particularly fond of Simon's uncanny ability to read her thoughts and debated whether she should confirm his only too accurate assessment. Finally she replied candidly, "Why didn't you tell me when you first heard the report, Simon?"

"I hadn't realized you suffered such anxiety with regard to Hull's whereabouts and activities."

Unable to ignore the heavy, sarcastic overtone to his reply, Melanie shot him a black glance, instinctively snatching her hand away, and not choosing to honor his comment with an answer, she stated firmly, "I still can't go, Simon."

A sudden flash suffusing his face, Simon's voice was carefully controlled as he spoke his next words. "Then I must insist that you give me your complete reason for not wishing to accompany me to New York, Melanie."

Suddenly furious with his imperious, high-handed manner, Melanie burst out angrily, her eyes blazing, "I'm surprised your superior intuitive powers have failed you so completely this time, Simon. The 'complete reason' I still refuse to go to New York with you is simply because of the fact that your *wife* is in New York! I simply do not wish to run the risk of running into your *wife!*" Turning quickly away, Melanie swallowed hard against the tears threatening to overcome her when she suddenly felt Simon's hands on her shoulders turning her gently to face him.

His face was contrite, his tone apologetic as he pulled her against his chest and whispered softly against her hair, "Melanie, darling, I'm sorry. But I still can't understand why—"

"Simon," pulling away from his comforting embrace, she looked fully into his eyes. "It is one thing to be your mistress in Philadelphia, when your wife is in New York and can pretend she knows nothing of your activities, but to come openly as your mistress into the very city where she resides—I cannot do that to her, or to myself."

"Melanie, I have told you, Charlotte cares very little what I do as long as I continue to support her in the style to which she is accustomed. As a matter of fact, she has told me on several occasions that my mistresses relieve her of a necessity to perform what she considers very unappealing duties."

"Simon, I can't believe that—truly I can't."

"Nevertheless, it is the truth, Melanie."

"But where would Sara and I stay, Simon?"

"With me, of course."

"Your wife, you and I, and Sara in the same house? Simon, you are insane!" Melanie drew as far away from him as his embrace would allow in an instinctive reaction to the unlikely arrangement.

"Melanie, my wife and I are estranged. We maintain separate residences within the same city. My house is across town from hers, and it is very unlikely that you will run into each other at all. Charlotte has never shown even the slightest interest in the women in my life."

Hesitating for a few moments, Melanie seemed to consider all he had said, and suddenly shaking her head, said emphatically, "I'm sorry, Simon, we will stay in Philadelphia and wait for your return."

Stiffening noticeably, Simon's hands dropped from Melanie's shoulders. "I will be absent from Philadelphia for a month, Melanie."

"Nevertheless, we will remain here."

His voice suddenly hard, Simon eyed her coldly. "I'm afraid I must insist that you accompany me, Melanie."

"Insist!" Melanie exclaimed heatedly, "Insist! You cannot insist, Simon. I am your mistress, not your slave!"

"And this is purely a business arrangement between us, is that not right?"

"Yes, a business arrangement."

"Payment due for services rendered, am I right?"

"What do you—"

"Am I right?" Simon demanded.

"Yes, you are right!" Melanie's voice was close to a shout.

"And do you expect to live here on my charity for the next month, or do you expect me to travel the distance from New York to Philadelphia each time I feel the need for your services?"

"Simon!"

"Answer me, Melanie!"

"How could you—?"

"I said answer me!"

"No, I do not expect you to travel from New York to Philadelphia, nor do I expect to live on your charity!"

Pausing for long moments as he stared silently and intently into her eyes, his glance frigid, Simon said quietly, with an air of complete finality, "Then you will be ready to travel tomorrow morning at six."

Jumping to her feet, Melanie looked down at Simon's coldly confident expression, her eyes blazing. "Yes, we will be ready! Damn you, Simon Young!" she shouted as she turned away and stomped toward the door, "We will be ready at six!"

Mrs. Walters took that moment to appear in the doorway with two glasses on a tray, and stared in an utterly bemused fashion as Melanie stomped past her and up the staircase. Her startled glance followed Melanie to the top of the stairs and returned to Simon as he stood calmly and walked toward her.

Taking one glass from the tray, Simon raised it slowly to his lips and took a small sip.

"Excellent," he murmured softly, and then more clearly, "Thank you, that will be all, Mrs. Walters."

Melanie retired early that evening, having supervised the packing and eaten a scanty, solitary dinner. Having heard the front door close behind Simon a few short minutes after she had stomped from the room, she had run to the window and watched his stately figure climb into the carriage, mumbling under her breath, "And good riddance," as he drove away. After having twisted and turned in bed for more than an hour, she had finally dozed off when a sound at her bedside awakened her to see Simon getting quietly into bed beside her.

"What are you doing here?" Her voice was resentful. "I thought you would be packing and attending to details."

"My valet is doing the packing and attending to the last minute details as well. Peter will be here at six." Simon's voice was soft and husky as he slid his arm under her rigid shoulders and drew her against him.

"It's too warm tonight, Simon," Melanie said irritably, still peeved at his behavior of that afternoon.

"And it will soon be a lot warmer, my darling Melanie," he whispered softly, pressing soft kisses against her lips and neck. When still she remained rigid in his arms, he whispered against her ear, "My darling, darling Melanie. Aren't you the least bit flattered that in a city as big as New York I can think of no woman whose services I could tolerate for even a short month now that I have found you?"

Unbending enough for a short laugh, Melanie

346

replied in a whisper, "You don't really expect me to believe that, do you Simon? It is simply your pride. You simply would not allow me to get the best of you, that's all."

"Melanie darling," Simon whispered as he continued spreading warm kisses along her cheek and neck and nibbling lightly at her earlobe. "You do me a dreadful injustice. Can't you see I'd be bereft without you?"

"Simon—"

"Absolutely bereft."

Unable to withstand his unusual cajoling mood any longer, Melanie finally relaxed in his arms, her own arms going around his neck, her hands sliding up into his heavy dark hair where she tightened her fingers in a slightly painful grip for a few brief seconds before loosening them again to move caressingly.

"Oh, Simon," she sighed against his cheek, "if I were to be completely honest, I'd have to admit I'd probably miss you like the very devil if I didn't see you for a month. I know no one else who can raise me to a heated frenzy as quickly and efficiently as you."

"And that is what I intend to do tonight, Melanie, darling, stir you into a heated frenzy."

"Simon! I didn't mean that," she laughed, slightly embarrassed with his interpretation of her remark.

"But I did, my darling," he whispered softly, his mouth moving to cover hers, "I meant every word . . ."

Chapter 8

Moving lazily, with the grace and beauty of a small, golden feline, Melanie stretched up her arms, relaxing suddenly to let them fall back against her pillow as she luxuriated in the comfort of the deep, downy mattress. The hot summer sun was just beginning to peep through the open balcony doors, and a cool morning breeze, fresh with the scent of flowers, stirred the air. With a small, serene smile, her topaz eyes traveled the luxury of the master bedroom. Large and airy, it was almost sinfully opulent with its dark, masterfully carved mahogany furniture and elegant touches of crystal, silver, and gleaming brass. The color of the sun was reflected in the yellow background of the delicately printed wall covering and repeated in the matching pattern of the fabric that covered the high-backed boudoir chairs and sofa. The same material was skillfully draped at the balcony doors and hung in a brilliant cascade of color from the canopy of the huge, ornately carved mahogany bed that dominated the center of the room. A rich Persian rug in deep hues of brown and gold ran from the elaborate marble fireplace, where the sofa and chairs were grouped, to the opposite wall, just short of the French doors to the balcony overlooking the garden. It was a splendid room, combining the perfect taste and elegance that was indicative of the entire ten room Georgian mansion that was Simon's New York home.

Contrary to her expectations, it had been a marvelous week! Simon spent only part of each day attending to business and the remainder showing her the diversity of the teeming city. He had taken her to the docks and escorted her through the offices of his shipping company with an offhanded pride, and with considerable amusement had pointed out the spot on the pier where a year before Captain James Chambers' ship the *London* had been boarded by irate citizens who had cast 342 casks of tea into the ocean. He had escorted her through countless waterfront shops, walking silently by her side as she had exclaimed rapturously over the unusual and often exotic items displayed, nodding lightly in approval of her selections.

This morning before leaving at an early hour for his offices, Simon had casually mentioned that he would return for her shortly before the noon hour so they could lunch as guests of Captain Wilbur Smythe aboard his own ship the *Eastern Queen* which had docked the previous day. All in all, she was secretly pleased that Simon had forced her to accompany him to New York, but with a small laugh, admitted she would die before she would confess that to him.

A sudden frown creased Melanie's smooth brow. Despite Simon's attentiveness, she knew that he became more and more concerned about the country's state of affairs as each day passed. Having returned from a meeting at the Fraunces Tavern late the previous night, he had confided that the prominent citizens comprising The Social Club that had met in the tavern's Long Room for many years, had met for the last time. Torn assunder by debate between its royalist and patriot members, the long standing club voted to disband, an act further demonstrating, in Simon's opinion, the strife that would tear the colonies apart when the inevitable war with England was declared. In the dark of the long night, with Melanie his attentive sounding board, Simon had decided to change the home port of his ships in his certainty that when war came, New York would be one of the first cities threatened.

With a slight shrug of irritation, Melanie attempted to ignore the thought that had been constantly recurring of late. War. Steve's association with Ethan Allen would have him immediately in the thick of battle. Why is it, she mused angrily, her eyes filling with frustrated tears, that despite his obvious contempt for me, I still cannot banish thoughts of him from my mind?

Determined not to allow herself to fall into that same trap again, Melanie arose from bed. She had lounged there longer than she should have dared, and lifting the long, shining spirals of hair that were just beginning to stick to her neck with perspiration, she walked to the washstand. Glancing quickly at the delicate French clock on the mantel, she began sponging herself lightly. In all likelihood, Sara had already awakened and was probably in her bath at the present moment. Molly's fondness for the bright, precocious child allowed her more and more latitude, a fact of which Sara was quick to take advantage. When they returned home to Philadelphia, she was going to have to do something positive in that direction, but for the time being, she would merely have to maintain the firm guiding hand that Molly lacked.

Hastily brushing her hair into a gleaming, fiery cascade, Melanie had just slipped into a soft, cotton batiste chemise when she heard a male voice in the hallway.

"No! It can't be Simon already! Something must have happened to bring him home at such an early hour." Quickly reaching for the gold Chinese silk banyan Simon had purchased for her the previous day, she pushed her feet into the matching high-heeled slippers beside her feet and, pulling it on as she ran, moved quickly across the hallway and down the stairs. She was halfway down the staircase when the well-dressed man in the foyer, just handing his hat to the maid, turned toward her.

Stopping suddenly, Melanie stared in surprise at the dark-haired stranger openly staring at her in return.

"Who are you?" Melanie burst out, clutching at the banyan that had been streaming out behind her as she ran.

"Good Lord!" the young man muttered softly as his eyes moved slowly over her small, pointed face, his gaze catching and clinging for a moment to the wide, amber glow of her eyes and continuing to move appreciatively with an intense, open scrutiny over the rest of her body while she flushed hotly.

"I said, who are you?" Melanie demanded again, beginning to anger at his open assessment of her physical charms.

Seeming finally able to speak, the young man said in a low, almost pleading tone, "You are not Melanie Morganfield?"

"Yes, I am!" Melanie's answer was a trifle sharp. She was not very pleased with the fellow's manner. "And I will ask you one more time, who are you?"

"Oh, I beg your pardon," the young fellow said at last, smiling to show well-shaped teeth in an embarrassed smile. "I'm afraid the sight of you knocked me senseless for a few moments. Please forgive me . . . I'm a friend of Simon's, Michael Searle. As a matter of fact, I'm his brother-in-law."

"Brother-in-law!" Flushing even deeper, Melanie hesitated on the staircase, uncertain whether to make as dignified a retreat as possible or continue down the steps. She found herself exceedingly embarrassed to do either.

"Oh, don't let that upset you. May I call you

Melanie?" Michael's manner was suddenly solicitous as he walked up two steps and extended his hand toward her.

Slowly descending to take his hand, Melanie said self-consciously, "I'm not really dressed for company. I thought you were Simon and . . ." Then blushing again at the implication of her words, Melanie's voice faltered to an awkward stop.

With a small laugh, Michael drew her to the bottom step. "Don't be concerned, Melanie. Everyone is aware of the state of affairs between Simon and my sister. If I may speak freely, Simon has had many liaisons in the past, without my sister's approval or disapproval, I might add. She has not felt any of them a threat to her marriage, such as it is. The only reason that brings me here unannounced and uninvited," he continued softly, slipping his arm around her slim shoulders and drawing her with him into the parlor in a disconcertingly familiar manner, "is Simon's altogether unusual conduct. You see, he is usually extremely conservative, conducts his affairs discreetly, never, never," he repeated emphatically, "never entertaining women in this house. It was built as his 'married bachelor' residence, so to speak, six years ago when he and Charlotte went their separate ways, and it has been sacrosanct—until now."

"I had no idea—"

"And now Simon has appeared again after a long absence from the city, bringing you openly to install you in this house, escorts you everywhere. Melanie, you can well understand my sister's concern. My dear, you are the talk of the city!"

"Surely you exaggerate!"

"Not in the least! It is that gossip that stirred my sister to summon me, and hence, I am here."

"Oh."

Observing her distress, Michael coaxed lightly, "Please don't be embarrassed, Melanie. I truly am Simon's friend. My sister is a cold, unfeeling woman and my sympathies are with Simon, I assure you, but she is my sister, after all."

"Oh." Melanie muttered inanely. Unable to think of an adequate response, she looked into his dark, boyishly handsome face wordlessly, unintentionally lifting the full power of her sober amber gaze to his eyes.

Visibly affected, Michael swallowed hard. "You need say nothing, Melanie. All my questions are answered just in looking at you." Then in obvious sincerity he whispered softly, "I find you far too beautiful for mere words—"

"Then it would be my suggestion that you stop talking before you make a complete ass out of yourself, Michael," came a cold, deep voice from the doorway.

Both sets of eyes flashed in the direction of the tall, slender, perturbed gentleman observing them from the doorway as they exclaimed in unison, "Simon!"

"Yes, Simon." His sarcastic reply was delivered with a sardonic expression that decidedly increased Melanie's discomfort. Suddenly very conscious of her appearance, Melanie pulled her banyan even tighter against her, causing Simon to wrinkle his brow in an exceedingly pained expression.

"Melanie, dear, you are only making matters

worse. Kindly allow the garment to fall free of you before poor Michael suffers a severe attack of apoplexy.''

"Come now, Simon," Michael's sudden laugh was hearty and sincere as he walked toward his friend, his hand extended in greeting, "I didn't look quite that bad, did I?"

Accepting his hand, a small smile finally breaking through his austere expression, Simon answered quietly, "My dear fellow, you were not in a position to see the expression on your face when I entered the room. I think I can safely say that you were about to make a very grave error in judgment that could possibly have had a serious effect on our friendship.''

The openness of Simon's rebuke stunned Michael into a moment's silence, while he slowly digested the fact that he had just been issued an unqualified warning about his attitude toward Melanie. Unable to hide the hurt tone creeping into his voice, Michael said lightly, "It isn't at all like you to be so sharp with regard to your lady friends. You are generally considered to be a very tolerant man.''

"Then it would seem that the general consensus of opinion is wrong, wouldn't it, Michael?" Without waiting for a response, Simon then turned to address Melanie.

"I would suggest that you go upstairs and finish dressing. We will expect you back as soon as you are suitably attired.''

With an angry intake of breath and an instinctive elevation of her small chin, Melanie shot Simon a coldly dark look before marching wordlessly from the room. Too incensed at his boorish manner to reply, she ascended the staircase without a backward glance.

Both men followed her with their eyes until she disappeared from sight in the hallway above. First to break the silence was Michael as he gasped incredulously, "Lord, Simon, she cannot be real! I've never seen a woman her equal. Damn you, you lucky fellow, where did you find her?"

With a small smile, Simon turned toward the smitten young man. "Oh, yes, Michael, she is decidedly real, and my old friend, Bill Tryon, has my undying thanks for sending me on that extremely tedious and unproductive mission up north in the spring of last year. I found Melanie in a colorless, barely civilized town where her beauty and intelligence were superstitiously regarded as works of the devil. A good many of the townsfolk actually believe her to be a witch! Can you comprehend such ignorance, Michael?"

Hesitating a brief moment, Michael replied in all seriousness, "I'm afraid I find that attitude far more understandable than you think. Were I not a more educated man, I would think myself bewitched. The first sight of her knocked me completely breathless, Simon!"

"I'm afraid I can't claim the same thing, Michael. The first sight of Melanie amused me immensely, but God, man, the second time I saw her . . ." Simon's voice drifted off as he retired into memory, and Michael urged quietly, "Yes, yes, go ahead, continue."

"Oh, no." Simon was laughing heartily now at his friend's avid curiosity, "that is a memory shared by

Melanie and me alone . . . suffice it to say that the occasion was memorable enough to keep her constantly lurking just beyond my range of conscious thought, and to make me return this spring and bring her back with me."

"But damn it, Simon, a whole year! Why did you wait so long?"

There was a moment's hesitation before Simon replied thoughtfully, "Yes, that was a mistake, I should have gone to claim her sooner, and that mistake may yet be my undoing." A dark frown had slipped over his face, and Michael declined to press the question any further.

"And where do you go from here, Simon?"

"I'm afraid I don't quite understand your question, Michael."

"Well, I may as well come out with it. I'm here at Charlotte's request, Simon." The earnest young man's face looked decidedly guilty as Simon turned a speculative glance in his direction. "She has become concerned about your behavior. To be very honest, it has become an embarrassment to her."

"That is unfortunate, is it not?"

"You know Charlotte is not really concerned that you have a mistress."

"That's quite generous of her."

"All she asks is discretion."

"You may take this message back to my faithful wife, Charlotte, Michael. I no longer choose to be discreet. I am thirty-six years old, and I am finished with punishing myself with endless, back-street, meaningless affairs that bring me nothing but the stimulus of a few stolen moments just for the sake of an unfeeling, loveless woman's sense of pride. Even if that woman happens to be my legal wife. I choose now to live in daily contact with my mistress, to be able to experience every facet of her engaging and," he added with a small, wry smile, "sometimes volatile personality. I choose to broaden myself by the mutual sharing of our daily experiences, not limit myself rigidly to the tasting of one small aspect of a warm, intelligent, witty, complete, and loving woman. In short, Michael, I will not allow Charlotte's wishes to mold me into a frigid, inflexible male replica of herself!"

"Simon!" Michael flushed brightly. "Those are very harsh words you speak of my sister—"

"Nevertheless, Michael, as we both know only too well, they are the absolute truth."

"Well," Michael's expression a bit sheepish, he continued, "since you are being completely honest, you force me into honesty in return. Charlotte is truly a cold bitch."

Bursting out into sudden laughter, Simon shook his head unbelievingly. "You do have a way with words, Michael."

"And you know she will never consent to a divorce."

"I have not yet asked her for a divorce."

"Well, don't. It would be a complete waste of time."

"Michael, my friend," all the laughter dropped from Simon's face as he stated in a firm voice, "we have come to the end of our discussion. Now, tell me, would you like some tea? Melanie should be down any minute, and from her state of dress, or should I

358

say undress, I should think that she had only arisen a few moments before. I doubt if she or Sara has had breakfast."

"Sara? Who is Sara? Simon, have you taken a harem?" Michael's brown eyes bulged in wonder.

"Come now, Michael," Simon's good spirits seemed to revive at the incredulous expression of deep envy reflected in Michael's open features, "don't let your imagination get the better of you."

Suddenly a loud, angry wail interrupted Simon, and he turned expectantly toward the steps. A few moments later Melanie rounded the corner of the hallway, followed by Molly and her petulant, teary-eyed charge. Melanie's expression as she entered the room was one of complete exasperation.

"I'm sorry, Simon, but Sara heard your voice and has expressed quite emphatically her desire to wish you a good day. Since Molly was about to bring her down to breakfast anyway, there didn't seem any harm . . ."

Melanie's voice trailed off into silence as Molly entered the room behind her, and Sara's gleeful shouts effectually drowned her out. A fine one I am to speak of a firm, guiding hand, she thought in self-disgust as suddenly all smiles, the beaming child stretched out her arms, almost jumping from Molly's weary arms as she called repeatedly, "Simee, Simee, morning, morning."

With a sincere attempt to hide his pleasure, Simon slowly took the radiant child into his arms. "Sara, dear, good morning."

Within moments the child's arms were wrapped around his neck and Simon caught his friend's incredulous stare.

"So, this is Sara." Taking a deep breath, Michael asked bluntly, "Is she your child, Simon?"

Simon's answer was delivered quietly, with a dark frown at his friend's impertinence. "No, she is not and—"

"Then where is her father?"

"Sara's father is dead!" Melanie's angry voice turned Michael around to her livid countenance. "And I will tell you now, I do not intend to answer any further questions, Mr. Michael Searle. Your relationship to Simon does not entitle you to play inquisitor into my private life. In the future, I will thank you to mind your own business!"

Completely taken aback by Melanie's set down, Michael ran his slender fingers nervously through his dark, curly hair. "Melanie, I'm so sorry, I didn't mean . . . it's just that it is such a shock. Simon has always showed a definite disinterest in children, and there is an obvious bond between them." With a small smile, he added quickly, "You are to be congratulated, Melanie, she is a beautiful child," and continued in apparently sincere contrition. "Please credit my obnoxious behavior to the many surprises I have had this morning. I assure you, I am not usually such a boor."

In the light of the truly penitent expression on his handsome young face, Melanie's anger softened and, hesitating a moment, she said slowly, "All right, Michael, I will forgive you this time."

The beauty of the small smile that slowly broke across her exquisite features as she spoke had him gulping like a schoolboy, and with a quick, fluid movement, Michael snatched her small hand into his, kissing the back as he whispered softly, "Melanie, dear, you are too generous with my absolute stupidity."

"Michael." Simon's tone held a warning quality that was unmistakable.

Turning candidly, Michael said in an annoyed voice, "Simon, you are not going to be tiresome about this, are you? Good heavens, man, where is your spirit of generosity? I only kissed her *hand!*"

The sudden entrance of the maid precluded the necessity for a reply as Rose announced softly, "Breakfast is served in the morning room, Mr. Young."

"Very good!" Michael's exclamation carried considerable enthusiasm. "And since Simon's arm is otherwise engaged, let me offer to escort you into the morning room, Melanie." Offering her his arm in a courtly manner, he stopped at her startled expression and added lightly, "Oh, you needn't worry. Simon has already invited me to tea this morning. Come on now," he urged, "we mustn't let your breakfast get cold."

With a tentative smile, Melanie accepted the arm held out to her, shooting a quick look at Simon's black scowl before turning back to Michael and proceeding into the morning room.

Breakfast moved along briskly, assisted by Michael's bright, lively chatter. Simon, having relinquished Sara into Molly's care so she might attend to her meal in the quiet of the kitchen, sat silently for the most part, his eyes moving between Michael and Melanie as they spoke animatedly, his gaze inscrutable. A stimulating conversationalist, Michael's sense of humor seemed to spark Melanie's wit, resulting in a spontaneous and easy banter between them. Several times Melanie made an attempt to draw Simon from his pensive mood but each time was forced to turn back to Michael without success. Michael, completely lost in Melanie's beauty and charm and absolutely insensible to Simon's darkening mood, prattled happily on.

At the conclusion of breakfast, finally excusing herself with the defense of attending to Sara's morning routine, Melanie bid a dejected Michael goodbye, and shooting Simon a small smile, retired from the room, amid a storm of Michael's vehement protests.

Maintaining her distance from the drawing room where the men had retired to talk, Melanie amused herself with household tasks for the remainder of the morning. Michael was a delightfully entertaining young man, but entirely too insensitive to Simon's changeability. She could not quite put her finger on the cause for Simon's irritation, unless it was Michael's irritatingly blunt manner of intruding into their private affairs. But he was, after all, admittedly Simon's friend, and he would have to handle the man himself.

Simon's reminder that they were to leave for the *Eastern Queen* within the half hour arrived by way of the maid later that morning. Melanie was greatly relieved their outing had not been cancelled. She had been anticipating meeting the bold Captain Smythe, whom Simon had described as one of his hardest but most capable captains, and eagerly looked forward to a tour of his vessel. Simon had voyaged to England several times aboard this particular ship, and spoke of a tour of the Indies when the present unrest within the country was settled.

At the appointed time, Melanie descended the staircase with enthusiastic expectations of the coming luncheon. She had chosen to wear one of her favorite frocks, and had taken particular care with her toilette in the hopes of lightening Simon's mood. Her gown, purchased the previous week in deference to the humidity of the city, was a light, almost transparent cotton batiste in a cool shade of orchid. The neckline, cut into a deep square in the front and back, exposed the white swells of her breasts to a daring degree, while still maintaining a semblance of decorum with the demure row of purple ribbon threaded through white eyelets that bordered the neckline. The sleeves, cut a bit more loosely than usual, tightened at the elbow to allow for floating tiers of the airy material that hung gracefully and moved provocatively when she walked. The wide, flowing skirt flared out from the tight point at the center of the waistline, and was caught up delicately with small clusters of white silk lilies of the valley tied with narrow purple ribbon. On her feet she wore soft leather slippers in dark purple and in her brilliant hair, swept to the top of her head in a soft pompador, from which little curling tendrils escaped to lie temptingly against her slender neck, she wore a single sprig of lily of the valley.

Glowing with eagerness for her adventure, Melanie was startled to see two figures move from the parlor to the bottom of the steps. Simon, taking in her appearance with a silent, appreciative glance, moved his clear, translucent eyes warmly over her figure, stopping briefly at the firm swells of her breasts, bobbing with her eager step. The first sign of a smile broke through his sober expression as Melanie seemed struck with sudden realization and deliberately slowed her step and the tantalizing movement that had ensued. Michael, in his open manner, watched with an all too apparent appreciation in his warm brown eyes, as he mumbled a trifle incoherently, "Lord, it is not natural to possess such complete perfection of physical beauty, it is just not natural!" And then as she reached the bottom step, he took her hand quickly before Simon could extend his own, and whispered solemnly, "Tell me, Melanie, are you truly a witch after all, who has conjured up this illusion to drive me wild?"

Contrary to taking compliment at his remark, Melanie frowned darkly, snatching away her hand in an angry gesture. "You'd do well to watch what you say, Michael. Such loose words as yours have caused me no end of difficulties in the past, and I would not enjoy a repetition of such dangerous talk."

Stunned at her rebuke, Michael stood in speechless remorse, and taking advantage of his garrulous friend's moment of silence, a bright smile finally breaking across his face, Simon extended his hand toward hers. "Melanie, this loose-tongued young man has insisted on accompanying us on our tour of the *Eastern Queen* this afternoon. Captain Smythe has already been advised of the added number for luncheon, so I suppose there is no way out for us but to be burdened with his presence for another few hours."

"Oh, come now!" Michael quickly recuperated from his moment of speechlessness. "Although I must admit I speak somewhat thoughtlessly at times, I am not quite that bad, am I? Melanie, let me apologize to you for my inappropriate remark before I direct that question to you. Now," he said with a small, coaxing smile directed intensely into her exquisite countenance, "remembering to be generous to a poor, smitten fool, please answer me, beautiful Melanie. I am not really that bad, am I?"

Unable to hold her anger against his overwhelming boyish charm, she smiled finally, a small dimple flickering across her cheek as she answered cautiously, "Well, I think I will reserve my answer to that question until the end of the day, just to make certain of my reply."

Laughing appreciatively, Michael moved quickly to her other side, taking her elbow with his hand and urging her forward. "Then, let us proceed to our destination. I am most anxious to redeem myself."

Walking lightly between the two good-looking gentlemen, Melanie was escorted regally to the waiting carriage, finally bursting out into startled laughter as Michael almost bowled Simon over in his rush to follow her into the carriage and assume his position at her side. Simon, a distinct expression of annoyance covering his distinguished face, assumed the seat facing them, forced to ride backward for the entire trip.

It was the end of a long, stimulating afternoon, and Melanie was completely and overwhelmingly smitten! But her new love was a huge, graceful sailing ship lightly riding the waves of New York harbor. Enthralled by the sway of the deck beneath her feet, the warm sea breeze in her hair, she was enraptured by the tales so easily and colorfully spun by Captain Smythe. Of medium height and extremely broad of chest and shoulder, the white-haired captain's weather toughened features brightened appreciatively at the first glimpse of Melanie, his capitulation to her charms becoming complete as she listened with rapt attention to his explanations of the workings of the ship, the problems of command, and over luncheon, his thrilling, but Simon suspected, often exaggerated experiences as master of a sailing ship on the high seas and in exotic ports. Michael, for the time being forced to tak a back seat to the captain, bore his burden with admirable restraint, while Simon, his clear eyes glued to Melanie's glowing countenance, savored her enjoyment more finely than he did his own.

The fare served at the captain's table was simple but delicious. Cold sliced meat and bright, golden cheese, served with hearty red wine and thick slices of a dark bread that invited healthy portions of fresh churned butter, purchased in their honor, to be spread liberally on its surface. Bright, colorful, fresh fruit provided the dessert, along with a moist applesauce cake that the captain confided was their cook's only truly great achievement, and reserved for the sorely few occasions when the ingredients were available to him.

When, at the end of the beautiful afternoon, Melanie realized the time had come to leave, she felt true reluctance. The amber glow of her eyes shining directly into his sun-reddened features, Melanie said sincerely, "Captain Smythe, I want to thank you for including me as your guest, and giving me truly one of the most memorable afternoons of my life."

Looking for a few wordless moments into the beauty of her shining countenance, the captain turned abruptly, and going to a huge seachest in the corner, returned in a few seconds holding a small, highly lacquered oriental jewel case.

"I would like you to have this, Melanie."

"Oh, I cannot accept it, captain. It most surely must have been purchased by you for someone special and—"

"It was, and has lain in my seachest for several years now. I finally have found the someone special for whom it was purchased."

Flushing with pleasure, Melanie averted her eyes and lifted the lid of the delicate box to hear a light, oriental melody coming from a small music box concealed beneath. Gasping with delight, she raised eyes filled with happy tears and said softly, "Thank you, captain. I will treasure it always."

Once again on deck, Melanie ran quickly to the far rail for one last look around the ship. With a caressing motion, she touched the well-worn rail, directing her glance hungrily around the ship as if storing into memory all that met her eyes. Gradually she raised her gaze to the top of the mast, imagining the thrill of the view from the vantage point of the crow's nest nestling at the top, her lovely face aglow with the glory of the imagined experience. Conversation between the three men waiting to descend the gangplank came to a complete halt as they watched her slight, graceful figure move along the empty deck, the sadness on her beautiful face woefully apparent as she bid the ship a silent farewell.

Captain Smythe's deep, vibrant voice was a whisper as he broke the silence that had settled between them. "For the first time in my life, I can truly say I envy another man, Simon. You are an extremely lucky fellow. If I were a few years younger, I would make you work to keep her, but my time for that is past, unfortunately. Guard her well, Simon, she is a rare treasure indeed."

Extending his hand with a smile, Simon replied softly, "I am not quite the fool you may think me to be, Willy. Thank you for an excellent afternoon."

Their goodbyes completed, they were once again installed in the carriage and traveling the streets of New York. This time Michael's efforts to gain the seat beside Melanie came to naught when Simon announced firmly, "You will ride backwards this trip, Michael, my friend." His grave expression showed he would suffer no argument.

They had been riding a short time, during which Michael chatted incessantly in his garrulous fashion, when Simon interrupted rudely. "Where may we drop you, Michael? I believe you sent your carriage home."

"Oh, that's all right, Simon. I'd be just as happy to come—"

"You most certainly are not coming back home with us!" Simon stated without the slightest effort to soften his statement. "I am quite certain Melanie should like to rest before dinner, and I, personally, have had my fill of you today!"

"Simon!" Melanie was aghast at his outspoken manner.

"Don't worry, Melanie," Michael consoled her in an offhanded voice, "I'm quite accustomed to Simon's blunt ways."

"There's no need for you to make excuses for me to Melanie, Michael." Simon's irritation was mounting. "I do believe you owe your sister a visit, and I would suggest you use this afternoon for that purpose." No longer waiting for his answer, Simon called out, "Peter, drive us to Mr. Searle's house!"

"Well, perhaps you are right, Simon." Michael's face still held a small smile. "I wouldn't want to wear out my welcome."

"Oh, heaven forbid!" Simon exclaimed, raising his eyes in mock horror, managing to break the tension by setting them all to laughing.

Within the half hour the carriage was in front of Michael's home, and standing on the walk beside the carriage, Michael made one last attempt to prolong the afternoon. "Why don't you come in for a drink? I can have Margaret make—"

"No!" Simon's unequivocal answer set both Michael and Melanie into hysterical laughter. Finally again in control of himself, Michael said in an amused voice, "Simon, you are a boor."

"Goodbye, Michael," Melanie began politely, "it has been a lovely day and I hope to see—"

"Melanie!" Simon interrupted in horror, "You will not conclude by saying 'I hope to see you again soon.' I absolutely forbid it!"

Ignoring their amusement, Simon continued,

"Goodbye, Michael. It has been pleasant seeing you again, but please do not give us the pleasure of your company too soon."

"How long will you be in New York, Simon?"

"Until the first week of September."

"Only another few weeks? In that case," turning to Melanie, Michael said softly, "I will be seeing you soon, Melanie, my lovely."

"Damn!" Simon exploded. "Drive on, Peter!"

As they drove away at a brisk pace, the sound of Michael's hearty laughter echoed in the street behind them.

Still frowning deeply, Simon assisted Melanie from the carriage. Walking briskly up the steps to their residence, he rang the doorbell with obvious impatience, greeting the little maid, Mary, with a show of irritation that set the poor girl to quaking and earned him one of Melanie's darkest frowns.

His first words spoken since leaving Michael in the street outside his house were uttered in a strained voice, directed at the openly shaken young servant.

"Mary, Mrs. Morganfield and I have had a strenuous day and intend to rest before dinner. We do not wish to be disturbed—for any reason!"

Grasping Melanie firmly by the elbow, he escorted her up the stairs, turning without hesitation toward their room, maintaining a steady forward pace that did not falter until he had followed her inside and turned to lock the door behind them. Turning back toward Melanie, he looked into her expectant face as she stood rigidly in apparent expectation of some type of somber declaration.

A slow, sheepish smile starting across his face, he relaxed suddenly with his back against the door, heaving a deep, silent sigh of relief.

"Melanie, dear," he said softly, "If I had been forced to listen to one more word of Michael's inane chatter, to one more fawning remark while he devoured you with those hungry, little-boy eyes . . ." Raising his eyes expressively to the artfully plastered ceiling, he finished through tightly clenched teeth, "I would have strangled him right there in the middle of the street, in full view of his complete staff of servants!"

Finally smiling as Melanie burst into spontaneous laughter, he continued softly, "As fond as I am of that young fellow."

Suddenly pulling himself erect, he strode forward to pull her into a close, warm embrace. Pressing his face against the fragrant softness of her hair, he closed his eyes for a few, brief seconds to savor the pleasure washing over him as her body pressed against his, almost crushing her in his desire to draw her ever closer.

"I've been waiting all day to hold you in my arms, Melanie, and suddenly . . . I just would not be put off any longer . . . for any excuse. You are a true confection for the eyes in that fortunate garment that has the honor to be worn against your skin. You look absolutely lovely, darling, and I have felt for most of the day like a hungry child who was given a huge bag of candy, with strict instructions not to touch a single piece until after supper! In short, my dear, the sight of you has been driving me wild!" Suddenly loosening his hold, he pulled back far enough to search her startled face for a few short moments before he lowered his mouth to cover hers with a deeply stirring kiss. His lips finally and reluctantly separating from hers, he whispered softly, "Well, I am happy to say you prove me right again, Melanie."

"I prove you right?" Puzzled, Melanie looked up into Simon's face as he continued to press light kisses against her cheek and temple. "Simon," she repeated again, "What do you mean I prove you right?"

"Simply that you prove how right I was in insisting that you accompany me to New York. Melanie, it would have been a damned dull visit without you! And now," he continued softly, his hands finding the fastening on the back of her dress, "I feel it is my obligation to use as persuasive an argument as possible to make you agree. As a matter of fact, it may take me the remainder of the afternoon to present my case in its entirety! Melanie, darling," pulling her close as his hands found the smooth skin of her back, he mumbled into her hair, "how I will enjoy convincing you."

"Michael, you will please not carry Sara around all morning. She is becoming increasingly spoiled, and will be past redemption by the time we return to Philadelphia."

Directing her remarks to the persistent young man who had made it a habit to drop by just an hour or so after Simon's departure several days a week, to spend the hours until Simon's return in her company, she surveyed him critically. Never a fellow to be unnecessarily formal, he had shed his coat and waistcoat immediately upon arrival, untied and removed his cravat after some energetic play with Sara, and stood listening to her reprimand with woeful eyes, his shirt unbuttoned to mid-chest and sleeves rolled up to the elbow in deference to the humidity of the day.

It is a good thing Simon trusts my integrity, Melanie thought with a small shake of her head. He had come home to this same compromising picture countless times in the past two weeks, his reaction being mainly exasperation as he announced each time after a short interval, "Michael, I believe it is time for you to leave for your appointment." On the first occasion having responded unthinkingly, "I don't have an appointment, Simon," Simon's answer had been delivered with a quick knitting of dark brows. "Then I would suggest you move quickly and make one!"

Even as she eyed him critically, Michael's heart beat a rapid tattoo in his chest. He gazed in return into the great amber eyes which looked at him from the splendidly sculptured face, its creamy complexion sparked with bright spots of color in her cheeks. She appeared not at all affected by the heat of the late August day in her pink and white striped cotton frock, which was low cut enough in the neckline to air considerable bosom and cause him considerable discomfort. Her brilliant tresses, piled high on her head in a casual manner, adorned with several small pink bows, displayed the smooth, tempting curve of her neck, and Michael swallowed tightly. His feelings were beginning to become dangerously more sincere than his light banter would seem to indicate.

"I don't wish to hear another word about your departure from this city." His expression was morose as he shifted Sara's weight from one arm to the other. "And kindly do not nag me, Melanie. If I am unable to hold one Morganfield woman in my arms, then I must content myself with the one available to me!"

"Michael, that is an absolutely scandalous remark!" Smiling widely at his petulant expression, Melanie continued reprovingly, "If someone were to hear you, they might not understand your sense of humor."

"And what makes you think I'm joking?"

Shooting him a quick glance, her smile faded slightly, "I know you are joking, because if you were not, I could not tolerate your presence during Simon's absence. And, Michael dear," she continued, her glance softening at his hurt expression, "We would all be the worse for that, wouldn't we?"

Choosing that moment to give his dark hair a firm tug, Sara efficiently eliminated the necessity for a reply as Michael reacted loudly, grimacing expressively with pain. "Ouch! Sara, you thankless child," he moaned, endeavoring to untangle his hair from the small, tight fist, "Unhand me, girl!"

Giggling wildly, Sara tightened her hand even further in expectation of even greater facial contortions to amuse her, and receiving the reward she sought, proceeded to laugh appreciatively.

"Sara, stop that now!" Melanie's voice was firm as she scolded the naughty child, and turning back to Michael, she sent her wrath in his direction.

"Michael, you encourage her in this misbehavior! Please stop at once! She is entirely too brazen!"

"Melanie, I did nothing whatsoever to encourage—ouch!" Once again tugging wildly at Michael's dark curls, Sara's anticipatory smile turned to wild shrieks of laughter as Michael grimaced even more vividly and crossed his eyes unexpectedly.

The doorbell rang loudly, and Mary started in its direction as Melanie said impatiently, "Michael, that is exactly what I mean! Sara is misbehaving with the specific hope of getting the exact reaction you provided her." Turning to Sara she said sharply, "You will loosen your hold on Michael's hair at once, do you hear me, Sara? Don't you see you are hurting him?"

Obliging Melanie by suddenly assuming a tearful expression for the benefit of the child whose gaze had flicked back to him for verification of her mother's remark, Michael received not the laughter he had expected. Instead, looking immediately contrite, Sara hesitated only a few moments before putting her arms around his neck to kiss him loudly on the cheek.

"My, that is truly a dear sight, isn't it?" A sharp voice from the doorway snapped all three heads in its direction as the lovely, dark-haired woman continued acidly, directing her remarks into Melanie's startled face, "You must be *Mrs.* Melanie Morganfield. It appears you are not content with flaunting my husband's infidelity before my friends and the entire city, but have decided to usurp my brother's attentions as well! Tell me, my dear, how do you manage the both of them at once?"

"Charlotte!" Michael's indignant outcry was simultaneous with the bright flush that suffused Melanie's face.

Simon's wife! With surprise, Melanie realized that the woman was startlingly beautiful. Of medium height with a splendid figure displayed tastefully in a green batiste gown, she had her brother's coloring and small, handsome features. Unfortunately, the resemblance ended there, for somewhere within the large, cold, dark eyes and tight humorless line of her beautifully shaped mouth, all the warmth of her brother's personality was absent.

"What are you doing here, Charlotte?" Michael's cold tone revealed only too clearly his anger at his sister's open insinuation.

"I should think the more appropriate question would be to ask what *you* are doing here, Michael."

"I am visiting a friend, Charlotte."

"And I have come to see my husband's latest whore!"

With a sharp gasp, Melanie took a step backward. She had no stomach for this type of scene; inwardly at a disadvantage as strong waves of guilt washed over her, and quickly taking an unprotesting Sara from Michael's arms, she made an effort to leave the room.

Moving efficiently to block her exit, Charlotte spat venomously, "The child is obviously yours—is it Simon's as well? I can only think it must be, or he would not tolerate its presence in the household, to be sure. Or perhaps I ask a foolish question, my dear. You probably have no real way of ascertaining her actual father."

Gasping at the calculated insult, Melanie suppressed the strong urge to claw the venomous sneer from the face looking into hers. Instead, answering sweetly in return, Melanie said softly, "My dear Mrs.

Young, you must try not to judge all women by your own standards."

Happy to see the convulsive jerk of the woman's mouth that her sally had hit home, Melanie was unprepared for her quick, snaking blow as the woman raised her hand and struck Melanie's face with a heavy stinging slap!

Sara's loud, frightened wail at the force of the blow to her mother's face drew Melanie's mind from the pain in her cheek, and attempting to quiet the startled child, she heard the woman hiss venomously, "Bitch, don't entertain the thought for a moment that I will ever consent to a divorce! I am far too accustomed to my role as Mrs. Simon Young!"

Seeming to snap suddenly from the shock that had held him immobile for so long, Michael stepped between the two women, directing a black stare into Charlotte's hate-filled countenance. "I asked you what you are doing here, Charlotte. You have never given even the slightest thought to Simon's mistresses in the past. Have you suddenly gone insane to come here and attack this woman? You will apologize to her immediately, do you hear me?"

"Apologize to this slut? You are the one that is insane—or are you just afraid of losing her favors, my darling brother?"

Too insensed to utter a word in defense, Michael said in a deep, warning voice, "Get out, Charlotte, get out of this house right now, or sister or not, I will throw you out that front door within five seconds!"

"Oh, I'm leaving to be sure. I have no desire to prolong this conversation. I've said all that I came to say." Turning to Melanie, she said insidiously,

"Don't think that you can embarrass me into consenting to a divorce. I can be very stubborn, and I play the martyred wife very well."

"People stopped believing your act years ago, Charlotte." Michael's response was delivered through tight lips.

"Perhaps, but I do want you to know, you are welcome to Simon's attentions, *Mrs.* Morganfield. I never could stand his rutting ways. I suppose it takes a woman of your caliber to put up with them. Certainly no decent woman—"

"Get out, Charlotte!" Michael's tone was truly vicious as he whispered into her face, "I suppose you can't be expected to recognize a decent woman when you see one. You've never experienced a decent tendency in your entire life!"

Her eyes widening in shock at her brother's deprecating sneer, Charlotte turned sharply and marched out the front door without another word. Turning back to Melanie, the flush of his rage still coloring his face, Michael said simply, "How can I ever apologize?"

Still attempting to quiet her frightened child, who mumbled repeatedly through hiccupping tears, "Bad . . . bad lady." Melanie avoided Michael's stricken gaze, and turned toward the staircase.

"I think I will take Sara upstairs for her nap now, Michael. It may take me a while to quiet her down."

An eternity later Melanie finally put Sara into her bed. Standing perfectly still, she watched until the child's last restless movement was done, and she lay sleeping restfully, before turning toward the door to leave. Walking forward, she was startled to see that

Michael waited outside the partially open door and had obviously been standing there quietly the entire time. Walking silently forward, she closed the door behind her and faced Michael for a few wordless minutes before moving forward into the arms he held out to her, to sob quietly against his comforting chest.

"I'm so sorry, Melanie." Michael's words were softly whispered against her hair as he held her warmly against him. "Can you ever forgive me for having allowed it to happen? I have no defense, except my shock at her appearance. It was the last thing I ever expected her to do. My dear Melanie—"

"What the hell is going on here?" Simon's sudden angry voice jerked them apart, and staring into Melanie's tear-streaked face, he saw the red welt on her cheek and demanded, tight-lipped, "What has happened here?"

"We have had an unexpected visit from Charlotte."

Michael's soft response drained the color from Simon's face as he stared at the mark on Melanie's cheek. "And?"

"Charlotte struck her."

Blinking hard, as if he himself had suddenly sustained the blow, Simon stared expressionlessly into Melanie's stricken face. Without moving his gaze, he said softly, "You will please go downstairs and put on your jacket and cravat, Michael. We will be leaving here together in a few moments."

As Michael moved down the stairs without comment, Simon continued to stare into Melanie's face, the muscle in his jaw twitching in quick, sharp spasms.

"Simon, she had no right to strike me, but she had a perfect right to be angry and to be here. She is, after all, your wife. I am the outsider here."

Moving forward in a quick, unexpected movement, Simon pulled Melanie into his arms, murmuring against her hair as he did, "She had no right . . . none whatsoever. She has never, never, been a true wife to me."

Simon was gone the remainder of the afternoon, returning alone in time for supper. Charlotte's name was not mentioned again by either Simon or Michael for the remainder of their stay in New York.

The sharp edge of impatience began to nudge her festive mood, and struggling to maintain an even disposition, Melanie stood perfectly still for the count of five long seconds. Then taking a deep breath in a determined effort to control her creeping irritation, she muttered softly through gritted teeth, "Where the devil is that shoe?" She was expecting Simon home any minute and wanted to be completely dressed when he arrived. Shooting another hopeful glance around her orderly bedroom to no avail, she closed her eyes, straining for a mental image of a possible location for the mate to the small silk slipper she held in her hand.

"Damn!" she groaned impatiently when the effort proved to be a dismal failure.

The shoes were the perfect accessory to the gown she had saved for Simon's and her last night in New York and she had planned on her appearance being faultless. They had spent countless exciting evenings in the city while Simon had indoctrinated her into its many diversions. Theatrical productions, cleverly billed as moral dialogues due to the ban on frivolous entertainments, had provided several thrilling evenings. The countless musicales they had attended had been intensely stimulating, and a day spent cruising up the Hudson River to return in the twilight of the glorious August day had provided her a glimpse of a world she had not realized existed. Her horizons had been broadened, her inquisitive mind stimulated, and her natural zest for life had grown proportionately. It had been a marvelous month, of which this was their last evening. They were spending it at the theater, and she was determined to make this last night as memorable for Simon as he had made their visit memorable for her.

With that thought in mind, the missing shoe suddenly assumed an importance all out of proportion to its significance merely because it was the first blur in the beautiful memory she strove to create. So obsessed was she with the missing article that she failed to realize so small an item as a pair of shoes could not hope to cast even the slightest shadow on the breathtaking picture she presented.

As lovely as a statue, Melanie was magnificent in a gown of floating aqua silk that hung vicariously on her slender shoulders, plunging daringly from its precarious perch to expose a heart-stopping swell of smooth white bosom. Closely molded against her upper arms for a short distance, the sleeves fell into two diaphanous tiers that swayed gracefully with each movement. The bodice clung enticingly, to dip to a deep point at her slender waist, from which the skirt flared out dramatically into endless shimmering folds just short of her ankle, where several ruffles of delicate white Belgian lace continued on to touch the toes of her small, unclad feet. Brilliants tastefully dotted the splendid garment, twinkling in the soft light of the room in close competition with the soft glow of her auburn tresses. Swept to the top of her head into graceful coils and loose curls, the upswept style was the perfect accent to the sculptured beauty of her face and the wide, golden eyes that searched the room so despairingly for the missing shoe. From her ears dangled glittering sapphires presented to her the week before by Simon, and around the slender column of her neck she wore the large, single sapphire which completed the set. Anticipation of the evening to come had added a flush of color to her flawless complexion and a sparkle to her already glowing eyes, combining to complete a picture of magnificence and beauty that was totally unforgettable.

Stooping momentarily, she slipped the lone shoe onto her foot before moving back toward the wardrobe with an uneven gait. A small sound at the door caused her to turn quickly, in time to catch Simon's brief, undisguisable expression as his eyes caressed her appreciatively. Wordless, he moved to her side to cup her face gently between his palms. His expression intensely serious, his translucent blue eyes held her amber glance as his lips moved slowly against hers with his whispered words.

"My darling, you are radiant . . . far more beautiful, more precious than the jewels you wear." Slowly closing the distance between, he pressed his parted lips against hers, firmly, lingeringly, before drawing away, a small wry smile crossing his face.

"Unfortunately, I was detained a little longer than I expected at the meeting this afternoon, Melanie, or I would show you in a more positive manner how deeply you truly stir me." Hesitating momentarily, his hand caressed her cheek lightly while his eyes roamed her lovely upturned face. "But perhaps it wouldn't matter if we arrived a little late at the theater this evening."

As his dark brows raised suggestively, Melanie's eyes widened, and stepping backwards unevenly, she said in a wary tone, turning simultaneously toward the door for a quick exit, "I'll wait for you in the living room, Simon. I wouldn't want to detain you with my presence."

A small quirk moving his lips, Simon replied softly, "Perhaps that would be wise, after all, Melanie, but I do think it would be a good idea if you put on your other shoe before leaving."

Stopping abruptly, Melanie turned back toward him, her brow knitted into a small frown as she flushed lightly. "Oh, I forgot! Drat that shoe! I can't find it!"

Amused by her obviously flustered state, Simon suppressed a smile and drew his brow into a mock frown of concentration as he mumbled thoughtfully, "Now, let me see. If I remember correctly, the last time you wore those shoes was at the musicale where we heard all that 'romantic' music you were so wild about. Afterwards we brought a bottle of champagne up here, and if my memory serves me well, your dress ended up near the door, your petticoat on the sofa, your chemise on the carpet by the bed . . . and, yes, you kicked off your shoes—"

"Simon!" Flushing a bright red, Melanie whispered in embarrassment, "Really!"

The small quirk broadening into a knowing smile, Simon walked toward the bed, continuing in an even tone, "and you kicked off your shoes . . ." In a quick movement he bent to reach behind the night table and turning, held the missing shoe in his hand. "And here it is!" Directing his knowing glance into Melanie's flushed face, his voice was soft and deep. "You seem to have forgotten that evening, Melanie, but I, on the other hand, remember every little detail."

The effect of Simon's intense, warm gaze was to deepen Melanie's flush even further as she limped forward and snatched the shoe out of his hand with a piqued air. Slipping it onto her foot, she finally raised warm amber eyes to his, a smile breaking through at last as she whispered in an intimate tone, "Simon, you are incorrigible!" Turning on her heel, she said over her shoulder, "I think it would be best if I wait downstairs until you are dressed or we surely will be late for the performance." Moving swiftly, she left the room and walked down the hallway toward the stairs, the heat of Simon's gaze following her every step of the way.

The John Street theater was crowded, each box filled to capacity for the production of *Othello*. The beautiful auburn-haired woman sharing a box with the handsome ship owner, Simon Young, caused a stir of interest that went unnoticed by the woman but was thoroughly enjoyed by the gentleman. Lively and entertaining, the performance moved quickly, but despite her enjoyment, a small veil of apprehension began to slip over Melanie. Too many times during the performance she had turned toward Simon to find his pensive gaze fastened on her. He was distracted, uninvolved with the events on stage.

Dismissing her questioning glance each time her eyes caught his, he returned his attention to the stage, completely failing to allay her concern with his brief smile. When finally they returned home and walked through the doorway of their room, Melanie's brow was knit in a light frown of apprehension.

Turning abruptly, she said in a level voice, "What's wrong, Simon?"

"Nothing is wrong, Melanie." Simon's voice was evasive.

"Well, tell me what's bothering you. I know you're concerned about something."

His face suddenly serious, Simon took her by the hand and led her to the sofa. Seating her quietly, he assumed a place at her side. His manner was strained and serious, and Melanie's heart began a slow pounding.

"I didn't want to tell you earlier for fear of spoiling your last evening in New York, Melanie, but I received an urgent summons from my solicitor this afternoon. You know he has been watching the situation with regard to Asa Parker's will."

As he spoke Asa's name, the color slowly drained from Melanie's face. Pressing her hand reassuringly, Simon continued. "The matter is finally to be brought to court. It will be decided next week whether his will stands or fails. My solicitor has kept his ear keenly tuned to the progress of the case. It seems Hiram Willis, Emily Parker's brother, has been active in raising the ire of the people against you, Melanie. You must realize that it was not difficult at all for him to convince the general populace of Salisbury that Asa Parker was bewitched by you into changing his will to your benefit and—"

"You know that isn't true, Simon!" Melanie protested avidly. "Asa left Aunt Emily well provided for until her death. He merely left a portion of the estate to Sara and me. Why is Hiram Willis so bitter? He certainly—"

"Hiram Willis wants everything, Melanie. Not just a portion of Asa's fortune!" His face reflecting his contempt for the grasping colonial, Simon made an obvious effort to restrain his emotions and continued quietly, "Since you were not Asa's legal wife and he is Emily Parker's only relative, he feels the estate should fall into his hands."

"But Sara is Asa's daughter! Surely she deserves her father's . . ." Melanie's voice dwindled off as Simon's gaze hardened, and realizing he had left something unsaid, she whispered, "Tell me the rest of it, Simon."

"It is simply this, Melanie. Hiram Willis maintains that Sara is not really Asa's child. He claims Stephen Hull is Sara's father."

"No! It's not true!" Melanie's spontaneous protest was emphatic, her eyes wide with shock as the remaining color faded from her pale face and her breathing became erratic.

"Don't get upset, darling."

"But it isn't true, Simon! Sara *is* Asa's child! He

loved her! Hiram Willis is a vicious man, hateful."

"No, Melanie," Simon corrected coldly, "he is merely a greedy man who will do anything necessary to get Asa's fortune."

"He can't do it, Simon! He can't have Asa's will declared void! If he wins the case, Sara will never be acknowledged as Asa's child. He is trying to take more than Sara's inheritance. He is trying to steal her heritage! Asa was proud of Sara. He wanted everyone to know she was his daughter. I can't let him do this, Simon. I can't let them take Sara away from Asa! I can't."

Trembling violently, Melanie mumbled over and over, "I can't, I can't . . ."

Suddenly taking her securely by the shoulders, Simon gave her a short hard shake, his tone of voice a sharp reprimand. "Stop this, Melanie, and get hold of yourself! If you are sincere about stopping Hiram Willis, hysteria will avail you nothing. There is only one thing you can do."

"What can I do, Simon?"

"You must go back to Salisbury to fight his petition."

"Back to Salisbury?" Melanie's response was a low gasp. She had no desire to face the criticism and hatred that was certain to be her welcome.

"The hearing is scheduled for Monday."

"But Simon, Salisbury is too far, and I wouldn't know what to do . . ."

"We can be there on time if we start early tomorrow morning."

"You are supposed to be in Philadelphia on Monday!"

"I am well aware of that fact, Melanie." Simon's voice carried a note of irritation at her needless reminder. "But I am quite certain the able men of the Continental Congress will manage to proceed without my presence for the first week of their fall session. In any case, I will send a representative to look after my interests while I'm gone. The hearing should last no longer than a day or so. I have already instructed William Moore, my solicitor, to make ready for the journey."

Astonished by his accurate anticipation of her reaction and his prompt action on her behalf, Melanie's voice was an incredulous whisper. "You would come with me, Simon?"

Annoyed by her obvious surprise, Simon's voice was gruff. "Well, I certainly won't allow you to go alone!"

"But . . ."

"Do you or do you not want to go to Salisbury, Melanie?" It was apparent from his tone Simon had had enough of talk and was impatient for her answer. Noting her hesitation, he repeated firmly, "Do you wish to go to Salisbury, Melanie?"

Taking a deep breath and swallowing hard, her eyes reflecting her trepidation, Melanie said softly, "Yes, I do."

Giving her a short, hard look, Simon stood abruptly, pulling her to her feet as well. "Then I suggest we retire now. We'll start for Salisbury at 6 A.M."

Nodding tightly, Melanie turned stiffly toward the great canopy bed, only to be stopped abruptly by a warm hand on her shoulder as it turned her back to face Simon. His expression suddenly warm, he leaned forward to press a lingering kiss on her lips. Drawing away, he whispered intimately, "But it's not so late that we won't have time for a little champagne first, darling."

Startled at his mercurial change of mood, Melanie merely blinked, bringing a small smile to Simon's lips as he whispered softly, "Here, let me help you remove your dress."

They had been traveling for two days, the roads becoming rougher with each mile. The warm, humid temperature of the final days of August did little to soothe their weary bodies or their ragged dispositions as they continued unerringly toward Salisbury. Helpless against the depression that had settled over her at the thought of the confrontation to come, Melanie was listless and uncommunicative. Unable to leave the same time as they, William Moore had opted to follow the next day in his own coach, promising to arrive in time for the proceedings. While at first unsettled by the fact the solicitor would not arrive in Salisbury with them, Melanie began to be thankful that the learned gentleman had declined to travel with them, for the additional space in the carriage allowed Sara the comfort of lying down when she tired. Having spent the first day on the road in an irritable, cranky mood that had worn Simon's and Melanie's patience thin and almost reduced Molly to tears while she struggled to restrain the uncomfortable child, Sara began to settle into the routine of the journey. By the third day she actually appeared to have begun to accept the constant rocking motion of the huge, black carriage and was dozing peacefully.

Gazing silently at her daughter as she lay opposite her on the seat beside Molly, Melanie could not suppress her pride. Her soft, round cheek pressed against the wine velour upholstery of the seat on which she lay, full red lips slightly parted in sleep, fiery curls framing her incredibly angelic countenance, Sara was a cherubic masterpiece. Shaking her head, she smiled sadly. Asa would have been so proud if he could see Sara now. Sara had been the fulfillment of his most cherished dream.

A sudden flash of anger tightened Melanie's mouth with determination. How dare that vile man attempt to steal from Asa the rightful honor of Sara's paternity? In another few hours they would be in Salisbury and the hatred and viciousness would begin again; but she would not run away this time. She would stay until Sara was acknowledged Asa's daughter. Her throat tightening with emotion, she felt the warmth of tears beneath her lids. She owed Asa that much. She would not . . . she *could not* allow anyone to rob Asa of his daughter.

Strengthened by her mental battle, Melanie drew herself up proudly. What had come over her the last two days? Had she forgotten the true beauty of the love Asa and she had shared that had resulted in the lovely child that lay sleeping opposite her? She had been proud to bear Asa's child, and she would allow no one to instill a sense of shame in her now. Sara would grow up to know that her father loved her and to revere his memory, and no one . . . no one would rob Sara of that!

Without her realization, a flush of color had come into Melanie's cheek as the return of her fighting spirit became obvious in her demeanor. Turning her face, she noticed Simon studying her intently through half-lidded clear eyes. His glance moved over her slowly for a few long seconds in open assessment. Finally speaking in a hushed tone, his voice was openly pleased.

"I see Hiram Willis is going to have a fight on his hands tomorrow." Leaning toward her, he kissed her lips lightly. "Welcome back, Melanie. I have missed you sorely these last two days."

Her eyebrows rising in surprise, Melanie was momentarily stunned at Simon's accurate assessment of her thoughts. Finally regaining her composure, Melanie whispered sincerely, "It is good to be back, Simon."

The main street of Salisbury echoed with the rattle of the large, black carriage as it moved at a speed calculated to allow the curious no doubt as to its occupants. Realizing she had been recognized immediately, Melanie held her head high, bearing the shocked expressions and whispers with a haughty disdain that she did not feel. When they were finally out of sight of staring eyes, Melanie said in a strained voice, "Was it really necessary for Peter to drive up the main street, Simon? We could just as easily have entered town far more inconspicuously."

To her surprise, Simon smiled, his expression very pleased. "Peter was merely following my orders, Melanie. I am afraid I derive considerable pleasure in knowing that Hiram Willis will soon be aware of our presence in town and will spend the remainder of the hours until the hearing tomorrow squirming like the worm he is!"

Within a few minutes the black carriage pulled onto Weaver's Row. The moment the corner was turned, Melanie's eyes fastened on the large brick house that dominated the far end of the street. Her throat filling with emotion, she struggled to form her words.

"Simon, do you think Martha and Tom will be there? You did say they were to remain in the house until the estate was settled, didn't you? Do you think they'll be happy to see us? Will they be surprised?"

Her heart thundering in her chest, Melanie's eyes remained glued to the brick structure as they drew nearer, and if Simon responded to her mindless queries she was not aware. She could think of nothing, feel nothing, but the myriad of memories washing over her.

Slowly the carriage drew to a stop. Stepping down, Simon raised his hand to assist Melanie from the carriage, cognizant of the fact that at that particular moment she was not even aware of his existence. Without conscious realization, Melanie ascended the familiar steps to the front door. Hesitating only a few seconds, she raised the brass door knocker and rapped loudly. Within a few minutes the door swung wide to accommodate the figure of the huge, gray-haired woman who answered its summons.

"Martha!" Gasping her name, Melanie unhesitatingly stepped forward to throw her arms around the motherly woman. "Martha, I have missed you so!"

"And we have missed you, Melanie." Martha's

tear-filled eyes attested to the sincerity of her response, and Melanie was still struggling to regain her composure when a familiar voice from behind Martha snapped her to attention.

"Melanie, is that you? Are you finally home?"

Stepping past Martha, Melanie's eyes touched on the source of the whispered query. It was the same Tom. Tall and awkward, with the same foolish little-boy expression covering his handsome face. In a few quick steps Melanie moved to embrace the shuffling creature warmly, her heart filled to bursting at his openly hopeful expression as he awaited her reply.

"Yes, it is I, Tom. Dear, dear Tom."

Thoroughly enjoying her embrace for a few short seconds, Tom turned toward his mother in an excited manner, his tone righteous. "See! I told you Melanie would come home, Mama! You said she wouldn't ever come back, but I knew she would!"

His lopsided grin widened broadly as he turned back to see the groggy, bright-haired child the young maid carried in her arms. With a short, spontaneous cry of happiness, he moved quickly down the steps in his awkward gait, to snatch Sara from the startled girl's arms, laughing wildly as he did.

"And we have Sara back now, too, Mama! Now Tom can be happy again!"

Tom's last statement proving too much for her control, Melanie could not suppress a soft sob and the tears that overflowed her welling amber eyes. Taking her arm firmly, Simon ushered Melanie into the living room, signaling the others to follow. When the great oak door was finally closed behind them, he announced solemnly, "Yes, my friends, Melanie has returned."

Despite the humid heat of late morning, the meeting room was filled to capacity. Row after row of the curious sat in silent expectation, apparently oblivious to the stifling humidity and the discomfort afforded by the overcrowding of the room. Directly in front of the spectators, at a long, low table, Judge Henry Rickman awaited the reading of the petition to have Asa Parker's will put aside, his heavily jowled face dotted with perspiration. Directly in front of him to his left was a small table, at which sat Hiram Willis and his attorney. To his right was a similar table where Melanie sat silently beside William Moore, her head high, exuding an aura of confidence she did not feel. She was inconspicuously attired in a fashionable sack dress, cut modestly in a high scoop neckline trimmed with white lace that afforded only a minimal display of her ample bosom. The bodice fitted softly to the waist to be gathered from there into wide box pleats that fell gracefully to the floor. The soft gray muslin, in keeping with the dull colors favored by most of the town matrons, failed in Melanie's case, however, to impart the drab, almost sexless appearance attained by many of the women present. Instead, the pale shade accented the softness of her flawless complexion, the abundant auburn hair swept to the top of her head in deference to the heat of the day, and the alert, topaz eyes that glittered so vividly in anticipation. Seated in the first row, impeccably dressed in a dark blue coat, with lighter blue britches and matching waistcoat, Simon was also in sharp contrast to those surrounding him. Unaffected by the weather or the many appraising glances cast his way, his appearance was cool and poised, as his unusual translucent blue eyes surveyed the scene dispassionately.

Raising his gavel, Judge Rickman brought it down in a practiced manner, its resounding crack still echoing in the room as his scratchy tones brought the proceedings to order.

"We will not stand on ceremony today, gentlemen." The man's voice echoed his obvious discomfort. "I suggest we get started before the day grows any warmer. Mr. Sloan, I believe you have a petition to read?"

Acknowledging the judge's direction, Wilbur Sloan slowly stood up. Casting a deprecating glance in Melanie's direction, obviously calculated to influence the judge's opinion of the beautiful woman across from him, he struck a dramatic pose, fingertips lightly touching the table in front of him as he gripped the lapel of his already perspiration-stained coat with his other hand. A short, gray-haired, balding individual whose good living was apparent from the width of his girth, he was obviously impressed with himself. Indicating a paper being handed to the judge by his clerk at that moment, he said pompously, "In the interest of expediency, Your Honor, I have given a copy of my client's petition to your clerk. My client has instructed me to make his appeal to the court in a more informal manner, which I shall commence straight away." Pausing briefly for effect, Mr. Sloan continued, "It is our contention that Asa Parker, whose last will and testament we are now contesting, was unduly influenced before the time of his death by this woman, Melanie Morganfield, with whom he was living illicitly, into changing his will in her favor while he heartlessly deprived his legal wife of sixteen years of her just inheritance. It is our contention that Melanie Morganfield's child, for whom she places the responsibility for paternity on Asa Parker, is actually the result of a former alliance, which she resumed immediately after Asa Parker's death. In short, we maintain Asa Parker was deluded into believing he owed this woman and her child a portion of his estate, and we sue to regain the house on Weaver's Row, which he left to Miss Morganfield, and the sums left in trust for both Melanie Morganfield and her daughter, Sara."

Quietly assessing the rotund, haughty individual presenting his client's case, Judge Rickman's response was low and even. "Do you have any facts to substantiate your client's claim, Mr. Sloan?"

"We would like to present the testimony of several individuals familiar with the events surrounding Asa Parker's and Melanie Morganfield's cohabitation, Your Honor. The first would be a person to testify as to the character of Melanie Morganfield. I would like to call Mrs. Harriet Sims."

Indicating his approval of the witness with a short nod of his head, Judge Rickman directed a quick glance to his clerk, who stood immediately at his position to the side of the room and called loudly, "Harriet Sims, you will please come forward."

There was a flurry of movement a few rows back as Harriet Sims stood quickly and made her way to the center aisle to walk forward with a rapid step surprising in a woman of her advanced years. Dressed completely in black, the thin woman's narrow, wrinkled face was dark, her visage more crowlike and ugly than Melanie had remembered. The small black eyes shot her a heated glance filled with hatred as she assumed her position before the judge, obviously anxious to continue the persecution which had been interrupted so abruptly months before.

Addressing her directly, Wilbur Sloan's tone was kindly, almost coaxing, as if urging testimony from a reluctant individual. "We would like you to tell us now, Mrs. Sims, all you know of Melanie Morganfield's association with the men of Salisbury, and with Asa Parker in particular."

"I will tell the court all I know, Your Honor," the woman said piously, working to hide the gleam of satisfaction that shone in her dull black eyes. "I will be able to contribute little before the time Melanie Morganfield and her father moved to Benson Road, but I will fill you in with the facts that are general knowledge. Melanie Morganfield and her father came to Salisbury four years ago. Both she and James Morganfield stayed temporarily with Emily and Asa Parker in his home until they were able to find a house of their own. That is where she first came into contact with Asa Parker, and all I know about that, Your Honor, is that Emily Parker resided in peaceful cohabitation with her husband, Asa, until that time. But it was no more than a year afterwards that Asa had Emily committed to an institution for the mentally incompetent." Pausing a moment to direct a vicious sneer in Melanie's

397

direction, she continued in the shrill, piercing voice that was burned into Melanie's memory. "It was when James and Melanie Morganfield moved into the house across from mine on Benson Road that I was finally in a position to see her daily and to watch her weave her evil spells."

Jumping to his feet, William Moore protested strenuously. "I object to that remark, Your Honor. The witness is merely speculating and using a great deal of imagination as well about my client's ability to weave spells! There is no basis in fact for her remarks!"

"Mrs. Sims is here to give us her impressions of your client, Mr. Moore," Judge Rickman responded quietly. "I will be the one to assess the veracity of her remarks."

The small smile that passed over the woman's dark face before she continued was frightening to behold, and a cold shiver crept along Melanie's spine. Addressing her remarks directly to Judge Rickman, her voice whined on. "Melanie Morganfield is the devil's spawn, ensnaring men with her beauty to bring them to their ruin. Each man she has been involved with has been brought to a violent end. She is evil, wily, using her beauty to bend men to her will. From the first day she moved to Benson Road, Martha White's idiot son, Tom, began visiting her just after James left for the foundry each day. He stayed in the house with her for indefinite lengths of time, and when he came out he was muddled and uncertain, looking to her for direction. He was completely under her spell! Many times I watched as she controlled him with her witch's eyes, changing his moods at will. He obeyed immediately any command she gave him without a word of protest. He was possessed!"

Sharp gasps came from the spectators, and the speculative buzzing of voices that ensued was stopped by the sharp crack of the gavel and the judge's call to order. When silence was once again established within the rows of spectators, he instructed Harriet Sims to continue.

"I warned James Morganfield countless times that the hand of God would smite him down if he allowed the girl to continue her evil practices, but he was deaf to my words. Asa Parker was under her spell even after she left his house. She wanted for nothing because anything that James Morganfield would not or could not give her, Asa Parker bought for her. After he put Emily into the institution, Melanie began visiting Asa Parker's home, and eventually Asa Parker assumed the same, mindlessness in her presence as Tom White. It was obvious to us all that she had bewitched him, too. Finally, the hand of God struck James Morganfield down, paralyzing him into immobility in punishment for his sin of refusing to stop his daughter's practices in the ways of darkness. I had warned him, but he paid no heed. I felt no sorrow when he was struck. Justice was done!"

The glow of hatred lighting her ugly face, Harriet Sims continued, "After her father was struck down, Melanie Morganfield remained in her own home for a short time to tend him, but she then managed to turn even her father's punishment to suit her own ends. She moved into Asa Parker's house, and from there into his bed. He was lost! He had no will to oppose her. He accepted the child she produced in his house as his own and continued in his submission to her until he, too, was struck down. Asa Parker was not dead a month before Stephen Hull moved into her bed and—"

"We are not concerned with Melanie Morganfield's actions after Asa Parker's death unless they are directly related to this will, Mrs. Sims. Do you have any further testimony to give in that regard?"

"Only to say that Asa Parker was not responsible when he changed his will. He was under Melanie Morganfield's spell."

The following person called to testify was Bernard Wipley, one of James Morganfield's coworkers at the foundry; and as the sober, nervous individual approached Judge Rickman, Melanie was at a complete loss as to the contribution he could make to the case. She hardly knew the man!

Approaching him slowly in an attempt to sustain the suspense that had built with regard to the witness, Mr. Sloan's nasal tones broke the silence that prevailed within the crowded room. "You, Mr. Wipley, worked at Asa Parker's foundry with James Morganfield and Stephen Hull, did you not?"

"Yes, I still work at the foundry."

"Tell us what you know of the relationship between Stephen Hull and Melanie Morganfield."

"Well, Steve always had an eye on Melanie Morganfield, even though he would never admit to it, so a few of the men began to ride him about it when she moved into Asa Parker's home after her father got sick. He just ignored them for the most part, but when one of the men suggested Melanie Morganfield was in love with the old man, Steve just laughed. He said he had given her something that the old man's money couldn't buy, and that sooner or later she would give up the old man and his money and come crawling back to him. When we all found out a little while later that Melanie Morganfield was going to have a baby, one of the men jokingly asked if that was the 'something' he had given her. All he did was laugh and turn away."

From his position in the front row, Simon Young shot a quick, surreptitious glance to Melanie's face. Drained of color, her countenance was stiff and unreal. He longed to comfort her. The hearing was proving to be more of an ordeal than he had anticipated, and he was anxious for it to be over, so she could dismiss all old agonies from her mind.

"How do we know that Stephen Hull's talk was not simple boasting, Mr. Wipley? After all, what's to stop any one of us from making the same claims?" Mr. Sloan's question was asked with a raised brow and a small smile that indicated complete confidence in the strength of his witness' answer.

"Because not even a month after Asa Parker's death Steve moved right into Asa Parker's house with Melanie Morganfield. He was proud as punch about it, too, I'll tell you. He even went so far as to go over to Charlie Moss who had been riding him the hardest about Melanie Morganfield and said, 'Well, Charlie, what do you think about Melanie Morganfield now?' I tell you, we all did a lot of wondering after that."

"Thank you very much, Mr. Wipley." Shooting a small, superior smile into the face of William Moore,

Wilbur Sloan signaled his witness to return to his seat.

Turning to face Judge Rickman, Mr. Sloan announced in a dramatic tone, "I would like to call Mr. Hiram Willis to testify, Your Honor."

Within a few minutes, Hiram Willis stood ready to speak. Obviously tense, the short, dark brother of Emily Parker shot a defensive glance to the beautiful woman in gray before beginning to testify in a troubled voice. His first words seemed aimed directly at her, and all eyes moved to her face as he spoke. Bearing the weight of their accusing glances, Melanie lifted her head a notch higher in protest of their silent accusations.

"Emily was a good woman, and a good wife to Asa Parker. She gave him a daughter that was taken by the Lord, and she suffered gravely in her grief. Until James and Melanie Morganfield came to town Asa was very content to allow her time to get over her sorrow; but it wasn't long after they came that I noticed Emily was being kept in her room more and more often. After a while she hardly left her room and Asa refused to let me see her at all."

"That's not true!" Melanie whispered vehemently to her solicitor. "Aunt Emily didn't want to see him. She hated her brother! He always upset her when he came!"

Covering her hand comfortingly with his, William Moore urged her silence and turned back to devote himself to Hiram Willis' testimony.

"After Asa put Emily in the institution, he told the administrator not to let me see her. When I appealed to him, he claimed Emily didn't want to see me. I know that was a lie! I'm her only relative!"

"What about the child, Mr. Willis? Do you have any information with regard to your claim that the child was not his?"

"Only that Asa lived with my sister for many years after the birth of their daughter. They both wanted more children, but my sister never conceived another child. When Melanie Morganfield came to live with Asa after her father was taken sick, she produced a child nine months later. Doesn't it seem strange to you that a man who couldn't create a child within his legal wife's womb for over ten years could so quickly create a child with the harlot, Melanie Morganfield?"

Once again a gasp issued forth from the spectators, and wrapping heavily with his gavel, Judge Rickman again called for silence as he reprimanded Hiram Willis sharply. "This is a court of law, Mr. Willis. We do not submit to name calling. You will watch your speech in the future or your testimony will end here and now."

"I have nothing more to say, Your Honor, except . . ." Hiram Willis' face had flushed hotly at the reprimand, but he continued stubbornly, "except to say that there is no proof that Melanie Morganfield's daughter was fathered by Asa Parker. My sister was his lawful wife and is entitled to his entire estate and to the full protection of the law so that that woman cannot steal it from her!"

Calmly assessing Hiram Willis' rabid expression, Judge Rickman slowly turned to address William Moore.

"What do you have to say to the testimony that has been presented, Mr. Moore?"

Standing quietly, Mr. Moore said in a low, even tone, "My client and I have some witnesses of our own that we feel will prove Asa Parker's state of mind and the paternity of Sara Morganfield."

Nodding his approval, Judge Rickman signaled Mr. Moore to continue.

"I would like to call Dr. David Pierce to give testimony."

Within moments Dr. Pierce stood before Judge Rickman.

"You were Asa Parker's physician, Dr. Pierce?" Mr. Moore began his questioning in a calm, quiet manner in direct contrast to the theatrics of Mr. Sloan.

"Yes, I was Asa Parker's doctor, as well as Emily Parker's and James and Melanie Morganfield's physician. I am, after all, the only doctor in town."

Small snickers broke out among the spectators, and ignoring their interruption, Mr. Moore continued. "Then you would be in a position to accurately assess the health, both mental and physical of those people?"

"I would say so, yes."

"All right. Then we will start first with Emily Parker's state of health. How would you assess her condition?"

"Emily Parker suffered severe depression after the death of her daughter. I was in constant attendance upon the woman and did all that could be done to help her, but despite my greatest efforts, her condition continued to deteriorate. Her mental condition degenerated to the extent that I advised Asa to put her into an institution for her own safety."

"What was Asa's reaction to your advice, Dr. Pierce?"

"He hesitated, and put off the decision for as long as he could, but when Emily almost set fire to herself and her room in a fit of depression, he was finally forced to have her institutionalized."

There was much buzzing and head wagging among the spectators that was immediately silenced by a brief warning from the judge, allowing Mr. Moore to continue his questioning.

"Were you the doctor in attendance at the time of the birth of Sara Morganfield?"

"Yes, I was. As a matter of fact it was I who pronounced Melanie Morganfield pregnant."

"And what was Asa Parker's reaction to the announcement?"

Hesitating briefly, Dr. Pierce turned to face Judge Rickman, directing his remarks to him in a soft voice. "Before I speak, Your Honor, I would like you to understand that Asa Parker was a close and cherished friend of mine. I would not be relating any of my conversations with him at this time, except that it is my desire to see that his wishes are carried out so his spirit might rest in peace." Swallowing tightly after his brief, emotional declaration, Dr. Pierce turned back to face William Moore. "In answer to your question, Mr. Moore, when Asa realized Melanie was to bear a child, he was inundated with guilt. He confided to me that Melanie Morganfield had been a virgin when he had first taken her, and that he felt that he had taken advantage of her vulnerability after her father's illness. But he also confided, Mr. Moore, that he could not truly say he was sorry the situation had worked out as it had because Melanie had made him happier than he had been in many years. He said that he was elated that she was to give him a child. His only regret was that he could not marry Melanie and give her and the child his name. When I advised Asa to send Melanie away to have her child in order to avoid gossip, Asa refused. He said that he and Melanie would face the town together. They did not wish to be separated."

Silent tears slipped down Melanie's cheeks as Dr. Pierce spoke. The memory of Asa was vivid in her mind, driving out her delicate hold on the present, and for a few brief seconds, Melanie felt the weight of consciousness drifting away. A strong grip on her shoulder brought the room abruptly back into focus as Simon slipped into the seat William Moore had vacated. Unable to face him at that particular moment, Melanie averted her gaze, but Simon was insistent, finally drawing her back to face him.

"Are you all right, Melanie?" The clear blue eyes assessed her sharply, noting her reluctance to face him squarely. "This is no time to weaken, Melanie. It is no time for regrets or recriminations, either, if you wish to insure Sara's future." Realizing he had hit upon the right note to bring Melanie around, he said sharply, "Then straighten up and pull yourself together. Things will not get easier this morning. You must grow stronger."

Realizing Melanie was once again assuming control of her emotions, Simon slipped back to his seat and directed his attention to William Moore, who was in the process of calling another witness.

"Please call Joshua Whitmore to testify."

Melanie's eyes snapped open wide at the mention of Josh's name, and turning quickly, she saw a tall, sandy-haired figure stand and walk toward the front of the room. A spontaneous warmth expanded in her breast at the sight of his familiar stride as he approached the judge, careful to keep his eyes averted from her gaze. He was more slender than she had remembered him, but then she was unaccustomed to seeing him formally dressed. In a light tan coat, with brown waistcoat and britches, Josh looked handsome indeed, and Melanie's heart swelled. Dear, dear Josh . . .

All trace of the wide contageous grin that Melanie remembered so well was gone from his sober face. His eyes fastened on Mr. Moore, he awaited the first question.

"Josh, you now manage the foundry that Asa Parker established, do you not?"

"Yes, I manage it for the cooperative that bought it after Asa's death."

"What was your relationship with Asa Parker?"

"Asa and I were friends. He was a wealthy man and didn't feel it necessary to be in constant attendance at the foundry, so I took over for him whenever he wanted some time to himself."

"Were you familiar with Melanie Morganfield during the time she lived with Asa Parker?"

"Yes, I was. Business affairs brought me to Asa's home on many occasions after business hours, and I was invited to supper at least once a week."

"Then you would be in a position to judge the relationship between them. How would you assess the terms under which they cohabitated?"

There was a brief hesitation before Josh replied. An expectant silence filled the room as the spectators awaited his response. His voice low, obviously affected by emotion, Josh replied simply, "They loved each other very deeply."

"And Asa's attitude toward the child?"

"Asa was extremely proud of Sara. The morning she was born, we drank to her birth, and Asa told me he was an extremely happy man."

"Do you have any reason to believe the child was not Asa Parker's child?"

"I do not!" Josh's reply was emphatic as a spark of anger lit his soft brown eyes. "Asa had no doubts that the child was his, and I am certain, too."

Swallowing tightly, Melanie strained to retain a hold on her emotions. Thank you, darling Josh.

Finally striding back down the aisle, Josh's eyes did not stray in Melanie's direction, for which Melanie was thankful. Her emotions were at such a pitch that just the smallest glance from his sober brown eyes would have crumpled her restraint completely. Oddly enough, she felt inwardly that the same situation existed for Josh, too.

"I have one more witness, Your Honor." William Moore's cultured voice broke the silence that had descended upon the room at Josh Whitmore's departure.

"Call him, please. The day is getting late and the temperature is rising." Judge Rickman was obviously feeling the weight of the humid summer day and was impatient to conclude the proceedings.

"Peter Benchly, please come forward."

The man who stood and walked toward the judge was a stranger to Melanie. Of medium height and slender build, he had the bearing of a gentleman, and Melanie's curiosity was greatly aroused.

Sensitive to the judge's call for haste, Mr. Moore's questions were brief and to the point. "You were Asa Parker's solicitor, were you not, Mr. Benchly?"

"I was," was the dignified reply.

"And it was you who made the changes in Asa Parker's will that are being contested today?"

"It was I who made the changes requested, yes."

"May I ask you to describe Asa Parker's state of mind when he approached you to change his will?"

"You may. Asa Parker was deeply concerned. He explained to me he was living with a woman whom he loved very dearly, and who had given him a daughter. He explained that he wanted to make provisions for them in the event of his death, and for those reasons he wished to change his will."

"Did you attempt to dissuade Mr. Parker from this action?"

"I did not! The man was obviously sincere, and I saw no reason to attempt to convince him to do other than what he wished. His legal wife was mentally incompetent but well provided for, and I felt, as he, that no one would be made to suffer by the change."

"Did Asa Parker have you institute any other action with regard to Melanie Morganfield or her child?"

"Yes, he did, but unfortunately he was fatally injured before the final legal proceedings could be followed through to a conclusion."

"And what was this action Asa Parker asked you to

initiate, Mr. Benchly?"

"Mr. Parker asked me to institute whatever action was necessary to have Sara Morganfield declared his natural daughter so she could carry his name."

Startled by the news, Melanie gulped, fighting to hold back the tears that threatened to overflow her wide, golden eyes. This was the surprise Asa had hinted at just before his death! She had forgotten! Asa's homely, well-loved face flashed vividly before her mind in that moment, almost succeeding in destroying her control. Closing her eyes, she whispered softly to herself, "Oh, Asa, why did you have to die?"

At a touch on her shoulder, Melanie's eyes sprang open to see a translucent azure gaze looking intently into hers. "Melanie, dear," Simon's voice was gentle, "this dreadful affair will soon be over. You must hold on a little while longer, darling."

Taking strength from his encouragement, Melanie nodded wordlessly and returned her attention to William Moore's placid features. Peter Benchley had already returned to his seat and both solicitors stood waiting for Judge Rickman to speak. There was total silence as the judge began, directing his words to Wilbur Sloan.

"Mr. Sloan, since your petition presents several contentions on your client's part, I will address them separately. First was your contention that Asa Parker was unduly influenced by Melanie Morganfield prior to his death, causing him to change his will in her favor. In this statement, Mr. Sloan, the key word would seem to be the word 'unduly' because certainly no man living with a young and beautiful woman could fail to be influenced in her favor. This point I will continue to take under consideration and will hand down my judgment at a later time.

"The second contention was that Asa Parker was not the natural father of Melanie Morganfield's daughter, Sara. It seems to me, Mr. Sloan, that the testimony you presented in this regard was merely speculation and heresay, whereas Dr. Pierce's testimony taken directly from confidential conversations with Asa Parker clearly showed Mr. Parker's satisfaction with the fact that he was the child's natural father. His desire to legalize that connection would appear to be further proof in that regard. After all, Asa Parker would be the one best to judge whether Miss Morganfield had been intimate with another before him, would he not, Mr. Sloan?"

Not waiting for a response, Judge Rickman continued. "The third contention ties in closely with the first, wherein you petition the court to return to Mrs. Emily Parker, or to you I would assume since Mrs. Parker is still adjudged incompetent to handle her own affairs, the house on Weaver's Row, left to Miss Morganfield, and the sums of money left in trust for both Melanie Morganfield and her daughter, Sara. Since I have already stated my conclusion derived from the testimony presented that Sara Morganfield *is* the natural daughter of Asa Parker, I will allow the bequest made to Sara Morganfield to stand. However, since I have not yet passed a decision insofar as Melanie Morganfield's right to inheritance, I will hold that matter in abeyance pending my decision on your first contention."

Melanie was no longer listening. The trembling

that had started deep inside her as the judge commenced speaking had increased to the point where she was uncertain she would be able to withstand its rigors. But it was done at last! Sara was officially adjuged Asa Parker's daughter, and nothing or no one could take that away from her! For the rest of her life, Sara would know she had had a father who had loved her dearly, and seizing upon that, Melanie exerted her last shreds of self-control to pull herself to her feet as Judge Rickman dismissed the hearing and left the room.

Suddenly so weak she could barely hold herself upright, Melanie looked neither right nor left, maintaining a firm grip on the consciousness that seemed so anxious to slip away from her. Within moments, Melanie felt a strong arm slip around her waist as Simon supported her casually. His voice noticeably gentle, he said softly, "It's over, Melanie. You were very brave, my darling. I'm—"

William Moore's apologetic tones interrupted his whispered speech at that point, turning both their heads to his contrite expression. "I'm sorry, Mr. Young. I had thought we presented a rather thorough case. I did not expect the judge to reserve his decision."

Shooting a quick glance into Melanie's eyes, Simon said quietly, "We are content to wait for the judge's decision as to Miss Morganfield's inheritance, William. We are quite satisfied with the results of the proceedings so far, are we not, darling?" At Melanie's weak smile of affirmation, Simon continued briefly, "You will please contact us in Philadelphia when the remainder of the decision has been

handed down. We will await your communication."
Extending his hand, Simon said with a smile, "You
did a marvelous job, William. You have both Miss
Morganfield's and my sincere appreciation."

Obviously pleased, the learned gentleman bowed
his head slightly. "My pleasure, sir."

Within the half hour, Melanie was lying on the bed
in her old room in the house on Weaver's Row.
Having arrived home a few minutes before, Simon
had assisted her upstairs and into the room, and
undressing her tenderly as he would a child, he had
slipped her arms into a light wrapper before coaxing
her to lie down for a rest. In truth, she needed little
coaxing. She was completely drained by the proceedings at the hearing and the reopening of old, painful
wounds. How tawdry everything seemed when
examined coldly without any reflection on the
pressures or passions of the moment.

A small noise at the door caused her to open her
eyes as Simon reentered the room. Stripped down to
his shirtsleeves and britches, he carried a glass which
he offered to her as he drew closer to sit on the bed
beside her.

"Here, darling, this drink will cool you." Slowly
lifting herself to a sitting position, Melanie accepted
the glass without comment and raised it to her lips to
drink. Allowing his eyes to move slowly over her pale
face, Simon was intensely aware of the emotions
kindled deep inside him as he did.

Having drunk her fill, Melanie placed the glass on
the table beside the bed, and dropped wearily back
against the pillow, averting her eyes from Simon as

she began to speak in a voice that was a choked whisper. "It was ghastly, wasn't it, Simon? I don't suppose you fully realized how dangerous and notorious a woman I truly am! I bewitch men at a glance, drive them to violent ends."

Driven by her own bitter words to a recollection of her father's and Asa's tragic deaths, Melanie suddenly covered her eyes with her hand, unable to face either the pictures in her mind's eye or Simon's pensive assessment. In a voice torn by her own agony, Melanie sobbed softly, "How can you bear to look at me! Surely the testimony furnished today has earned me your complete contempt and disgust. I cannot."

Forcibly removing the small hand shielding her from his glance, Simon held it tightly in his own, gently wiping away the tears that stained her pale cheeks with his other hand. "Listen to me, Melanie, and try to understand what I say right now." His thin distinguished face intense with concern, he continued quietly, "How could you possibly consider that the word of ignorant, prejudiced individuals such as those who testified against you today could affect my feelings about you in any way? Was I not completely aware of all the facts concerning your background from the first? I told you then and I will repeat it once more. I do not care about your past Melanie. Surely if witnesses were brought forth to testify with regard to my past misdemeanors, the picture painted would be far blacker still than yours. But aside from that, darling," moving closer as his hand tangled gently in the long auburn curls streaming across her pillow, he whispered in a voice heavy with emotion, "my feelings for you transcend all the vile, malicious gossip that naturally follows a woman as beautiful and desirable as you. I wanted you from the first time I saw you, and I want you now. Nothing has happened to change my feelings except to make you dearer to me still for the courage you displayed today in the face of the jealousy and hatred that obviously abounds against you within the minds of the ignorant bigots of Salisbury."

Her eyes riveted on his intense expression, Melanie swallowed briefly, still unable to speak.

"No man in his right mind, Melanie," Simon continued in a husky tone, "having held you in his arms, having made violent love to you, having slept beside you to awaken with your glorious beauty the first thing his fortunate eyes touched upon in the morning, or having seen you now, more appealing and desirable than ever in your obvious vulnerability and pain, could do else but consider himself fortunate indeed to have you a part of his life."

A lone tear trickled down Melanie's cheek at the conclusion of Simon's whispered confession, and unable to restrain himself a moment longer, Simon swept her close against him, covering her mouth in a deep, passionate kiss that adequately confirmed his heartfelt words.

Himself trembling with emotion, Simon lay Melanie back against the pillow, whispering softly as he did, "Rest now, darling. You have well earned a rest this afternoon. We will leave for Philadelphia in the morning."

Standing in a quick movement, Simon moved to the door, turning back for one brief glance before leaving and closing the door silently behind him.

*   *   *

Awakening a few hours later, Melanie was groggy and disoriented. The room was warm and stuffy, and she had slept badly, with all manner of worrisome dreams combining to haunt her troubled mind. The lovely room with its hand-painted, rose-bordered furniture seemed to be closing in on her. Shooting a quick glance to the clock on the chest, she gasped lightly. It was after six! She had slept for hours! Moving quickly to the wardrobe, she was momentarily startled to see her old dresses still hanging as they had before she had left Salisbury with Simon. Fingering the simple garments with affection, she suddenly succumbed to whim and removed a pale blue cotton from the wardrobe. Slipping out of her wrapper and into her chemise, she slipped the frock over her head and adjusting it quickly, went to stand in front of the mirror. Strangely, she looked the same as she had the last time she had worn this dress. But so much had happened since then. She really wasn't the same person anymore, was she?

Possessed of a sudden impulse, Melanie pushed her small feet into her soft black slippers and moving quickly to the door, opened it and started down the hallway. With a quick glance down the staircase, she saw no one about, and taking her opportunity to leave unobserved, she ran quickly down the steps and slipped silently out the front door.

She had to get away for a while! Her mind was muddled, her emotions tearing her apart. She needed time to walk and settle her raging thoughts. It was after six and she realized she would run little risk of encountering anyone if she avoided the more heavily

416

traveled lanes, as most of the residents of Salisbury would be gathering at home for their evening meal. Without conscious realization, Melanie found herself heading in the direction of the foundry. The huge wooden structure finally came within view, and Melanie's heart gave a little lurch. It was Asa's creation. He had sole responsibility for building it into the flourishing enterprise it had become. Quickly running her eyes over the building and yard, she saw that everyone had left for the day and the building was deserted. Moving swiftly to the rain barrel, she extended her hand into the small niche behind it. Within seconds her hand closed on a key. Smiling softly when she found the spare key in the same place Asa had left it, Melanie walked slowly to the office door. Unlocking it, she slipped inside to close the door behind her.

The darkness of the unlit room was blinding after the brilliance of the late afternoon sun. Gradually her eyes adjusted to the light and began touching on familiar objects as they moved around the room. Her heart twisting in her chest, she walked over to the desk and fingered the old inkstand and pens that Asa had used. She ran her hand slowly along the back of the worn leather desk chair, picturing Asa seated there as she had seen him so many times. A wealth of memories flooded over her and Melanie's eyes filled with tears. Darling Asa . . . The love they had shared had been so pure, so different from the raw emotion that Steve and she had shared; but each in its own way had been powerful and consuming. She . . .

The sudden sound of a door closing behind her snapped her from her reverie, and turning quickly,

417

Melanie saw a tall male figure silhouetted in the doorway. The light coming through the small window pane behind him kept his face in shadow, and unable to identify the figure, Melanie said hesitantly, her heart beating rapidly with apprehension, "Who—who is it? I can't see your face."

Several long moments of silence followed her whispered question before a familiar voice said softly in response, "It's me, Melanie."

Almost overwhelmed by the moment of panic the voice produced, Melanie managed an astonished gasp. "Steve!" Managing to subdue the unreasonable fear that had closed her throat, Melanie whispered hoarsely, "What are you doing here? Simon said you were at Fort Ti with Allen. He said—"

"Well, it looks like the all-knowing Simon Young was wrong, doesn't it?" In reality, Steve had just returned from Fort Ti on a chance errand for Allen, but irritated by her reference to Simon Young, he refused to give her the satisfaction of an explanation. Despite himself, again he experienced the welling of deep, senseless anger at the strength of the emotion her beautiful face inspired within him. Would he never be free of her? He had arrived in town just a few hours before, while the hearing was still the main topic of discussion in the tavern. Helplessly drawn to the house on Weaver's Row, he had remained there unseen, hating himself as he waited for a glimpse of the beautiful woman who haunted his thoughts so relentlessly. Surprised to see her stealing out of the house, he had followed her.

The same light that kept his own face in the shadows, illuminated Melanie's frightened countenance. Stifling the anger that flared anew at her reaction to his presence when his own reaction was an overwhelming desire to sweep her into his arms, he walked closer, reaching out to touch her pale cheek in a tentative caress. Shaking off his hand, Melanie took a step backward out of his reach as anger flared in her eyes. Incensed as she avoided his touch, Steve said harshly, "What's the matter, Melanie? The calloused hand of a backwoodsman isn't good enough for you anymore? Are you so accustomed to the soft hands of that dandified ass that you can't stand the touch of a real man?" Stepping forward abruptly, he roughly slid his hand into the length of hair at the back of her neck, grasping it tightly, effectively holding her prisoner in his grasp. Pulling her face close to his, he whispered unevenly, "I remember the time when you couldn't get enough of my touch, couldn't get enough of the sensation of my hands on your body—"

"Stop! Stop this immediately!" Melanie demanded, beginning to squirm even as his other hand came out to grasp her shoulder and hold her more securely. "I was a fool then, a stupid, trusting fool! All the while I earnestly tried to show you my love, you were laughing at me! Bernard Wipley told everyone at the hearing the way you bragged about me to your friends!" With strength born of fury, Melanie jerked herself free of his grasp. Taking a few short steps backward, she felt the sofa touching the back of her knees and knew she could retreat no further. In one swift movement, Steve was again close to her, his face only inches from hers as he whispered passionately, "What difference does all that make now, Melanie? You know I want you. I've never stopped wanting you . . . and you want me too, I can feel it." Lifting his hand, he caressed her cheek with his palm as his other arm slid around her waist to pull her tight against him.

"You want me to make love to you, to make things the way they were before. You want to feel me inside you." Slowly his lips moved over her face, pressing a shower of kisses against her eyes, her cheeks, her temple, her mouth. His passion rapidly mounting, he drew her closer still, moving his hand sensuously in her hair, moving the line of his kisses across her cheek and down the gleaming whiteness of her throat. But despite his impassioned lovemaking, Melanie remained stiff and unyielding in his arms. Gradually drawing back, he searched her expression for the slightest trace of a reciprocal passion; but there was none.

"Let me go, Steve." Her voice cold and even, Melanie's expression was stiff, unaffected by emotion, and Steve flushed hotly. Suddenly possessed of a blinding fury, Steve drew back his hand and struck her hard across the face, the force of his blow knocking her back against the sofa to sprawl helplessly on its worn surface. Within seconds he was on top of her, the weight of his body crushing her into submission as he continued pressing kisses against her cheek, her lips, her throat, mumbling as he did, "I'll make you want me, I'll make you." When his frenzied kisses drew no response except the renewal of her struggles to be free of his embrace,

Steve's caresses became more intimate. Finding the soft roundness of her breasts, he caressed them, cursing the impediment of the clothing that lay between them. Still she was impassive to his touch. Tightening his grip on her hair, he pulled her head back, forcing her mouth open to cover it with his as he plunged his tongue deeply inside. Within moments Melanie felt his hand on her bare thigh. Her loud, prolonged scream was muffled by the pressure of his mouth on hers as he relentlessly pushed aside her skirt and pulled away her undergarment.

"No, please . . . Steve, no." she sobbed, her vain struggles weakening as he exerted the power of his superior strength. There was the briefest second of pause before Steve plunged deep inside her, a long, low groan issuing from his lips as he came to rest within the intimate warmth of her body, savoring fully the ecstatic moment of complete possession. The beauty of possessing her was intoxicating, more rapturous than he had remembered. "Darling, my darling Melanie," he whispered softly against her neck as he resumed his deep penetrating motions, the impetus of his motion gradually accelerating with the swiftly widening scope of his passion.

A few moments later his large, masculine frame was shuddering atop hers as he climaxed in a brief, lightning jolt of ecstasy, to collapse weak and spent against her. Still joined to her body, Steve lifted himself slightly to look into her face. His whispered caress was stopped abruptly by her cold, hard expression as she said in a lifeless voice, "Are you finished now, Steve?"

Drawing back, jolted from his euphoric state by her coldness, he mumbled questioningly, "Melanie?"

Her voice hard and strange to his ears, she repeated, "I said, are you finished now, Steve?"

His face suddenly flushing a deep red, he jerked himself free of her. His voice a vicious snarl, he murmured, "You bitch!" Getting up, he fastened a venomous gaze on her vacant expression as he struggled to straighten his clothing. "You cold, black-hearted bitch!" he hissed again, his glance holding hers with intense hatred. "Damn you, you witch! You have bewitched me! But before I let you take complete possession of my soul, I'll make you suffer, too. I'll take you again, as often as I want, and if the illustrious Simon Young cares to dispute that, tell him I'll be waiting for him at the boardinghouse tonight!" Pausing a moment longer to stare down at her malevolently, he said softly, insidiously, "In answer to your question, yes, I'm through with you for now, but perhaps not for long. I'll find you when I feel the need of your body again."

Turning abruptly, he strode out of the office, slamming the door behind him.

Melanie jumped as the slamming of the office door startled her out of her bemused state, the sudden noise effectively shattering the shield of semiconsciousness behind which she had retreated during the ordeal of the past half hour. Once released, her grief and shame knew no bounds. Her body quaking uncontrollably as she sobbed without restraint, she found that she could not seem to control the convulsive weeping that shook her to the soul. The realization that she was near hysteria did not serve to diminish the violent trembling or the heartrending sobs that threatened to overwhelm her. Still lying on the couch, her dress pushed up to her thighs, she continued to sob out her grief.

Admist her storm of tears, Melanie did not see the tall male figure that came into the room; did not know of his presence until a heavy hand touched her shoulder. Suddenly jerking her face to the side, she saw the broad figure crouching beside her. Immediately recognizing the sandy blond hair that caught the last of the light reflected through the window, she turned her face away.

"Please, please don't look at me, Josh. I can't—I don't want anyone to see me now."

Taking her chin gently in his hand, Josh turned her face back toward his and assessed her darkly. Her tear-ravaged face confirmed his suspicions. Slowly running his eyes the full length of her, he reached down to cover her legs with her dress, his expression hardening as a deep, shuddering anger began deep within him.

"Tell me what happened, Melanie. I just saw Steve coming out of here. What did he do to you, Melanie?"

The tears still streaming down her face, Melanie sobbed incoherently, "I didn't know he was watching the house, Josh. I just wanted to walk. I wanted to come back here to see Asa's old office. How could I know he would follow me? I told him to leave me alone, but he just became angrier and angrier. He said I still wanted him. I don't know . . . maybe I did, Josh, but I wouldn't have let him touch me, I swear it! I'm not like they say I am, Josh! I'm not a witch either. I'm . . ."

Suddenly enfolded within Josh's embrace, Melanie's rambling words came to a faltering stop and she clung to him desperately.

"Melanie . . ." Josh's agonized words reflected the depth of his own despair at the wretched course of events that he had been too late to prevent. "Melanie, Melanie . . ." Caressing her tenderly, Josh held her against him until her sobs had stopped, managing to control his own violent reaction to the despicable act he was certain Steve had committed upon her. There would be time for the settling of that debt later. Right now Melanie needed his full attention.

Finally pulling herself slightly away from him, Melanie strained to see his expression in the fading light of the room. Appealing to him in an urgent tone, Melanie said softly, "Please don't tell anyone what happened here, Josh . . . please."

"Of course I won't tell anyone."

Interrupting him quickly, Melanie continued in the same urgent tone, "I mean not anyone, Josh. I don't want Simon to find out that Steve—" Swallowing tightly, Melanie took a deep breath and continued determinedly, "I don't want Simon to find out about Steve's threats or that he—"

"Raped you? That's what you mean, isn't it, Melanie? Steve raped you and you expect me to do nothing about it? And he threatened you, too? Did he warn you not to tell anyone? That dirty bastard, did he?" Fury flooded Josh's senses, inundating him with a desire to find Steve that very minute and beat him until he could no longer raise his fists.

"No, Josh. He said he *wants* me to tell Simon what

he did! And he wants me to tell Simon that if he objects, he'll be waiting for him at the boarding-house tonight! Josh, please help me! I can't let Simon find out. He'll go there to kill Steve, I know he will. He threatened to kill Steve if he ever insulted me again. If he found out what happened—Josh, please help me! I don't want Harriet Sims' word to become the truth! If anything happens to either one of them because of me, I couldn't live with it, Josh! First my father, then Asa. I couldn't live with it! Please, Josh, please help me!"

Suddenly sobbing anew, Melanie clung tightly to Josh's broad frame, and unable to stand her pain, Josh closed his arms tightly around her, his own eyes moist as he struggled to overcome his raging emotions. Managing to maintain control, Josh murmured softly against her hair as he caressed her gently, "Don't worry, Melanie. I won't say anything, I promise. But if you really expect to be able to convince Simon Young that nothing has happened to you, you had better get control of yourself now."

Pulling herself away from him, Melanie nodded her head lightly in a supreme effort of restraint. Finally able to speak, she mumbled hoarsely, "Thank you, Josh. Yes, I'll pull myself together and maybe you could walk with me back to Asa's house. I, I don't think I want to walk back alone."

"All right, then, Melanie." Pulling her gently to her feet, he smoothed the tears from her cheek. "You're going to have to think of a really convincing story to cover your condition, you know." With a small laugh that didn't reach his eyes, he said softly, "You are a mess, you know."

Shooting him a quick look, Melanie bent down to smooth her dress. Realizing it was a hopeless endeavor, she ran her fingers quickly through her hair, and taking two deep breaths, faced him again. "I'm ready now, Josh. Let's go."

Within a few minutes they were on Weaver's Row. Holding tightly to Josh's arm as they approached the house, Melanie's mind was racing. She still was not certain what she was going to say when she entered. The sheer strength of her desire to get within the safety of her room consumed her thoughts. Glancing quickly up into Josh's face, she caught his sober scrutiny and managed a meager smile. What would she have done if Josh hadn't come and extended the strength of his presence? Dear Josh, always seeming to appear when she needed him.

Going around to the back of the house, Melanie approached the kitchen door. Taking a deep breath, she opened it and took a step inside, her disheveled appearance bringing a gasp from Martha's lips.

"Melanie, what happened to you?" The large, anxious woman moved swiftly toward her.

Stepping back, Melanie stammered, "I . . . I fell, Martha. I tripped and hurt myself, and Josh found me and brought me home. Isn't that right, Josh?" Her eyes begged for his corroboration. She repeated again in a pleading voice, "Isn't that right, Josh?"

Unable to resist her silent appeal, Josh responded tonelessly, "Yes, that's right."

Moving her wise eyes between them, Martha finally responded in a voice that held an element of disbelief, "Well, if you say so, Melanie. The only thing I can say is that you're lucky Mr. Young isn't

426

here right now. He's been gone all afternoon, so he won't even realize you've been out if you can manage to get upstairs and cleaned up before he comes home."

Melanie glanced around the room searchingly, and reading her thoughts correctly, Martha said softly, "Tom is on an errand and Sara is still napping. You must move quickly, Melanie."

Turning back toward Josh, her eyes showing a gleam of hope, Melanie said softly, "I must hurry, Josh." Her eyes filled with tears as she slowly perused his sober face, taking in the warmth of his brown eyes, his pleasant, comforting face. Swallowing tightly, Melanie lifted herself on her toes and threw her arms around his neck, hugging him with all her strength. Finally slackening her grip, she pulled herself slightly away. Lifting her face to his, she kissed him lightly on the lips. "Josh, I will never forget you, never. Thank you for . . ." Choking on her words, she managed to croak out a soft, "Goodbye," before turning away and running from the room.

Listening until she reached the top of the steps, Martha turned back toward Josh. Her question was straightforward. "What really happened, Josh?"

Avoiding her question, Josh said in a tone of controlled menace, "You needn't worry, Martha. I'll take care of everything."

Startled by the blackness of his glance, Martha called after him as he turned on his heel and started out the door, "Josh, wait!"

Her call went unheeded, and within seconds Josh was out of sight.

*   *   *

Still fully dressed, Steve lay sprawled on the bed in his room, his face dark with anger. Tortured by the vision of Melanie's cold expression, he once again felt fury exploding inside him. Choking with frustration and abounding hatred for the beautiful face that haunted him, he mumbled under his breath, "Witch! She is a witch! She will not be satisfied until she owns me body and soul, but I won't let her win!" God, he wanted her! What had really happened at the foundry? He hadn't intended . . . he had just wanted to talk to her. He had intended to apologize for his behavior at their last meeting; but the moment he was close to her, everything seemed to go wrong. He had just wanted to touch her cheek. She was so beautiful. He wanted her so much that it drove him wild. Why had she pulled away from him? Why had she said all those things, irritated him, stirred his anger? It was her own fault! He had just wanted to hold her for a while, just . . .

A harsh pounding at the door startled Steve from his thoughts, and frowning blackly, he got to his feet as the pounding continued. Slowly pulling himself to his full height, he started toward the door, a menacing smile on his face as he thought with bitter amusement, "Simon Young, you surprise me. I hadn't expected you to lose control."

Quickly turning the lock, Steve jerked open the door. Startled to see Josh's angry face, he opened his mouth to speak as a powerful fist crashed against his jaw, knocking him to the floor. Before he was again able to focus his eyes, Steve felt himself being jerked upright, only to be knocked backward against the bed as heavy, angry fists pummeled his body and face. The bitter taste of blood filled his mouth. He could not see for the blood that streamed into his eyes, blurring his vision, but the blows continued, crashing into him again and again until he could no longer distinguish between the bright flashes of pain that rained upon him. Finally the pounding blows stopped, and the wave of blackness that had swept over him began to recede. He strained to open his eyes, but it hurt . . . it hurt. Exerting the last of his strength, he strained to make out the shape that loomed over him. His vision finally clearing brought a broad, furious face into view.

Realizing Steve was fully conscious and able to understand him, Josh grabbed him by the shirtfront, jerking him upward until their faces were level. "You filthy, no good bastard," Josh mumbled, the hatred flashing from his eyes giving added emphasis to his heated words. "I could kill you without a second thought right now for what you did to Melanie today, except that Melanie would be the one to suffer the most. I won't allow you to add to her grief by making her feel responsible for your death. But hear me now, Steve, and remember what I say! If you ever dare to touch Melanie Morganfield again, to hurt her in any way, I *will* kill you with my bare hands! You are the cause of all her problems! You! If you hadn't taken advantage of her loneliness to satisfy your lust, she would be married to me right now! You didn't want her, you were afraid of her, she was too beautiful, too lovable, she was breaking you down. You had to get away from her before you surrendered completely, so you abandoned her to the hatred and jealousy of this town. But you didn't want anyone else to have her either, did you? You scum! Now you want to ruin her life again because she won't take you back!"

His mouth swollen and bleeding, Steve was barely able to speak. With a supreme effort he whispered hoarsely, "She's no good, Josh, like me. We belong together."

With a gasp of fury, Josh shook Steve's limp body like a rag doll, finally throwing him back against the floor with a grunt of complete disgust. "Listen to me, you filth, and listen to me well." Josh's voice was filled with menace as he lowered over the bloodied face of his former friend. "The next time you touch Melanie Morganfield, you seal your own death. Forget her, you bastard!" Josh hissed softly, "Or you are dead!"

Leaving him where he lay, Josh turned abruptly on his heel and walked out the door, slamming it hard behind him. With the sound of his departure, the black, creeping darkness finally overcame Stephen Hull.

Her hands shaking with anxiety, Melanie stripped off the devastated blue cotton dress and stuffed it into the corner of her wardrobe. Quickly removing her torn undergarments, she was slipping into her wrapper when a soft knock sounded at the door.

"Who is it?" Melanie's voice was anxious. She wasn't ready to face Simon yet.

"I've brought you some warm water, Melanie," Martha's voice answered from outside the door. Opening it quickly, Melanie smiled her gratitude.

"You must hurry, Melanie. Supper is ready and Mr. Young said he would be home at seven to eat."

"All right, Martha. Take Sara downstairs with you. She is sleeping far too long and will detain Simon for a few more minutes should he return. Please hurry, Martha!"

Turning away as Martha nodded her head and slipped out the door, Melanie poured the water into the washbowl. Wetting the washcloth in the tepid water, she worked up a good lather with the lavender scented soap and began scrubbing herself fastidiously. She needed the time to cleanse herself, to remove the scent of Steve from her nostrils. She wanted to feel clean again. With a soft sob she scrubbed her soft skin even harder.

Within a few minutes she was done. Running to her dresser, she pulled out a fresh chemise and underdrawers. Putting them on swiftly, she ran to her wardrobe and pulled out the soft yellow cotton and slipped it over her head. Turning back toward her vanity mirror she brushed her thick auburn curls into order, and unable to spend any more time dressing her hair, she picked up the two front locks of hair and pulled them to the back of her head, securing them there with a small length of ribbon from her drawer.

Surveying herself critically in the mirror, she frowned darkly at her reflection. She was far too pale, and her eyes were still swollen, but Simon would not be suspicious at that. Satisfied that her appearance was passable, she slipped her feet back into her black slippers and was walking out the door of her room as the front door opened and the sound of Simon's voice reached her ears. Fixing a small smile on her face, she slowly descended the stairs.

Hours later Melanie lay silently in bed. Lying quietly beside her, Simon searched her face intently in the light of the small lamp at bedside. He was worried. Melanie was disturbed and anxious, far more so than she had been directly after the hearing. He had expected that the afternoon's rest would settle her nerves, but it seemed to have had the opposite effect. Frowning lightly, he touched her cheek. Jumping at his touch, Melanie appeared to stiffen all the more, causing him to whisper in a concerned voice, "What's wrong, Melanie? You can't seem to relax tonight. I know you've had a hard day, but it's all over now, darling. It's time to put everything behind you and to go on from here. We'll be back in Philadelphia within three or four days and you'll be back in your own home. You'll be relieved to leave Salisbury, won't you, Melanie?"

Lifting her golden eyes to his for the first time, Melanie said in a quick, earnest voice, "Oh, yes, Simon. I'm anxious to leave Salisbury behind me. There is nothing but grief left for me here, only . . ."

"Only what, darling?" Simon encouraged, relieved to see her responding openly once again.

"Only I will be sorry to leave Martha and Tom again. I love them both dearly, and Martha has been a great . . . comfort to me."

Looking at her strangely, Simon ignored her comment and whispered softly, "I think it is best you try to sleep now, darling. This day seems to have taken more out of you than I had realized."

Lowering his head, he pressed his mouth lightly against her soft lips, his brows drawing together in a dark frown as she stiffened noticeably at his touch. Deeply disturbed, he said softly, "What is it, Melanie? Tell me what's wrong."

Suddenly on the verge of tears, Melanie moved closer to him, burying her face in his neck as she pressed herself against him. Her voice was choked and ragged. "Nothing is wrong, Simon, nothing. I just want you to hold me for a little while . . . just hold me."

Too filled with emotion to respond, Simon slid his arms under and around her, holding her tight against his chest, close and safe within his arms until she fell asleep.

Chapter 9

Storming across the hall in quick, angry strides, Simon entered the study to slam the door violently behind him. He was at the end of his patience, irritated almost beyond control by an indefinable quality that he had trouble putting a name to even in his own mind. But it was there—as much as Melanie denied a change in her attitude toward him, it was there—ever present since their short stay in Salisbury. Now, in retrospect, Simon realized it had been a mistake taking Melanie back for the hearing, for obviously her brief exposure to the faces from her traumatic past had affected her far more than he had realized possible. But he had been so secure in their relationship, so certain she shared his enthusiasm for their situation. Their month in New York had been idyllic, and he had begun to believe that he was becoming as necessary a part of Melanie's life as she had become a part of his. His own growing affection for Sara had not allowed the child's future to be jeopardized by the greed of Hiram Willis. Even though he, himself, was slowly securing the child's future financially, he felt the child deserved to know she was conceived in love, and was not merely an accidental outcome of a faded passion. But somehow, all his good intentions had fostered the first obstacle in the completely honest exchange that had existed between Melanie and himself. Try as he might, he could not recall a specific instance to mind where Melanie had been neglectful or short with him since their return to Philadelphia, but she was not the same as before. The difference was there, in the reluctance of that golden gaze in meeting and holding his; the almost forced gaiety she exhibited at social gatherings where she was achieving even greater success while seeming to enjoy herself less and less; the restraint on her part when he baited her so relentlessly, hoping for the spark of temper that now appeared to be buried in an avalanche of pensive wanderings; and most of all, in the absence of the glowing eagerness with which Melanie had always greeted his advances, and in the honest, spontaneous response she had always exhibited in their lovemaking. While still spending a part of each day since they had returned to Philadelphia with her, Simon was painfully lonesome . . . lonesome for the old Melanie who had seemed to disappear, leaving only the beautiful outer shell of the complete, glorious woman she had been.

This very evening he had spent some very unsatisfactory hours in Melanie's company at the City Tavern, a familiar haunt of many of his old friends. Melanie had held court as usual, her beauty drawing many admirers, while her keen mind and sharp wit held them entranced. His dissatisfaction had not stemmed from the fact that Melanie had charmed so many, however. Quite the contrary, he had always found considerable amusement in the fact that so many men were utterly devastated by Melanie, while only he could call her his own. His irritation stemmed from the fact that when they were alone in the carriage on their return from the tavern, he and Melanie had not indulged in the easy banter of the past wherein thoughts and impressions were easily exchanged. Somehow she had felt it necessary to continue the same type of gay facade and repartee with which she had entertained his friends. He felt hurt, shut out now that she had no longer allowed him free access to her quick mind. At first avoiding his intimate glances, she appeared finally to force herself to respond, setting off a sensitive appeal from Simon that had resulted in a particularly heated exchange.

Staring at Melanie's incredibly lovely face in the semidarkness of the carriage, Simon had appealed to her honestly.

"Melanie, darling, something is wrong. Why

won't you tell me what has happened to change you toward me?"

Avoiding his eyes, instantly confirming in his mind the veracity of his suspicions, Melanie responded, "Simon, nothing is wrong. Why do you continue to plague me so?"

Angered at her continued evasiveness, Simon's tone had been sharp. "You are hiding something from me, something that is obviously affecting our relationship adversely, and I do not intend to put up with your secrecy any longer! I demand to know what it is that is bothering you!"

Responding with spontaneous heat at his tone of imperious command, Melanie exclaimed with a spark of her old hauteur, "You demand? How dare you assume that you have the right to *demand* anything of me? I have told you before, Simon, I am your mistress. I am not your *slave!*"

Encouraged by her spirited response, Simon pressed her further. "Nevertheless, I insist you tell me what is troubling you! Ever since that afternoon in Salisbury, you have not been yourself! As it stands now, you are merely the milk toast version of your old self!"

"*Milk toast!* How dare you?" Amber fire flashed from golden eyes as Melanie eyed him in obvious astonishment.

"Yes, milk toast!" Simon's clear blue eyes assumed a hard, glacial quality as he refused to renege on his adament demand for an explanation. "You will tell me immediately what has you so upset! Do you understand me, Melanie?"

Drawing herself up haughtily, Melanie had replied in an angry, even tone, "Do not speak to me, Simon Young! Do not waste your breath with another word. I have nothing whatever to say to you!"

The remainder of the ride home had passed in an angry silence.

Unable to penetrate her icy reserve, he had assisted her from the carriage with stiff formality upon their arrival at the Walnut Street address. Without a moment's pause or a glance in his direction, Melanie had preceded him up the front stairs and through the entrance, continuing up the staircase to her room without a break in stride. Unwilling to follow her up the stairs like a chastised pet, he had stormed across the hall and into the study, slamming the door violently behind him. His anger and baiting had availed him nothing except Melanie's anger in return, and seated alone at his desk, he began to feel the first rise of panic with his silent admission that he was at a complete loss for a way out of his dilemma.

Huffing angrily, Melanie entered her room and slammed the door behind her. Within a few seconds another slamming door downstairs echoed her own, and she straightened up indignantly. How dare he! That insufferable man! How dare he! He had been at her constantly since their return to Philadelphia, watching, assessing, his clear blue eyes reading only too clearly the underlying anxiety that was her constant companion. She dared not explain that Stephen Hull's black heated gaze haunted her, followed her through each day, casting a pall over every facet of her life. Try as she might, she could no more forget the hatred in Steve's last glance than she could forget Harriet Sims' heinous words. But it was not true! She had not been responsible for her father's or Asa's deaths, and Steve would not come to a violent end because of her! Vainly she had sought to deny the truth of Harriet's Sims' words in her own mind while the very violence of Steve's attack on her had seemed to be the first proof of the hateful woman's words. Was she really the Devil's spawn? Was there truly something wrong with her? Did she really drive men to violence? Had she somehow driven Steve to the point where he had forced himself upon her?

Angry and confused, there was only one thing of which she was certain. She need have no fear for Simon. Unlike Steve he was superbly controlled. While allowing himself to completely and fully enjoy her intimate companionship, he still maintained his own particular sense of dignity and aloofness. No, she need have no fear for him . . . damn him! He was such an irritating man when he chose to exercise his "proprietary rights" as he was fond of calling his demands on her. Milk toast indeed!

Despite herself, a small smile crossed Melanie's lips, and shaking her head lightly, she made one concession to Simon's statement. She had not really been herself since their return to Philadelphia, of that she was fully aware, but she simply could not seem to put Steve out of her mind.

A small sound at the door to her room snapped Melanie around to meet Simon's sober expression as he entered the room and closed the door quietly behind him. Subconsciously, she compared the man walking toward her with the man whose face haunted her so relentlessly. Tall, dark, splendidly built, and moodily handsome, Steve exuded a sensual appeal to which most women were helplessly drawn. She herself was proof of that fact. But Simon was another matter. As tall as Steve, he gave the impression of slimness, which was in reality the trim, muscular physique of an athlete, which he appeared to retain as effortlessly as he drew women's glances with his cool aloofness. Where Steve was a perpetual threat, Simon was an endless challenge. Exact opposites, both held an appeal for the opposite sex that was strong and undeniable.

Within moments Simon was beside her. Silencing her haughty remark before she could speak, with the power of his mesmerizing gaze he said softly, "Melanie, the time has come when we must talk coolly and sensibly." Taking her hand, he led her to the lounge chair where he urged her to be seated. Assuming the place at her side, he continued holding her hand as he spoke earnestly.

"We have come to an impasse between us, Melanie. Despite all your denials, something in Salisbury upset you sufficiently to cause a change in your attitude toward me." Stopping her brief protest with the raising of his hand, he continued softly, "I do not intend to allow this to happen, Melanie. I will not submit passively to whatever has inspired this change within you, be it guilt, fear, or any other mediocre device that has preyed on your mind. I would have some things clear with you here and now."

Swallowing hard, Melanie kept her gaze cool as

she answered quietly, "Is this to be considered in the nature of an ultimatum, Simon? Perhaps you feel the pleasures of our relationship insufficient to support the aggravation involved." Averting her eyes, she continued softly, "If you feel it would be best to conclude our arrangement, I will understand perfectly and will be—"

"Melanie!" His face white, Simon's icy words stopped her short. "You will please stop attempting to anticipate me and listen quietly until I am finished, or I will gag you here and now! When I am ready to end our arrangement I will say so in no uncertain terms, you may be sure."

Melanie's quick response was stifled by the obvious anger in Simon's eyes. Silently she awaited his next words.

"Since you are so adamant about refusing to tell me the problem that is driving you away from me, I must cover all points; and there are several things I would have you know here and now. The first is that there is nothing in your past, no matter how dark or despicable you may think it to be that could turn me against you. To me your past is dead, gone, forgotten, as if it never existed. The only thing I am interested in is having you with me here and now, totally and completely, with no reservations on your part. You need not tell me anything that you do not wish me to know as long as you do not allow it to come between us. Having held the complete, beautiful woman, Melanie Morganfield, in my arms, having had her respond to me with the depth of her sensitive, passionate nature, I can no longer abide having just a portion of her, even if that portion is

441

her body. It is very easy to obtain a female body for a night's pleasure, Melanie. I don't say that with any particular conceit. It is merely a statement of fact. But it has never been that way between us, Melanie. From the first time we made love it was a passionate, loving exchange that far outdistanced a casual meeting of bodies. It can be and will be that way again. I will have you know, now," Simon's voice was husky with emotion, his expression serious and intense as his startlingly clear azure eyes held her glance with a burning intensity, "that you mean more to me than any woman I have ever known, Melanie, and I do not intend to sacrifice myself or you to any senseless guilts, fears or uncertainties that you may be harboring in your mind. You belong to me, Melanie, and I do not intend to give you up."

"But Simon," Melanie began in a choked whisper, "you heard Harriet Sims. She said—"

"Damn Harriet Sims to hell, for that is certainly where she belongs!" Simon interrupted heatedly. "Put that evil witch out of your mind!" Cupping Melanie's face in his hands, Simon continued gently, "Think only of me, darling, and I will exorcise your fears." Still holding her captive with his mesmerizing gaze, he lowered his head slowly toward hers, gently pressing his lips against her mouth in a light, lingering kiss that deepened gradually as the passion he held so tightly in check assumed control. Slowly Simon's arms slipped around Melanie to draw her close, the magic of his touch once again striking the spark that had lain dormant during her long month of anxiety. Immediately sensing her response, Simon's mouth plunged deeper, separating her lips to taste the warm, welcoming sweetness within as his senses exulted in the new awakening of Melanie's acceptance. Slowly Melanie's arms slipped around his neck, encouraging the kiss that deepened to explore her mouth. Reveling in the pressure of their bodies against each other, Simon's hands roamed her back hungrily, his one hand finally tangling in her glorious auburn curls in an effort to press her mouth even closer against his.

Finally tearing himself away, Simon's breathing was ragged. Unable to tear his gaze from her tremulous lips, he stood up, and bending in a swift movement, scooped Melanie into his arms. In a few rapid strides he was at the bed, and laying her down gently, he sat beside her. Slowly he began removing the pins from her hair, glorying as each lock that fell free of the upswept coiffure added to the gleaming beauty that covered her slender shoulders. His hands trembling, he reached around her to free the buttons on the back of her dress, his breath catching as the smooth whiteness of her perfect breasts were revealed to his eyes.

Experiencing an overwhelming tenderness for the woman before him, Simon reached out to run his hands lightly along the graceful line of her shoulders, finally moving to touch the beautiful breasts that invited his caress. Lifting his gaze back to her face, Simon rejoiced in the warmth smoldering in Melanie's golden gaze. Within moments, the barrier of clothing removed, the mutual spark that ignited with the touching of their bodies burst into a blaze that consumed all other thoughts but that of assuaging the desire that burned brightly between them. Reveling in the touch of her flesh, he exulted in her spontaneous gasp as he pressed warm, moist kisses against the gleaming whiteness of her breasts. Stimulated to even greater passion by the tremors of delight that shook her slender body, he extended his trail of kisses along her narrow rib cage to the delicate skin of her stomach. Caressing her slender hips tenderly, Simon circled the delicate triangle of shining auburn ringlets that nestled between her thighs with light, butterfly kisses. Gradually raising the heat of their mutual emotion, he rained passionate kisses on the shining curls, until the gleaming white thighs separated of their own volition to allow him access to the delicate lips awaiting his kiss. Unable to resist their appeal a moment longer, Simon pressed his mouth against them, his tongue slipping into the glorious crease to taste the sweetness awaiting within. Melanie's spontaneous gasp of ecstasy pushing him over the edge of restraint, Simon began a violent, loving attack on the body of the woman who had become an indispensible part of his life. Kissing, tasting, exploring, his voracious appetite for her could not be appeased. Allowing his passions full rein, his hands caressed, touched and titillated every portion of her body as his mouth continued seeking, drawing, indulging, devouring her private inner reaches. In a bursting jolt of ecstasy, Melanie's slender body shuddered convulsively, abandoning itself to the passionate release of the glorious emotion that had held her on the brink of suspended ecstasy, for long, rapturous moments.

Glorying in his reward, accepting it with an all-consuming desire for more, Simon continued his tempestuous pursuit, bringing her up and over the summit of her passion again and again as he gloried in his renewed power to arouse her, carry her with him to the heights of the unsurpassable beauty they achieved so miraculously in the meeting of their flesh. Once again Melanie's slender body trembled, her shuddering growing until gasping in the throes of her seemingly endless ecstasy, she again climaxed in a blinding burst of searing beauty that left her weak and spent.

Tangling her hand gently in Simon's dark hair as his mouth lay intimately against hers, Melanie whispered in a soft, breathless voice, "Please Simon, no more. I want to feel you inside me now . . . now, darling, now."

Suffused with a joy that brought the heat of tears to his light eyes, Simon moved to cover Melanie's body with his, his own soft groan mingling with hers as he plunged deeply within her at last. Carried high on the wings of the brilliant emotion that held them within its grasp, Simon plunged again and again inside her, his supreme joy building and accelerating out of control until it rushed them in a breathless, reckless ascent to the pinnacle of their passion, where they poised for a long, endless moment of incomparable beauty before careening in a headlong spiral of ecstasy from its glorious summit.

Finally stirring, suddenly humbled by the overwhelming emotions they had shared, Simon drew Melanie close, pressing the small, perspiring body that brought him such joy against his, possessively, protectively. Breathing deeply of the sweet, womanly scent of her, Simon whispered softly against her ear in a voice that was deeply affected by the passion of the last consuming minutes. Suppressing the words he so wanted to say with his deep, instinctive knowledge that she was not yet ready to hear them, he said simply, "Melanie, my dearest darling, never draw yourself away from me again, but remember what I say to you right now. Within us we have the power to create for each other a glorious world where only the two of us abide. We are able to glimpse together a beauty few others will ever hope to see or are even aware exists, short of heaven. Surely you realize, darling, that to confine an emotion of such magnitude, to turn away from it or seek to suppress it in any way is the true evil, for truly, such a pure, sharing experience as this must be considered a gift of God. My darling, darling Melanie, you must feel only joy between us, for truly, that is the emotion you bring to me."

Looking up, Melanie assessed Simon's ardent expression silently. Her eyes clinging to his clear, warm gaze, her own golden glance mingling with the azure stare that seemed to search out and purge her very soul, she said softly, in a voice that was hoarse with the emotions of the past hour, "Perhaps what you say is true, Simon, perhaps not. I only know that you manage to put to rest within me for a while some of the evils of the past, and surely, that in itself is a gift. We are fortunate in that, are we not, Simon?"

Swallowing deeply, Simon pulled her close again in an effort to hide the eyes that had become suspiciously bright with her last statement. Holding her tightly within his embrace, he said softly and simply, "Yes, we are fortunate, my darling, indeed we are."

With the dawning of their new understanding, Melanie lived in an armed truce with her emotions. Still unable to completely drive Steve from her thoughts or overcome the fears Harriet Sims had managed to implant in her mind, she succeeded in relegating those thoughts to the back of her mind where they occupied a second place to the elements of her daily life.

Aiding her resolution was the gradual change that had overcome the house on Walnut Street. Upon their return from Salisbury a month before, Simon had returned to their former living arrangements, wherein he maintained his own residence, visiting Melanie each day and several nights a week as was his former custom. On the day following their tempestuous reconciliation, however, he left to reappear a few hours later, announcing his intention to stay for a "short term." By the end of the second week, he had spent only two nights in his own house and had taken to moving more and more of his clothing into the master bedroom at Walnut Street.

As they lay abed one night and the night grew darker, Simon frowned in the direction of Melanie's wardrobe.

"Damn, Melanie! Why have you never told me that your wardrobe was so small? I am having endless problems fitting my clothing in without their becoming wrinkled beyond belief. You should have mentioned that you needed another one for this room."

With a look of feigned innocence, Melanie said

softly, "It is big enough by far for one person's clothing, Simon."

Shooting her a scrutinizing glance with a raised brow that broke Melanie into instant laughter, Simon said in a sober voice that made Melanie instantly ashamed of her poor joke, "Do you find my residence here a burden, Melanie?"

Raising herself up slightly, she pressed a light kiss on his unsmiling mouth, saying softly in way of apology, "Simon, I could not resist."

Before accepting her apology, Simon noted the puzzled expression that had drawn her brows together in a small frown. In a soft voice he ventured, "I can see you have more than jocularity on your mind, Melanie. Wht is it that is bothering you?"

Taking advantage of the opportunity to pose the question that had bothered her the past two weeks, Melanie began falteringly, "I was just wondering, Simon . . . I mean . . . how do you . . . what of your other mistresses? In spending every night here, do you not find it difficult to . . . I mean, do they not object?" As she continued to stammer in posing her question, Simon's smile grew gradually wider.

"Melanie, dear," he said lightly, his clear blue eyes staring directly into hers, mesmerizing her with the impact of their penetrating power, "Surely you realize from the consistency of my attentions that I no longer have any other mistresses, in fact have not had any others since you first came to me." Melanie's mouth fell open in shock as Simon continued seriously, all trace of a smile removed from his face. "You fill all my needs more than adequately, Melanie. I have no use for another woman, nor

448

any desire."

When still she continued to stare in open-mouthed amazement, he broke into sudden laughter. "Surely you realized this, Melanie. We have rarely gone three nights in succession without making love at least twice since the first day we lay together. Did you think me superhuman, perhaps, to maintain this type of activity while other mistresses also shared my association?" When she still did not answer, he began to laugh loudly, his body shaking with mirth as she colored hotly. Finally settling down to kiss her mouth lightly, he said in a soft voice, "My dear Melanie, I am extremely flattered."

Working quietly in the kitchen a few days later, much to Helga's annoyance, Melanie was startled to hear Simon's voice in the hallway. Glancing quickly to the kitchen clock, she realized it was far too early for Simon's usual return, and stifling a short siege of anxiety, she began moving in the direction of the hallway as Simon entered the kitchen. A quick look at his expression reassured Melanie there was nothing wrong, and slightly annoyed with herself for her wrong assumption, she said shortly, "What brings you home at this time of day, Simon? You startled me. I . . ."

Taking her arm as she talked, Simon ushered her toward the hallway, almost dragging her along with his long stride. Annoyed by his handling of her, Melanie exclaimed sharply, "Simon! You will please desist pulling me this way! I am quite able to move under my own power, and I resent being pulled like a horse on a lead! If you will kindly—"

Already approaching the foyer, Melanie's words stopped short as she caught a glimpse of two figures standing stiffly by the front door, their faces in the shadow of the light streaming in behind them. Certainly, the tall, broad proportions of the woman left no doubt as to who she might be, instantly indicating the identity of the tall, slouched figure standing beside her. Unable to wait a moment longer for absolute confirmation, Melanie said in a soft, disbeliving voice, "Martha, Tom, is it you?"

Martha's familiar voice replied lightly in return, "Yes, Melanie, Tom and I both."

With a sob of happiness, Melanie flew into the soft, plump arms extended to her, exclaiming happily, "I can't believe it! You are truly here!" She hugged the woman tightly, and then turning to the broad-shouldered figure beside Martha, she said with a soft catch in her voice, "Tom, my dearest, dearest Tom." Hugging him wildly, she heard Tom's familiar stumbling voice in her ear, "I told Mama you would send for us, Melanie. I missed you so much."

"But I didn't send—"

"It just took longer than we thought to get settled, Tom." Simon interrupted her hesitant reply.

Sara's arrival on the staircase in Molly's arms then drew their attention from his response. As the sleepy child rubbed her eyes wearily, Martha murmured in a husky voice, "My little darling, Sara."

The sound of the familiar voice snapped the child's head in their direction, and finally identifying the two shadows, Sara shrieked loudly, almost throwing herself from Molly's grip in an effort to reach Martha's outstretched arms.

Overcome with excitement as Martha and Tom exclaimed over Sara in the manner of true family, Melanie sobbed openly with happiness. Finally turning to Simon who stood silently behind them, watching the proceedings with a somber face, Melanie threw her arms around his chest and hugged him tightly, unable to do more than mumble incoherently, "Thank you, Simon. Thank you so very much."

His arms closing around her in a warm embrace belied his casual tone as he said quietly, "Well, perhaps now we will have some semblance of order in this household!"

Lifting her tear-stained face in surprise, she met his amused glance. Openly lifting her mouth to his, she said with a small shake of her head, "Simon, you are incorrigible!"

Simon's full-time residency at Walnut Street provided daily updates of the action of Congress, and Melanie found herself awaiting anxiously Simon's nightly recitations while still refusing inwardly to admit the true cause of her concern. In an action that surprised no one, Congress voted to authorize the attack on Canada advocated by Ethan Allen, but the news that followed was a considerable shock to everyone. Her eyes wide in amazement, Melanie was hardly able to believe her ears.

"Do you mean to say Ethan Allen was voted *down* as leader of the Green Mountain Boys? I don't believe it!"

"It's true, nevertheless, Melanie. Seth Warner was chosen by overwhelming vote!"

"Whose overwhelming vote?"

Smiling lightly, Simon shook his head. "You are a clever girl, Melanie. That is the crux of the matter. It was reported that the vote was not put to' the Boys themselves, but to the farmers in the area of the grants. It seems Ethan's enemies have finally gotten their revenge."

"But what of the Boys? They'll never stand for this action. Steve said . . ." She was about to continue with Steve's comments but stopped self-consciously in mid-sentence as she was about to quote her former lover.

Conscious of her discomfort, Simon fought the wave of jealousy assailing him to say softly, "You need not be afraid to mention Stephen Hull in my presence, Melanie. You were about to say, I am sure, that the Boys would serve under no other leader. Well, you're right. They didn't take the news lightly, even if the man chosen was Seth Warner. For that reason Ethan was kept on as a civilian scout working with the operation and is presently in Canada recruiting Indian and white alike to the American cause. You must be well aware of the fact that Allen will probably serve better in this capacity than any other man alive. He is after all, Melanie, a firebrand who draws men to his cause like bees to honey. He is a legend among the Indians, and no man demands greater respect than he among them. In short, he is where he is needed most."

Melanie listened closely to all Simon had to say, and then dropped her eyes from his without speaking a word. With great gentleness, Simon raised her chin until she looked straight into his all-knowing eyes.

"Stephen Hull elected to travel with Allen, Melanie, and is presently with him somewhere near St. Johns, just south of Montreal."

The expression in Melanie's eyes at that moment said it all, and Simon knew a pain so deep in his vitals that he was almost overcome. With a small smile, he turned from Melanie's sad face and left the room. Entering the library, he closed the door firmly behind him and moved slowly to the desk, where he sat to rest his elbows on the surface and cover his eyes in a weary gesture.

Retreating into dark oblivion for a few moments, Simon suddenly uncovered his eyes to stare unseeingly into space in front of him as a small voice in the back of his mind nudged him, Come out of hiding, Simon, old fellow. Admit it to yourself. Be honest. You love her . . . you are hopelessly in love with the beautiful Miss Melanie Morganfield . . . and she does not love you in return. Her feelings for you have progressed from actual dislike to a warm affection. You have conquered the sensual side of her nature. She is utterly yours in bed. Simon could feel the swelling of his body with just the reminder of her soft flesh against his, but his common sense nagged on. But in her heart and mind she loves Stephen Hull. You have finally managed to convince that virago you married with the sheer force of your rage at her actions against Melanie, to give you a divorce, and even now that the proceedings are in progress, you will not tell Melanie. You know she still dreams of being reunited with Hull and fear she will sever all connection with you should she sense you wish to make the relationship permanent. Isn't that why you forced Michael to swear that he would not inform Melanie of the divorce, earning his contempt by appearing to want to avoid a permanent commitment to the one person you want most in the world? In short, it is Melanie . . . dear Melanie . . . lovely Melanie . . . passionate Melanie . . . witty Melanie . . . loving Melanie. She is everything, everything you had dreamed in the idealistic, long-gone days of your youth of finding in a woman, and long ago despaired of ever finding. Running his slender fingers through his thick brown hair, his thin, handsome face twisted into a deep frown of frustration.

It is unjust, unjust! his mind countered angrily. But for the hesitation of a few months, I would be first in Melanie's life. But Stephen Hull didn't hesitate. He moved boldly, and now, even hundreds of miles removed, he is still first to Melanie.

But wait, Simon . . . Reason prevailed in Simon's raging mind. Each day Melanie turns a little more freely toward you. You don't know for certain if she will ever see Stephen Hull again, and in the meantime she holds nothing back from you, or almost nothing. She shares the beauty of her body and mind, if not her heart, freely and with full fidelity and devotion. You can ask for nothing more except that over which neither she nor you have any control. You will have to wait, Simon, and hope . . . and enjoy her now while she is still yours. His stomach tightening unmercifully at that last bitter thought, Simon rose from his desk, unconsciously pushing his ruffled hair back into place. Taking a deep breath, he walked briskly to the door, and opening it, strode into the hallway to see Melanie standing motionless a few feet away, a disturbed frown creasing her beautiful face as she searched his expression warily.

His full lips spreading into a small smile, he walked forward, sliding his arm around her shoulder as he reached her, to bend and press a short kiss on her unsmiling lips.

"I'm especially tired tonight, darling," he said softly. "What would you say to our retiring a little early?"

For a few, short moments Melanie searched Simon's face, trying desperately to read the thoughts behind his impenetrable facade. Finally smiling briefly, she touched his cheek gently with the tips of her fingers in a tender gesture, and whispered softly, "Yes, that might be a good idea, Simon. Let me bid Martha and Tom goodnight, and I'll join you upstairs in a few moments."

Watching as her slight figure turned the corner of the hallway, Simon made no attempt to go upstairs without her. Somehow he could not face that empty bedroom alone, without her . . . not tonight. Not tonight or any night . . . not ever again.

"Damn him . . . damn Major Brown!" Steve mumbled with breathless vehemence as he stumbled again in his flight through the heavy underbrush. His buckskins sweat-stained and blackened with gun powder, perspiration dripped down the sides of his face as he maintained his rapid, stumbling pace through the virgin woodlands of Canada. Glancing over his shoulder, he saw the remains of their attacking force following in rapid retreat, but not quickly enough. The British were gaining on them steadily, not having the disadvantage of carrying wounded, and moving sharply to the left, he called to the tall, broad man beside him.

"Ethan, do you suppose there is any hope that either Walker's or Brown's forces could arrive in time?"

Turning toward him as he continued steadily forward, Ethan's face showed the contempt he felt for the two commanders who had abandoned them to the British. "Those damned cowards are busy making their way south by now, Steve. May they rot in Hell for their parts in this betrayal. My concern is for these loyal men with us now. Most of them are Canadians, and if we are captured, it will go hard for them. I don't—"

"Watch out!" Shouting a warning, Steve simultaneously pushed Allen to the ground and out of the path of a burst of fire from the British soldiers already overwhelming them. Scrambling for his rifle, Allen got off a wild blast that failed to do any damage, and with only a few yards separating the opposing forces, Allen came to a quick decision. Suddenly moving boldly into clear sight, he called in a loud voice.

"Gentlemen, you will have an orderly surrender if you will assure me of decent treatment for me and my men."

An authoritative voice called back from beyond their range of vision. "Colonel Allen, I can promise you treatment that befits honorable prisoners of war."

"That is all we ask." Turning wearily to his men,

his dark, perspiring face drawn into a dispirited frown, he signaled them to draw around him.

Slowly the men grouped around their leader, while the huge man eyed them sadly. Thirty-eight remaining out of one hundred and ten. Standing rigidly beside the great woodsman, Steve could hear the sounds of his ragged breathing. Ethan did not take defeat lightly, especially when dealt to him by betrayal. The capture of Montreal has been a military tactic that both he and Ethan had believed in equally, and Steve's own dark eyes mirrored the fury of Ethan's raging gaze.

"Come forward slowly, with your men." The British lieutenant's command echoed on the heavy air while his men kept avid watch, their muskets poised to fire, "And present your sword, hilt first."

Following the orders precisely, Ethan had advanced and turned over his sword, when a quick movement to the side of the group caught his eye as an Indian leaped from behind the British line with a savage war whoop, advancing wildly toward him, his musket poised and ready to fire. Grasping the red coat of the British officer, Ethan whirled the officer between himself and the advancing Indian, providing a living shield for his large, brawny frame. Moving quickly to the other side, the Indian leveled his musket again and Allen swung the officer around again, using him as cover. As the Indian turned, Allen turned, switching back and forth, keeping the British lieutenant continually between them.

Up from behind came another Indian, but before anyone could shout a warning, Allen saw him from the corner of his eye and whirled the confused officer wildly from side to side like a rag doll, jerking him this way and that, effectively blocking all attempts to fire.

"By Jesus!" A disgusted shout sounded from outside the wild foray as an Irish soldier, advancing steadily, directed his heated words and the point of his bayonet at the threatening Indians. "If you damned heathens so much as touch that prisoner, I will part your damned souls from your bodies where you stand!"

With a quick assessment, the wild-eyed Indians considered the advancing musket and the determined countenance of the burly Irishman. Realizing their only alternative was to buck the entire British force, they slowly moved backwards to fade into the surrounding foliage.

As soon as the frustrated Indians had backed off, Allen freed the British officer. Shaking himself lightly, the young man turned to Allen, regaining his composure with remarkable speed to say with typical British cool, "I'm happy to see you, Colonel Allen."

Still filled with bitter frustration, his massive chest heaving from the exertion of the encounter, Allen took just a moment to look into Steve's outraged face before turning back to say darkly in return, "I'd be a damn sight happier to be seeing you in Montgomery's camp!"

Turning back once more to his men, he signaled them to fall in behind him, and the two mile march to the British garrison commenced.

"You say you are Colonel Ethan Allen of the Green Mountain Boys?" His voice tinged with scorn,

General Richard Prescott, commander of the British forces in Montreal interrogated Allen while he trailed his eyes contemptuously over his rough, stained garments, a slow flush suffusing his distinguished countenance. "The same Colonel Allen who took Ticonderoga?"

"The same." The proud ring in Allen's voice was effective in pushing General Prescott over the edge of fury. Standing to his full but meager height, General Prescott advanced, suddenly enraged and waving his cane menacingly at Allen's head. "Traitor, rebel, you would steal from the King and make your own that which belongs to him! Wastrel! Thief! And murderer to boot, to be sure! You have failed this time, and now you will suffer full punishment for your acts of rebellion!"

Continuing his raging torrent of abuse, General Prescott swung his cane ever closer to Allen, his last swipe coming alarmingly close to Allen's face.

Allen's temper, held so closely in check, suddenly erupted as the cane swished dangerously near his face, and his black brows knitting together over dark eyes widened in fury. Projecting the full power of his anger into the General's face, he raised his huge fist and his voice as well, as he looked down into the man's livid countenance. "You had better stop waving that cane around, general, because if you touch me with it, you are damned well going to meet your maker this very minute!"

With an enraged bellow General Prescott raised his cane, only to have his aid pull him backward with the skirt of his jacket as he whispered into his ear, "Sir, it is most unseemly to strike a prisoner."

Quivering with rage, the general then turned his attention to the Canadians who stood beside Allen. "Lindsay!" he called in quick command to the sergeant of the guard, "these men are Canadians! Shoot them!"

Allen gasped aloud. He had bargained fairly for decent treatment for his men and would not allow such a miscarriage of justice. Before the sergeant could react, Allen moved forward, effectively blocking immediate access to the men, and baring his chest said forcefully, "General Prescott, if you are going to kill these men, it would be safer to have the first bayonet thrust into my breast!"

Rage and better judgment waged an open battle across the features of the furious general and, common sense winning out, the general made a small signal to the sergeant to desist.

Turning, he eyed Allen coldly. "I will not execute you now," he said in a soft, calculating voice, "but you shall grace a halter at Tyburn, God damn you!"

News of Allen's capture in an attempt to take Montreal virtually single-handed shocked the Continental Congress. Meanwhile, the British waged an active war of propaganda with factual stories of his confinement in thirty-pound chains with the most brutal of treatment, in an attempt to shake the rebels' spirit. To Simon the news was doubly ominous, and while others reacted in horror, he spent the remainder of the afternoon attempting to discover the fates of Allen's men.

With a slow, measured tread, Simon climbed the steps to the Walnut Street residence. As he reached the door, it swung open to reveal Melanie smiling broadly. "You're late, Simon, and I've been waiting most anxiously all day to tell you something." In a soft batiste dress of pale lemon cotton, her shimmering hair piled high and decorated with small pale bows of the same shade, she looked like a delicate yellow flower, her golden eyes the softest amber velvet, small dimples winking in her cheek as she purposely prolonged the announcement.

"Yes, Melanie wants to tell you something," Tom's heavy voice echoed from behind Melanie's small frame. "She has been waiting all day to tell you that Sara has finally walked across the room unaided today!"

"Tom!" Melanie's voice carried her obvious dismay.

"What's the matter, Melanie?" Tom was truly oblivious to his offense.

"You told him! I wanted to tell Simon myself!"

With a small, sheepish smile, Tom mumbled, "Well, you should have said so, Melanie," and turning, made haste to escape her possible wrath.

Turning back to Simon, Melanie firmly closed the door behind him, and taking his hat, placed it on the table. "Oh, well," she said softly, shrugging her shoulders philosophically, "whether Tom or I told you, the news is the same. Sara is finally walking, and—" Suddenly realizing Simon had made no comment at all, she stared into his face. "Is something wrong, Simon? You look unusually sober today."

"Well, we received some rather disturbing news at the State House today."

Melanie's face paled lightly, her lip developing a slight quiver as she awaited his next words.

Unable to think of any way to lessen the shock, Simon stated quietly, "Ethan Allen and his men were captured in an attempt to take Montreal. It is rumored that they are to be returned to England to be tried."

"Is . . . Steve . . ." The words seemed to stick in her throat, and unwilling to put her through the torture of another moment's doubt, Simon said quietly, "Yes, Stephen Hull is among the prisoners."

"And if they are tried in England and found guilty, what then, Simon?" Melanie's words were a raspy whisper, her eyes glued to Simon's face.

"If they are found guilty, they will be hanged at Tyburn."

"No!" An agonized sound escaped Melanie's throat. Harriet Sims' hateful words echoed in her ears as a vision of Steve's body swaying at the end of a rope appeared before her eyes. "Steve will die . . ." Taking an involuntary step backward, trembling ever so slightly, Melanie's small body suddenly slumped forward into his arms. Catching her quickly, Simon scooped up her limp form and called loudly as he started up the steps, "Tom! Martha! Quickly! I need your help! Quickly!"

The progress of everyday life at Walnut Street from that point on contrasted sharply with the affairs of the nation. Simon's conscientious concern surrounded Melanie and her "family," cushioning each threatening political incident with the comfort of reason and knowledge, allowing her life to proceed smoothly, with a surface calm that was remarkable for such unsettled times. Using his many business contacts to great advantage, he managed to secure periodic updates on the fates of Allen and his men, providing Melanie, without thought for his own personal feelings, with the solace that Stephen Hull was still alive.

By the end of the year circumstances appeared to be worsening immeasurably. General Montgomery's death and the failure of the invasion of Canada had plunged American spirits steadily downward, while the arrival of General Benedict Arnold and his forces on the St. Lawrence the month before had forced the British to make new arrangements for their important prisoners.

Separated from his men since his early confinement, Ethan stepped aboard the British dispatch carrier *Adamant,* manacled and under heavy guard. Having been informed by one of his friendlier guards that he was to rejoin his men incarcerated aboard and be shipped to England for trial, he felt a strong measure of apprehension. Fortunate enough to have been turned over to a more sympathetic jailer in the past month, he was anxious to learn how well his compatriots had fared. Descending slowly into the bowels of the ship, flanked on either side by armed guards, the skin on Ethan's broad, muscular neck began to crawl as a horrendous stench arose to greet them. Ushered to a small door, he felt a moment of overwhelming disbelief as the guard opened it to reveal the horror chamber that had housed the remaining thirty-four of his men for the duration of their confinement.

In a compartment no larger than twenty feet square, unlit and poorly ventilated, the men were crowded together with two large tubs of their own excrement, shrinking the inadequate space even further.

Almost gasping from the nauseating odor, Ethan stood firm as bayonets jabbing the soft flesh on his back nudged him into the filthy hole. There was complete silence from within as Ethan released an enraged bellow.

"So this is the treatment that befits honorable prisoners of war, loyal soldiers in the Army of the United Colonies of America!"

"It is the treatment that befits traitors, rebels against the King of England!" shouted one of the King's men.

"I will not enter!" Shaking off the hands of his jailers as they attempted to force him through the doorway, he shouted, "I demand you remove my men to better quarters. I insist—"

"You will insist on nothing!" Turning, Ethan faced Brook Watson, commander of the ship and a sworn enemy of his brother, Ira, whose shrewd nature had made him play the fool on an earlier encounter. Anxious to wreak his revenge on the Allen clan, he had anticipated Ethan's arrival and made his plans accordingly. Accompanied by a group of friendly Tories, he had come to view Allen's incarceration in the hell-hole and was eager to see the door shut tight behind him.

"I will not enter!" His deep voice firm, Ethan resisted the attempts to force his manacled form into the hold.

Stepping from behind Watson, a medium-sized, slender young man spat out contemptfully, "Traitor! You are a traitor, Allen! You should have been executed on the spot for your rebellion against New York!" And taking a deep breath, the Tory spat full into Ethan's furious face!

With a heart-stopping growl, Ethan's eyes widened in rage as he threw aside his captors' restraining hands, moving forward still manacled, and sprang on the petrified Tory. Knocking him to the ground, he moved after him again as the coward, screaming loudly, scrambled between the legs of the guards who pushed Ethan back with the points of their bayonets.

Pushing forward in a wild rush, the guards then shoved Ethan forcibly through the compartment doorway, knocking him to the floor as they slammed it shut behind him! Brook Watson's loud laugh echoed in the hallway as Ethan attempted to raise himself to his feet, his hands slipping on the slime covering the muck-ridden floor.

With a grunt of disgust, Ethan wiped his hand against his britches in an attempt to remove the foul-smelling filth.

"It's useless, Ethan. But don't worry, in a short time you'll become accustomed to the feel of it on your skin and will hardly notice it is there."

Recognizing the voice, Ethan turned toward Steve, barely able to subdue his horrified reaction at the obvious physical deterioration of his friend. Hardly recognizable, Steve's face was gaunt and spotted with filth, his sallow skin stretched tight over protruding cheekbones, with deep, dark circles underlining his lusterless eyes. A wild, shaggy beard, the equivalent of two months' growth, hung from his chin, and his hair lay in uncombed, greasy strands on his shoulders, housing an army of lice that moved visibly within. His buckskins, the same he had apparently worn since his imprisonment, were crusted with the slime that indeed appeared to cover the entire surface of the room.

"Steve! By God, man, you look terrible! How long have you been here in this filthy pit?"

"How long has it been since we were captured, Ethan?"

Swallowing hard at the obvious suffering of his friend, Ethen squinted his eyes, sending his glance around the walls, nodding briefly at the familiar faces. Feeling the sting of tears in his eyes at the criminal deprivation of the men, Ethan swallowed hard. Finally able to trust his voice, he said in a low, determined tone, directing his powerful gaze into the dulled eyes returning his gaze.

"By the Almighty, I swear, they will pay for the mistreatment of you all, God damn their black souls, they will pay!"

Moving again to the window, Melanie peeped through the lacey curtains and emitted an excited gasp as the door of the carriage that had pulled up in front of the house opened to discharge a familiar figure. Running toward the door, she shouted loudly, "Simon, he's here! He's finally arrived!"

Not waiting for Simon to emerge from the library where he had been secreted most of the afternoon, she ran to the front door, throwing it open wide, despite the cold December air and the light flurrying of snowflakes that had begun a short hour before. Barely giving the man time to enter, Melanie threw her arms around his heavily bundled back, hugging him with all her strength.

"Michael! You're here at last! We were beginning to believe you would not make it in time for Christmas! It is just like you to keep us waiting right up until the last minute like this!"

Smiling broadly, his little-boy face red with cold, he said hoarsely, "You must blame that blasted wreck of a carriage for my tardiness, not I, Melanie. We broke down not once, but twice, mind you, and damned cold it was too, trying to fix a broken wheel in this weather, you may be sure. But," he continued, directing his warm gaze into her glowing countenance, finally having struggled out of his heavy overcoat, muffler, and hat, "I'm finally here." Pulling her against him in a crushing embrace, he breathed deeply of her fragrance, his eyes closed blissfully.

"All right, Michael, let's not take advantage of Melanie's welcome. It is time that you release her and shake the hand of your old friend."

Opening his eyes, Michael smiled at Simon's slightly impatient greeting and released Melanie with obvious reluctance to take the hand extended to him.

"Simon, my friend," Michael's smile was a trifle wry as he shook his hand, "you could have waited a few minutes longer to put in your appearance so I could have greeted Melanie properly."

"Which is exactly the reason I did *not* wait to put in my appearance, Michael. I am not a fool!"

Laughing heartily, Simon slapped his shoulder companionably and urged him into the parlor. "You look like you could stand a warm toddy. Mrs. Walters!" he shouted festively, "Bring on the rum, our guest has arrived!"

Melanie's eyes rested contentedly on the scene before her. Christmas morning! It could hardly be more perfect. Snowflakes floated past the windows in the dull light of morning, as an air of suppressed excitement filled the warm sitting room. A huge Yule log blazed in the wide fireplace, and it seemed each chair gathered around its warmth was filled with someone she loved. Michael, smiling with obvious anticipation, held his presents on his lap as he sipped his tea, awaiting the signal for the festivities to begin. Martha, her huge form amply filling the large, upholstered chair, watched lovingly as Tom held Sara on his lap, his pale eyes adoring the excited child who could not tear her eyes from the huge stack of presents lying beneath the brilliantly lit tree in the corner. Honoring a long-standing family tradition, Melanie had requested an evergreen be cut and set inside the sitting room, and they had proceeded to decorate it the night before with strings of popped corn, dozens of brightly colored gingerbread cookies that had kept Martha in the kitchen for days, and tiny handmade ornaments which, to her surprise, each of the servants had contributed to the festivities. The tantalizing fragrance of roasting goose and pine mingled in the air while the dozens of candles on the tree flickering softly added to the festive scene an intangible, intoxicating aura of excitement that titillated the senses.

Noticing Simon beckoning her from the doorway where the servants waited expectantly, Melanie moved quickly toward him. They had decided to distribute their gifts to the servants first so they might open them before starting the full day's work the holiday festivities entailed, and she was anxious to see how well she had chosen.

Molly, her eyes wide, was obviously overwhelmed by the soft gray fur muff Melanie had selected. Although she exclaimed that it was too fine a gift for her, Melanie thought it simply inadequate for the many hours of endless patience the girl had shown to her beloved and very spoiled Sara.

Rose, shy and quiet as always, could not suppress the small gasp of surprise when she uncovered the delicately embroidered shawl that had seemed so right for her.

Helga, with a rare smile of genuine pleasure, took the delicate ivory and gold pin in the shape of a single rose that Melanie had chosen and pinned it with a great flourish to her dress. She was obviously pleased.

Last was Mrs. Walters. The very proper, somewhat reserved woman had been the hardest to choose for, and Melanie watched with particular expectation as she opened her gift. The woman's sober expression turned momentarily to one of delight when she viewed the small golden filigree bird pin that nestled within the velvet box. Her eyes filling with unexpected tears, she nodded a brief thank-you and turned to move the others back to their chores.

Directing a small, pleased smile into her eyes, Simon stooped to place a light kiss on Melanie's lips.

"Darling, they are delighted. Now, let's exchange our gifts before Michael bursts from suppressed eagerness!"

Within the hour all gifts had been exchanged. Sitting contentedly on the floor, Sara was surrounded by the many boxes and wrappings that had contained her gifts, delighting as much in the chaos she had created as she had in her presents. Martha, proudly wearing her new delicately carved cameo, watched with tear-filled eyes as Tom stroked his handsome new leather waistcoat, his chest puffed with pride. Michael examined with obvious appreciation the masterfully engraved watch fob she and Simon had selected. Glancing quickly to Simon, she saw he, too, was pleased and a warm happiness flooded over her. She had worked hard, with great determination in an effort to make this a special Christmas. With a silent, steadfast resolution she had decided she would not allow the uncertain times or her personal worries for Steve to dampen the holiday festivities. Her inner apprehension at the impermanence of her own situation further strengthened her zeal to enjoy and show appreciation for the richness and ease of the life she was presently living . . . for as long as it endured.

Simon, despite his capricious temperament and moodiness, was thoughtful and generous and tender . . . oh, so tender. A small chill ran up her spine as Melanie recalled their personal Christmas Eve celebration the night before. Having chosen to give Melanie her present in the privacy of their room, Simon had first presented her with a small box, which opened to reveal a huge topaz ring, the soft, mellow gold color of the perfect stone winking warmly in the dim light of the solitary lamp.

"Simon, it's beautiful!"

"The topaz is your stone, darling," he had whispered softly, taking it from her hand to slip it on her finger. "The color of your eyes, but not quite matching their brilliance, I'm afraid." Slowly lowering his head, he kissed each of her eyelids as they fluttered momentarily closed, and when they once again opened, he was looking wordlessly into her face, an odd sadness momentarily visible within his glance.

Noting her puzzled expression, he smiled softly, and reached behind him to take a long, narrow box from the dresser. "And this, also, my darling, for a very happy Christmas."

Lifting the lid of the second box, Melanie gasped. Taking out the magnificent bracelet within, Simon fastened it around her wrist. Set in a wide golden band were topaz stones of various sizes, combining to circle her wrist with a burning, golden glow.

Overwhelmed by the magnificence of his gifts, Melanie's words tumbled ineffectually from her lips. "Simon . . . what can I say? How can I tell you how much—you shouldn't, you are too generous. My gift is so insignificant in comparison to these." In an almost embarrassed manner she looked at the hand-tooled leather and brass cigar box she had discovered in a shop in New York and saved specifically for the holiday. She had filled it just recently with extremely expensive, hand-rolled cigars that had been recommended highly at the tobacconist shop and had until this moment been very proud of her gift.

Her small deprecating glance directed at the box did not go unnoticed, and Simon lifted her chin so that her eyes might look into his and said determinedly, "Melanie, dear, I am the one whose gifts are inadequate if we were to balance out that which we have given each other. I am not referring to the very lovely cigar box which I will treasure among my most precious possessions, but the many other gifts you have so magnanimously given me without your realization." At her puzzled expression, he continued softly, his clear, almost transparent eyes covering her face hungrily before he continued in a whisper. "Someday I will list for you all your many gifts to me, but not now, darling, not now." His lips covered hers for a long, deep kiss that started her blood rushing through her veins in throbbing anticipation. "I want to make love to you now, Melanie, this very minute. With your family and all your dearest friends sleeping under your own roof, I want to lie here in our bed, our flesh touching and joining, and know that you belong to me alone, just me, Melanie."

"Simon . . ." Her hesitation mirrored on her face, and Simon lifted his finger to her lips to silence her response with a quick gesture.

"Say nothing, darling," he whispered, his voice throbbing with passion, "just love me now."

Lifting her eyes, the memory of their exquisitely tender, passionate exchange of the night before still vivid in her mind, Melanie met Simon's glance, and for a moment their minds merged in silent communication. The touch of his burning glance was almost physical in intensity, and Melanie flushed hotly. Moving to her side, Simon took her hand and raised her open palm to his lips. Kissing the warm softness lingeringly, he raised his eyes slowly, his glance moving from her arm across the white swells of her breasts, the slender column of her neck, lingering warmly for the briefest second on the full, slightly trembling lips, to look into the glowing, molten gold of her eyes.

"My darling," he said softly, "you have made this a Christmas I shall never forget. My deepest thanks, my very dearest love."

The filthy, lice-ridden scarecrows stumbled up the steps of the ship, finally reaching the deck, to shield their eyes against the bright light of the sun as their eyes reacted painfully to the first true light they had seen in forty days. Fed primarily on salt pork and beef, all but the minimal quantity of water had been withheld from them for the duration of their voyage in a criminally cruel torture devised by their jailer, Brook Watson, to wreak his revenge. Dysentery and fever had run rampant through their number, fouling their prison compartment even further, with one small gill of rum dispensed to each prisoner per day as a cure-all for the multitude of ills besetting them.

"Barton, quickly, move them to the far side of the ship! I cannot bear the stench of them!" Holding a handkerchief over his nose, Brook Watson directed the prisoners' removal to the far side of the deck. "They smell like the foul creatures they are—no better than animals. They will be a pretty sight for Falmouth to view when we march them through town tomorrow. Hah!" he laughed jeeringly, "The infamous Ethan Allen and his band—cut down to size at last!"

A chorus of laughter accompanied his last remark. Exchanging short glances, Ethan and Steve breathed deeply of the fresh air, savoring its sweetness. In their deteriorated conditions, it was not a time for response or action. It was merely a time for thanksgiving that they had managed to arrive in England with none of their number having succumbed to the extreme harshness of their treatment. Drawing deep, full breaths into their deprived lungs, they remained silent and bided their time.

". . . And I will not stand silently by another day while you enjoy the fruits of her sweet and loving nature and deal with her in a dishonest and underhanded manner!"

"Michael, what has come over you? You are being ridiculous! Why do you accuse me so falsely of dealing unfairly with Melanie?" Having suddenly been set upon by Michael in his own library just a day prior to his scheduled departure for New York, Simon was stunned by the vehemence of his friend's verbal attack. Obviously upset, the young man had stormed into the room, his pleasant face drawn into deep, angry lines.

"Falsely, Simon? I have just been speaking with Melanie. You still have not told her of your divorce. Why do you hide it from her?"

"The reason I have not told Melanie of the divorce proceedings is my own concern, Michael, and I will thank you to respect your word and not mention it in her presence." Moving to the desk, Simon poured two glasses of port from the decanter resting there, and offering one brimming glass to Michael, said softly, "Take this, Michael, you need something to calm you down."

"I don't want it, Simon. What I want I don't think you'll be willing to part with too easily."

With a narrowing of his light, clear eyes, Simon stiffened, lowering the glass to the tray as hostility tinged his voice for the first time. "If you refer by that remark to Melanie, you are correct, Michael. I will not give her up to you or anyone else without exerting every effort within my power to keep her."

"If you value her so much, if you truly realize her worth, then why will you not tell her that you will soon be free?"

"I don't wish to discuss it, and I have your word—"

"I must know, Simon." Michael interrupted persistently, his dark, sober eyes earnest. "I have hesitated before speaking and considered the circumstances carefully before coming here, but I must know your intentions toward Melanie. If you do not intend a relationship of a permanent nature, I must ask you to put aside personal considerations and consider Melanie's future. She is a beautiful, intelligent woman with the responsibility of a young child's future. If you are not prepared to offer Melanie marriage, Simon, I am. This week has only confirmed in my mind a conclusion I had previously reached during the summer in New York. Melanie looks on me now merely as a friend, but she is a loyal, honest woman who has not allowed herself to consider her protector's friend in any other way. You have her complete fidelity, Simon, and in my opinion have proved unworthy of her trust."

"Michael, I advise you to be cautious of your words. The agreement Melanie and I contracted between us made no mention of my marital status. There has been no betrayal of a trust." The heat of anger was rising in Simon's face; but deliberately disregarding the deepening flush, Michael continued.

"I love Melanie, Simon. That is no particular surprise to you, I am sure. Were you intending to do right by her, I would stand aside and never mention my own feelings."

"Michael, you are mistaken in your assumption."

"If I am mistaken, then you must explain my error, Simon, because I am determined not to leave this room until this is settled between us."

"I could order you out of the house, my friend—"

"You could order me out, Simon, but it would settle nothing. We must talk this thing out now."

For long, silent moments Simon stared into Michael's solemn face. Finally speaking, he said in a low voice, "You truly are my friend, Michael, and for that reason alone I will honor your request and tell you where your mistake in reasoning lies. You assume the reluctance for a permanent relationship to be on my part, when in reality the reluctance lies with Melanie."

His face registering shocked disbelief, Michael exclaimed, "I can't believe that, Simon. I saw Melanie's embarrassment when she faced Charlotte. I have seen her loyalty and obvious devotion to you. What possible reason could she have for resisting legalization of a state that already exists between you two in every other possible way?"

"She loves someone else, Michael."

"No! I don't believe it! You're making that up, Simon!"

"I wish I were."

"But who?"

"I have no desire to discuss the fellow, Michael, but believe me, he does exist. It is not something I have found easy to accept."

"But where is this fellow? Why is Melanie with you instead of him?"

"They quarreled and became separated. There are bitter words and feelings between them, but Melanie still loves him. She met him before she and I came together and her love for him is something over which neither of us has any control."

"Are you certain, Simon? I mean, perhaps you are wrong. I still cannot believe . . ."

"Melanie has no hesitation in acknowledging that ours is purely a business relationship based on her dire circumstances and my desire. That is not to say there is no feeling between us, Michael, and I do not think it necessary to go into any further intimate details. Suffice it to say that she bears a true affection for me, I am sure, understandably of a more personal nature than she holds for you, but there is no mention of love in the relationship."

"On either side, Simon?" Michael's keen, discerning glance took in the almost imperceptible slip of Simon's guarded expression and eliminated the necessity for a reply.

Lowering his eyes, Michael murmured softly, his

grave disappointment mirrored on his unhappy face. "I see. There is no chance for me then, is there, Simon?"

Glancing up finally, Michael continued with a brave attempt at cheerfulness, "Well, I suppose I shall have to be patient and bide my time until Sara grows up. Damn! What will I do with myself for the next sixteen years?"

Shaking his head, the unhappy young man turned and left the room as unexpectedly as he had entered, leaving Simon frowning slightly at the closed door.

Smiling lightly to himself, Steve reclined against his straw bedding, his eyes wandering absent-mindedly around the room. One thing was certain at least. Their circumstances since their confinement in Pendennis Castle had seen a change for the better. Still lodged in a common apartment, they were provided with a type of Dutch bunks and were sharing the same food as the British soldiers, three very respectable meals a day with a bottle of wine provided at noon. Proper bathing and laundry facilities had enabled them to wash their clothes and rid themselves of the lice that had caused them no end of discomfort, and after two weeks of decent treatment, although they were all still in irons, he was actually beginning to feel human again.

"And Ethan has certainly been putting on a good show for them," he snickered to himself, recalling that afternoon. To his amazement and amusement, Ethan found himself to be somewhat of a curiosity in Great Britain, and stunned with the number of people willing to travel many miles to meet and talk to him, he had decided to become as accommodating as possible. The number on certain days was so great that the guards had taken to bringing the prisoners up to the spacious green inside the castle, where the visitors could see and talk to them. Standing as he usually did, boldly in front of his men, his impressive frame clothed in the Canadian dress he had been wearing when captured; a short fawn jacket, with undervest and britches of sagathy, worsted stockings and a red stocking cap; Ethan was a colorful sight indeed, and he made the most of his outlandish appearance.

A few minutes after arriving on the green, a serious gentleman stepped forward from the crowd, addressing Ethan directly. "We have come a long distance for the sole purpose of speaking with you, Mr. Allen, and would like to make free with you in conversation."

Smiling broadly, Ethan responded, "I choose freedom in every sense of the word, my friends!"

A second man, speaking up suddenly from behind inquired, "What was your occupation in America?"

"In my younger days I studied divinity," Ethan responded truthfully, adding with a twinkle in his eye and a broadening grin, "but I was a conjuror by profession."

"Well, it seems that you conjured wrong at the time you were captured, Mr. Allen," the first man commented dryly.

"Ah, yes," Ethan sighed good-naturedly, "I mistook a figure at that time, but I did conjure you all out of Ticonderoga, didn't I?"

His response surprisingly brought a chorus of

laughter from the group assembled, and truly astounded that the joke had been received so well, Ethan laughed the loudest of all.

Earlier in the week when a large group of the curious had gathered, Ethan saw the opportunity for a lengthy discourse on the impractability of Great Britain ever conquering the American colonies. His throat having become slightly parched from his wild harangue, he directed his glance over the crowd, spying a gentleman whose servant had prepared a large bowl of punch.

"I find I would greatly benefit from a bit of that punch your servant has served up for you, sir. Are you generous enough to quench the thirst of a visitor to your country?"

Without answer, the surprised gentleman signaled his servant to bring the bowl forward, and serve up a cup.

Turning back to the silent Britisher, Ethan looked him in the eye. "I will not consider the offer genuinely made unless it comes from a gentleman's hand, sir."

Surprisingly, the man hesitated only a moment before walking forward to give him a cup, to which Ethan said companionably, "Will you join me in a drink?"

Speaking for the first time, the gentleman responded in a slightly annoyed tone, "I do not drink with state criminals, Mr. Allen."

Hesitating only a brief second, Ethan said in his most resonant tone, "Then I suppose I shall have to drink by myself!" Ignoring the cup and taking instead the huge bowl into his hands, Ethan raised it to his mouth, and holding it there, continued drinking until it was drained dry. At the open-mouthed gasps and laughter from the amazed observers, and, Steve suspected as a result of his lengthy drink as well, Ethan grinned widely, adding yet another brilliant facet to his already legendary character.

But those interviews, conducted so lightly, served a useful purpose as well, as Steve was well aware. Completely cut off from all outside news, the prisoners had no knowledge of the action being taken on their case in Parliament and relied solely on the remarks of the visitors to tell them how events were progressing. Having heard from one visitor that Brook Watson had not received the reward he had expected when arriving in London, but was treated rather coolly, the prisoners' hopes soared, only to be brought thudding back to earth with the later comment whispered in confidence into Ethan's ear that the odds in London were two to one that they would be hanged.

Realizing the uncertainty of their fates, Ethan had not been able to rest without taking some positive action in their behalf. Not having received replies to letters directed to two different prominent Englishmen pleading their case, Ethan devised an ingenius plan.

Granted permission to send a communication to the Continental Congress, Ethan wrote a lengthy missive, describing only briefly his ill-treatment on the voyage and instead stressing his and his men's status as declared criminals in Great Britain. Brilliantly pleading the patience of Congress, he asked that they hold off sentencing their British prisoners and wait to see the conclusions reached by British Parliament on his and his men's case before passing the same judgment on their prisoners.

The following day, accusing him of impudence, the commander of the castle faced him haughtily. "Do you think we are fools in England to allow you to send such an inflammatory letter to your Congress? For your information, I have forwarded your letter to London, and it is now on its way directly to Lord North!"

Turning from the commander with a dark frown, Ethan left the room, glowing inwardly with the satisfaction of knowing his letter, presenting precisely the concept he wished to have considered by Parliament, was on its way to the exact person for whom it was intended, and he now had merely to sit back and await the results.

The days dragged slowly on, and Steve began to realize that the waiting was indeed going to be the hardest part of their confinement. His health having almost returned to normal, he was capable once again of clear thought, which was proving to be a more competent enemy to his peace of mind than the English. For when he thought of home, he thought of only one person. Warm, golden eyes that seared his heart even in memory; smooth white, unbelievably fragrant skin, as soft to the touch as velvet; slender, clinging arms that clutched him close in the mutual joy of intimate moments; the quick, brilliant smile, so full of the appreciation of life; and that small, beautiful body that welcomed him, drew him in and brought him incomparable ecstasy, leaving no room in his heart for another.

Then, with a clarity dangerous to his peace of mind he remembered another time and the fear in Melanie's eyes as she searched his face. The quick, instinctive withdrawal from his touch; the humiliation on her face as she described the testimony given by Bernard Wipley in court; the stiff coldness in her body when he kissed her. Most of all he remembered her small, flat voice and emotionless expression after he had taken her. "Are you finished now, Steve?"

Filled again with the pain of her rejection he realized that it had been his own jealousy and fear that had forced the only true happiness he had ever experienced to an abrupt and brutal end and the only woman he ever loved into another man's arms.

"Fool, fool, I was a fool, Melanie," he whispered to the pale, golden image in his mind's eye that had become his constant companion. Closing his eyes briefly against the pain, he recalled Simon Young's protective, possessive gesture that last day in Philadelphia, and he groaned inwardly at the stupidity of his own vicious attack on her in Salisbury.

"I was jealous and angry, Melanie. I wanted you so badly, and you were so cold. I acted like an animal, darling, but I didn't mean any of the terrible things I said to you." The haunting image did not respond. "God knows, I want you back," he continued earnestly. "I want you back more than anything in the world. And I *will* have you back. With the Almighty as my witness, if I regain my freedom I will have you back, darling . . . and I swear to you, I will never hurt you or leave you again."

*   *   *

The sudden loud clang of the prison door startled the prisoners out of their slumber. His eyes darting to the small window high upon the wall, Steve saw the first light of dawn had not yet creased the sky.

"All right, everyone up!" The sergeant's loud shout echoed in the early morning stillness. Ignoring their startled state, he added in a grim tone, "You are leaving Pendennis immediately. You will no longer be our guests."

"But where are we going? What has been decided?" Dozens of mumbled questions filled the air as the groggy men stumbled from their bedding and moved forward awkwardly. When no answer was given, and only sober stares met their questions, Ethan exchanged a brief, apprehensive glance with Steve before addressing the guard. "I demand that you tell us where we are being transported. It is our right as honorable—"

"You have no rights, damn you!" the sergeant shouted maliciously. "You are rebels, criminals, and you will do as you are ordered now, or you will not live to reach your destination! Now, move on, damn you all, move on!"

Chapter 10

Gasping, struggling for breath, Steve dragged himself out of the water to run in a headlong dash for the cover of trees edging the shore. Once in the protection of the heavy foliage, he dropped wearily to the ground, shivering slightly in the cool, May breeze and groaning as the screaming muscles of his arms and legs throbbed, knotting painfully from the strain of his long and rapid swim. Turning watchfully toward the sea, still struggling to regain his breath, he stared at the outline of the *Solebay* floating quietly several miles out in Cape Fear. Squinting, he studied the deck and water surrounding the vessel, and satisfied at last that there appeared to be no unusual activity on deck or boats being lowered, he dropped to his back and heaved a silent sigh of relief. His escape from their prison ship was yet unnoticed, which meant he probably had another hour before his presence would be missed. By then he should have enough of a head start to make his recapture impossible.

The preoccupation of the guards with Ethan once they had reached American waters had been obvious, and carefully awaiting an opportunity, he had finally been able to slip over the side of the ship unnoticed. For the first time in six long months he was free! Free! A sudden sense of exhilaration overwhelmed his senses, and Steve had a wild desire to laugh and shout. He had made it! He was free! God, it felt good—too good to believe. Darting a quick look back to the vessel, he strained his eyes to confirm the fact that the water was still clear of small craft, and then dragged himself to his feet wearily. He wasn't in the clear yet, and wouldn't be until he was finally behind his own lines. He had been able to hear the sounds of battle from the ship and had estimated that the American forces shouldn't be too far away.

With one last glance at the *Solebay* still peacefully riding the waves in North Carolina's harbor, he turned his back with renewed determination and started moving again. Just a little way further and he would be among friends, and then he would head homeward, homeward to Philadelphia, or wherever it was that Melanie was now residing, because he had finally determined that the only thing worthwhile returning to in his life was Melanie.

Not having heard her enter the library, Simon continued to stare moodily out the window, his sharp profile etched brilliantly against the startling colors of sunset in the darkening room. He was dressed casually in his shirtsleeves, his shirt front partially undone, exposing a lightly furred chest, his well cut britches fitting smoothly against the athletic flatness of his waist and hips. His dark hair, sprinkled with a bit more gray than had been apparent at their first encounter almost two years before, was tousled as if he had run his hand through its thickness in an impatient gesture.

"He is short tempered again today," Melanie thought worriedly. It was a situation that seemed to be occurring more and more often of late. Something was bearing very heavily on his mind, of that she was certain, and she feared it had little to do with the politics of the country. A subtle change in Simon had become apparent shortly before Michael's departure at the turn of the year, and relations had been so strained between them on the day of Michael's departure that Melanie was almost happy to see Michael leave. Suspecting that they had had words, she had never inquired into the cause, but had expected it was a matter that time and distance would eventually fade.

But a month ago she came to realize all too clearly that she had been entirely wrong. Having written a brief, social note to the dear fellow who had managed to win a very definite place in her affections with his endearing, boyish charm, Melanie had just prepared the letter for the post when Simon suddenly appeared behind her.

"What is that you are doing, Melanie?" Simon's demanding tone immediately raised the hackles on her back, and Melanie's reply was delivered with especially haughty sarcasm.

"You did say at one time that what I did in my own time was my own affair, Simon, as long as it didn't interfere with your plans; but since you ask so *sweetly*, I will answer your question. I have written a letter to Michael to inquire as to his well being. We have not heard from him in the three months since he left and I have become quite concerned."

His brow slightly raised, Simon stated with an air of finality, "I do not feel there is a need for concern, Melanie, and I do not feel it is necessary for you to correspond with Michael."

An immediate flash of anger heated her face at his officious tone, and Melanie retaliated with increased sarcasm, "I find it no end of relief that *you* are not worried, Simon, but unfortunately, I *am* concerned, and I *do* feel it necessary to correspond with Michael!"

A small muscle twitched warningly in Simon's cheek as his mouth tightened into an uncompromising line. "You will not post that letter, Melanie."

"I shall do as I damned well please, Simon!" Melanie exclaimed vehemently, too incensed for further politeness.

His eyes narrowing in what had progressed to suppressed fury, Simon snatched the letter from her

488

hand in a swift movement and proceeded to tear it into little pieces as Melanie stared open-mouthed, shocked into speechlessness by his unexpected action and his low, angry tone as he said emphatically, "Now the matter is settled once and for all!"

"How dare you do that? How dare you tear that—"

"I told you, Melanie, and I will say it again. You will not communicate with Michael, do you understand me? I forbid it!"

The coolly ominous sound of Simon's voice completely escaped Melanie in her advanced state of agitation and she exclaimed hotly, "You forbid it! You forbid it!" Her eyes widened in astonished fury, she continued slowly, "Well, just so we will understand each other completely, Simon, I will make *myself* clear. I will write to Michael if I so choose, and if you rip up the next letter, I will write again and again and again, until you tire of—"

"Melanie!" Suddenly grabbing her by the shoulders, Simon shook her roughly, his hands biting into the soft flesh of her upper arms as he repeated in a furious voice, "You will obey me, Melanie Morganfield, and do as I tell you! You will not write to Michael Searle! You will not write to him, do you hear?" Shaking her again violently, his voice a near shout, he stated forcefully, "I will not stand for it!"

Suddenly, as if shocked by his own loss of control, Simon dropped his hands from her arms without waiting for her reply, his face whitening as he saw the tears that had sprung unbidden into her eyes.

When he spoke again he was in full control of his temper and said in a softer tone, although his glance was still unwavering, "You will not write to

Michael, Melanie, and that is my final word."

Unable to comprehend his behavior, Melanie burst out bewilderedly, "But why, Simon? Why? I don't understand. Michael is your friend, our friend . . ."

"And that is precisely the reason, Melanie, because he is my—our friend."

That day had passed without further explanation, and Melanie had acceded to Simon's wishes, but his tenseness and anxiety only appeared to increase. Experiencing a deep pang of regret at her inability to help him, Melanie closed the library door quietly behind her and moved softly in his direction.

The sound of Melanie's unexpected step snapped Simon around to reveal a brooding, unhappy expression that changed in the few, brief, unguarded seconds his eyes touched on her to one of such complete vulnerability and pain that she was momentarily stunned. Finally walking toward him, her sympathy apparent, she slid her arms around his neck and pressed herself tightly against his chest, her voice pleading softly, "Oh, Simon, please tell me what's wrong. Why won't you let me help you?"

His arms gradually moved to seal her in the circle of his embrace as he murmured softly in return, "My dear Melanie, we are both powerless against the problem confronting me. Both of us." And with a small groan, he pulled her closer still.

Managing to extricate herself from his crushing embrace, Melanie searched his tortured expression for a few, endless moments. Sliding her hand inside his shirt front to move it slowly over his smoothly muscled chest in a caressing motion, she whispered,

"Let me help you, Simon. I can at least console you. Let me at least give you consolation, Simon."

His heart began to pound heavily under her hand while his eyes moved warmly over her beautiful, upturned face, and he whispered hoarsely, "You are more than my consolation, darling."

Turning quickly, he moved to the door and, snapping the lock, walked back to her in three quick strides. Scooping her into his arms, he carried her to the heavy rug before the fireplace and lay her down gently. Within moments they were lying together, their clothes a small heap beside them as Simon drew her against him. Moaning slightly as their flesh touched, Simon pulled her closer still, savoring the ecstatic sweetness of their intimate embrace.

"Melanie . . . Melanie, my darling," he whispered softly against her hair, almost overcome with the myriad of emotions overwhelming him, "Oh, God, Melanie, if I could only express the complete and utter joy of you."

Hours later in the darkness of the night they both lay abed unsleeping. Turning toward her, Simon moved to his side to gaze thoughtfully down into her face as the bright moonlight streaming through the window illuminated her delicate features. Running his fingertips lightly down the side of her cheek, he continued the gentle caress across her full, inviting lips, stopping to kiss them lingeringly before beginning to speak.

"Darling, I have something I must tell you . . ." He began hesitantly, his reluctance apparent in his tone of voice. "We received word a few days ago, about the prisoners."

With a spontaneous gasp, Melanie stiffened, her heart suddenly racing. There was no question in her mind to which prisoners he referred, and unable to bear her rioting apprehension, she whispered, "What happened, Simon? Please tell me quickly."

"The prisoners were in the process of being returned to North Carolina for transferral to the British authorities in New York. One man managed to slip overboard and escape enroute. It was Stephen Hull." At her frightened expression, he hastened to add, "He is well, and has been detained for the past week for questioning, but he is due to arrive in Philadelphia tomorrow morning to testify before Congress as to his imprisonment."

"Tomorrow? He will be here in Philadelphia tomorrow? But why didn't you tell me sooner, Simon? Why did you wait until the last minute?"

Still caressing her cheek lightly, he hesitated while his eyes moved over her face as if memorizing each lovely detail. "I saw no need to give you cause for any more sleepless nights than the one you will have tonight, Melanie. And . . ." he paused briefly before adding in a husky voice, "if I'm to be completely honest, I didn't want to share you with him, even in your thoughts, for any longer than necessary."

"Simon, I . . ." Melanie began haltingly.

"Shhh, don't say anything, darling," Simon whispered against her lips. "Just try to get some sleep now. I'll take you with me in the morning to hear the testimony in person. You'll see him then. Just try to sleep now, darling."

* * *

Her knees quaking violently, Melanie ascended the State House steps on Simon's arm. It was strange, but she couldn't seem to think straight this morning. Perhaps it was because she had gotten so little sleep as Simon had predicted. She hardly remembered getting dressed. Her mind racing ahead to the time they would enter the assembly room and she would see Steve at last, she had paid so little attention to what she was doing that she was hardly certain she looked at all well. Glancing down quickly at her dress, she fingered the material nervously. The pale gold silk had seemed appropriate enough at the time, but looking down at it as they approached the assembly room, its soft scooped neckline seemed suddenly too revealing, its perfect fit perhaps a bit too tight against her softly curving body, and her hair—that soft yellow rose Molly had insisted on pinning in her hair—it was hopelessly out of place. Her anxieties suddenly assuming immense proportions, she stopped. They had reached the inner hallway when she decided she just could not go any further, and raised her anxious eyes to Simon.

Efficiently reading her thoughts in his usual manner and smiling encouragingly, he said simply, "You look absolutely lovely, Melanie. You have lost none of your powers. I am absolutely bewitched, I always have been."

Flashing him a grateful smile, she clutched his arm even tighter as they progressed forward, nodding politely to their many acquaintances as they passed. The State House was extremely crowded.

"Do you think we'll be able to get a seat, Simon? It appears everyone in Philadelphia is here today!"

"I doubt that very highly, darling," he responded softly. "But even if it is so, there are two seats reserved for us. You needn't worry."

Within minutes they were safely installed in the second row, Melanie's fingers knotting and unknotting nervously as she awaited Steve's arrival. A debate appeared to be in progress between a few of the congressmen, but Melanie could not seem to focus her attention on what they were saying as her mind whirled in hopeless confusion. Gone from her mind was the terrifying experience of her last encounter with Steve. In its place loomed her anxiety to see him alive and well. How would he look? Had he suffered during his imprisonment? Had he changed much?

Suddenly the side door opened, and a low buzz filled the room as a tall, dark-haired man walked slowly forward, waiting to be summoned to the chair for his statement. Melanie clutched Simon's arm tightly, her nails digging into the soft gray fabric of his coat. She could not seem to tear her gaze from Steve's sober, strained face. He looked the same, still breathtakingly handsome, although a bit pale and considerably thinner than before. His black hair looked to have been freshly cut and gleamed darkly; his black eyes were still bright and sharp, although perhaps a bit more serious than before. The breadth of his shoulder and chest and his proud, erect stance; even in his simple homespun clothing and fawn jacket he was a beautiful man, the same . . . the same Steve.

Melanie's heart was beating so rapidly she could hardly breathe as her throat tightened with emotion. Steve! Back at last!

Her eyes glued to Steve's face for the duration of his

testimony, her heart bled at his apt description of the harsh treatment Allen and his men had received at the hands of the British. If only she could make it up to him—all his suffering—if he cared anything at all for her, anything at all, she would make it up to him.

So engrossed was Melanie in Steve's appearance that she could not spare a thought for the distinguished gentleman at her side whose eyes never left her. Watching every emotion that flashed across her expressive face, he read her thoughts well, and his heart dropped into hopelessness. There was no doubt she loved Stephen Hull still, and if the fellow had any wits at all, he would take the first opportunity to spirit her away. It was, after all, what Melanie truly wanted. Stephen Hull could bring her complete happiness—but God, what of himself? How could he return to the empty, shallow existence he had led before Melanie had brought him to life? Melanie, darling . . . Without realizing, Simon reached to cover the hand clutching his sleeve so tightly, and she flashed him a quick, careless smile before returning her attention to Steve, her eyes not moving from his face again for the remainder of his testimony.

His statement concluded, Steve rose from the chair. For the duration of his statement, his gaze had never faltered, never left the faces of the congressmen as they reacted violently to the description of the often times inhuman conduct of his captors, but at the conclusion, as the spectators began to file out of the room, Steve's eyes searched the crowd hopefully. Finally meeting and clinging to the familiar amber gaze that burned steadily in his direction, he held her eyes unwaveringly until the majority of the spectators had filed out of the room. Moving slowly in her direction as she stood there alone, his pace quickened gradually until he was almost running, and finally at her side, he hesitated only a brief second before pulling her hungrily into his arms in a crushing embrace.

"Oh, Melanie, darling, can you ever forgive me?" he whispered against her hair. "My darling . . . darling," he murmured as his mouth sought and captured hers in a deep, searching kiss. Without giving her a chance to respond, he continued softly as he stared down into her flawless beauty, "We'll start over again, Melanie, the past will be forgotten, canceled as if it never happened. I've come to realize a great many things in the past six months, most of them my stupidity and—"

But Melanie did not appear to be listening. She was pulling herself out of his embrace, struggling to be free of his tenuous grip. Finally speaking, she stammered uncertainly, "But the past did happen, Steve. It exists and . . . it can't just be forgotten."

"Melanie, what's the matter? You're still angry with me, is that it?" Steve's handsome face was drawn into anxious lines as she stared soberly into the dark eyes that had mesmerized her so many times into unqualified forgiveness. But strangely, Melanie herself wasn't certain as to what was truly wrong. Her smooth brow knit into a troubled frown as she searched Steve's concerned expression for her own answer. But the fact remained. Steve's arms were uncomfortably foreign to her now. Those black, wicked eyes that had held such a power over her seemed merely a shadow of her past, a part of her that had diminished as she had grown mature. Somehow, astonishingly, looking closely into the troubled face that she had believed she loved, she felt merely a lingering affection and a deep, overwhelming relief at his safety.

Suddenly feeling a deep sense of release, she recognized the feeling for Steve that she had been harboring inside her for what it was—anxiety for the man who had held a strong place in her past. But it was all in the past now. Her future lay in another direction, in another man's arms.

Hardly believing her own actions, Melanie gently removed Steve's hands from her arms and stepped back slightly to lift the steady, sober, golden glow of her eyes to his. "No, I'm not angry, Steve. I'm happy you're well and free again, but," she continued hesitantly, not wishing to cause him any additional grief, "but the past is past, Steve, a long ago time that's just a memory. It truly is good to see you again, to know you are safe and well." Retreating slowly as she spoke, she continued just before turning away, "If you see Josh, tell him I still think of him, too. He was a true friend. I will never forget either of you, Steve. Goodbye. Good luck."

As she turned, all thoughts of Steve were immediately dismissed from her mind. Searching the room for a certain face she thought anxiously, "Where is Simon? Where did he go? Darn that man."

Running quickly to the door, she glanced down the hallway in time to see his tall, distinguished figure moving slowly toward the exit of the building. Her heart suddenly thudding heavily in her chest, she began running after him, calling hesitantly, "Simon! Wait! Where are you going?"

Snapping around at the sound of her voice, Simon

stared disbelievingly at her as she drew nearer, seeming transfixed by the sight of her beautiful face as tears brimmed in her glowing eyes. Finally reaching his side, she caught his arm breathlessly.

"Did you really expect to be rid of me so easily, Simon? Whatever made you think of me as an inconstant woman? We have a business arrangement, do we not?"

Still he did not answer, but continued to stare down into her face, his ice blue, clearly penetrating eyes slowly beginning to glow with a brilliant warmth of their own while he searched her face avidly for verification of her words. Suddenly unwilling to wait any longer for his response, Melanie demanded, stamping her foot in anger as the tears threatened to overflow the huge, topaz gold of her eyes, "Simon Young! Answer me this minute! Do we or do we not have a business arrangement between us?"

His incredulous expression finally breaking into a small smile that gradually widened into a magnificent grin, Simon scooped her into his arms and crushed her tight against him for a few seconds of silent, blissful thanksgiving. Finally releasing her, he said softly into her shining face, "Well, I suppose, my darling, if you're still uncertain about our arrangement after all this time, we shall have to see what we can do about formalizing it so we may put an end to any further confusion on your part once and for all. Shall we go home now and discuss it, my beautiful little witch?"

"Oh, yes, Simon," Melanie murmured, looking deeply into his eyes, her voice a soft, loving caress, "Do let's go home."

1781

Mrs. Melanie Morganfield Young lay abed in the master bedroom of her Walnut Street residence in Philadelphia, although it was already mid-morning. Having arisen two hours earlier, she had slipped into her sea-green silk wrapper and started for the door, only to have the general feeling of malaise with which she had awakened cause her to turn around and return to her bed without even bothering to remove her wrapper. Now, hours later, finally having discouraged all solicitous visits by the members of her staff and "family," she lay completely still. Glorious auburn hair streaming across the pillow, her eyes were closed. The dark lashes lying against pale cheeks were unmoving, while faint bluish smudges beneath her closed eyes silently attested to her fitful night's sleep. Contrary to outward appearance, however, she was not sleeping. In the past hour she had silently run the events of the past few years across her mind in a soundless parade, and suddenly restless, she opened her eyes testily. Catching a quick glimpse of her reflection in the mirror as she did, a small, exhausted chortle of amusement escaped her lips. Running her palm slowly up the ridge of her greatly distended abdomen, she finally rested her palm on the highest point of the rise, smiling gently at the rapid movement of the child within as she stared at her awkward outline in the mirror.

"Oh, Mrs. Young," she whispered to her artless reflection, "I'm afraid your appeal is practically nil at this point in your life. And you, my little darling," she whispered, her voice softening as she patted the baby who squirmed so endlessly within, "had better make your appearance soon before you bruise my innards beyond repair."

In the final days of her pregnancy, Melanie was anxious for the birth of her child, and anxious for the release of the burden she carried so laboriously before her.

"Well," she mused, in an attempt to take her mind away from the uncomfortable present, "at least the war is finally over." Circumstances were finally beginning to return to normal in Philadelphia, or were at least moving in that general direction. All trade restrictions were removed, and new markets would soon be opening for Simon's ships. There was even talk of trade with the Orient. If that was so, Simon would undoubtedly be sailing with the first of the ships. Hmmmmmm, he had promised her a sea voyage of her own choosing when she was completely recovered from her lying in.

Strange how long it had taken to conceive Simon's child. She had begun to worry that Simon's and her heart's desire would never be realized when the accomplishment of the fact had eliminated her fears. Succumbing to her strange weariness, Melanie closed her eyes again, remembering with a glowing warmth the night of their marriage.

It had been a small affair, attended by her adopted family, a few of Simon's close friends, and the entire staff at Walnut Street. Dressed in a gown of glowing oyster silk and lace, Melanie had joined Simon at an altar fashioned in the parlor of the Walnut Street home. Simon's clear blue eyes had not left her person from the moment of her arrival in the room on the arm of a beaming and surprisingly dapper Tom. Simon's voice had been clear and sure in repeating the vows, but the expression on his handsome face had been so intimate as to void the room of spectators in her mind's eye. His eyes had remained on her lips as she had repeated her vows, his glance so loving and filled with commitment when he lifted his eyes to hers at her conclusion, that she had been brought to the edge of tears.

She had not been allowed to indulge her sentimentality for long, however, for Simon's deep, searing kiss was soon interrupted by an impatient voice in their ears.

"All right, Simon! Give over now, will you?" Turning they saw the outright impatience evidenced on Michael Searle's face as he continued in an annoyed tone, "You will have the rest of your life for that kind of thing, whereas I have only today in which to take advantage of the situation. I have been waiting far too long already to get my arms around Melanie, and I do not intend to wait any longer!" Elbowing Simon aside, Michael took up a stance in front of Melanie, his bright, boyish smile not quite overshadowing the sadness in his brown eyes. "My darling, Melanie," he said softly, "since you have persisted in this monsterous bit of foolishness by actually marrying this pompous oaf," shooting a short look sidewards at Simon's astonished face, he continued, "then I suppose I shall have to extend you my good wishes for your happiness, which I do most sincerely. But remember, my dearest Melanie, should you feel the need at any time for a buffer between yourself and his arrogant demands, I will be available for your call."

"I think that will be enough for now, Michael." Simon's haughty tone was spiced with amusement as he shot his friend a quick, deprecating glance.

"Oh no you don't, Simon!" Quickly slipping his arms around Melanie's waist, he pulled her close. "I have not yet kissed the bride!"

Starting to show a true edge of impatience, Simon said quickly, "Then be fast about it, man! You are not the only one who wishes to express congratulations!"

Contrary to Simon's demands, Michael took Melanie slowly into his arms, and brought his mouth down firmly upon hers in a deep, searching kiss that was almost his undoing. Feeling a firm hand on his shoulder, Michael pulled away reluctantly to face Simon's sober expression. Unable to disguise the note of true sympathy mixed with his irritation, Simon said softly, "All right, Michael, you have kissed my wife well enough."

With a small smile Michael quipped lightly, "You used to be such a generous man, Simon, but you are so very niggardly with Melanie's attentions."

"And you may rest assured I will remain that way, Michael." Simon's sober tone took the remainder of the light out of Michael's warm eyes. Suddenly snapping back in the manner so characteristic of his garrulous personality, Michael turned quickly to Melanie.

"Then I'm afraid I must take advantage of this opportunity to ask for the hand of Miss Sara Morganfield soon-to-be Young when the adoption papers are completed. I have missed out on the opportunity for one of the Morganfield women, and I will not miss out on the other!"

A surprised laugh broke from Melanie's throat, and Michael reprimanded quietly with an expression of mock severity, "I am quite prepared to wait fifteen years for her, Melanie, but not a day longer."

Addressing him with a serious air, Melanie returned with a small smile, "Then you may rest assured I will keep in mind you are the first to ask for Sara's hand. I do fancy having you for a son-in-law, Michael!"

"Son-in-law! Gad! I hadn't thought of that!'

Giving it a moment's consideration, Michael snapped back cheerfully, "Well, better an ignominious relation than no relation at all!"

Snorting disgustedly, Simon pushed Michael aside to allow the rest of the well wishers an opportunity to speak. At the conclusion of the brief but emotion-filled congratulations, Simon took Melanie's arm under his. Shooting a quick look at Michael, who was speaking animatedly to another guest, he ventured quietly, the warmth in his voice taking the edge from his sharp words, "Sometimes I wonder what I see in that young idiot!"

"Do not dismiss him lightly, Simon." Melanie whispered in return as they walked toward the banquet table in the dining room. "You see in that smiling young man the first suitor for Sara's hand and a possible son-in-law."

"Heaven forbid!" Simon's brief exclamation was delivered with a raising of his brows and a pleading glance heavenward that broke Melanie to laughter, and set the mood for the truly joyous reception that followed.

It had been a beautiful wedding and their lives had been eventful since that day. Forced to flee Philadelphia when it was taken by the British four years before, they had moved their entire household to New Jersey for the duration of the occupation. Simon's political connections would not allow him to remain in Philadelphia, for he surely would have been thrown into prison for his connection with the Continental Congress. But they had returned once again on the heels of the British retreat to reassume their residence, and in September had been on hand for the triumphant march of the Continental Army, followed by six thousand French soldiers up Front Street and down Vine to the Center Square enroute to join Washington in the ultimate triumph at Yorktown. Behind the long, lean line of homespun-clad Continentals, France's General Rochambeau and his troops marched in their dress whites, the different regiments distinguished by the facings of blue, rose, green and pink on their uniforms. The Soisonnais wore pink plumes in their caps, their appearance that of "effete aristocrats," as remarked by an impressed Governor Morris. Philadelphia was enthralled by the French, and as yet the fever had not died down.

Unable to convince Melanie to move their residence to his larger home, formerly his bachelor quarters, Simon finally concurred in making Walnut Street their permanent residence while in Philadelphia. "I think, my dear," he had responded to her heated resistance to moving, "you enjoy the upper hand in having me under *your* roof!"

To which Melanie responded lightly, "I suppose that could be true, Simon, but you must remember, we will still be sleeping in *your* bed."

"That is true, isn't it." A small smile lurking at the corners of his mouth, Simon had assumed a posture of consideration. "I had quite forgotten that! Well, in that case, compromise is the winner. We will stay at Walnut Street."

Truly at home in the surroundings, Melanie's gratitude for his concurrence was obvious in her glance, and in the fervor with which she fulfilled her wifely duties while the household slept that night.

Restless again, Melanie reached for the newspaper that lay on the table at bedside. As she picked it up, her eyes fell on the name of Ethan Allen, and intrigued, she read on. Always the prolific pamphleteer, Ethan Allen's experiences were being reprinted by almost every newspaper in the newly formed United States of America. His harsh treatment during captivity formed the basis for his railing words against the British government's handling of Continental prisoners, and reading of his experiences, Melanie was thankful Steve had escaped the prison ship when he had, for Allen's treatment by his jailers from that time on had not improved.

Transported from the *Solebay* to a prison in Halifax, Allen related the brutal treatment he received while incarcerated there. In the meantime, New York had fallen to the British, leaving thousands of Continental soldiers in British hands. Eventually moved to New York, Allen was paroled in his own custody and allowed the freedom of certain sectors of the city, and it was at this point that Allen's resourcefulness again came into prominence.

His appearance marked considerably by the poor treatment he had received at the hands of his jailers, Allen appeared somewhat sickly and emaciated. Still a great figure of a man, however, standing almost a head and shoulders over the average man, the deep hollows in his cheeks and the dark circles under his eyes, as well as his hacking, deep rooted cough, did not detract from the power of his penetrating glance. To the contrary, it added a somewhat fanatical gleam to his dark, purposeful stare, and fully aware of the change in his own appearance, Allen used it to his advantage. Pretending a degree of madness when the situation merited, he gained access to areas of the city that were off limits within the terms of his parole.

Experiencing the seething heat of Allen's fury in reading his vivid account of the dire circumstances under which wounded Continental prisoners were housed and the inadequacy of their treatment, Melanie frowned as her own anger mounted. Describing in forceful terms the barbaric treatment prisoners received at the hands of their British captors as they slowly starved to death while being encouraged to join the British Army if they wished to better their conditions, Allen allowed his talent to arouse the human spirit full range. The pitiful spectacle of an endless procession of carts transporting dead Continental soldiers, moving slowly to the laughter and jeers of heartless Tories and remorseless jailers tore at her heart and led Melanie to an understanding of Allen's secret counseling of all Continentals still in a condition to recover, to enlist in the British service and desert at their first opportunity for the American lines.

Managing to confound his British captors for eight months while he conducted his own mission within the occupied territory, Allen was finally arrested for breaking his parole. Placed in a provost jail in New York City, he was held there for nine months before finally being exchanged for a British colonel. Conducted immediately to a conference with General Washington on his release, Allen related all the information he had gained with regard to the enemy before returning to Bennington and a rousing welcome from his Boys.

Allen's narrative concluded with a pledge of loyalty to the new United States of America, as well as the young Vermont, the name by which the lands of the Hampshire Grants were known in deference to the French pronunciation of green mountains.

Never having been completely sure of her feelings for the volatile Ethan Allen, Melanie nonetheless felt a great sense of relief that the unconventional backwoodsman was back in his home territory and safe at last. But in the back of her mind, she could not help but wonder what the wily revolutionary would be up to next.

Her reverie was interrupted by the opening of the bedroom door, and Melanie smiled as Simon entered the room.

"What are you doing home at this time of day, Simon?" Embarrassed to be found still abed, she began to rise. Reaching her side in a few swift strides, Simon gently pushed her back against the pillows. His expression concerned, he said softly, "Martha sent Peter with the message that you were not well this morning."

"Oh, bother!" Melanie exclaimed heatedly. "It is nothing more than my laziness to carry around the load that has attached itself around my waist!"

His eyes still showing his concern, Simon responded with mock indignation, "Remember, Mrs. Young, it is *my* child you refer to so blatantly as that 'load'!"

Laughing at his expression, Melanie said lightly, "Somehow, Simon, I feel you will be just as happy as I when the child is born and I am once again fit to look at."

"Melanie, darling," Simon bent forward to kiss

her pale lips, "you are quite right that I am anxious to see my child born. I ache to hold him or her in my arms. But, my darling, please do not demean yourself by inferring you are not fit to look at in your present condition. Quite the contrary, you are lovely beyond words. You are a temple of creation for my child, darling. You will never be more beautiful to me than you are right now."

Slowly Simon bent to press a warm kiss on the rise of her stomach, smiling lightly as the child within moved beneath his lips.

A sudden noise at the door broke into their intimate moment as a small, flaming-haired bundle burst through, exclaiming as she did, "Papa! I told Martha that I heard your voice! She said I was mistaken and I should leave Mama alone, but I can run faster than she can now, so I came to see for myself!"

As if in confirmation of her statement, an angry, panting Martha appeared at the door behind her. With a small squeal, Sara scooted out of her grasp, and running forward, threw herself into Simon's arms with a burst of spontaneous giggles. Amused despite himself, Simon hugged her warmly while struggling to subdue a smile and assume a severe facade.

"I am glad your hearing is so acute, Sara, but I do wish your behavior was as superior. You have obviously put Martha to much trouble by having to run after you. And since I have some important matters to discuss with your mother right now, I think it would be best if you return to the nursery with Martha."

"But it's boring in the nursery all alone, Papa!"

Shaking her head silently at her daughter's sulky expression, Melanie deferred to Simon who responded with a smile, "You will not be alone there for long, Sara. Now be on your way!" Slapping her backside playfully, he watched as Sara made her way slowly to the door, mumbling as she did, "When Mama has the baby, it will be a boy. And we will name him Simon. Then I will have a Simon of my own and won't care if Papa tells me to go away!"

Managing to hold her tongue until the door closed behind Sara, Melanie said in amazement, "The child is a hellion, Simon! Wherever does she get it from?"

Barely able to hold a straight face, Simon returned quietly, "She is certainly nothing like her mother."

Deciding from Melanie's expression that it was time for a change of subject, Simon reached into his pocket to retrieve a letter which he put into Melanie's hands. "This letter arrived today. I thought you would want to read it."

Smiling at the familiar script, Melanie opened it quickly. Asa Parker's will had been upheld a few years before, and having inherited Asa's house in Salisbury, Melanie had asked Josh Whitmore to use it as his residence while he continued to manage the foundry. Presently living on Weaver's Row with a small staff, Josh wrote regularly to keep her appraised of the passage of events in Salisbury.

After reading for a few, short minutes, Melanie raised her eyes to Simon, her gaze pensive. "Many changes are coming about in Vermont now, Simon. Perhaps we should visit there after the child is born. I've not seen my father's homestead since I left as a child of thirteen."

Startled by the fleeting expression of apprehension

that passed over Simon's face, Melanie inquired worriedly, "Simon, is something wrong?"

"No, darling, nothing is wrong . . ." Simon's voice trailed off hesitantly as his eyes moved slowly over her flawless features, lingering for a few short seconds on her full, parted lips before he bent to kiss them lightly. "It's just that I can't help remembering the last time we returned to Salisbury. That hateful town seems to have a negative effect on you, and I don't think I care to risk your slipping away from me again as you so nearly did the last time we visited. Having had you to myself these past five years, I realize that nothing is worth the risk of losing you. I love you beyond measure, Melanie, darling." Bending swiftly to scoop her tightly against him, Simon whispered against the softness of her flaming hair, "You are not merely a part of my life . . . you *are* my life."

Slowly sliding her arms around his neck, Melanie moved her fingers caressingly in the thick, brown hair. Closing her eyes, she tensed spontaneously in reaction to the recurring pain that had been gripping her systematically in the last half hour. Immediately conscious of her stiffening, Simon gently disentangled himself from her arms to look hesitantly into her face.

"Melanie?"

In answer to his unasked question, Melanie whispered softly, "Yes, darling, I think it has begun."

Fear, anticipation, joy, excitement—all chased their way across Simon's ordinarily sedate expression in a fleeting second. Paling slightly, he burst out with uncharacteristic animation, "I must call Martha now, and Dr. Martin."

Holding him firmly in his position at her side, Melanie responded calmly, amused despite herself at his obvious agitation, "You needn't rush, Simon. The pains have only just begun."

"Nevertheless, I will call them immediately, and—"

"But we haven't finished our conversation!"

Turning back, Simon exploded with exasperation, "Blast, Melanie! This is no time for conversation! There will be plenty of time to talk later!"

Barely able to suppress the smile lurking at the corners of her mouth, Melanie allowed Simon to remove her restraining hands from his arms, saying with uncharacteristic meekness as he did, "Yes, darling, whatever you think best."

Stopping abruptly as he turned toward the door at her placating tone, he caught the amusement in her eyes. Suppressing his own answering smile, he turned toward her again to lean over the bed.

"Woman!" he said with mock severity, "this is no time for levity! My child is about to be born! We will talk later!" Planting a quick, hard kiss on her lips, he turned away once again and within moments he had disappeared through the doorway.

In the grip of another pain, Melanie whispered softly to the empty room, "Yes, I suppose you are right. It would be better if we talked later, my love."

Approximately four and one half hours later, Simon Elliot Young, Jr. gave forth his first lusty cry.

It was indeed many, many hours later before their conversation was resumed.

512